'You're not going anywhere without me.'

She was breathing hard, angry and still shocked that he had found her. There was no way to be forceful with the man when she was flat on her back and he was standing over her. She struggled to her feet.

'This is my room and you get out.'

'You have the same choice tonight you had last night. You're coming with me or you're going to jail. And judging from the way you're dressed,' he drawled, studying her as if she were a bug under a microscope, 'you've been up to something.'

Her heart lurched again. She didn't want to go to jail. She didn't want Jason around when the news came out about Dorian.

'Call the sheriff. I'm not going with you anywhere,' she snapped, trying to give herself a minute to think and to get out from under Jason's blue-green gaze.

'Suit yourself,' Jason drawled and strolled to the telephone, punching the number for an outside line, then punching more numbers.

The Bachelor Takes a Wife
by Jackie Merritt

ෆ ❧ ೧

'I know what you said.'

'Well, how would I know if you still love to laugh when we rarely see each other? Andrea, when you really think about it, isn't it silly for you and I to be anything but the closest of friends?'

Instantly wary, Andrea covered her fluster by picking up the pitcher of tea and refilling their glasses. She had to say something, give him some kind of reply, but what?

She finally said, rather stiffly, 'It's not so silly, Keith. We didn't part on the best of terms, you know.'

'But that was a hundred years ago! Andy, I have so many feelings for you. What should I do with them?'

'They're all *old* feelings, Keith, part of the past! Leave them there.'

Available in July 2003 from Silhouette Desire

The Playboy Meets His Match
SARA ORWIG

The Bachelor Takes a Wife
JACKIE MERRITT

SILHOUETTE®
DESIRE™

Silhouette, Silhouette Desire and Colophon are registered trademarks of Harlequin Books S.A., used under licence.

First published in Great Britain 2003
Silhouette Books, Eton House, 18-24 Paradise Road,
Richmond, Surrey TW9 1SR

The publisher acknowledges the copyright holders of the individual works as follows:

The Playboy Meets His Match © Harlequin Books S.A. 2002
The Bachelor Takes a Wife © Harlequin Books S.A. 2002

Special thanks and acknowledgement are given to Sara Orwig and Jackie Merritt for their contributions to The Millionaire's Club series.

ISBN 0 373 04871 8

51-0703

Printed and bound in Spain
by Litografia Rosés S.A., Barcelona

THE PLAYBOY MEETS HIS MATCH
by
Sara Orwig

SARA ORWIG

lives with her husband and children in Oklahoma. She has a patient husband who will take her on research trips, anywhere from big cities to old forts. She is an avid collector of Western history books. With a master's degree in English, Sara writes historical romance, mainstream fiction and contemporary romance. Books are beloved treasures that take Sara to magical worlds, and she loves both reading and writing them.

With thanks to Joan Golan and Stephanie Maurer.
Also, to all New Yorkers, God bless…

One

"**D**on't tell me I'm the club expert at seduction," Jason Windover grumbled good-naturedly, glancing around the circle of friends and fellow members of the Texas Cattleman's Club as they sat in one of the elegant private meeting rooms. Thick carpets, dark paneling and polished wood flooring graced the spacious room, built over ninety years earlier. A boar's head was mounted above the stone mantel, and a Tiffany chandelier glittered brightly.

The Texas Cattleman's Club was one of Texas's oldest and most exclusive clubs. Usually, it was a place where Jason could relax and enjoy his friends, but at the moment he was mildly annoyed. He crossed his jeans-clad legs, resting one booted foot on his knee, and arched his brows.

"*Au contraire*," Sebastian Wescott said, turning to his longtime friend. "You're the one who excels at seduction, so I nominate you to get this Valkyrie out of our hair."

"I second that motion," snapped black-haired Will Bradford, a partner of Wescott Oil Enterprises.

Jason looked into Sebastian's silver-gray eyes and shook his head. "If nothing else, she's not my type," Jason said coolly, certain this foolishness would pass. "I like tall, long-legged, sophisticated blondes. Beautiful blondes who are poised and sexy. This wildcat sounds like five feet of pure trouble and anything but sophisticated, sexy or poised. Forget it, guys. It ain't gonna happen."

"The woman is unhinged. She belongs in a mental hospital," Dorian Brady added sharply. "She's got this vendetta against me—at the moment it's me. No telling who it will be tomorrow. She's mentally unstable, and her fixation could switch to any one of you. Lord knows, I haven't done the wild things she's accusing me of."

Studying Dorian, Jason felt cold distaste. Other than Dorian, Jason liked all the members of the Texas Cattleman's Club, an exclusive, prestigious facade which allowed members to work together covertly on secret missions to save innocents' lives. While most of the men had grown up in and around Royal, Texas, Dorian was a relative newcomer. There was an arrogance about Dorian that rankled him, but Jason knew he needed to get over his dislike. Dorian was, after all, Seb's half brother.

"You're elected," Rob Cole said dryly to Jason. "You're the rodeo guy. You can handle wild bulls and wild horses. I'm sure you can handle a wild woman."

"You're the detective—you should know how to handle her."

"Nope. You have a way with women, and I already have my hands full trying to find out what I can about our unsolved murder here in Royal." Rob studied the circle of men. "We have someone trying to frame Sebastian for the murder of Eric Chambers. We don't need this woman in our hair while we're trying to find out who's behind this."

"I wasn't here when she burst in on y'all, but I've heard what an unholy commotion she caused here at the club. Dammit, don't dump this on me." All of the men looked at Jason. "C'mon, y'all," Jason argued.

"You have to be the one," Sebastian replied. "You're the CIA-trained operative, so you've dealt with difficult people before. Frankly, I've been through enough lately, and I have a new bride to devote myself to."

Jason sighed and waved his hand. "Save your excuses. I can guess all of them. All right. I'll try to keep the little wildcat out of our hair."

"That problem solved, let's adjourn to poker," Keith, the computer expert, suggested, his brown eyes twinkling.

The men agreed swiftly, and Jason knew the matter was settled. Morosely, he joined them, getting a fresh drink, going through the motions while he contemplated his assignment. He didn't like one thing about it. He was not accustomed to forcing a female to do something she didn't want to do—in this case, he was going to have to do exactly that in order to keep this little wildcat out of the other guys' ways.

Will, Rob and Sebastian were all recently married. Marriage had become an epidemic, except he was safe—no marriage for him—at the moment there wasn't even a woman in his life. Maybe Keith should be the one to take care of this nuisance. Jason wondered whether Keith had ever gotten over his old flame, Andrea O'Rourke. He said he had, but he sure didn't act like it. Jason sighed. He could understand why this assignment had been dumped on him, but he didn't like it. Thank goodness he wasn't involved with anyone right now because this would be a very unwanted complication in his life. He wished he could just haul this Ms. Silver down to jail and ask Sheriff Escobar to lock her up and throw away the key until all their mysteries were solved.

When Jason realized he was losing the first round of the poker game, he shifted his thoughts to cards and forgot about Meredith Silver, hoping she had left town and he would never have to deal with her.

It was almost midnight when Jason pocketed his winnings and told his friends goodbye. Stepping outside, he inhaled the cool May air. A silver moon hung in the inky sky while stars were blotted out by the lights of the parking lot. As he crossed the lot to his black pickup, Jason's boot heels scraped the asphalt. As he reached for the door handle of his pickup, he heard a faint sound behind him.

The hairs on the back of Jason's neck prickled, and he stood motionless beside his pickup. His experience in the CIA had trained him to be a keen observer, and he knew he had heard the scrape of a footstep on the asphalt.

Jason stood in a row of empty cars and pickups. When he had walked from the clubhouse, there hadn't been another person in sight. In spite of the seemingly empty lot, Jason doubted he was alone in the parking lot. Should he look under the next car? he wondered, or would it be better to try to discover what the person intended? Jason pocketed his keys and headed casually back to the club.

He went through the front door, down a hallway past the cloakroom and rest rooms, and cut through the giant kitchen, touching the brim of his Stetson with his finger in silent greeting to the skeleton cooking crew still on duty at this late hour. They were familiar with the members of the club, and none of them questioned his presence in the kitchen as he passed through and went out a side door. He stepped into a flower bed, creeping behind cedars and flowering crape myrtles. Glad now that he had worn a dark blue Western shirt and his dark jeans, he moved stealthily even though he was wearing Western boots. He paused, his gaze sweeping over the empty lot and then settling on the car parked next to his.

He knew to whom it belonged—Dorian. As he watched, a shadow separated itself from the darker ones around it. Jason focused on a black-clad figure that had slithered out from beneath Dorian's car and now knelt beside the back tire.

Something glinted in the moonlight. There was a clunk and then a swift hiss of air. When the vandal moved to the front tire, Jason sprinted from his hiding place, determined to catch the rascal who was vandalizing club member's tires in their private parking lot.

Seeing Jason, the culprit dropped the knife and ran. From the short stature, Jason decided it was a teen. Jason's long legs gave him the advantage, and he stretched out his stride. As they raced across the lot, Jason made a flying tackle, wrapping his arms around the miscreant's tiny waist.

"Gotcha!" he snapped triumphantly as they both went crashing to the asphalt.

The high yelp didn't indicate anything about the vandal, but the moment they landed on the asphalt, and he felt the soft, curvaceous body beneath his, surprise rippled through Jason. A female! And then he guessed who it was. The crazy woman who was stalking his fellow club member, Dorian Brady—the wildcat who was his assignment.

"Oh, damn," he muttered. Never in his life had he hurt a woman and remorse filled him as he groaned and moved off her. "Are you all right?"

Light from one of the tall lamps spilled over him, although the brim of his hat shaded his face, but her back was to the lamp and her face was completely hidden. She was covered in black with a black cap and some black goop spread on her face, so that he couldn't distinguish her features. Jason hunkered down on the balls of his feet as she started to sit up.

Her fist shot out. Catching him completely by surprise, five feet of female did what few six-foot-plus, some-two-hundred-pounds of male had never done. Her blow landed squarely in his middle, knocking the breath from his lungs as she followed with a swift push that knocked him off balance. Springing to her feet, she tried to run for it.

Jason's surprise lasted only a second and then his natural reactions set in. He rolled forward, snaking his hand out, caught her by the ankle and yanked. For the second time in his life, he sent a female sprawling facedown.

He wasn't giving her another chance. Unceremoniously,

he grabbed his hat, scooped her up and slung her over his shoulder.

For someone who was up to criminal activities and packed a vicious punch for her size, her epithets and name-calling fit a five-year-old's vocabulary. Heck, some five-year-olds could do better.

Ignoring her harmless blows on his back and her sputtering fury, Jason carried her to his pickup, unlocked the door and dumped her inside. Like a cat springing back into battle, she came up fighting, but he was ready this time.

Tossing his hat into the back with one hand, he clamped her wrists in a tight grip with his other hand, pinning her against the locked door and the seat with his body. In spite of her struggles, he became aware of several things at once: an enticing perfume, a body whose topside was even more curvaceous and soft than her backside, a wiry strength he wouldn't have believed possible and short, guttural moans of battle that made him think of something far removed from their struggle. Against all wisdom, he was curious and wanted to see what she looked like.

"You just slashed a club member's tire, and I can call the sheriff and have you hauled to jail."

"Go ahead and call, you warp-noggined manhandler," she snapped. "They can't put me in jail for slashing a tire. I'll call my lawyer."

"Why do I doubt you even have a lawyer? *Warp-noggined?*"

This was the Valkyrie who Dorian said had been stalking him. Jason had suspected Dorian had been stretching the truth a bit, but after the past few minutes, he decided the man had been correct. Everything about her seemed amateurish, and he didn't think there was a lawyer, a plan or much sense. From the few minutes of dealing with her, he figured he had a crazy person on his hands, or perhaps a woman emotionally unhinged by a man who had done her wrong. Was this some ex-lover of Dorian's, and he didn't want to admit it?

"Settle down, wildcat. Fighting won't do you any good. You're not catching me by surprise ever again."

In the darkness he could see her jaw lift in a stubborn gesture. "That's what you think. Let me go. I can charge you with assault—"

"Hardly," he stated dryly. "I just caught you in a criminal act." She wiggled, struggling to break free, but it was having a far different effect on him. Jason had been a longer time than usual between women. She was soft, curvaceous and she was squirming and gyrating against him. His body was pressed over hers, pinning her down, but she was doing things that were setting him on fire in spite of his annoyance.

"Wildcat, do you know what you're doing?" he rasped.

She stilled instantly, and he knew she had become aware of his natural male response to a warm, sweet-smelling female rubbing sensuously against him.

When he reached down with his free hand and unbuckled his belt, her struggles became wild. Swiftly, he yanked his belt free, bound her wrists together and secured her to the door handle. "I'm not going to hurt you. You're just not going anywhere. You've caused enough trouble around here. Now, you make a choice. I take you home with me—I lock you in a room by yourself for tonight. I have no evil intentions, I promise. Tomorrow you go on your way and get out of Royal. Or I can take you to the sheriff. You decide."

Why he was taking her home with him, he wasn't altogether certain about, except he had been assigned to keep her out of the way of the rest of the club members, and it was the best way to keep an eye on her.

She struggled, and Jason tightened his grip. "Look, you're just going to get yourself in deep trouble. There are laws against stalking someone—"

"Stalking! I'm not stalking that rotten lowlife varmint. He's mean and vindictive and dishonest."

Jason was intrigued. "I've given you a choice. Make

your decision. Or it'll be the sheriff because I'd be glad to dump you into someone else's lap.''

They were both breathing hard—his ragged breath was not from exertion. Erotic thoughts were tempting him and she was the cause. She might be five feet of trouble, but she was definitely all woman and a very sweet-smelling one at that. Jason fished a handkerchief from his pocket and began to wipe the black stuff off her forehead.

''How do I know you won't hurt me?'' she asked so softly that he had to lean closer. And got another deep whiff of her perfume. A little pesky wildcat shouldn't wear seductive perfume.

''You have my word on it,'' he said, and she gave a bitter laugh. ''The sheriff or my house,'' he repeated.

''Your house,'' she whispered, her breath sweet, lightly brushing his skin.

Keeping up his guard, he moved away and fished for his keys, starting the pickup. Now she was hunched into a ball in the corner between the door and the back of the seat. As he drove out of the lot, he glanced at her again. She looked pitiful all huddled over, but his bruised midriff warned him not to be taken in by appearances. This was not a cringing, frightened little waif. The wildcat had a punch that had knocked him flat.

Jason worked out over an hour every day. He shouldn't have been felled by a blow from a female of her size, and he vowed he would increase his workouts tomorrow.

He opened the glove compartment and pulled out a flask of whiskey, opening it and offering it to her. ''Need a drink?''

''Now you want to get me drunk so you can have your way with me,'' she snarled.

''Great grief,'' he grumbled, wanting a stiff drink himself, but resisting, since he was driving.

''Where did you get your vocabulary—out of some 1920s dime novel? Outside of melodramas, I didn't know anyone used that phrase *have your way with me*.''

"You're too young yourself to know anything about 1920s dime novels, and I certainly don't. And you know full well what I meant."

"I gave you my word. You're not my type anyway."

"I can imagine your type."

He glanced at her again, his curiosity growing. Silence stretched between them as he drove down Main Street, Royal, Texas, the place where he had grown up and lived a good part of his life. "So, what type do you imagine I'd like?" he asked finally.

"Someone beautiful, sexy, sophisticated and easy. *Real* easy."

Amused, he looked at her, still unable to see anything except a huddle of black.

"You don't think I have any charm to win over someone who isn't easy?"

"You tackled me twice," she said in the same haughty, aloof tone that he could recall early grade-school teachers lecturing him with. "That isn't a winning approach."

"I wasn't trying a winning approach. I never intended seduction. I was trying to stop a criminal act. That's not a fair judgment of me," he remarked, amused by her in spite of his annoyance at being saddled with responsibility for keeping her away from the others.

He drove past Pine Valley, the exclusive, private-gated, residential community that held mansions, including one belonging to his family where his brother was currently residing. Jason could take her there, but he preferred her out on the Windover Ranch—far enough out of town so that she would have a hell of a hike if she decided to run away.

"It might be a good idea if we knew each other's names. I'm Jason Windover."

"I'm Meredith Silver," she said.

"Well, hi, Meredith. Where are you from?"

"I'm from Dallas," she said.

"And what do you do in Dallas?" he asked, slipping

into old patterns of interrogation, avoiding the hot topics or accusations.

"I'm a computer programmer. I'm a freelance consultant."

"Interesting profession—and gives you freedom to keep your own hours sometimes."

"Yes, it does," she answered while she stared out the window. "We're out of town."

"I'm taking you to the Windover family ranch."

"You're a cowboy?"

"Yes, I am. I've been with the government, but I recently retired to the ranch. So, Meredith, who's your current boyfriend?"

"There isn't one," she replied. "But I'll bet there's a woman in your life."

"As a matter of fact, there's not at present."

"I'm sure she's not far in the past and there's another lined up somewhere in the near future."

"Now why do you think that? You don't know me."

"You have that easygoing manner of a man accustomed to always having a female in his life."

"Do I really?" he asked, amused by her observations.

"You know darn well you do. You're also egotistical and overbearing."

"Golly gee whiz. I'll have to work on that."

"You can save the charm because it won't work on me."

"Now is that a challenge or what?" he asked, his voice dropping as he shot her a look.

"It's definitely not a challenge. Besides, I'm not your type remember?"

"Point taken." He drove quietly for a few minutes and then asked, "Do you have a hotel room in Royal or did you intend to drive back to Dallas tonight?"

"I'm staying at the Royalton Hotel," she replied, naming Royal's oldest and finest hotel.

"Do you still have family in Dallas?"

"Yes. My sisters and my mom are in Dallas. I have an older brother who's in Montana, I think."

"Silver," he said, remembering a stocky, wild guy from the rodeo circuit. "I've met a bull rider—Hank Silver."

"That's my brother," she said with what sounded like reluctance.

"Well, small world. He's a tough cowpoke. I'll bet that's where you got the punch you pack. You have a big family," he said, curious to see what she looked like. Her voice was soft, low and soothing. A sexy voice that didn't match her volatile personality. If he had talked to her on a telephone and hadn't seen her in person, he would have conjured up an entirely different type of woman in his mind. The voice definitely didn't fit a little five-foot wildcat with a vocabulary as old-fashioned as his grandmother's. Her enticing voice didn't fit someone who could deliver a jab that knocked the breath from your lungs. But with Hank Silver as an older brother, Jason could well imagine, she'd had to defend herself growing up. From what Jason could remember, Hank Silver was in trouble with the law more than once over barroom brawls.

"I have two older brothers," he said. "Ethan and Luke."

"That's nice," she said, not trying to hide her anger. for the next hour they lapsed into silence, a new experience for Jason with a female.

Jason turned south between large posts with the Windover brand carved on the front of each one and drove swiftly along a hard-packed road until they pulled up behind the sprawling ranch house that had belonged to his family for four generations. Moonlight splashed over a combination of red sandstone, rough-hewn logs and glass. A porch with a sloping roof ran along the front and a well-tended lawn was surrounded by a picket fence. Beyond the house were outbuildings, a guest house, a bunkhouse and a barn.

Jason stopped near the back gate and untied the belt, taking her arm to lead her inside. When they entered the house, he switched on lights in a back entryway that held a coat rack, pictures of horses and potted plants. He turned and punched buttons on a keypad to disengage the alarm system that was beeping steadily. As soon as he had finished, the tiny red alarm light changed to green and the alarm was silent.

In the large kitchen he switched on soft lighting that fell over whitewashed oak cabinets and a pale-yellow tiled counter. Jason caught Meredith's wrist lightly. ''Come here,'' he said, leading her to the sink. She wore black boots and black, lumpy sweats that hid her figure. And he knew from falling on her and pinning her down in the car that she definitely had a figure. Pulling out a towel, he ran warm water over it and then turned to scrub her face.

''I'd like to see what you look like. You've been a dark blob from the first moment I saw you,'' he said, looking down at her as he tilted up her chin. At the sight of her in the light, he drew a sharp breath and remorse filled him because she had a raw scrape on her cheek and he knew he had caused it. When he touched her jaw lightly, she jerked her head away.

''I'm sorry you're hurt. I thought you were a boy.''

Thickly-lashed, large, stormy gray eyes gazed up at him, and the moment his gaze met hers he received the second stunning blow from her. Her eyes took his breath and held him mesmerized. He couldn't recall ever seeing eyes exactly the color of hers. But it was something more than color that held him breathless. He felt as if he had touched a live wire and sparks were flying all around him. Silence stretched; he realized she was as still as he and he didn't want to break the contact.

She took the cloth from his hand and began to rub black off her face. He retrieved it, wanting to touch her, wildly curious now to see what she looked like without all the junk on her face. And still neither one of them had spoken or moved or looked away.

''We need to clean up your scrapes quickly. Just a minute and I'll be back." Silently, he called himself all sorts of names for causing her face to be scraped raw as he hurried to the nearest bathroom. He returned with a bottle of peroxide. "Lean over the sink and let me pour this over your cheek. It'll clean your scrape and disinfect it. How long since you had a tetanus shot?"

"Only a year ago."

She tilted her head and he poured the clear liquid, dabbing gently. "Sorry, if I hurt you."

"Oh, yeah, sure," she grumbled, and he felt worse than before. Finally he patted her cheek dry. "Let's see your hands."

"I can take care of my hands."

"Put your hands out and let me help," he ordered. When she held them over the sink, palms up, he winced, hating that he was at fault for her injuries. He washed the scrapes, cleaning and disinfecting them. "I wouldn't bandage those scrapes tonight. Maybe tomorrow when you'll be out in the world, but let them heal tonight. Now, let's get off the rest of whatever you have smeared on you." In slow deliberate strokes he wiped her face gently, while he continued to look into her eyes. The longer he rubbed her face, the faster his pulse beat.

Finally, he had to rinse the cloth because it was covered in whatever she had spread over her face. In silence he rinsed it and returned to a task that was ever so pleasant, slowly stroking her face free of smudges. Besides the fabulous eyes, she had a slightly upturned nose, full pouty lips and prominent cheekbones.

She yanked the cloth from his hand. "I can wash my own face," she snapped and turned to wash over the kitchen sink. She slanted him a look. "If you'll tell me where the bathroom is, I'll wash in there."

"You're fine where you are," he said, not giving a rip about the sink and interested in the smooth, rosy skin beginning to show.

As she shook water off her hands, he handed her a clean

towel, and she scrubbed with it vigorously, something he had never once seen a woman do.

Big gray eyes peeped at him over the towel, and he wondered if he should get ready to dodge her fist again, but she merely folded the towel.

Reaching out, he pulled the cap off her head. When long, slightly curly auburn locks spilled out, he drew a swift breath. Unruly, silken strands curled around her face. From what little he already knew, she was fiery, impetuous and fearless.

"You want anything to eat or drink?"

"No, thank you," she replied with disdain.

"Come here," he said, taking her wrist again and leading her through the kitchen, down the hall, into the spacious family room. He led her to a wide, brown leather couch that faced a large brick hearth. With a little tug he got her to sit down and he faced her, releasing her wrist. "Now, why were you slashing Dorian's tires? What's going on between the two of you?"

Two

Meredith Silver thrust out her chin stubbornly. "I don't have to answer any of your questions," she snapped. No man should look so sinfully handsome. He had black curly hair that he wore long, and it gave him a wild, dangerous look. His features were slightly rugged with a strong jaw, prominent cheekbones and straight nose. It was his thick lashes and blue-green eyes that had stopped her in her tracks in the kitchen.

Meredith wished she hadn't stood there like a starstruck teen looking at a movie idol, because she suspected Jason Windover drew women the way flowers drew bees.

She glanced beyond him to study the windows. This was no fortress, although he had turned off an alarm system when they entered. She knew how to hot-wire a car, and later tonight she was getting out of this house and away from this man who was becoming a big interference in her life.

"I can still call the sheriff and have you locked up. This

is a small town and most of us know each other pretty well. He can come up with some charges to hold you in a cell for a while.''

Her mind raced. She knew lawyers because she had solved computer problems for various ones, but not recently and she had never made lasting friendships with any of them. She didn't know a single lawyer to call for help. Besides, compelling bedroom eyes were staring at her, an invisible push to get her talking.

''I've been trying to find Dorian Brady. Now I've found him and he's telling everyone that I'm crazy and that everything I'm saying about him is a lie.''

''Well, is it or not?''

''I'm telling the truth, but he's your friend and your good-ol'-boy fellow club member. Y'all are a bunch of snooty male chauvinists, and I know you'll believe him over me, so what's the point in even discussing this with you?'' she said, becoming more annoyed as she talked because a twinkle had come into his eyes.

''What's the point in slashing his tires?''

''I just want him to know that I'm here. That I'm in his life and I'm not going to go away. I want to cause that man some grief.''

''He knows you're in his life, and you are causing him a little grief. But I'll tell you what, all those good-ol'-boy male chauvinists have voted that I'm to keep you out of everybody else's hair, so that's just what I'm going to do. Tonight, you can just stay here under my roof until you simmer down. And tomorrow you can go back to wherever you came from.''

''That's what you think, mister.''

''Jason is the name, remember?''

''Mister is sufficient. We're not going to be friends.''

''Now that's another challenge you've just flung at me,'' he drawled, and she definitely saw the twinkle in his eyes that time.

Thrusting out her jaw, she leaned closer to him. "I will never be friends with a man like you, buster!"

He looked as if he was making an effort not to laugh out loud. He leaned close. "Why not, Meredith?"

Oh, my! She was going to have to watch it around this one. He was sexy and too handsome and his voice sent shivers skittering around inside her. And those bedroom eyes of his! She moved back and drew herself up. "I'm sure most women just melt when you bat your eyes at them, but I'm not melting, nor will I. I—"

"Challenge number three," he stated, this time speaking in a slow drawl and looking at her with a speculative gleam in his eyes that made her draw a swift breath.

"I'm not flinging sexy challenges at you. I'm telling you. You probably can't believe that a female in this whole big state of Texas is immune to your charm."

"Darlin'," he drawled in a tone that did curl her toes and sent a flash of heat that threatened to melt her, "I haven't even begun to turn on any charm. Knocking the wind out of me doesn't exactly draw out the best aspects of my personality."

"You attacked me."

"I stopped a vandal from escaping," he reminded her. He took her wrist again. His brows arched. "Your pulse is racing, Meredith."

She glared at him while crimson flooded her cheeks. "Don't flatter yourself. It's fright."

"You—*afraid?*"

"There's good reason to be," she snapped, pointing at her scraped face and annoyed that her pulse was reacting to him in a wild, uncontrollable manner.

"I'm sorry I hurt you," he said, and to her surprise, he sounded truly contrite. "Come on. Let's get something to drink. I definitely want a drink."

"I'll come without you holding my hand," she said, attempting to yank free.

"I think I want to keep one hand under control. You

have a wicked punch there. Besides, I don't want you heaving one of the family heirlooms at me and breaking some favorite vase.''

''I wouldn't think of it.''

''Not much you wouldn't.''

He was tall, broad-shouldered and a very sexy male. Having him hold her wrist made her nervous, even though his grip was light. When she had tried to get free, he had held her without effort, but she knew that wasn't what bothered her. It was the physical contact with him, however slight, that set her pulse racing.

Maybe if she humored him until he locked her in a room—and she was certain that's exactly what he would do sooner or later—then she could try to escape. Once they were in the kitchen, he released her wrist. While he pulled a cold beer out of the refrigerator, Meredith studied the windows and latches, which looked quite ordinary. And she had watched when he had turned off his alarm, so she could remember the series of numbers he had punched in. She was certain Jason wouldn't think she'd try to escape, especially since they were so far from town. He had left his pickup near the back door and if she could get outside to his pickup, she would be on her way.

''Want some pop?''

''I am not drinking or eating with you.''

''Suit yourself,'' he said, and turned to open the bottle of beer. They returned to the sofa where he sat too close for comfort. She could detect his aftershave, see the faint dark stubble on his jaw.

He set his beer on a coaster on the large cherrywood table standing in front of the sofa. He pulled off a boot and set it aside and then pulled off the other one. ''We might as well get comfortable.''

She was half tempted to say she wanted to go to jail, but his house was cozy and there weren't any bars on the windows and she stood a far better chance of escaping from this ornery Texan than she would from a jail.

"Now tell me why you want to cause Dorian grief."

"He's a wicked man. But I know you don't believe a word I'm saying because he's in your good-ol'-boy group."

"Let me decide that."

"One of my sisters was engaged to him."

"He denies that. Do you have any proof?"

"Proof of their engagement? No, I don't."

"Did he give her a ring?"

"He told her that he was having his grandmother's diamond ring reset. He kept putting off why it wasn't ready and at the time, he sounded convincing. He can be charming and he's good-looking and he's clever. Everything sounded logical, so I didn't doubt what my sister was telling me. Twice I had dinner with them, and I had him at our house," she said. As Merry talked, she had to constantly gaze into those sexy eyes and she could hear how lame her story sounded. There wasn't a flicker of emotion in Jason's expression, so she had no idea what he was thinking.

"*Our* house? Are you married?"

"No, I'm not. I live in an apartment in Dallas, but I go home often to the house where I grew up. My mom is a Dallas news anchor and I grew up in Dallas."

"Another well-known family member." He tilted his head to study her. "Your mom isn't Serena Dunstan, is she?"

"Yes, she is. Her real name is Therese Silver, but Serena Dunstan is her professional name. How did you guess?"

"She's the right age and she's done some controversial reporting—and won awards. Hank Silver, Serena Dunstan—you're from a whole family of feisty daredevils."

"My sister Holly isn't. She's a little on the shy side."

"I would have to see it to believe it," he remarked dryly.

"Mom's certainly more well-known than my brother. I'm really close to my three younger sisters, so I'm at our house most of the time. My youngest sister, Claudia, is in high school now, but she graduates this spring."

"I hope she's not the one Dorian was supposedly engaged to."

"It isn't supposedly," Merry said darkly, knowing he was friends with the creep and wasn't going to believe a word she said. "Dorian was engaged to Holly, who finished college early and has a great job as an engineer."

"Do you have pictures of them together?"

"No, I don't," Merry answered flatly, realizing how flimsy her accusations were beginning to sound up against Jason's practical questions. "There was always a reason why Dorian did or did not do something. When I wanted to take their pictures, he'd put me off and then we'd forget all about it." The more she talked, the more her anger built again. "I thought Dorian just decided all of a sudden to dump her, but now that you're asking all these questions—reasonable questions—he must have planned to do this from the very start. She really was in love with him," Merry said, remembering Holly sobbing and shaking and refusing to eat far too many times. For the past few months she had watched her sister lose weight steadily.

"Holly believed Dorian and was taken in by him. She had bought a wedding dress—"

"No ring, but she bought a dress?" Jason asked doubtfully, as if Holly were lost in fantasies.

"I can't tell you how believable he made it all sound."

While blue-green eyes studied her, she wondered what was running through the lanky Texan's mind.

"Men can be very convincing when they want to. Even in the biggest of lies," she added.

A shuttered look altered Jason's expression slightly. "I don't think you should limit that to men," he said in a cynical tone that surprised her.

"I can't believe any woman ever hurt you. I'll bet you draw them like flies to honey."

The twinkle returned to his eyes. "Whatever makes you think that?" he asked with great innocence.

"Stop fishing for compliments! You know you're a good-looking and sexy stud."

"Son-of-a-gun, darlin'," he drawled. "You will turn my head. So you think I'm a sexy stud?" The words rolled out like soft velvet sliding across her skin, and Meredith wished she hadn't said anything. When would she learn just to keep quiet? But then, how could she sit in silence when he was looking at her with an eagle-eyed intentness that made her nervous and made her want to chatter?

"Why don't we go out to dinner tomorrow night? I can drive to Dallas," he said.

"Thank you, but I have other plans. And I'm not leaving Royal."

"You have friends here in Royal?"

"No, I don't know anyone except Dorian, and now you. I'm staying right here in Royal. You can't make me leave town."

"You plan to slash Dorian's tires again?"

"No, I won't," she said, annoyed with him and trying to ignore the little nagging voice inside that wanted to accept his offer of a dinner date. "I wouldn't tell you anyway, but I don't have other plans. I just don't care to go to dinner."

He grinned, a full-fledged, heart-stopping grin with perfect white teeth, and she tried to catch her breath and not stare. With an effort she shifted her gaze to her fingers laced together in her lap. She had just turned down a date with that grin. Just sitting there doing nothing, the man was handsome, but when he smiled, he was to-die-for gorgeous. His smile could melt the coldest heart. She just knew it had better not melt hers. And she knew he had an ulterior motive in asking her to dinner because he was trying every which way to learn her plans about Dorian and to keep her away from him.

"I'm sure you're unaccustomed to any female turning down an offer of a date with you, but I'm not interested."

"Well, in that case, we'll sit right here at my house. You

can go with me tomorrow to pick out a computer and we'll have dinner at home and you can help me set up a new computer—''

''You're kidnapping me!''

''No, I'm not. You're free to go. You want to leave, I'll take you straight to the sheriff. After all, I caught you in a criminal act.''

She glared at him. ''I don't want to go to jail. I'll think about it tomorrow.''

''I wouldn't want to go to jail, either. My house is far more comfortable, and I'm better company that any of those deputies and you can have something to eat or drink whenever you want.'' He gave her a speculative look. ''You know, men have been breaking women's hearts and vice-versa since the beginning of time. Your sister got jilted by a low-down lying rascal—as you would say—but that happens. When it does, you pick up and go on with life.''

She bristled. ''How easy that is for you to say! You're a playboy and I'm sure you're incredibly experienced at breaking hearts. I'll bet you've left a path strewn with them back to when you were just out of elementary school.''

''Grade school? I don't think so!'' he said and rewarded her with another fabulous grin.

''And I'll bet no female has ever broken your heart. So don't even talk to me about how unimportant a broken heart is!''

He tilted his head. ''Another swift punch—somewhat undeserved, I think. I've always made it clear that I'm not a marrying man. I'm not into commitment and I always state that up front. I have never been engaged to anyone and never hinted at engagement. So don't lump me in with broken promises of engagement. There's a difference. Anyone who dates me knows exactly how I feel about marriage. I'm very open about it. Most of the women I date feel just the way I do.''

''Why aren't you a marrying man, if I may ask?''

Again, she caught that brief shuttered look and a muscle

working in his jaw. He had some touchy point, something that had happened to him that had soured him on marriage.

"My brothers have had disastrous marriages that have torn apart their lives and hurt their children. I don't ever want to go through that."

She suspected there was more to the story than he was telling her, but they were little more than strangers and she could understand why he would be reluctant to tell her about himself. As he talked, he unbuttoned his shirt and rolled up his sleeves. She didn't think he was aware of what he was doing, but she was certainly aware of the slight glimpse of a tanned, well-sculpted chest.

"Those sweats may be rather warm for this time of year. Want something more comfortable?"

"That would be nice," she said and he stood, reaching down to take her wrist.

"You don't have to hold me."

"Only your wrist. I can keep up with you better this way," he answered lightly, but it made her stand closer to him than was comfortable. He had to be a couple of inches over six feet tall. The top of her head reached his shoulder and she felt as if tiny currents of electricity were jabbing her when she was close to him. The prickly awareness put her on edge because it was so uncustomary for her. What was it about him that caused the sparks? Surely not just his movie-star looks. She shouldn't be susceptible to bedroom eyes and a high-wattage grin. Something about him had her heart skipping way too fast and she could just imagine the broken hearts he had in his past.

They entered a large hallway decorated with Western art and he directed her back across the kitchen to another hallway. "The east wing of the house has spare bedrooms, my office and a workout room. We don't use these bedrooms unless everyone is home."

"Who is everyone?"

"My brothers and their families. They've remarried and have kids. We spend a lot of time here," he said switching on lights and she entered another large, comfortable room with leather-upholstered furniture. A pool table was in the center of the room with a Ping-Pong table in a far corner and an immense stone fireplace along one wall. A wide-screen television stood at one end and one wall was lined with shelves filled with books. Two large gun racks were against another wall with an antique sword mounted over the fireplace.

"I can see why. You have everything you need here at home."

"Not quite," he drawled, and she knew he was referring to a woman companion.

"Don't you get lonesome here?" The moment she asked, she knew it was a ridiculous question, and she answered before he could. "I know you don't get lonesome anywhere. I'm sure I'm keeping you from some woman's company tonight, and I'll bet she's quite unhappy about it."

"No, I told you. There's no one in my life right now."

"If there's not, she must be only a day away. I can't imagine you going ten minutes without a woman close at hand."

"Tonight I've got you, darlin'," he drawled lightly, and she knew he was teasing her.

"And I know full well you didn't want me."

"I didn't say that. I'm just assigned to keep you out of trouble."

"To keep me away from Dorian is the truth. You can't watch me forever."

"Nope, I surely can't, but for tonight I can do my assignment."

She was acutely aware of his fingers still circling her wrist. Moving close at her side, he led her to another large room where he switched on a light. "Here's my office."

"What a beautiful desk." When she wriggled her arm, he released her. As soon as he did, she crossed the room to look closer at the satinwood-and-ebony desk. "This looks old."

"It is. My grandfather brought it home from Europe on one of his travels. I've tried to add some antiques to this home since I've had the house."

"This is a beautiful desk," she said, running her fingers along the smooth wood. Antique glass-fronted cases held books, but before she could read the titles, he took her arm lightly and led her back through the kitchen toward the center of the house and the west wing. "We'll be staying in this end of the house."

While they sauntered down the hall, Meredith considered escape. Maybe if he drank a few more beers, he would sleep dead to the world and her escape would be even easier.

"I'm surprised you don't keep a dog out here."

"There are several dogs on the ranch, but they're down at the bunkhouse with the men."

"Don't tell me dogs don't like you."

He glanced at her with amusement in his eyes again. "I get along fine with the dogs. They're just shut in the bunkhouse at the moment. Want me to get one of them up here?"

"Heavens, no! I just found it unusual to be out in the country and not see a dog."

"Well, city girl, the dogs are here. I'll show you tomorrow. Right now, I'll show you around the house. Here's the dining room."

She looked at a large room with a Texas-size carved, mahogany table that held ten chairs on each side and two arm chairs at each end. A sparkling crystal chandelier caught the light and silver gleamed on the buffet. Another brick fireplace was at one end of the room.

"Do you actually eat in here?"

"Sure. The table is over one hundred years old and my great-great-grandfather had ten kids. The Windover descendants are all over Texas. We have big family get-togethers, and each of my brothers has four kids, so that's at least twelve people when they come home. There's a guest cottage in back for the overflow.''

''What about your parents?''

Again she caught the briefest shuttered look before he turned his head away and switched off the dining-room light. They moved down the hall. ''My parents were divorced. I haven't seen my mother since childhood, and my dad died last year.''

''I'm sorry you lost your father. My dad died when I was eleven.''

''I miss my dad,'' he said gruffly. ''Eleven must have been a rough age to lose your father.''

''It was, but my parents were always very involved with each other and not as much with us kids. Particularly my mom. My mother was just not meant to be a mother. I was always mother to my sisters and that was all right with me and good for Mom. Dad helped with the girls.''

''So you were mother to your sisters. Was your brother Hank the second dad?''

''Hardly,'' she answered dryly. ''Hank's wild. When Dad died, Hank got more wild. He's in trouble half the time and he's out of touch with the family. I haven't seen him in over a year.''

''I sort of remember that he'd been in some scrapes,'' Jason said politely, and she could imagine that if he knew her brother, he knew some of the predicaments Hank had been in.

''If you know Hank, you must ride in rodeos.''

''I used to, but I haven't had time in the past few years. I was a saddle bronc rider. I did a few months of bull-riding, broke my arm and quit.''

''I don't know how many bones Hank has broken.''

''Here's the living room,'' Jason said, switching lights on in a formal room that was exquisitely furnished and looked as if no one ever used it, much less a houseful of men. It was the one room that did not appear to hold any antique furniture, and it struck a slightly strange note with the rest of the house.

"This is a nice room," she said, noticing that the blue satin drapes were faded, but still looked elegant.

"Yeah, well, we don't spend time in here," he said, switching off the lights. His voice was harsh, and she realized there were undercurrents in his family that he didn't talk about. She suspected he didn't talk about a lot of the facets of his life. She was beginning to decide the real Jason Windover might be hidden from the world.

"Here are the bedrooms," he said, switching on lights and moving down the hall as she looked into rooms that were spacious, masculine and comfortably furnished. "My bedroom is the master bedroom at the end of the hall and I'm going to put you in here tonight, right next to me, so I can hear you."

He switched on a light and crossed to the closet. She looked at an elaborate Louis XVI bed of dark, hand-carved mahogany. A tall chiffonier matched the bed. The room had pale-green and off-white colors, and, as she looked around, she wondered how many other women had stayed in it.

He tossed out a cotton robe. "Here's a robe. I'll give you some of my T-shirts so you can get into something cooler. There's the bathroom and towels are in the cabinet. Change and we'll get something to eat."

She nodded and he motioned to her. "First, come see my bedroom, and I'll give you the T-shirts."

She followed him to a spacious bedroom with a brick fireplace, shelves of books, another large television, a tall, rosewood armoire with an ornate cheval glass beside it. A second keypad for the alarm system was in his room, so he could switch it on or off from either end of the house. A king-size four-poster bed dominated one end of the room and a stack of books stood on a table beside the bed. She strolled over to see what he read and looked at titles about the Second World War.

"You like history."

"Yes," he answered while he rummaged in a drawer and handed her a stack of folded T-shirts. "My grandfather was in the landing at Normandy in the Second World War. He kept a diary of sorts and because of that, I got particularly interested in that war."

Jason thrust the pile of shirts into her hands.

"Thanks. I'll need only one."

"Take them all. After we say good-night, don't try to leave the house. I have the alarm turned on. If you open a door or a window, it will trigger the alarm. When we go to bed, I'll change the setting and the alarm will go off if you step into the hall. You're in a cell here. It's just much nicer than the one in Royal."

She nodded again, left his room and went to hers, closing the door behind her. She showered and washed her hair. She found a dryer and dried her hair. It had a natural curl and was unruly, but tonight she didn't care. She pulled on a navy T-shirt and slipped back into her sweatpants and then left to find him, returning to an empty family room and then going to the kitchen where he was making sandwiches.

He glanced over his shoulder and then turned to look more carefully at her, and she wished she were back in the lumpy sweatshirt. The T-shirt clung, and the look he was giving her was making her tingle all over.

"My goodness, Meredith, you clean up good."

"My friends call me Merry," she said breathlessly, knowing she needed to re-engage her brain. The man was definitely *not* one of her friends. Nor would he ever be one.

He crossed the room to her, stopping only inches away, and she hoped he couldn't hear her drumming heartbeat.

"So we're going to be friends," he drawled in that deep, sexy voice. He reached out to touch her hair, letting locks slide through his fingers, and she was aware of the faint contact. "That's interesting."

"I spoke before I thought," she admitted.

"You don't want to be friends?"

"I don't think it's possible."

He focused on her face, moved closer and tilted up her chin. She was too aware of his finger holding her chin, too aware of all of him. "I am sorry about your scraped cheek and hands. You shouldn't ever have something like that happen. I hate that I caused your scrapes and bruises. I'm sorry."

"You should be," she said, wishing he would move away, but unable to move herself. Another one of his riveting looks nailed her and she gazed back, too aware of the silence stretching between them. "You're standing too close," she said, aware she was hemmed in by him and the kitchen cabinets behind her.

"I am? I disturb you?"

"You're not adding me to your list of broken hearts, Jason, so just move back and give me room."

"All those challenges," he said quietly without moving an inch, placing his hands on the cabinets on both sides of her and moving even closer. "Now do you really expect me to ignore them?" he asked softly. "You're the one who brought them up."

"I didn't mean any of them as challenges to you. I'm not impressed. I'm not interested. I don't want to go to dinner or anything else with you."

"You might hurt my feelings."

"There's no way I can do that," she said, finding every word more difficult to get out. He stood entirely too close and he was entirely too handsome. And she was being far less than truthful when she told him she wasn't impressed. Oh, my. She'd bet the house that his kisses would melt any recipient into a bubbling blob.

"I have a heart that can be broken just like anyone else's."

"I think your heart is locked away behind impervious armor and no woman will ever get to touch it."

He ran his finger along her throat, a faint touch that sizzled. "I'm not invincible."

"I don't care to find out. I think you said we were going to drink something," she reminded him, trying to look away and glancing first at his mouth, fleetingly wondering what it would be like to kiss him. Why would she wonder something like that about a man like Jason Windover? Had her brain gone completely to mush?

"Oh, sure," he answered as if that were the last thing on his mind. "What would you like?"

"Just some pop."

He moved away, and she could breathe again. Watching him as he walked around the kitchen, she was thankful his attention had shifted from her. He brought her pop poured over ice in a tall glass, and he carried another beer and she hoped it would knock him out for the night, yet he had a way of slowly sipping them that made them last.

Finally they were settled back on the sofa in the family room. Jason sat too close with one arm stretched on the back of the sofa and one leg bent, his knee on the sofa only inches from her thigh. He offered her a sandwich which she declined. He helped himself.

"I think you should forget about Dorian and go home," he said, taking a bite of his cheese sandwich.

"Maybe so."

"You don't mean that. You're just patronizing me until I'm out of your sight. You can't change him. You can't accomplish anything. You're just a fly buzzing around his head annoying him."

"Maybe that's all, but he deserves to be annoyed."

"Merry, I said it before and I'll say it again. Women have jilted men and broken their hearts. Men have jilted women and broken their hearts. When it isn't a deep commitment, you just pick up and get over it."

"I'm sure that's the philosophy of your life," she said, becoming aggravated with him again. "My sister is losing weight. She's broken-hearted. Her work is getting neglected. Her life is suffering.''

"She's got to get over him. Introduce her to new guys," he said, finishing his sandwich and taking a sip of beer.

"She doesn't want to meet any guy right now."

"I'll repeat, when there hasn't been too deep and too lasting a commitment, then broken hearts mend."

"Thanks, Abby, for that bulletin."

"It's the truth. They weren't married. They hadn't known each other for years."

"That's so easy for you to say! She's heartbroken and I want him to know he can't walk all over someone and then turn his back and walk away. I want to cause him some grief. He's hurt her and taken her money—"

Jason turned to look at her. "Dorian took money?"

"Yes. Holly didn't have a lot, but she's very thrifty. She has a good job and she's saved quite a bit for having just been out of a college a few years."

"Are you certain he took her money?"

"Now you're interested," Merry said, once again annoyed with him. "Money's important to you, but Holly's broken heart isn't."

"There's a difference. If he took money, he may have broken the law," Jason said quietly, and she realized she had his undivided attention now.

"Tell me exactly what Dorian did," Jason said.

Three

A broken heart was one thing—but missing money was quite another. All of Jason's cold, negative feelings about Dorian returned. Suppose he had been right about the man all along? Money was missing at Wescott Oil and some of it had turned up in an account in Sebastian's name. Someone had taken that money and tried to frame Sebastian for murder. A man had been killed, and the guilty party was a cold-blooded murderer.

Jason realized Merry was studying him intently. "What?" he asked.

"What's going through your mind? Dorian taking Holly's money disturbed you."

"We've had something going on here in Royal," he said, choosing his words carefully. "You've met some of the Texas Cattleman's Club members," he remarked dryly, and she did have the grace to blush.

"I just wanted to find out where Dorian was. I'm sure it

was a dreadful shock to have a woman violate the inner sanctum of your precious club.''

''You weren't exactly quiet about it,'' he said, thinking that was all he'd heard about the day after Merry had burst into the club demanding to know Dorian's whereabouts. Merry was a fiery, feisty, Texas tornado, stirring people up everywhere she went. Was she that way at home in Dallas? He found it difficult to keep his mind on the conversation, on Dorian, on problems, when she was sitting close and looking so enticing.

Since her shower, Merry's hair was silky, springing free to curl slightly around her face and spill onto her shoulders. Its deep auburn color held highlights of gold and fiery orange. In the kitchen he had wanted to kiss her. And he had almost tried because he thought she wanted him to, but the moment had passed. Now he wanted to stretch his arm out about three more inches and touch her. He resisted the urge, focusing on their discussion.

''Do you remember meeting Sebastian Wescott?'' he asked.

''Dorian's half brother. I thought he was nicer than Dorian.''

''Ahh, we agree on something,'' Jason said, having resisted touching Merry as long as he could. He wound locks of her hair around his fingers, letting her soft curls slide over his hand. There was a flicker in her smokey eyes and pink tinged her cheeks, so she had noticed and she wasn't objecting. Was the lady feeling the same sparks that he was?

''Sebastian inherited the Wescott Oil empire and when Dorian arrived in Royal and let his presence be known and that he was a long-lost half brother, Sebastian took him in and got him a job at Wescott Oil in computer services.''

''Sebastian Wescott should know that he has taken in someone who is deceptive and unscrupulous. Dorian is a real snake.''

''We've inducted Dorian into the Texas Cattleman's

Club because he's Sebastian's half brother. He seems to have fit himself into life in Royal.'' Only half thinking about Dorian and Sebastian, Jason talked while his thoughts were on Merry, her big eyes, her soft hair that he was winding around his fingers. She sounded sincerely annoyed with him. His usual ability to charm a woman seemed to be failing. But, he reminded himself, they hadn't gotten off to the best of starts. Still, for whatever reason, he wasn't accustomed to women disliking him and it bothered him. It also bothered him greatly that he was the cause of her skinned cheek. Her skin was as soft as a rose petal and he wished he could undo the harm he had done.

"And—"

He realized he had stopped talking as he studied Merry and wondered about her.

"Sorry. My mind wandered. Where was I?"

Her brows arched while her gaze filled with curiosity. "Where did your mind wander?" she asked softly.

His pulse jumped. "To you. What you're like, your soft hair—"

"Your attention better wander back to Dorian Brady."

"That's not nearly as much fun."

"It's safer."

"Scared, Merry?"

She gave him a sultry look that sent his temperature soaring. "Not at all. I'm not your type, so let's get back to facts. What were we talking about, Rob Cole?"

"Don't be in such a rush to change the subject, now that it's on us."

"There is no 'us.' Tell me about Rob."

He was tempted to keep flirting with her, but good sense took over, and he knew she was right.

"Rob Cole's wife, Rebecca," Jason continued, trying to disengage himself from a spell that Merry seemed to weave effortlessly, "found the body of Eric Chambers, a man who worked at Wescott Oil and was murdered."

"How awful!"

"Eric had been strangled. Eric was Vice President of Accounting at Wescott. Money was missing at the company. When some of it was found in a private account of Sebastian's, he was arrested and accused of the murder. There was a very incriminating e-mail that Sebastian supposedly sent to Eric."

"That sounds terrible," Merry said. "At the trial Sebastian must have walked, or I wouldn't have met him at the club." She shook her head, causing the locks wound in Jason's fingers to slip free and he wondered if it really bothered her that he was touching her hair. The last thing he ever intended to do was force even the slightest unwanted attention on a woman. Yet, when they had locked gazes, Merry had been as immobile as he. And in the kitchen when he had moved close, she had been breathless. Just minutes ago, she had flirted with him. Curious about his effect on her, he ran his finger across her knuckles while he watched her face.

When he saw the faint flicker in her eyes, his pulse jumped. Maybe his attention wasn't unwanted after all.

He took her hand in his gently, careful not to touch her scraped skin. "You have small, delicate hands, Merry."

She yanked her hand away and balled it into a fist in her lap. "What happened after Sebastian was arrested?"

"The case was dismissed. He had an alibi that he couldn't talk about, but his attorney found a way to prove that he couldn't have committed the murder, so someone was obviously trying to frame him. Someone planted evidence in Sebastian's office that indicated he was responsible for the missing money."

"That's dreadful!"

"Dorian might stand to gain a lot if Sebastian were out of the way. It's one thing for a man to break your sister's heart. It's another to cross the line and steal her money."

"The money isn't as important as deceiving her."

"Maybe not, but it tells me more about Dorian's character."

"It doesn't say one thing more about him than what I'm telling you that he did in deceiving Holly."

"All anyone knows about Dorian's past is what he's told us," he said. "Tell me about the money."

"All right. Holly let Dorian talk her into opening a joint account. He said that when they married everything would be jointly shared anyway. He told her he didn't believe in keeping things separate. What was his was hers and vice versa. So she did."

As Merry talked, Jason watched her. If he had good sense, he wouldn't flirt with her or touch her. This was definitely not a woman he wanted to date. Not in the next million years. And yet—what was it about her that drew him? A few casual touches shouldn't hurt anything. She was going to ignore them anyway.

"By your standards I'm sure she didn't have a lot," Merry continued. "Holly worked hard and went without things and saved. She had several thousand dollars, and he just cleaned it all out and was gone."

"That's an entirely different matter than running out after telling a woman he loved her."

"It's different if you think money is more important than love!" she snapped indignantly and he knew he had just lowered himself in her sight again, but he was lower than a snake already so another notch wouldn't matter.

"Do you have records of this joint account and of the withdrawal?"

She flushed again, and he wondered whether she was making everything up. "Dorian kept the records. He told Holly that he was moving the account to a bank where they would get better service. She gave him all the receipts. I don't have proof of anything he did. He was very clever." Big eyes stared at him. "You don't believe me, do you?" she asked, sounding resigned as well as aggravated.

He thought before he answered. "I sort of believe you, but I sure as hell wish you had proof. Do you know how much better it would be if you could pull out bank statements, that sort of thing?''

"He took the money," she said stubbornly. "And I'll bet he's tied in with whatever is going on at Wescott Oil. The man is greedy, ruthless and totally unscrupulous.''

Jason stared at her while he mulled over his own negative feelings about Dorian. He shouldn't let them color his judgment now, though.

"I'm not convincing you," she said and she sounded discouraged and resigned.

"I'm listening and thinking about it, but proof would make a world of difference. You know the old saying about a woman scorned."

She stood. "I'm exhausted and I'd like to go to bed.''

"Sure." He came to his feet. "In the morning do you want to sleep in or do you want me to call you?"

"I would much rather sleep in."

"Suits me fine," he said, thinking of appointments he would have to juggle to stay home with her. Yet the thought wasn't unpleasant. "I'll be up early. I work out first thing. You may use my exercise room if you want."

"Thanks. I usually work out in the morning, too."

"I'm not surprised at that," he remarked dryly.

Switching off lights, he walked down the hall with her. He glanced at her out of the corner of his eye. He had rarely dated short women and hated to have to stoop down to kiss one. It was much more pleasant to have an armful of tall, soft woman than to have to bend himself into a pretzel shape to get a hug and a kiss. "Are you between jobs right now?"

"That's right."

"So you can take time to get out and slash tires and break into men's private clubs and all that?"

Her eyes narrowed and she shot him a look that should have dealt as big a blow as her fist, but he wasn't one to be intimidated by looks.

"Dorian Brady is evil, and I don't think he should do his wicked deeds and not have some comeuppance."

"Maybe you should let the law worry about comeuppance."

At the door of her bedroom, she turned to face him. "You can't keep me here indefinitely."

"I don't intend to. I got you off the street tonight and as long as you leave Dorian alone, you can go your own way. Will you leave the man alone?"

She seemed lost in thought. "I suppose," she said with a sigh.

"I think he's suffered."

"You are birds of a feather," she remarked darkly.

"I told you before that I've never promised a woman marriage, never taken a dime of a woman's money. Please do not lump me with Dorian Brady," Jason said, annoyed with her again. She was like eating hot peppers—tasty, but full of sting.

"All right. I apologize for lumping you with him," she said.

"Thank you." He placed his hand above her head, resting his palm against the jamb. Moving closer, he tilted her chin up. "You know, the night doesn't have to be wasted."

"Wasted?" she asked, sounding breathless. He slipped his hand to her throat and discovered her racing pulse. He wasn't waiting for her arguments or protests that he was sure would be coming. Pretzel twist or not, he wanted to kiss her. He slipped his arm around her waist, stepped closer and leaned down.

The moment Jason's arm went around her waist, Merry opened her mouth to protest, but his lips covered hers and it was as if she had stepped into space and was into a dizzying free fall—and on fire at the same time. When his tongue touched hers, her heart thudded. His tongue slipped across hers, stroking and exploring her mouth, melting her into a trembling mass of breathless woman.

Mouths together, tongues together, bodies together. She

couldn't resist him even though she knew she should. His kiss was dynamite with a million tiny explosions, yet beneath the fireworks, something seemed great.

Standing on tiptoe, she slipped her arm around his neck and held him. Lordy, the man was tall. And breathtaking and a heartbreaker. A world-class heartbreaker who always let women know they wouldn't be permanent fixtures in his life.

Clinging to him, she trembled, kissing him eagerly in return as his kiss became more demanding and passionate. She was lost in it, drowning in heady sensations. This couldn't be happening, but it was. It was all too real, all too intense, making her want so much she knew she could never have. Where were her wits?

She stopped kissing him back, pushed against his chest and then was standing facing him once again. The moment she pushed, he moved away.

There had never been a kiss like his. Not once in her lifetime, and she was shaken badly. She wasn't widely experienced with men, but she suspected if she had been widely experienced, she still would have had the same reaction to Jason. Breathing hard, he looked down at her.

Words failed her, and she simply entered the bedroom and closed the door in his face.

Then she felt idiotic. She should have said something and not acted like a kid with a first kiss. But it was too late to open the door and start a conversation now.

Dazed and flustered, she stared at the closed door. No wonder he left hearts broken everywhere. It wasn't fair. He was too handsome, had a smile that would melt a glacier and had kisses that could seduce the coldest and wisest heart.

She moved to a rocker and sat down, staring into space. Closing her eyes, she remembered his kiss. He probably hadn't even enjoyed kissing her. Goodness knows, he had stopped fast enough! *Oh, my.* What a kiss! She had turned down a dinner date with him. She wanted to jump up, run to his bedroom and tell him yes, she'd go to dinner with him. Except she couldn't. She didn't want to be just another one of his conquests, and she suspected if the number of them were known, it would be a Guinness record. Maybe not that many. He seemed sort of a nice guy. Her lips still tingled, and she had other things to think about, but for the next hour, she was just going to sit here and remember the best kiss of her life.

An hour later the house was quiet and dark. Her eyes had adjusted to the darkness and she had rummaged around and found little things she thought she might use: a paper clip she straightened, a nail file. She dressed in her dark sweats again with a cap on and she opened the door of her bedroom and lay down on the floor. Carefully, taking time, she slithered into the hall. The alarm system would either be one of those heat-sensor ones or it wouldn't. If it was a garden-variety motion detector, it might not pick up movement very low to the floor.

Expecting the siren to scream at any second, she inched her way, moving her arm so carefully and then the other arm. Next she slid her body, trying to stay pressed as close against the floor as possible and to move as slowly as possible. Her ears felt as if they were growing as she strained for the slightest sound.

She was thankful his hall floor wasn't carpeted. Instead, he had a plank floor that made it easy for her to slide along. With her body weight spread, there were no creaking boards either. Pray the man slept soundly and for hours longer!

If the alarm went off, she was going to make a run for it, but after covering five yards and no alarm, she thought maybe she would make it all the way to the back door and the alarm keypad.

Sleep, sleep, she silently urged Jason. Perspiration poured off her face and she was on fire in the hot sweats and clinging cap. It seemed hours and miles to the back door.

When she reached the back entryway, she wondered how long it had taken her. She was afraid the sun would be coming over the horizon. As a rancher, he probably rose before the sun, so she wanted to be out of the house as soon as possible. She wiped perspiration from her face on the sleeve of her shirt. She was hot, miserable and tense.

She neared the keypad. If the alarm system was typical and this door was keyed in as the entry door, she would have some thirty seconds to turn it off before the alarm would go off. But with her first movement, it would begin emitting tiny beeps that might wake him. She thought about the numbers she had watched him punch. If she got them wrong, all her effort would be for nothing and he would be after her and catch her before she could reach his pickup. The man was a very fast runner.

Taking a deep breath, she stood and swiftly punched the combination of numbers she had watched him use. As her fingers flew over the keypad, there were four tiny beeps from the alarm, and she prayed he slept soundly.

Without looking back, she unlocked and opened the door. As soon as it opened, it set off another three small beeps, but no loud alarm went off when she stepped into the cool night. Taking a deep gulp of air and half expecting him to clamp a hand on her shoulder or tackle her again, she raced to his truck. Thank Brother Hank for teaching her how to hot-wire a car.

Seconds later, the motor roared to life, and she grinned.

"Whoo hoo!" she yelled when she put the pickup in gear. "So long, cowboy. You'll get your pickup back later today!"

She floored the accelerator, skidded and settled to a speed that stirred up a plume of dust as she laughed triumphantly and raced away from Jason's house.

While she drove into town, she planned her next move—another little annoying reminder to Dorian Brady that he had not gotten away with his schemes without any reprisals.

Sometime soon, she intended to confront Dorian about

Holly's broken heart, but she knew he would just deny that he knew anything about Holly and say that he had never been engaged.

Her smile of triumph over escape vanished as she thought about Dorian and Sebastian and all Jason had told her about Wescott Oil. Could Dorian be behind a murder and the attempted effort to frame Sebastian Wescott?

Feeling chilled, Merry realized she might be dealing with a very dangerous man. If he was involved in murder, then his dirty dealings went far beyond lying to Holly and stealing Holly's money and trying to frame Sebastian. Holly was fortunate the man was out of her life. Merry hoped the day would come when Holly would see that.

The more Merry thought about Dorian and Wescott Oil, the more certain she became that Dorian had to be the murderer. No one would believe her, though. She didn't have one degree of proof; just because he had deceived Holly and taken her money, that didn't make him a murderer. Merry wished now she had asked Jason more questions about the murder.

When she reached town, the eastern sky had the faintest gray tinge. She parked the pickup in front of the Royal sheriff's office. That way, if Jason reported it stolen, they would find it quickly. She climbed out, locked the pickup and walked swiftly down Main Street to the Royalton Hotel where she left word at the desk that under no circumstances was she to be disturbed. So much for Mr. Jason Windover.

In the dark of his bedroom Jason slept, dreaming an erotic fantasy about Merry Silver until dreams spun into empty reality. In the dim recesses of waking he was aware of a motor. And then he was fully awake.

For a full two seconds he stared into darkness while he listened to the roar of a motor that was rapidly fading away. Then Jason lunged out of bed because he recognized the sound of his own pickup.

He didn't think it was one of the hands leaving in the

dead of night, and none of them would have taken his pickup without asking. Jason yanked on briefs, glanced at the house alarm and stopped in his tracks as he stared at the steady green light that meant the alarm was turned off.

"What the hell?" he asked no one. He ran, yanking open the door to the bedroom next to his and staring at the neatly made empty bed. He raced down the hall in his briefs, plunging through the back door and outside to stare at where his pickup had been parked. A cloud of dust still hung over the road.

"How the hell did she get out?" he snarled, running his hand through his hair. "Dammit, wildcat."

She couldn't be far down the road. As he hurried inside and returned to his room to yank on his jeans, he mulled over his choices. He could turn in his pickup as stolen and have her thrown in jail. He could go after her, but she had a head start and he suspected she would drive fast.

"Dammit," he swore again. The woman was more trouble than a basket filled with snakes. She might not even return to Royal. She might be headed to Dallas. He didn't think she would keep his pickup, though, and she had a car somewhere in Royal, he was certain.

He yanked on a T-shirt, pulled on his boots and began to stuff his pockets with his wallet and keys. He could drive the car into town. He didn't know how she had managed to get to his keypad to turn off the alarm without setting it off, but he realized that when they'd arrived at the ranch, he had been careless in turning off the alarm. He hadn't tried to hide the code from her because he didn't think she was paying attention anyway. And he hadn't thought she would have any chance to use the code.

What was one of the first things he had been taught? Don't underestimate the enemy. Well, he had grossly underestimated this little enemy. Damn, she was trouble! She wasn't doing anything except annoying Dorian and the rest of the club members. Jason grimaced. She was annoying the hell out of him. He remembered kissing her. He didn't want to remember because her kiss had all but melted his teeth. Her kiss had gone deeper than just hot—stirring some feeling that was totally foreign to him. He had to get her out of Royal and out of his hair.

He locked up and jogged to the garage, swearing under his breath. Here he was in the dead of night, his pickup stolen, outsmarted by a five-foot bit of trouble—that was embarrassing. He thought of the foreign assignments he'd had, the assignments with the Texas Cattleman's Club. He had been up against the toughest of the tough and here this little five-foot wildcat had outwitted him—his own damn fault for underestimating her.

He should have slapped handcuffs on her and made her spend the whole night beside him. And then he *really* wouldn't have gotten any sleep. He didn't want to think about her kisses or her body or those great big smokey eyes or her soft lips that set him on fire. He was not going to think about any of that. He backed out of the garage, turned the car and raced up the road for the highway, trying to shake thoughts out of his mind that he didn't want there.

He should just call the sheriff and turn her in and let her rot in a jail cell. It would serve her right. He thought about her silky skin that was raw and skinned because he had tackled her and he knew he couldn't have her arrested and thrown in jail.

"You're getting soft, Windover," he told himself. The hell he was. He was getting hard just thinking about her and her delicious mouth. He swore and pressed the accelerator and wondered what she would do next.

As he cruised Main Street, he spotted his pickup. In spite of his aggravation, he had to grin because she had parked it squarely in the sheriff's reserved parking spot.

Watching for her, Jason cruised down Main until he reached the Royalton. He turned into the lot and let a valet have the keys. Inside the quiet hotel with its potted palms, plush oriental carpets and high ceilings, Jason strolled to the desk, his pulse jumping with satisfaction when he recognized the stocky blond clerk behind the desk.

"Morning, Mr. Windover."

"Hi, Stan. I didn't know you worked here."

"Yes, sir. I've been here almost a year now."

"Do you like it?"

"Yes, sir."

"Stan, what room is Meredith Silver in? I need to talk to her."

Stan frowned and looked uncomfortable. "She said no one was to disturb her. I'm sorry."

"All I want to do is talk. You know I wouldn't harm a woman."

"Oh, no, sir!"

Jason pulled out his wallet, withdrew a fifty-dollar bill and carefully folded it and slid it across the counter. "Just tell me the room number. I'm not asking for a key. I just want to slip a note under her door or talk to her if she will talk."

"Mr. Windover, gee." The fifty had already disappeared into Stan Fogarty's hand. "It's room three-one-seven. But I didn't tell you."

"Thanks, Stan. She won't ever know that you told me. I promise, no trouble."

"I hope not, sir."

Jason crossed the lobby, entered the hall and took the stairs. In minutes he was in front of her room. He pulled a small wire from his pocket, picked the lock and quietly turned the knob.

The room was dark and he slid inside, closing the door behind him without a sound. Ready to get revenge, he switched on the light.

Jason blinked and stared at the smoothly made bed. He spun around, looking into the bathroom, the closet, the rest of the room. There was no luggage, nothing. Had she gone back to Dallas? In the early hours of the morning? Where was she? And had she given up pestering Dorian? She hadn't checked out or Stan would have told him. She had left orders not to be disturbed. He had a gut feeling the woman was still right in Royal, but if so, where was she?

Jason knew that he had underestimated her at every turn and it was beginning to annoy him. He better start thinking that he was up against a very intelligent operative instead of five feet of aggravating fluff. He circled the room again. He could smell her perfume. He glanced in the bathroom. A wet cloth hung over a rack. She had been in here, but was gone.

Feeling ridiculous, he looked under the bed and searched the closet that held nothing except extra pillows and an ironing board. Finally, he switched off the light and went downstairs.

"Stan, has Miss Silver checked out?"

"No, sir. She just said she didn't want to be disturbed."

"Well, I didn't disturb her, so you can relax. Tell you what," he said, pulling out a ten-dollar bill. "If you see her again," Jason scribbled on a piece of paper and handed it with the ten to the clerk, "will you call me on my cell phone?"

"Sure. You don't have to give me any more money."

"Keep it. Thanks for your help."

"Yes, sir, Mr. Windover. Anytime."

Jason walked out and waited to get his car. When the valet brought it and stepped out, holding open the door, Jason noticed a small square of white paper fluttering beneath the windshield wiper. It was not the time of night or day for anyone to be advertising or selling something. And he hadn't been parked illegally. He pulled out the note and looked at the neat printing. "Your pickup is in front of the jail. Thanks for the loan of it."

He wanted to kick a tire, but he had the disgusting feeling she was somewhere watching him and laughing and he didn't want to give her the satisfaction. He swore quietly and steadily, every word in his native tongue and a few in other languages that he knew.

"Sir, is something wrong?" the valet asked.

"Sorry, no." He tipped the man and climbed into his car, then looked up at the Royalton. Every window was either dark or if a light burned, the drapes were pulled. He couldn't spot anyone looking out a window, but he couldn't see them all from inside the car. He hit the steering wheel with the palm of his hand. "Dammit!" Where was the wildcat? And what would she do next?

Four

Filled with reluctance, later that morning Jason strode into the quiet, elegant meeting room at the Texas Cattleman's Club. Coffee was served in the tall silver samovar on a sterling silver tray. Thin-bone china cups edged in gold with the club crest were beside the silver service.

Within a few minutes all eyes were on him as Sebastian stated, "Dorian's tire was slashed. We assume you apprehended Meredith Silver after that. Now, have you sent her back to wherever she came from or is she still out at your ranch?"

While the question hung in the air, Jason could feel his face flush. He rubbed his fingers along the soft denim covering his bent knee. "She's not at my ranch."

"So?" Rob coaxed. "Where is she?"

Jason faced ten pairs of curious eyes. "I don't know where the hell she is," he grumbled, and Rob let out a whoop.

"Could it be a woman has gotten the best of our resident playboy?"

"Dammit—" Jason started, but then they were all laughing.

"Our CIA agent has been given the slip by a slip of a girl—" Sebastian said, grinning.

"By a little wildcat," Jason remarked, knowing he would have to endure their teasing. "I sort of underestimated her. I'll find her—"

"How long ago did you 'lose' her?" Rob asked, grinning broadly.

"I'll find her soon enough."

"Find her before she does some other damn mischief. I had to buy a new tire," Dorian snapped, looking less than amused, but the others were still laughing.

"You may have to go back to the CIA for a little more training on how to secure and hold your prisoner," Rob needled, still chuckling.

"When did you last see her?" Sebastian asked with a twinkle in his eyes.

"Last night she was at my ranch—"

"She got away from you at your ranch?" Rob asked incredulously. "How'd she do that? I thought you had an alarm system."

"I do—"

More laughter drowned out his statement, and Jason grinned. "I'll find the wildcat today," he assured them.

Rob's smile faded. Looking relaxed, he sat back in his leather chair, but Jason noticed that Rob was intently studying each man. "On a serious note, there's something we have to discuss. We're trying to discover what we can about Eric's murder. Sebastian has been cleared of the charges against him, but there is still a murderer loose in Royal. And for reasons I don't want to go into right now, it looks as if there may be a mole in our organization." The words wiped all amusement off every face and felt like an icy wind sweeping through the room. A chill ran down Jason's spine as he instantly thought of Dorian, but kept his attention on Rob who continued to gaze solemnly at each of them in turn.

"How can we discover who it is?" Keith Owens asked, his brown-eyed gaze circling the room.

"I suppose all suspicion lands immediately on me," Dorian announced. "The rest of you have known each other for a lifetime and now this crazy woman is accusing me of things I haven't done."

"No one is making any accusations at this point," Rob said. "We just need to be more alert."

They continued discussing the problems at Wescott Oil, but the conversation wasn't as free as before, Jason noted and the group soon broke up with suggestions on how to catch his quarry and more good-natured teasing. Before they disbanded, he managed to ask Rob to wait a few minutes.

As soon as they were the only two left in the room, Jason closed the door. "I want to tell you what I learned from Merry."

Rob burst out laughing again. "How'd she get past your alarm?"

"It's a thousand years old, and I'm having a new one installed today. Dad put that other one in when I was a kid."

"You didn't take her car keys?"

"Shut up, Rob, and let me tell you something."

Grinning, Rob nodded. "Go ahead."

"She told me about Dorian jilting her sister."

"Which he denies. Is there any proof?"

"Not a shred. She said that he always had reasons for what he did or did not do. He avoided leaving any incriminating trail: no pictures, no ring, nothing. She'd bought a wedding dress and was planning her wedding when he left. He cleaned out her account."

Rob's brows arched. "Any proof of that?"

"No, but I wanted you to know what Merry said."

"Merry? You're on a first-name basis. That's good."

"I'm telling you, shut up."

Rob laughed and then sobered. "Do you believe Meredith Silver? Slashing Dorian's tires and bursting into the club doesn't give her much credibility."

Jason remembered big smokey eyes, her earnest voice. "I think she's telling the truth."

"We'll keep an eye on Dorian. In spite of his rock-solid alibi, it's beginning to sound suspiciously as though he's our man. And if he is, I don't need to tell you, he's dangerous." Rob clamped a hand on Jason's shoulder. "There's a good rookie cop I can get when he's off duty to help you keep an eye on the Valkyrie."

"Go to hell, Cole. I'll find her today." Jason snapped, knowing he would be in for teasing for the next few weeks, if not longer.

The two men walked out together and parted in the parking lot. As soon as he slid behind the wheel, Jason turned the ignition, driving out of the lot and heading for the Royalton Hotel. He was going to find Merry Silver and when he did, she wasn't getting away again.

Two hours later, as he sat in a hot car across from the Royalton, he swore under his breath. "Where is she?" he asked himself, climbing out of the car and deciding to take another approach to locating Merry.

Merry spent the morning looking at apartments, finally deciding on one a block off Main Street. She met the landlord at the office, a tall, gaunt man named Willard Smythe who was unhappy to discover she didn't have a regular job. For once in her life, Merry tossed out a mention of her mother's vocation and as she expected, she won Mr. Smythe's grudging approval.

He reminded her of a crane, with his long legs and tufts of blond hair and a peculiar way of jutting his head out, and she suspected he would have liked to turn her away.

"This is a very quiet area, Miss Silver," he stated firmly.

"I lead a very quiet life," she said, or she had until Jason Windover had crashed into it.

"Hmpf. Most of our tenants are widowed or married. We don't have young singles. Now on Berry Street there are two apartment complexes you might find more to your liking."

"I like this place. It's quiet and charming. May I see the apartment that's available?"

He sighed and stood. "Come this way." He stopped at the door to look at her. "Miss Silver. Let me repeat—this is a very quiet place. There are no wild parties."

Since when did she look like the wild-party type? she wondered. "I promise that you'll never know I'm here except when I pay my rent."

"Yes. Well, we'll hope," he muttered and turned to lead the way to a small apartment that faced the front gates.

The two-year-old apartment had lots of glass that gave it a sunny, spacious look even though it was small. The entryway opened onto a living area, an adjoining small dining room, a kitchen that was bright and cheerful in blue and white. She liked the cozy, high-walled patio, although she didn't expect to have the apartment for a long time.

The security of twenty-four-hour armed guards at the gates was reassuring. After cajoling, holding firm and finally making a deal with Mr. Smythe to help him get his records into computer files, she made arrangements to rent the apartment for a month. She made a deposit and drove back to the Royalton, circling the block and spotting Jason's black pickup parked along the curb across from the hotel.

Jason wasn't in the pickup, but she couldn't be certain he wasn't close by, watching for her, so she kept driving, circling around and approaching the hotel from the back entrance. She turned into the hotel parking, gave the valet the car key and entered the hotel, stepping into a gift shop to survey what she could of the hall and lobby. She didn't see a tall Texan, a broad-brimmed hat or any other sign of Jason.

Moving carefully to the stairs, she hurried up and in minutes closed the door behind her as she entered the second room she had rented at the hotel. It was expensive to have two rooms, but it had enabled her to escape being found by Jason last night. This room was rented under her youngest sister's name: Claudia Barclay. Claudia Barclay Silver had an old family name as her middle name and it was serving Merry well now. She didn't want Jason to find her again soon, so extra precautions were in order. She didn't think he believed one word of what she had told him about Dorian Brady.

"Men!" she said aloud. She set down the bag of items she had in her arms and began to plan for the evening.

That night Merry sat in a corner booth in the almost empty Royal Diner. Only one waitress was working and Manny was cooking. The short time she had been in Royal, Merry had heard about Manny's hamburgers and his pork chops. She had also heard about Jason Windover's playboy reputation.

Through the window of the grill kitchen Manny was visible in a white undershirt that revealed muscled shoulders and arms. At the long Formica countertop, red, vinyl-covered bar stools stood empty which was a relief to Merry because a crowd would interfere with her plans. An old sentimental ballad played on the ancient jukebox.

Excitement bubbled in her because she was going to strike again in Dorian Brady's world. And she was exuberant because the entire day she had eluded Jason Windover. At various times she had seen him watching the hotel. She was tempted to leave another note on his pickup, but by doing so, she might be pushing her luck.

Almost an hour ago, she had ordered a burger and fries and pop and had a book propped in front of her so it looked as if she were reading while she ate. No one seemed interested in her, and she surreptitiously watched the single waitress and now the only other customer at the diner, Dorian Brady, who sat three booths away from her. The whole time he had been there he had flirted with the waitress and the woman was constantly at his table, hovering over him and giggling at things he told her. Merry caught the name Laura.

Dressed in navy slacks and a blue sport shirt, Dorian looked handsome, yet Merry could only feel anger every time she looked at him. She wished she could warn the waitress, who seemed as taken with him as Holly had been.

Merry touched the blond wig she wore and adjusted the fake glasses on her nose. When he'd entered the restaurant, Dorian had glanced her way, but he had never looked at her again. And he shouldn't recognize her even though he knew she was in town. The blue sweats she wore were well padded, adding lots of pounds to her appearance.

Motioning to the waitress, Merry asked for her check and in minutes the woman brought it to her.

As soon as the waitress left, Merry pulled a cellular phone from her pocket. It was nine o'clock and dark outside. Dorian should be just into the first few bites of his dinner. Merry had seen them bring him chicken-fried steak, which suited her purposes fine. She placed a call, turning her back on the room.

"Royal Diner," the waitress answered.

Merry whispered, "Tell Dorian Brady he better check on his car." She broke the connection quickly and slipped her phone into a pocket.

As the waitress hurried to Dorian's table, Merry slid out of the booth to cross the diner to the cash register to pay her bill. She heard the brass bell over the door jingle and glanced around to see Dorian leaving.

"Was everything all right?" the waitress asked as she stepped behind the register to take Merry's cash.

"It was fine," Merry said.

"Good. Thanks for eating here. Come back again."

"Sure. Thanks," Merry said. She collected her change, walked back to her table and left a tip. Then she strolled toward the door, looking at the empty diner and the waitress with her back turned while she brewed a fresh pot of coffee. Manny was bent over with his head in a refrigerator.

Merry passed Dorian's plate and paused to shake the contents of an envelope over the thick gravy covering his chicken-fried steak. With one more glance at Manny and the waitress, Merry picked up Dorian's fork. Ignoring her pounding heart, she stirred the gravy and then replaced the fork and strolled out into the cool night. Heading back into the diner, Dorian passed her, but he didn't glance her way.

She climbed into her car and left. "Now, Mr. Dorian Brady, see how you like that!" she said. Soon the man would realize that his misdeeds wouldn't go completely unpunished.

She returned the back way to the hotel, took the stairs and whipped out her key. She would stay in her room tomorrow and maybe venture out the next day.

She stepped into her darkened room, heaving a huge sigh of relief as she reached for the switch. The light came on and her heart lurched.

"Howdy," drawled Jason, who sat with his long jeans-clad legs stretched out in front of him.

In shock, she stood immobilized. "How'd you get in here?" she asked in stunned amazement that he had found her.

"It wasn't difficult. Now that's an interesting outfit."

She began to pull her wits together and come out of her shock. All she wanted to do was get away from him.

She spun around, grabbing the door and yanking it open. With her heart pounding, she ran.

Hearing him behind her, she headed for the stairs.

An arm snaked around her waist, and she was yanked back against a rock-hard, lean body. He tossed her over his shoulder again and strode back to her room, kicking the door closed and locking it.

Crossing the room to the bed, he dumped her on it unceremoniously and stepped to one side, out of kicking range.

"You're not going anywhere without me."

She was breathing hard, angry and still shocked that he had found her. There was no way to be forceful with the man when she was flat on her back and he was standing over her. She struggled to her feet.

"This is my room and you get out."

"You have the same choice tonight you had last night. You're coming with me or you're going to jail. And judging from the way you're dressed," he drawled, studying her as if she were a bug under a microscope, "you've been up to something."

Her heart lurched again. She didn't want to go to jail. She didn't want Jason around when the news came out about Dorian.

"Call the sheriff. I'm not going with you anywhere," she snapped, trying to give herself a minute to think and to get out from under Jason's blue-green gaze.

"Suit yourself," Jason drawled and strolled to the telephone, punching the number for an outside line, then punching more numbers.

"Is Sheriff Escobar in?" he asked.

Merry's heart thudded as she dashed across the room and broke the connection. Better Jason Windover's ranch than a cell. And she didn't want to be sitting in jail when they got word about Dorian eating a dinner laced with chili peppers.

"I'll go to your ranch."

"Fine." he said, replacing the receiver. He stood too close and his gaze was too intense.

He touched her blond wig. "This is interesting," he said, carefully removing her wig and tossing it on a desk. He removed the fake glasses. "Blond wig, fake glasses, makeup that isn't like you at all." He ran his fingers through her hair and tingles shot through her in the wake of his strokes.

"And this," he said, holding her shoulders and stepping back to look her over. His finger punched her waist, but she felt nothing because he was poking the padding she was wearing.

"My, my. No one would look twice at you, would they? It's a pretty good disguise. Did it work?"

"I don't have to answer you."

"No, you don't. You've been up to something. You've done something to Dorian. Am I going to read about it in the papers?"

As her cheeks burned, she moved away from him.

"Pack your stuff. You're moving to my ranch."

Glaring at him, she watched him move to the chair and sit down as if he had no cares in the world. How could the man look so relaxed and then move so fast?

"I want to shower."

"Go right ahead. I'm in no hurry. There aren't any windows in the bathroom and the air vent is too tiny for even you to wiggle through."

She gave him another glare and began gathering up her things.

"If I am going to read about Dorian in the paper—or worse—hear about him on the late television news, you might be better off to tell me."

"I don't have one thing to tell you."

He shrugged, and she continued gathering her clothes, too aware of flimsy lace underwear in her fist. She hurried to the bathroom and locked the door, thankful to escape his watchful eyes. How had he found her?

Annoyed and worried, she showered, washed her hair and took her time. She dressed in jeans and a blue T-shirt and when she finally emerged from the bathroom, he was reading a magazine.

Her suitcase lay open on a bed. Wordlessly, she flung her things into it as he watched every move she made.

"I had a new alarm installed today. You won't get past this one."

"I didn't intend to," she answered as haughtily as she could.

Amusement flared in his eyes while he came to his feet. "Ready to check out of both rooms? You won't be needing them."

"I think I will just go home to Dallas. You can follow me."

"No way, lady. Today you rented one of the most exclusive apartments in Royal."

"How did you find out—" She clamped her mouth shut, determined she wouldn't give him the satisfaction of knowing how shocked she was that he already knew about the apartment. The man wasn't as out of it as she had first thought. She couldn't guess how he had learned about the apartment because she knew he hadn't been following her. If he had, he would never had let her get near Dorian tonight.

"Do you want to call home and tell anyone where you'll be? A boyfriend? Your sister? Your mother?"

"There is no boyfriend. I'll call my sister."

She called and got the answering machine. "Holly, I'll be at Jason Windover's ranch. The number is—" She handed him the phone and he said his number and gave her back the telephone.

"I'm fine and staying at the Windover Ranch. I'll let you know any developments." She broke the connection.

"Ready, Merry?" Jason asked.

When he said her name, another tingle slithered along her nerves. She nodded and headed for the door. He took her arm and she knew that, in the next few minutes, there wouldn't be any escaping him.

She checked out and they left. "What about my car? I can't leave it here."

"You won't have to. Give me the keys. I've already made arrangements to have the hotel keep it tonight and tomorrow one of my hands will pick it up and bring it out to the ranch.''

Silently she climbed into his pickup and sat far against the door while he drove.

''I'll say it again—you should let me know now if you've been out doing something evil to Dorian.''

''I don't have anything to say to you. You don't believe me about him, anyway.''

''I'm open-minded about it. It would be nice if you could come up with some proof, so keep thinking back. Seldom do people avoid leaving some kind of trail. Where did he work when he was dating your sister?''

''At Denworth Technology.''

''There, we can check on that.''

Merry watched Jason as he drove. His answer implied he was thinking about her accusations. ''Tell me again about the murder,'' she said.

While Jason talked, she watched his hands resting on the steering wheel and then she looked at his handsome profile. The man was sinfully good-looking and she had to keep up her guard because she didn't want her heart to become another trophy.

''You're trying to find a murderer. I think it might be Dorian.''

Jason shot her a glance. ''You don't like the man, but don't hang a murder charge on him when you have no proof.''

''You don't like him either, do you?'' she asked, feeling an undercurrent when Jason talked about Dorian. Jason's head whipped around in another swift glance.

''No, I don't,'' he admitted. ''I don't have a reason either, which is bad. I usually like everyone I know. There's just something about him—I don't know what it is—''

''It's probably his insincerity. He's as phony as they come. Why don't you let me help on this murder investigation?''

Jason smiled. ''You'll have to ask the police.''

"Cat's whiskers! You and those Cattleman's Club member friends of yours are investigating this, aren't you?" The idea just occurred to her and the more she thought about it and the little things he had said, the more certain she was.

"What gave you an idea like that?"

"You're not denying it, Jason. You know what I think— you said Sebastian had an alibi, but he couldn't tell people at first. That snooty club of yours is a front. You're involved in other things. Are you all a bunch of detectives?"

Silence stretched between them while he shot her another speculative glance. "No, we're not. That's rather perceptive, Merry. Rob is a private detective and most of us have military backgrounds with several of us having done some foreign work."

"I'm right, aren't I?"

"Look, most people don't know what we do. Let's leave it that way."

"I can keep my mouth shut."

"Then please do. It'll be safer for everyone concerned."

"I will, but not around you. You're not all detectives— so what's the deal?"

Again, he was silent a long time and she waited, watching him—which was oh, so easy—while he got an answer formed in his mind. At least he wasn't lying to her about it.

"We try to help people when they need help. We can go places and do things that officials can't always do. But that's strictly off the record and for your ears only."

She nodded. "I'll keep it to myself. It does raise my opinion of you somewhat."

He grinned that fabulous grin and shot her another quick look. "I thought I was right down there with the snakes in your book."

She had to smile in return. "Nope. Dorian's down with the snakes. You were a little higher in my esteem, but you've gone a little higher still since I know you are something besides a spoiled, rich playboy."

"Ouch! Look, I work. I hope I'm not spoiled—shoot, I might as well save my breath because I know I'm not changing your opinion." Another quick look shot her way. "I take it you're not exactly on poverty row since you booked two rooms at the Royalton and rented an apartment. You can choose your work assignments as you please."

She flushed and was glad it was dark inside the pickup so he couldn't see her. "I earn a living," she said.

"You graduated from college about five years ago?" he guessed.

"No. As a matter of fact, I enrolled at Texas University, went one year and landed a part-time job. Then I went home to a summer job that paid so much I never went back to college. But I'm going to get my degree," she said, fierce determination welling up in her. "I'm taking a correspondence course now. I'll get my degree."

"I'm sure you will if you put your mind to it."

"What did you major in?" she asked.

"Political science with a minor in animal husbandry."

"That's a weird combination."

"I needed both in my life."

They talked about college years and earlier until Jason turned the truck into his ranch. This time he parked in the garage, a distance from the house. When they entered his kitchen, he punched the alarm so swiftly, she wasn't certain of the numbers.

"It doesn't matter whether you got that combination or not—you won't slip past this one when it's set."

"I don't intend to try," she said, drawing herself up and receiving a disarming grin.

He reached out to brush her jaw lightly with his knuckles and she drew a deep breath. "I'm glad that scrape is healing."

"It's fine."

"We're not enemies?" he asked, his voice lowering a notch and a heated look warming his eyes.

"No," she said, aware he stood too close and she should move away, but she was rooted to the floor.

"Friends, then?" he asked, his hand stroking her throat.

"I suppose so," she whispered. Summoning all her will-power, she turned away from him. "Where do I put my things?"

"I'll put them." He picked up both suitcases and carried them to the bedroom that she had stayed in before. In a short time she was seated on his large leather sofa again, curled up in a corner and he was seated facing her only a little over a foot away.

"I've been thinking about all you told me. Did anyone question where Dorian was at the time of the murder?" she asked.

"He has an alibi—he was at the Royal Diner. Laura Edwards, a waitress there backed up his story."

"Another woman in love with Dorian."

"How do you know that?"

"You only have to look at the two of them together." Merry took a deep breath. "Why don't you let me help you catch Dorian?"

He gave her a smile that was as condescending as a pat on the head. "Thanks, but I don't think so."

"Why not? It looks to me as if you could use a little help."

"Your style is a little flamboyant. Right now he doesn't know he's under suspicion."

"It doesn't have to be flamboyant. I can be subtle."

"Thanks, anyway."

Jason was beginning to annoy her again. "If you can get me into Wescott Oil, I can get into Dorian's computer files."

Jason lowered his bottle of beer, set it back on the table and gazed at her patronizingly. "In a word—no. Thanks, anyway."

"You don't think I can do it," she challenged.

He shrugged broad shoulders. "No, I don't. You're into slashing tires and bursting into private clubs."

"I slipped out of here without your knowing it and got away with your pickup and eluded you all day."

"It was the luck of the amateur."

"Well, it sounds to me as if you guys are suffering the incompetence of the too-well-trained."

Amusement flashed in Jason's eyes while he shook his head. "Tomorrow I'll take you to town with me and buy a new computer. You can help me set it up here in my ranch office. I'll pay your going rate, of course. Okay?"

"Yes. Now back to Dorian. If you'll get me into Wescott, I can look at his files and I might learn something none of you know."

"You can't get into his files."

"Hah! It's an oil company."

"They have their computer people who are specialists."

"I can get into his files."

"You're mighty confident."

"I know my abilities and my limitations," Meredith said, hoping she could live up to her promises, but she thought she could.

The ring of the phone interrupted their conversation and Jason stretched out his long arm to pick up the receiver. He stood and turned his back to her, lowering his voice and moving a few feet away so she couldn't hear what he was saying.

He turned, glancing over his shoulder at her with a direct, annoyed look.

Dorian. Intuitively, she was certain the call was about Dorian. The man deserved a little upset in his life. If what she suspected were true about him, he deserved far worse than anything she had dealt him.

Jason replaced the receiver and turned to face her, his hands on his hips. "You're not accomplishing one thing except to aggravate Dorian."

She raised her chin and refused to bother defending herself.

"You put chili peppers in Dorian's dinner. What in blazes did you think that would do other than make him angry?"

"What makes you think I did any such thing?"

"Oh, come on—that was Keith, who was in the pharmacy when Dorian charged in. He was breaking out with hives because someone had laced his dinner with chili peppers. You're wasting your time, aggravating him and getting his guard up, and getting in the way of our investigation."

"So you *are* investigating what happened?"

"That's between you and me—if you can be trusted."

"You can trust me, but why don't you let me help you?"

"Why don't you stop doing these ridiculous things?" he shot back, sitting down again to face her. "You're not solving anything or helping your sister either."

His words stung because she knew he was right. Meredith wound her fingers together and looked at them. "I know you're right, but it was so terrible to watch Holly suffer and know that Dorian was getting off scot-free."

"Give it up and leave him to us," Jason said grimly.

"Maybe I'm going about this all wrong, but I didn't know Dorian might be involved in murder. I'll stop annoying him."

"Good. Do I have your promise?"

"Yes, but you should let me get to his computer. You're trying to catch a murderer here and whatever has happened is tied into Wescott Oil in some manner. Money was taken, a man was murdered. Let me look at Dorian's computer files."

"Dorian has an alibi. He couldn't have committed the murder."

"Yet you suspect him anyway."

"Yeah, maybe so. But breaking into his computer is illegal."

She gave him a look. "So is murder."

As Jason raked his fingers through his hair, Meredith watched dark locks spring back into place and remembered when she had touched the back of his head and his hair had curled over her hand.

He turned to stretch out his arm and snagged the phone again, placing a call.

"Sebastian, it's Jason. I've got Merry Silver here with me." He paused, listening. "That's right. I want to ask you something. Is there any way you can get us into Wescott Oil so she can look at Dorian's computer files?"

She waited, unable to fathom much from Jason's side of the conversation except that Sebastian was not enthused. Obviously, neither man believed she could get into Dorian's computer files and neither thought it worth the trouble to let her try.

Finally Jason replaced the receiver and turned to her. "How badly do you want to look at his files?"

"How badly do you want to catch him if he's the murderer?"

"Sebastian will help us, but he said there is no way he can get us into the building after-hours. We're on our own."

"What do you mean—'we're on our own'?"

"If you want into Dorian's office, we're going to have to break into Wescott Oil like burglars."

Five

"**W**hy can't Sebastian just let us in?"

"He doesn't want to be seen with us. I don't blame him and I don't want him involved. Remember, he was recently arrested and I'm certain he's still being watched, so he shouldn't be seen with us."

"I understand."

"Up to a point, if we're caught, you've got a reputation in town for doing wild and crazy things, so I think we can talk our way out of trouble with the law. If a security guard finds you looking at Dorian's private files, that's another matter. And I don't want us to get caught. If Dorian has done what we suspect, we're crossing a dangerous man."

A chill raced down her spine as she thought about how much she had already antagonized Dorian. "So we're on our own."

"Basically. Sebastian will come out tomorrow and bring a map of the offices and building. He'll go over everything with us and he's going to unlock a back gate, but we have to get ourselves in and out of the building. Sebastian said you'll never get into the files. They have a highly sophisticated, hacker-proof system.''

Eagerness bubbled in her to get her fingers on Dorian's computer. ''I'll bet you a steak dinner that I get in.''

''Deal,'' he said, studying her. ''You're sure of yourself.''

''When it comes to computers.''

''I know computer types—you'll get engrossed in what you're doing and lose all sense of time. You can have twenty minutes to get into his files. If you can't access them during that time, we're getting out of there.''

''If we get past the guard, we should have plenty of time.''

''I don't want to take that chance. Twenty minutes. That's it.'' Jason lifted locks of her hair and curled them around his fingers. ''Still game?''

''Yes, I am. If Dorian's guilty of murder, I want him caught,'' she said forcefully.

''You have strong feelings, Merry.''

''I shouldn't have done what I did to him. It was foolish, but I hate how he hurt my little sister. I couldn't watch her suffer and not do anything.''

''You have to let go. She's all grown up now.''

''I know, but it's hard,'' she said, thinking of Holly. Jason pulled her into a gentle embrace and Merry looked up at him, relishing his arms around her, knowing he was right. She had to let go. Holly was a grown woman. As Merry gazed into Jason's eyes, all thoughts of Dorian or breaking into Wescott Oil fled.

What had been a comforting hug transformed. Sparks ignited, and her breath caught.

Jason's green eyes darkened, desire as easy to see as if he had spoken his feelings. Her pulse drummed. She wanted him desperately with a need she had never known before. This man was special, incredibly appealing no matter how dangerous he was to her well-being.

As he watched her, Jason wrapped his hand behind her

head and pulled her closer, leaning toward her while her heart jumped. Her hands went up to rest on his arms and then his mouth was on hers and he was kissing her.

Heat swept over her, and she leaned into him, kissing him in return while his strong arm banded her waist and he shifted her to his lap. His tongue stroked hers, and her roaring pulse shut out all other sounds. When her hand drifted to his chest, she felt his pounding heart. She wanted this tall, strong Texan, but she knew it was impossible and a threat to her future happiness. She would end up like her sister, with a broken heart and hopeless longings. Jason had made clear his feelings on commitment and Merry knew, even as she kissed him back passionately, that the only kind of relationship she wanted was one that would be permanent.

She pushed against Jason's chest and slipped off his lap. "Jason, you'll complicate my life, and we're not remotely compatible. You and I can't date each other."

"I don't know why not," he said gruffly, looking at her with so much scalding desire in his eyes that her will turned to slush.

"I want one thing. You want another. You don't want commitment. I do."

A shuttered look altered his expression, she could feel him withdrawing from her even though he hadn't moved a muscle. "Whatever you want, Merry," he said roughly. "I never go where I'm not wanted."

"I'm sure that's the truth," she stated, thinking it was a sin for him to be so handsome and charming when his attitude was so solitary.

"We'll talk tomorrow," she said, standing and leaving the room in a rush, afraid if she stayed any longer to talk, she would be right back in his lap.

The following night, butterflies danced in Merry's stomach as Jason slowed the truck behind the block that held the Wescott Oil building.

Landscaped grounds spread in front of the building and there were parking lots along one side and in the back. At the deserted side of the building, they stepped out of Jason's truck and crept to a locked chain-link gate. Jason reached through and carefully removed the partially open padlock.

Sebastian had said the back gate was rarely used and he would unfasten the padlock, certain the guard would merely give it a cursory glance when he did his rounds.

They slid through the gate, hurried to the dark shadows by the building and crept around to the front, which was well lit. They were both dressed in black. Merry's first glimpse of Jason in the dark shirt, black jeans and boots that emphasized his black hair, and made his blue-green eyes seem deep green had sent her heart hammering overtime.

In spite of the danger, it was difficult to keep her attention focused on their mission.

"You stay here," he directed, leaving Merry in the shadows near the front door.

Jason had purchased a cheap, noisy horn that he could easily activate. He had set it up with a battery operated timer, and she watched as he disappeared behind a car in the almost deserted lot. In minutes he came sprinting to join her.

"It should go off in one more minute. Your suggestion to put a couple of empty beer cans nearby should make the guard think kids were playing a prank. He'll have to get down on his knees to shut the thing off."

As Merry stood beside Jason, she could see the night guard sitting at the front desk, thumbing through a magazine.

While they waited, Jason stood close, his hand on her arm and she was only half aware of the danger of their situation, more aware of the danger to her heart from the cowboy at her side.

As they had made their plans, Merry had considered that these first few minutes would be their most vulnerable, and now her racing pulse could not slow.

Shattering the quiet night, the horn began a continuous, raucous blast. The security guard moved cautiously around the desk, paused at the door to peer outside and then stepped out. With his hand resting on his pistol, he crossed the parking lot. Moving cautiously he peered between the two cars and then disappeared as he knelt down.

"Let's go!" Merry said without waiting. Jason ran beside her and they made a stealthy dash, sliding through the front door and racing around a corner out of sight. At any second, she expected to hear a yell from the guard, but the only sound was their footfalls.

When Jason stopped abruptly, she bumped against him. He steadied her, pulling her close against his side as he pointed toward a door to the stairs. They moved more slowly, opening and closing the door without a sound. She was surprised how easily Jason managed all this—as if it were second nature to him.

They made the long climb to the executive floor, the tenth story of the building where the offices were spacious, elegant and locked. At the top floor she noticed Jason wasn't winded. He glanced at her. "You weren't kidding about working out. You just climbed ten flights without difficulty."

"So did you."

"I should have known from that first night," he remarked dryly and she grinned, remembering how she had caught him by surprise and knocked him flat. Her grin vanished as he hurried to a door and efficiently picked the lock.

In seconds he was through the outer door to the offices and then he was through Dorian's locked office door. Silent and dark, the empty office made Merry realize she was crossing a line now herself—taking risks to catch a criminal, but involving Jason, too.

He moved with the quiet certainty of a cat, and, again, she wondered about Jason's past. Then her thoughts shifted to the office and the task at hand. Walnut paneling, sheer drapes, oil paintings, crushed velvet upholstery surrounded a mammoth oak desk.

She studied Jason as he moved unhesitatingly to the desk and checked the drawers. "For a cowboy, you're very adept at breaking and entering."

She received another fabulous grin. "I retired recently from another job. I worked for the government," he said with a wink, and she realized how very little she knew about the man.

"Here's the computer," he announced, opening a cabinet and swiveling Dorian's chair around. "Do your thing. I'll stand guard. If I say someone's coming, you get out of here immediately. Just get out and get back to my car no matter where I am or what I'm doing. Agreed, Merry?"

"Yes," she answered, looking into his solemn gaze.

"Promise me."

"I promise. I don't know what you think I'll do."

"We don't have time for me to tell you."

She thought about the map that Sebastian had given them of all the offices on this floor. She knew the ninth floor held the accounting offices, but it was Dorian's office and computer that she was interested in. She had spent an hour late in the afternoon with Jason, both of them studying the Wescott Oil building map while she had been more aware of him than of the map.

Merry slid behind the desk and sat down, at home instantly when she was facing a computer. She switched on the CPU, watched the screen ask for a password and began to type.

She was unaware of Jason watching her or of him slipping out of the office and leaving her alone. The only light was from the screen, a bright glow that reflected on her hands as they moved on the keyboard.

Merry knew she had only a few tries to get this right.

It took her five minutes, but then the screen asking for a password disappeared and she was in. She scanned the menu and pulled up a file.

Merry lost track of time, but her pulse raced as she discovered that Dorian kept an electronic journal. She scanned it swiftly, her gaze skimming over words, searching for anything that might incriminate Dorian until the words: "...you don't want them to know..." jumped out at her.

The door opened and she looked around to see Jason. "Your twenty minutes are up."

"I'm in. Leave me alone."

She went back to what she was doing, unaware that he had closed the door and left. Slowing so her hands wouldn't shake, she inserted a floppy into the CPU and copied the file, skimming more lines while her pulse raced.

The moment she finished that file, she copied another one.

The door swung open and Jason thrust his head inside. "Someone's coming. Shut down!"

"One more—"

"You promised," he snapped, looking over his shoulder.

She clicked on another file from Eric Chambers to Dorian, hit Save and watched, standing while her pulse raced.

"Merry!"

She yanked out the disk and hit the close button.

"Stop what you're doing. I hear footsteps. Come on!" Jason urged, motioning to her. She dashed across the office.

"It isn't shut down."

"Don't care. Run!" Jason grabbed her hand and raced down the hall, still keeping sound to a minimum until they yanked open the door to the stairs and stepped inside. Jason closed the door silently behind him, and gasped, "We've got to get out of here."

While she clutched the floppy disk, they raced down the stairs. By the fourth floor the alarm had gone off, a high, ear-splitting shriek that turned her blood to ice.

"They know someone's in the building," Jason said. His hand tightened on hers and they moved even faster until Merry felt as though her feet weren't touching anything solid. The stairs seemed interminable, but finally they reached ground level. Releasing her hand, he sprinted ahead. They raced through the building, bursting through a back door. Now Jason wasn't making any effort to keep quiet. Alarms were blaring, all the lights on the grounds were on and she could hear sirens approaching.

"Suppose they shoot? We'll be easy targets."

He caught her hand. "If it's the Royal police, they'll fire a warning shot first. Then you stop running. Let's go."

She ran, aware that Jason was behind her. Was he trying to shield her in case anyone did open fire? she wondered.

They raced across the open parking lot, expecting at any moment to hear the guard charging after them, but they reached the gate without incident.

Gasping for breath, she yanked off the lock and rushed through to the truck, looking back to see Jason grab the padlock.

He stretched out his long legs, running to the truck to slide behind the wheel and they were off, spinning around a corner. In minutes they moved into traffic along Main Street. Jason had slowed to a sedate speed and her pounding heart was beginning to return to normal.

"We got away," he said at last. "Was it worth the risk?"

"I think it was," she said, holding up the disk. "There are things on here that I think incriminate him, but I'm not certain. I looked at everything so fast, it was almost a blur. I'm not certain I got the computer turned off. If I didn't, when Dorian comes to work later today, he'll know someone was in his office and into his computer."

"He'll know now. He was the one who came in."

"How on earth do you know that?"

"I heard him talking to the security guard as they were coming down the hall."

"Now Dorian will know someone was trying to get into his computer files," she said, chilled by the realization. "I backed out of his files. I just didn't get the computer off. He won't know for certain that someone got into them."

"He'll guess it was you."

"I suppose he will," she agreed.

"Don't try to get away from me now," Jason warned. "You may be in a lot of danger."

She shivered and locked her fingers together. "Now I'm glad Holly didn't marry him. When I can, I want to tell her all I've learned about him."

"Don't tell her yet because we don't know for certain. He knows you're at my ranch, but as long as I'm there with you, I don't think you're in danger."

"I could go back to Dallas."

"You stay right where you are," he said in a no-nonsense tone. He had been calm and in control through the entire episode while she was still shaking from their close call with security and with Dorian Brady. She took a few deep breaths and looked at the houses they were passing. She realized the foray was over. They had gotten into Wescott Oil, she had looked at Dorian's files, and she and Jason had escaped unscathed.

Fear changed to relief that was touched with jubilation. They had succeeded!

Impulsively, she turned and flung her arms around Jason and gave him a hug. "We did it! We got in and got out in one piece and I think I have something you can use."

"Hey!" he yelped, startled and glad they were on a deserted block at the edge of town and not speeding along the highway. He pulled the truck to the side of the street, turned to wrap his arms around her and hug her. Her face was inches away, and even in the dim lights on the dashboard, he could see the sparkle in her eyes. He wanted her and leaned forward to kiss her hungrily.

For one startled moment she was still and then her arms

tightened around him and she kissed him back, long slow kisses that made him forget they needed to get out of town, needed to avoid drawing attention to themselves, needed to resist touching and kissing and stirring up one iota more of the sparks between them.

She was fiery, wild and passionate and he wanted her with a need that shocked him. He wanted to shove her down on the car seat and take her right here, but for a dozen reasons he knew that was impossible.

As her tongue stroked his, Jason's senses were stormed. His pulse roared and he was hard, eager, ready. He wanted all of her and he was losing arguments with himself about holding himself in check. His hands slipped over her, following soft curves, resenting the jeans and shirt that were in his way. When he tugged her shirttail out of her jeans, she straightened, pushing against his chest.

Her breathing was as ragged as his. ''We're in town and we should get out of here.''

Jason couldn't answer. Fighting his urge to reach for her again took all his concentration. Yet he knew she was right, so he tried to get a grip on reason. He turned his attention to the road, glanced in the rearview mirror to see if they were being followed or if anyone had noticed them. Houses were dark, lawns undisturbed, the street deserted at this early-morning hour.

He put the car in gear and drove in silence, not trusting himself to speak, trying to get his thoughts away from Merry to something neutral, something that would take Merry Silver right out of his mind.

Chattering to him about the disk, she bubbled with excitement, yet he didn't hear a word of what she was saying. He wanted her desperately, and it took all his willpower to keep his attention on the road and head for home.

As they drove through the dark night Jason finally began to follow what she was saying and realized she thought she had something that could tie Dorian to the murder.

The moment they reached the ranch, she would want to look at the disk, he knew. That wasn't the urgent matter on his mind, but he was certain she was intent on discovering what she had copied from Dorian's files.

Jason turned onto his ranch road, and then he lowered the window and tossed out the padlock that he had removed from the back gate at Wescott Oil. It sailed high in the air and then dropped into a heavily wooded area with a tangle of underbrush. He had large uncleared areas on his ranch and few people ever bothered to explore them. He didn't want the police to speculate on why the padlock had been unfastened. Seb had enough problems to deal with.

The moment they entered the kitchen at the ranch, Merry waved the disk at him. "Can we look at this right now?"

"I kind of thought you'd want to," he drawled and they went to his office where she switched on the computer while he pulled a chair up beside her.

Jason watched her fingers fly over the keyboard and suspected she had already forgotten his presence. He openly studied her, knowing her attention was wholly elsewhere. He was curious about the files, but they were secondary to Merry herself. Since she had wrapped herself around him in the car, all he could think about was wanting her.

He ached to pull her into his arms, but he knew he should resist. Besides, he had a feeling he wouldn't be able to get her attention away from the computer right now. The damp night air had made her thick mane of hair curl more than usual and he touched her curls slightly. Just as he had expected, she didn't notice.

Leave her alone, he argued with himself. This was a woman who had told him she wanted commitment. He had no intention of having a long-term relationship with Merry or anyone else. Resist the lady, he reminded himself, yet still fingering locks of her hair in his hand and not wanting to break the physical contact with her.

He wanted Merry as he had wanted few women in his life and the thought scared him. He didn't want a broken heart—something he hadn't suffered for a long, long time. He didn't want to get hurt that way ever again.

"Look!" she whispered, and he tried to pull his attention from her to the screen.

He forced himself to read what she had on the screen, and then his attention focused on a daily journal by Dorian.

"I can't believe he kept records like this at the office," Jason said, looking at hints that Dorian was pleased with the way things were going and that he was getting money from Eric Chambers to keep something covered up. There were references to moving money and Jason whistled.

"There's not enough here to go to the police with, but it sounds to me as if Dorian was blackmailing Eric Chambers."

"I agree. Why would he keep this in his computer files?"

"He might not have had a chance at work to get them off his computer. With his alibi and the evidence pointing to Seb, there wasn't a reason for anyone to suspect him. And for a while after the murder, he might not have wanted to go to the office late at night to work because he might have been afraid of drawing attention to himself. He could have gone there tonight to get rid of his files," Jason said, knowing men often tripped themselves up, and Dorian was arrogant enough to think he could outsmart everyone.

"You can tell the two men knew about company money that was being shifted around, but there's no absolute proof that proves what was going on."

"You're right," he agreed, reading another file that she opened. In emphatic words, Dorian had told Eric to stop sending him messages with attachments, to get anything off his computer that they wouldn't want others to see.

"But there's enough here to point more suspicion at Dorian. A whole lot more suspicion," Jason said, too aware of the scent of her perfume as he moved closer to read the screen.

She tilted her head, studying Jason. "You said you used

to work for the government. You were at home with what we did tonight. What branch of the government were you with—Secret Service, Special Forces, CIA—what?''

''CIA.''

She closed her eyes as if she had received a blow, and he wondered if, in her eyes, that was another mark against him. Smokey eyes studied him again. ''Why did you quit?''

''I took a bullet in my side and spent some time in the hospital. It gave me time to think about what was important in my life. I took some time off and spent a few days in a little town on the coast of Spain. If the shot had been a few inches to my left, I wouldn't be here. I decided life is pretty good, and being a cowboy was a damned fine life.''

''Why did you want to be in the CIA in the first place?'' she asked, as if she couldn't imagine a single good reason.

''I got into the CIA because I wanted to do all I could for my country and I wanted the excitement. For a few years I had all that. Then home and ranch life and being a cowboy looked good again. Leave the wild stuff for the younger guys.''

''You're *so* old,'' she teased.

''I'm twenty-eight now. There are younger guys who are eager and good at their jobs.''

''I suppose your father was glad to see you come home.''

''He didn't live long enough to know,'' Jason replied, gazing past her as if lost in his own thoughts. ''My dad had a coronary occlusion and died suddenly while I was deciding whether to get out or not. He left the ranch to all three of us. I'm buying out my brothers' interests because they don't care about ranching.''

Merry realized there were depths to Jason she hadn't guessed. His CIA background was sobering.

''Make about four copies of those files, will you?'' As soon as she finished, Jason took two disks. ''I want to get one of these to Rob tomorrow and one to Sheriff Escobar. Now, enough about Dorian Brady. Let's get a drink,'' he said gruffly.

They went to the kitchen where a low light burned over the sink. With deliberation Jason set the disks down on the counter. With every move his gaze was on her, and his eyes had darkened with desire. She was lost in his gaze, drowning in the longing in his expression, so intense it was doing things to her heart and other, more intimate parts of her.

He reached for her, his fingers closing on her slender arm. The moment he touched her, her heart thudded.

"Come here, Merry. I've waited all evening for this."

Six

His words echoed the silent message in his eyes and added to the heat and desire building in her. How could he do this to her with just words and a look? But he was. He was turning her inside out without so much as the brush of his fingers.

Merry knew he wanted to kiss her. She wanted him to, wanted to kiss him, wanted more of him than she could possibly have.

As he leaned down, he pulled her close against him. She tilted her face up, standing on tiptoe, closing her eyes. Heat flashed through her. Desire was scalding her skin while she tangled her fingers in his shaggy hair and kissed him. Instantly, his arms tightened around her, pulling her hard against his lean body. The taste of him, his touch, all his lean hardness was a wonder that shook her.

He picked her up in his strong arms, carrying her to the sofa and cradling her in his arms when he sat down. Why did she feel she had waited a lifetime for this moment? He held her in the crook of his arm while his other hand slipped beneath her T-shirt. When he touched her breast, she gasped with pleasure, lost in sensations so intense that the world vanished. Lights burst behind her eyelids and the roar of her pulse shut out all sounds.

She was barely aware when he released her to tug off his T-shirt, but then her hands were on his muscled, bare chest. She ran her fingers over scar tissue, realizing how close the wound had been to his heart.

"Jason," she whispered, knowing there was a chasm between this wild man who took risks and her very ordinary life. Yet differences couldn't stop her aching desire. He was hard against her softness. His body was warm, fascinating to her. She ran her fingers across his chest and heard him groan while he kissed her.

Jason swept her T-shirt over her head and tossed it away, his gaze searing as he unclasped her bra and pushed it aside to cup her breasts in his large hands. His warm hands were big, rough, tantalizing, his fingers driving her wild.

His callused thumbs stroked her nipples. Merry shook, wanting so much with him. She knew there had to be a stopping point, but not yet, ah, not yet. For a few delicious, stolen minutes, she was going to touch him and kiss him.

Then he leaned down to take her nipple in his mouth. His tongue stroked the taut peak, a velvety wetness that sent her into another dizzying spiral and she moaned softly, her fingers winding in his hair while her other hand played over his chest.

He was giving her pleasure, giving her memories, creating longings she hadn't expected.

In minutes he shifted her so she was lying on the sofa as he moved between her legs to unfasten her jeans and pull them off. Now the look in his eyes was filled with the same heat that was melting her. The temperature had soared and every inch of her body was sparking with ultra-sensitive awareness of his touch.

Watching her, holding her immobile with his heart-stopping gaze, he caressed her legs and gently spread her thighs, moving between her legs.

Aware how deeply she wanted him, Merry tried to summon caution, knowing in seconds they would both be beyond stopping. With stormy reluctance, she pushed against his chest. With all her being she desired this incredible, appealing man, yet wisdom urged caution. When she pushed lightly, he paused to look at her.

"I want you," he whispered hoarsely. His jeans bulged with evidence of his physical needs, but the hoarse note in his voice was filled with emotion.

Her heart thudded when she met his dark gaze. "I want you, Jason, but there are other things I want, too, and I can't have them. We have to stop now while we both can."

"I want you, Merry," he repeated.

Trying to get her breath, she pushed hair out of her eyes as she sat up. "This isn't what either one of us wants." She wriggled away from him, yanking up her T-shirt to hold it in front of her.

"I can't agree with that. It seems to me that it's exactly what both of us want." His voice was husky and raw. He stretched as if struggling to regain his control.

"My sister was devastated by a broken heart. I don't want the same thing to happen to me."

"Scared you might fall in love with me?" he asked with a challenging note in his voice.

She tilted her head to study him. "As scared as you are to fall in love—period. With me or anyone else."

His blue-green eyes turned icy, and she could feel a wall come up between them. When he wanted to, he shut himself off, keeping part of himself entirely private. Sometime in the past someone had hurt him badly, but he didn't want to share who or when or how with her, and she wasn't going to pry.

"Merry, I know this won't last and you know it won't. But why not enjoy the pleasure we find in each other? You've kissed guys before."

"Not like you," she answered honestly, and he drew a deep breath.

He moved to the end of the sofa away from her and raked his hair away from his face with both hands. Shaking his hair back from his face, he seemed to be gulping for breath.

She pulled her T-shirt swiftly over her head and jammed the wispy lace bra into a jeans pocket. As she stepped into her jeans, she saw him watching her intently.

"You're a beautiful woman," he said in a low voice.

"Thank you," she replied while her heart drummed with pleasure. She reminded herself he had told that to plenty of other women and not to be bowled over by sweet talk and hot kisses, but her heart wasn't listening to her head. When he caught her wrist lightly, she looked at him in surprise. The touch was casual, merely done to get her attention, yet it sent shock waves reverberating through her. Her body ached for his touch, for his kisses, for him to finish what he had started.

That wasn't something she wanted to let him know. Unable to summon words, she looked at him quizzically.

"Don't go. I'm not sleepy and I know you're not. Let's just sit and talk," he said, releasing her wrist.

"Just sit and talk—you promise?"

"Sure," he answered. He wiped his brow, beaded with sweat, and she still felt hot, too. "You say you want commitment, Merry. How much commitment?"

Surprised by his question, she sat and put her bare feet on the sofa, hugging her knees and facing him while she mulled his question.

"An affair—long-term? Marriage?" he asked. "What do you really want when you talk about commitment?"

"I'm very old-fashioned, Jason," she answered, knowing this would be the answer that would send him running or bring that cold wall higher between them. "I want it all. I want marriage. And for me, marriage is sacred and special."

"How'll you know when you meet the right person?"

"I'll know," she said quietly, trying to avoid looking too deeply into her feelings now as she studied the handsome cowboy facing her. She didn't want to admit the bald truth, but her heart was screaming her feelings.

"Just like that?" he asked quizzically. "Like lightning striking or what?" He sounded sincerely puzzled, as if she were the expert and he the novice in dealing with sex and love.

"I'll know the way anyone knows when she or he is in love. Surely you've been in love?"

He looked away, but not before she caught a strange flash that was almost a grimace. "I've loved, and I don't believe you if you tell me you've never been in love. You've dated, haven't you?"

"Yes. I haven't ever been truly, deeply in love. I don't want what you're accustomed to—flings that hold no strings of any sort. That's different."

He pulled at his jeans stretched across his knee and glanced at her, then looked back at his knee. His scowl hinted at some inner turmoil raging, but she remained silent, knowing if he wanted to say something to her, he would.

She put her head back against the sofa and closed her eyes, aware that they were at an impasse. And aware that she already cared too much about him. He was attracted to her, but did she want to give what was between them any chance to bloom? Could she risk her heart in dating him? Questions swirled in her mind and there were no easy answers except the one that tore at her every time she came back to it—go back to Dallas and get away from him. Even given the few people she knew in Royal, she had heard talk about Jason being such a playboy.

"Merry, I loved someone and I got hurt badly once," he admitted. She raised her head to listen. "I don't ever want to get hurt like that again," he said.

As she heard him talk about someone he obviously must have loved deeply, pain cut deep in her heart. At the same time, she realized he had just opened a part of himself to her that she suspected he kept closed from nearly everyone else.

"I'm sorry," she replied quietly. "Love carries risk and sometimes loving means hurting. Were you engaged?"

He was silent so long, she wondered whether her question had intruded too much. He shook his head finally. "No. When I was five, my mother left my father and my brothers and me. She remarried."

"Jason!" Merry said softly, shocked and caught by surprise, never guessing the shuttered looks had been because of his mother. A muscle worked in his jaw, and his fist was clenched on his knee. He had already told her his parents had been divorced, but she didn't realize those old hurts still plagued him.

"My father never got over her. Never. That's what hurt so damned badly. He loved her every day all his life, and he drank too much to drown his sorrows. It hurt to lose her, but that pain never diminished because my brothers and I had to watch our dad suffer. My brothers have had bad marriages, and I vowed I would avoid loving someone the way my father and brothers did. No commitment—no great hurt."

"Jason, love doesn't always bring hurt," she said, aghast at his dismal view of love.

"It makes you damn vulnerable," he said with rough cynicism.

"You want to go through life alone? There are so many joys when you share life. Children are wonderful."

"I have my nephews and I haven't exactly been lonely."

She hurt for him and she hurt for herself because she suspected his life was settled the way he wanted it, and he was in no danger of risking his heart. That realization spread pain deep inside her, because he was a strong-willed man who was old enough and experienced enough to know what he wanted and to control his impulses when he needed to. Hurt and sadness filled her. She was aware of the invisible barrier between them.

She thought about the living room that didn't seem to fit the rest of the house. "Your mother decorated the living room, didn't she?"

"Yes, and my dad never wanted to change it. It was the one room that held her touch. That and their bedroom, but he changed the bedroom. I suppose it was too painful for him the way it had been when she was here. But the living room is the same. I intend to change it, but I just haven't gotten around to it. None of us has ever used that room and now I don't give it much thought."

Merry moved close to him and put her arm around him. "I'm sorry. Do you remember her?"

He turned to look at her. He was only inches away now, and she realized moving close to hug him in sympathy was the wrong gesture if she wanted the attraction between them to cool. In the depths of his eyes, desire flashed as hot as a consuming blaze. When she met his gaze, her pulse jumped. His arm tightened, and he leaned the last few inches to kiss her.

Mouths touched, and that flash of heat and desire came, but along with it was more. Jason had just given her a part of himself that she knew he seldom had shared and it made the kiss more important. There was more of a closeness. And desire was building, igniting into heat that melted and shook her. The man could kiss. She didn't need to know his past to know she was with an expert. His mouth, his tongue were doing things to her, with her, that shattered her cautious resolve.

She wanted to kiss him in return, to give in return and to do to him even half of what he was doing to her.

She broke away finally, both of them gasping for breath. "We're going in circles. I should go."

He caught her wrist, turning her hand to kiss her palm. "Just stay and talk. We're not going to sleep. I promise I'll keep my distance if that's what you want."

"It's what I want," she said, knowing that wasn't the full truth at all. It was fast becoming less than a half-truth. She wanted him with so much of her being that it frightened her.

When she moved to the corner of the sofa, he looked amused. "I think I asked you if you remembered your mother. You don't need to answer me if you don't want to," she said.

"Oh, yes. I remember her," he replied. "Lots of memories that have grown fuzzy over the years and that I no longer try to dredge up. When I was little I thought she loved us all. I was wrong."

"I'm sorry you were hurt, because I think loving someone would be pretty wonderful."

"Yeah, if they always loved you in return."

"True enough. Are your brothers happily married now?"

"Yes. Ethan, who is thirty-five, has two boys from his first marriage and two from his second. Same with Luke."

"See, sometimes you can marry and live happily ever after."

"Maybe." A muscle worked in his jaw and she regretted his hurts and his attitude that she didn't think would ever change.

"So what's the next step with the disk?" she asked, trying to get away from a discussion of marriage.

"I'll give those copies of the files to Sheriff Escobar, to Rob—actually to several of the club members. I'll call them around seven to set up a meeting."

He scooted closer, stretched out his long arm and wound his fingers lightly in her hair. There were faint tugs against her scalp that should have been insignificant, but were not. Instead, desire that had been steadily burning, sparked and danced across her raw nerves. Her gaze drank in his thickly lashed eyes and sensual mouth. She longed to be back in his arms. Everything in her screamed that this man was important to her, yet she knew her reactions to him were dangerous to her well-being.

"If I meet with my friends tomorrow, will you stay here?"

"If you want me to. Yes."

"Is that a promise?"

"If it makes you happy, I promise to stay. I'd like to hear what everyone else thinks after you meet with them, but I should go home soon."

"You don't have to go yet. You rented an apartment, so you didn't plan on heading back to Dallas in the near future."

"Tell me again about the murder."

Jason talked softly, his hand stroking her nape or winding through her hair. The conversation shifted and changed and time passed until she glanced at her watch. "It's almost dawn."

"Well, we had a late start on the night."

"I'm going to bed." When she stood, he came to his feet.

"One good-night kiss, Merry," he said softly, a honeyed warmth that stole her resolve.

When he pulled her to him, she went willingly into his arms, relishing his lean, hard body against her softness. Mouths together again, and the same wild sensations and needs flaring. Winding her fingers in his hair and holding him, she kissed him passionately for a few minutes before stopping him.

"Now I go." She could feel his eyes on her as she left the room, and she suspected even though they had been awake almost the entire night, she would still have trouble sleeping.

She needed to move out of his house. Their kisses were escalating wildly into hot passion, and she didn't want that to happen. This was not the man with whom to become seriously involved.

"Sleep in, Merry," he called after her.

"Sure," she replied, glancing back over her shoulder at him. He stood with his hands on his hips, watching her as she walked away. His chest was bare, all hard muscles, tempting, special. The feel of him could turn her to quivering jelly. How easily she could turn around and walk right back into his arms and he would make love to her as long as she would let him.

Was she already falling in love with this tough, hardhearted cowboy? Was he changing just a little? He had told her about his childhood pain, something she suspected he had told few people in his life.

"Don't get soft now," she warned herself, yet all she could think about was Jason: his touches, his kisses, his laughter, his sexy good looks. And beneath the scary moments tonight, the risks they had taken, she realized they had worked well together.

"That doesn't mean anything," she whispered, closing the door to her bedroom. "You've got me talking to myself, Jason Windover," she said. "Get out of my head. Get out of my heart," she added, moving to the bed to shed her jeans and shirt and slide beneath the sheet. She was exhausted, but not sleepy. Every nerve in her body was wired and she could still feel his hands on her, still remember too vividly his kisses. She'd better remember his dire views of marriage.

She came up out of sleep to bright sunshine pouring into the room. After she showered and dressed in cutoffs and a T-shirt, she went to the kitchen to find a note from Jason stating that he had gone to town.

Midmorning, he called, asking her to meet in him Royal for lunch and to help him select a new computer. Merry rummaged through her clothes, finally wearing jeans and a blue plaid shirt, letting her hair fall free.

They were to meet at the Royal Diner and when she turned to park at the curb, she saw Jason leaning against his pickup, waiting for her. As he straightened and sauntered over to open her car door, her pulse raced. How handsome he was in his black Stetson, jeans and a white T-shirt.

Over juicy hamburgers, she asked him about his morning meeting with other Texas Cattleman's Club members.

"I didn't get to talk to them. Dorian saw Sebastian and Will as they left the office and asked them where they were going and then wanted to go with them. I'll try again to talk to all of them when Dorian isn't present. But we were delayed getting together because the execs at Wescott Oil were busy with the law this morning. Will told me that someone broke into the place last night. Then, when we met at the club, Dorian was there, so little was said. Sebastian, Will and Dorian are eating lunch there now."

"What about Dorian?"

"He avoided my gaze most of the time, but a couple of times we made eye contact, and if looks could kill, I wouldn't be here."

"How can he suspect *you* of breaking in?"

"It may just be an old antagonism that has always existed between us. Anyway, I did get to talk to Rob and Keith as we left. I gave Rob and Keith copies of our disk. Keith was impressed with your getting into Dorian's files."

She shrugged. "That's my business."

"Well, after lunch you can help me get the right computer, and then please get it all set up for me, and in exchange…" His voice changed to a sexy huskiness that made her draw a quick breath and lose what little appetite she had. She waited while he paused and his eyes devoured her.

"In exchange?" she asked, prompting him and waiting breathlessly.

"Whatever your fee is plus dinner at Claire's plus a little romancing back at the ranch." He reached across the table to take her hand, stroking her knuckles with his thumb. "Want me to tell you what I'd like to do to you?" he asked wickedly in a husky voice.

"Not here. Not now."

"Later then," he drawled. "How's the evening sound? Do we have a deal?"

"I think so, yes," she said, knowing she was mush whenever he turned on his sexy charm.

"Good." He sipped his drink and looked at her partially eaten hamburger. "You're not eating."

"I'm not hungry."

"Neither am I. Not hungry for hamburgers," he said, his searing gaze telling her exactly what he wanted.

"Jason, we're in town in public."

"I don't care, and besides, we're just holding hands. It's not like I have you in my lap or any of a dozen things I wish I could do to you right now."

"Let's get that computer," she said, trying to get back to being impersonal, casual and merely friendly, yet finding it difficult to catch her breath.

He slid out of the booth, leaned down beside her. "If that's what you want, Merry," he said in a husky drawl that was like a stroke of his hand over her.

She waited while he paid for their lunches and then they left to shop.

She tried for the rest of the day and later, as they worked on the new computer, to keep distance between them and to keep things on an impersonal basis.

Around ten that night, Jason got a phone call; when he replaced the receiver, he looked at her grimly. "That was Rob. He's looked at the disk and he thinks the same thing we do—that more suspicion is pointed at Dorian. He said that Dorian knows someone was trying to look at his files. And Dorian suspects you, which makes him now suspect me. Rob said to be careful. Dorian probably feels safe at this point because there's nothing in his files incriminating enough to cause his arrest."

"Would he inherit Wescott Oil if something happened to Sebastian?"

"No. Rob has already checked into that, so I don't see what he has to gain. That's another big question—if Dorian is the murderer, what is his motive?"

Pondering the question, they sat in silence until they went back to the computer. At midnight, they closed it down and walked to the kitchen for a cool drink of lemonade.

Their good-night kisses escalated again until she stopped him and closed the door to her room at two in the morning.

She undressed swiftly, pulling on a frilly short red nightie and skimpy matching panties. In minutes she slid beneath the sheet.

Merry lay awake, knowing that she was falling in love with Jason. She just hoped she wouldn't leave Royal hurting the way Holly hurt, with a broken heart that threatened never to mend. And she knew she must move out tomorrow. She had already told Jason, and they had argued about it, but she had held firm and told him she was going to return to Dallas tomorrow.

Even though she desperately longed to stay, and she was curious to see what happened to Dorian, she knew it was time to go home unless she wanted a deluxe broken heart.

She was going to get out of the agreement to rent the apartment because now there was no reason to stay in Royal. She didn't want to harass Dorian further. It was time to stop seeing Jason, and she didn't want to risk her heart more than she already had.

She tossed and turned restlessly, knowing another reason to leave with the dawn—she couldn't say no to him much longer. More and more, she wanted to know him intimately, wanted his lovemaking. She didn't know what time she dozed into a light and fitful sleep.

An ear-shattering blast shook the house and her bed, tossing her to the floor.

Instantly awake and terrified, Merry jumped up and dashed across the room, yanking open the door. When she stepped into the hall, orange flames filled the east end of the house as an inferno roared and crackled.

''Jason!'' she screamed.

Seven

The entire east part of Jason's house was in flames. She could feel the heat.

"Merry!"

Wearing only briefs, Jason grabbed her and pulled her to his room with him. He yanked on jeans and jammed his feet into his boots. Merry saw his T-shirt on the floor and grabbed it, realizing how she was dressed. Swiftly she tugged the T-shirt on over her nightie.

"C'mon, Merry!" he shouted, taking her hand again.

Bolting for the patio door, he paused at his desk to open a drawer and get a cellular phone and his pistol.

As he punched 911 and relayed a call for help, he thrust Merry to one side of the door. They both were flattened against the wall. The moment he broke the connection on his phone, he held her behind him with one arm and kicked open the door with his foot. He held his pistol at the ready.

When she realized he expected someone to shoot at them, her fright changed to an icy chill. Beyond the door was the dark night while behind them, she could hear the roar and crackle of flames and smell the acrid smoke. "Let me go first. You come right behind me," he said.

With the gun leveled, he ran through the doorway, and she followed.

The night was transformed. Men ran from the bunkhouse, dogs barked, and lights went on all over the grounds.

Jason sprinted ahead, and she followed him while he shouted directions to the first man to reach him. She glanced over her shoulder to see flames roaring and a huge column of black smoke billowing and mushrooming over the house.

At the sight of the conflagration, she felt weak and sick inside.

"Merry!" Jason snapped, catching her wrist and pulling her with him to run to his pickup. He opened the door and shoved her inside. "Stay in here and stay down so you're not a target."

"A target?" Startled, she looked at the men passing them on their way to the fire. How could she be a target now with so many people all around her? "There are men who work for you everywhere."

"A sniper could still get you."

Her shocked mind began to function. She realized then the possibility that the explosion had not been an accident and someone had been trying to kill her. Shivering, she looked at the brilliant flames. Anguish was stronger than fear as she remembered Jason's family heirlooms and antiques.

"Jason, your house!"

"It's just things, Merry," he said roughly. "We're alive. That's what's important, and let's keep it that way. Stay out of sight unless you want the press all over you."

"Jason, I thought it was a gas line."

"It was a bomb," he said bluntly.

"A bomb? Why?" The moment the words were out of

her mouth she thought of Dorian, of breaking into his computer. Was this because of last night?

She looked at the men who worked for Jason who were already fighting the fire. The first shocks receded further when she thought about the danger she might still be in, the police who would want statements and the press who were sure to arrive.

Jason was society and old money. The fire could be seen for miles and when word got out that it was from a bomb, the news would be nationwide. Her mother would want every tidbit and she would be livid to know that Merry hadn't called her the first moment.

Jason slammed the truck door, and Merry saw that he had pushed the lock.

She tried to stay low in the pickup so she would not be a target, yet she sat up enough to watch what was happening. All of the east wing and the center of the house were gone. If someone had been trying to kill her, he had bombed the wrong end of the house. If the bomb had gone off about three hours earlier, neither she nor Jason would have survived.

In spite of the stuffiness of the interior of the pickup and the balmy May night, she shivered. She heard the wail of sirens and she rolled down the window to get fresh air. The smell of smoke took her breath, and, with the window lowered, the roar of the fire was louder. Sparks shot high as wood crackled and popped.

"He's lost almost everything," she said softly. If it had been a bomb, it had been intended for her. She was the one to blame for Jason losing his family belongings and his house. She had stirred up Dorian who was a dangerous man, pushed him to this destruction and now Jason had lost so terribly much that could never be replaced.

She shook and wrapped her arms around her middle, unaware of tears streaming down her cheeks. Vehicles with flashing lights poured into the yard and men were everywhere. A news helicopter circled overhead while the media trucks rolled in.

Pumper trucks sent streams of water pouring onto the house. When pickups appeared and men jumped out, she realized Jason's friends and neighbors had come to help.

She could see Jason with the firefighters now. She wanted to go help, but she wasn't dressed for it and she wouldn't be that much more help now because there appeared to be at least fifty men fighting the blaze.

Firefighters, reporters, cameramen, lawmen, friends, neighbors and employees filled Jason's yard. The bright lights of the media lit up a place that now looked like a war zone.

Time was suspended. One moment she thought she had been watching for hours, the next, it seemed only minutes from the explosion until the flames had disappeared.

To her relief the fire was finally doused and the conflagration never reached the west wing of the house. Men still poured water over the smoldering ruins, but some of the volunteers began to get back into their pickups and go. When the television vans departed, she opened the door and swung her legs outside to get some air. She couldn't imagine being in danger now.

It seemed an eternity before she saw Jason's dark silhouette come striding toward her.

"You're making yourself a target."

"I'm safe," she replied. "What exploded?" she said, knowing his answer, yet praying his first assumptions were wrong, and it was a malfunctioning gas line.

"I told you earlier—and the fire chief agrees with me although they'll make an official investigation—someone detonated a bomb."

She shook her head in agony. "Jason, I'm sorry about your house. This is my fault for staying here. Whoever did this was after me."

"Forget it, Merry. I've made plenty of enemies before. And I wanted you here. I knew the risks we were running."

"I didn't." While she shivered, he put his arms around her.

"We can stay in the guest cottage. Let's go up to the house. I want to get a few things and then we can move. Some of the firefighters will hang around to make sure nothing flares up again."

As they walked toward the house, he draped his arm across her shoulders, and she walked close beside him.

"Merry, when the media interviewed me, I said I thought the explosion was from a gas leak."

"You told me—"

"I wanted that out in the news. I know Chief Blanton, and he only told them there would be an investigation into the causes of the blaze. It'll buy us some time before the truth comes out—if it ever does—that the blaze was caused by a bomb. I don't want that much attention focused on us yet. If Dorian was behind this, I don't want him brought into it in any way prematurely."

As they entered through Jason's bedroom, he removed his pistol and placed it on his desk. She could see down the hall and out into the night. Men moved around, and now, instead of walls and rooms, there was just open space. The smell of the fire and water was stifling, and she shook again.

"Jason, I did this to you. You could have been killed! Your wonderful house—"

"Merry," he said quietly, drawing her into his arms and tilting up her chin, "I keep telling you that we're safe. That's what's important. We're both all right. Things and houses can be replaced."

"You had all those family heirlooms and antiques. The family belongings can't be replaced."

"They don't matter that much. I told those guys that we'd be out on the porch at the guest house. Let's go down there. I want you to sit with me."

"Don't you want to look at the damage?"

"I've seen it with the fire chief. I've talked to my in-

surance agent and an adjustor will be out in the morning—
in a few hours, actually. I'll see the ruins more than I want
to.''

"How can you be so casual about it?" she asked,
amazed at his calm reaction.

"Because we're both alive. Let's get our things and
move. The guest house will smell better."

In a few minutes she had her purse and clothes. She had
pulled on shorts and kept on his T-shirt. When she joined
him, he had a bundle tucked under his arm. He put his arm
around her. As they walked to the door, he stopped to pick
up his pistol.

"You want to sit outside to keep watch, don't you?" she
asked. "You think he might come back."

"I don't think so, but I want to watch in case he does."

"We're talking about Dorian, aren't we?"

"I think so more than ever. You got into his computer
and he knew it," Jason replied as they crossed the yard to
the guest cottage.

"The minute the sun comes up, I'm going back to Dallas
and maybe your life can get on an even keel. You should
be safe."

Jason halted, turning her to face him. "I'm not worried
about being safe. I can get this place under guard and get
an alarm for the grounds around the house. You can't go
back to Dallas now. You could be in all kinds of danger."

"Stop it, Jason. You're scaring me. I have to go back
because if I stay here I put you at risk."

"Do you want to put your family at risk?"

"No!"

"Merry, I've been trained for this sort of thing. You stay
here." There was a steely command in his voice that made
her hold back any argument.

She nodded, and they continued walking in silence to the
guest house. Inside, when he switched on lights, she looked
at a spacious knotty pine room with Navajo rugs and Western art, bronze statues and forest-green leather furniture.

"You call this a cottage?"

"It's smaller than the house," he replied casually. "Come on, I'll show you where you can stay." She placed her things in a bright, cheerful bedroom with a brass bed and more Western art on the walls. Then she joined Jason on the porch. He switched off lights in the house and returned, bringing two chilled bottles of pop.

They sat close to the house with their backs only inches from the wall. A shaggy black-and-tan dog wandered up, sniffed Merry's feet and moved to put his head on Jason's knee.

"This is Tiger."

"He doesn't act like one."

"If you see him in daylight, you'll see he has stripes." The dog curled at Jason's feet and placed his head on Jason's boot.

"I guess he does like you."

"You didn't give a rip whether I had dogs that liked me or not when you asked that first night. You were planning your escape, weren't you?"

"As a matter of fact, I was. I wanted to know what I might run into outside your house."

"Now that I've had time to think about it—if Dorian did cause the blast tonight, you may not have been the target. Any computer disks we had could have been what he hoped to destroy."

"I hope you're right."

"Think about it. I met with my friends, but nothing was said about anyone stealing anything from Dorian's computer. He didn't even mention that anyone got into his computer. I didn't mention disks. I asked Rob to take a disk to Sheriff Escobar. If Dorian followed me, he would know I didn't go to the police. Besides, the files by themselves are not that convincing—it's just that with the suspicious things Dorian has done, the computer files are more evidence that points to Dorian."

"If all he intended to destroy were the computer files—why do it when we were home?"

"He might have wanted to send a message. He might have wanted to scare you off. Scare both of us off, maybe. If he knew which end of the house we were in, then all he wanted was to destroy my disks and my computer—which he did. But Rob and Keith already have copies."

"It makes sense, Jason. Unless he knows nothing of the layout of your house."

"I suspect whoever set the bomb knew the layout as well as we knew the layout of Wescott Oil. As a matter of fact, I had a party several months back and the Texas Cattleman's Club members were out here. Dorian would know his way around here reasonably well."

"Maybe I'm not in as much danger then."

"Maybe, but let's not take chances. Not for a while."

As they talked quietly, she noticed Jason kept his pistol on a table beside him and all the time they talked, he was gazing into the dark night.

"Mr. Windover?" A fireman spoke from the dark shadows to the east of the porch, and Jason stood.

"I'm here." He left her, crossing the porch and striding to the fireman to talk quietly to him.

"Jason," she heard another man say and join the two of them. From the jeans and boots he wore, she judged the other man worked on the ranch. She could hear their low voices, catch phrases as they talked. Tiger had followed Jason and sat at his feet. Another dog meandered up to sit beside them.

Finally Jason shook hands with the fireman and thanked him again. As the man left, Jason turned to his employee and they talked in even lower voices. When they parted, Jason came back to join her.

"Let's go inside."

"What about keeping watch?"

"My men are spread out all around here. No one will get past them tonight. I promise—you're safe here."

He draped his arm across her shoulders, but then he paused and turned. "Ben," he called.

A deep voice came out of the darkness, and she could see the cowboy yards away.

"Call the dogs and keep them with you."

As a whistle broke the stillness, both dogs trotted away and Jason led her inside.

He closed and locked the door and then switched on a small lamp. As he crossed the room to her, the look in his eyes made her forget the events of the night. Her breath caught and each step closer he came, her pulse jumped another notch.

"Jason," she whispered while her heart thudded.

"There's something I want to know, Merry," he said solemnly. His voice was husky, causing more jumps in her pulse.

A thick fringe of black lashes framed sexy blue-green eyes that blazed with desire. He placed his hands on either side of her face while he gazed down at her. "Tonight, when we talked right after the fire, you sounded like you care what happens to me."

Her heart thudded at the implications of his question. She could answer it flippantly—tell him that she would care about anyone being hurt. That was the answer if she wanted to walk away. But not one tiny inch of her wanted to walk away from him. The night had changed her, brought everything around her into sharper focus. Made her more aware of the frailty of life and of the gifts of love. She could give him one of those casual answers now, or she could tell him the truth.

"Yes, I care a lot."

Something flickered in the depths of his eyes and as he inhaled swiftly, his chest expanded. "Ahh, Merry," he said softly.

He leaned down to kiss her, and her heart thudded. She had been terrified for his safety tonight, crushed over the damage he had suffered—loss and danger that she had brought on him. In spite of all his losses, his concern had been their safety and the safety of the men who worked for him.

This tall cowboy was incredibly special to her, and she was thankful he was safe. She was thankful that they were both alive. Wrapping her arms around him, she leaned into him as he embraced her.

When his lips touched hers, she kissed him passionately in return. Her kisses were hungry, a confirmation of life, a sharp awareness of how precious life was—and how special Jason was to her.

All her reservations fell away. Someone had tried to kill them tonight, yet they had survived. They were alive and caution and reason seemed foolish where her heart and Jason were concerned. Priorities shifted. Life was infinitely precious, and love was a gift to give.

Jason was special, and she wanted to show him, wanted all of him, wanted him as she had never wanted anyone else. They had been on the brink of death tonight, and now she wanted an affirmation of life, a chance to love.

Considerations and terrors of the night vanished.

Her tongue went deep, stroking his as he kissed her passionately, and she slid her hands over him, feeling his body, all hard, lean planes and corded muscles. Excitement exploded in every nerve in her body.

As he trailed kisses along her throat, his hands peeled away her T-shirt. Her nightie went with it. When she unfastened his jeans, he cupped her breasts, looking down at her. His hands were large, dark against her pale skin, his fingers warm, setting her aflame.

"You're beautiful," he whispered hoarsely, and her heart thudded.

All the time he balanced on one foot and tugged off a boot, then yanked off the other one, tossing them aside, his gaze never left her. Clothing fell swiftly, but invisible barriers seemed to be tumbling as well.

He made her feel like the most desirable woman on earth.

When he straightened, she pulled away his briefs to free him, drinking in the sight of his strong male body that left no question of his desire and readiness.

His large hands cupped her breasts again, and his thumbs circled her taut peaks. Pleasure swirled while she clung to him, feeling the thick muscles of his upper arms. His strength was exciting, his touch electrifying.

She closed her eyes, letting him caress her, wanting his hands all over her, wanting to touch and know him.

She slid her hand to his chest, trailing her fingers down over his flat, muscled stomach, touching his manhood.

"Merry," he ground out her name when her hand closed around his thick shaft.

He swung her into his arms to carry her to his bed. She was dimly aware of light spilling from a hallway, of a four-poster bed, a rocker, but surroundings were dreamlike and unreal. What was real was warm flesh against warm flesh, kisses that sent her temperature soaring, looks that made her tremble.

Why did she feel she belonged in his arms forever? She ran her fingers along his jaw, feeling the bristles, aware of all he had been through in the night and all he had lost, aware too of that walled-off part of his heart that was keeping him from truly loving and being loved. Didn't he realize that real love could heal hurts?

Placing his knee on the bed, Jason lowered her gently and leaned down to kiss her breast, his tongue stroking her nipple as he sucked and teased. Exquisite sensations stormed her senses, and she gave herself to him. His hands were everywhere, his tongue driving her wild.

"Merry, I've wanted you so damned badly," he whispered. His magic words were as seductive as his caresses. He turned her on her stomach, trailing kisses from her nape to her ankles. He stroked between her thighs and she rolled over, coming up to kiss him hungrily, knowing no matter how much he desired her, she wanted him more.

"Let me love you, Jason," she whispered, certain that he would never realize the true depth of her request.

She did want him with all her being, even though she was honest enough to know that he would never love her deeply in return. Tonight she wanted to give and take and have it all. Tonight, she was willing to risk a broken heart.

Strong shoulders, smooth back, narrow waist, his manhood: she wanted to explore and touch and kiss all of him. As she did, she heard his groan and was surprised that he shook. She was amazed what she could do to him, expecting him to be jaded and accustomed to women as expert at loving as he. But that wasn't the case. He was coming apart in her arms until he grasped her and shifted her roughly. "Merry—"

He cradled her in his arms, kissing her as passionately as she kissed him. His hand caressed her thigh, sliding to her inner thigh and she opened her legs to him. While she caressed him, his fingers trailed higher, reaching the juncture of her thighs and then touching her intimately. He stroked her, taking her to a new height, finally lowering her to the bed. He moved down to trail his tongue where his hand had been. He was between her legs, watching her as he kissed her.

She closed her eyes, arching and gasping, lost in scalding sensations, yet fully aware this was Jason who was loving her and who wanted her.

Thought spun away while lights flashed behind her closed eyes, and she dug her fingers into his shoulders, arching and wanting more of him, wanting him deep inside her.

"Jason!"

She rocked with spasms that only made her want more. With an effort, she moved, turning to take his manhood in her hand, to kiss and caress him until he groaned and shoved her back to the bed, moving between her legs.

"Are you protected, Merry?"

"Yes, I'm on the Pill."

He was on his knees between her legs and she inhaled, feeling breathless as she looked at him. Virile, handsome, so incredibly sexy, he knelt, poised, ready to love her. His blue-green eyes were dark with need, a look on his face that heated her blood to boiling. Then she closed her eyes as he lowered himself, the velvet tip of his shaft teasing, moving against her.

With a cry, she wrapped her legs around him and arched beneath him, pulling him closer. His mouth covered hers, and she clung to him, writhing and wild with her need.

Jason tried to hold back, to drive her to the highest point of need. Sweat covered his body, and his pulse drowned out all sounds. She was silk and softness and a marvel to him. She was a wildcat, more passionate than he could have imagined.

The fire in her auburn hair only hinted at the fire in her body. He kissed her deeply, wanted to plunge himself into her softness, to feel her moving beneath him, crying out in ecstasy.

He slid into her and then felt the barrier where he hadn't expected one. *She was a virgin.* Something he hadn't considered. He couldn't take her or hurt her. He raised his head to gaze down at her.

Her eyes opened, dark, yet caught with pinpoints of fiery, age-old desire. ''Jason…'' she urged.

''Merry, I don't want—''

''Love me,'' she said, moving against him, arching her hips, her hands sliding over his bottom and pulling him closer while her legs tightened around him. ''Jason, now. I want you.''

''I don't want to hurt you. I don't—''

''I *do* want,'' she whispered. ''Come here, now,'' she coaxed.

He couldn't argue. He had given her a chance and his control was flying away. He thrust slowly into her, feeling the barrier, knowing he had to be hurting her.

She gasped and he kissed her, stopping whatever sound

was caught in her throat. Then the barrier was gone, and he went deep inside her, moving slowly, trying to keep from hurting her. Thought and effort shattered, and he had to move, to take her completely.

Merry clung to him, feeling torn apart, swamped for an instant in pain, but as he moved, the pain was replaced by a driving need and she moved with him. She held him tightly, crying his name, yet the cry was only a sound in her throat because his mouth covered hers. While they rocked together, desire thundered in her.

"Merry!" Jason cried, his arms around her, and then his head lowered again, and he kissed her again while all she knew were wild sensations tearing her apart before she crashed into release.

Rapture exploded in her, carrying her further into oblivion while Jason shuddered with his release.

She held him, moving with him, their hearts pounding in unison. He kissed her as hungrily as before and she returned his kiss as passionately, feeling a bond between them now, an intimacy that she could not have known before.

"Merry, my love," he whispered, smoothing her hair away from her face.

Even while his words thrilled her, she knew better than to believe them. The man was in the grip of passion and she would not hold him accountable for what he said to her now.

She trailed her fingers down his back, wet with a sheen of sweat. Her hand moved up then to tangle in his thick, coarse hair.

He raised up to look at her, a slight frown on his brow. "Did I hurt you?" he asked solemnly.

She traced the outline of his lips, trailing her finger to his jaw and feeling the slight stubble of his beard. "Only a little."

"Next time will be better. I promise."

"Next time?" she asked, arching a brow.

"Yeah, next time," he said, turning on his side and taking her with him. He let out a long sigh and held her close against him. "Merry. Did you get that nickname because you were always cheerful?"

"No. When she was a very small child, Holly couldn't say Meredith and my name became Merry." While she talked, Jason's fingers trailed over her. He stood and leaned down to scoop her into his arms.

"Come here, darlin'. We'll shower."

He carried her into the bathroom and set her down in the shower, stepping in with her to close the door. He tilted her chin up to look at her quizzically. "You told me you were on the Pill, but you were a virgin."

"It was because of medical reasons. The Pill regulated me."

He nodded, satisfied by her answer as he turned on the water and it sprayed over them. In minutes, as they rubbed each other's bodies, desire rekindled until he turned off the water and stepped out, taking a towel to rub her dry. "I want this to last and be good for you, to really take time."

"Jason, you take more time than we did before and the sun will be high over the house!" she said, wondering how near dawn it was now. And then, as he moved the thick terrycloth towel lazily across her nipples, down between her legs, over her bottom, she forgot about the time altogether.

She caught the towel to dry his body, relishing touching him, exploring every fascinating inch of him. He carried her back to bed to kiss her from her mouth to her ankles while his hands drove her wild. And then she returned the loving, kissing him all over. He moved between her legs and took her slowly. This time sensations rocked her, causing her to arch against him as she clung to him, her hands splayed on his smooth back.

Intimacy united them. She was one with him, body and soul, a deep joining that forged bonds. Their shared, hot kisses held promises of love.

They moved wildly together and finally crashed over a brink. Merry settled slowly with Jason sprawled over her. She wanted to feel the weight of his body and wanted to be one with him as long as possible.

When Jason rolled over, he pulled her into his embrace, his legs tangling with hers, her head on his chest. He held her tightly against him with one hand while he stroked her back with the other.

"You're a very special woman, Merry."

His words strummed across her heart, and she raised her head slightly to kiss his chest, looking into his eyes.

"And you are a very special cowboy," she answered, wanting to say so much more.

He brushed her damp forehead and lifted locks of hair away from her face. "We'll go shower in a little while, but right now I just want to stay here and hold you close."

"I want you to hold me," she whispered, holding him in turn, wanting to take away his past hurts and toss aside his fears of love, yet knowing she could only take him as he was.

She put her head down on his chest and held him tightly, shutting out reality and problems as long as she could. "Whatever the future holds, neither one of us will forget this night for the rest of our lives."

"No, we won't." Jason kissed the top of her head while he continued to caress her with his free hand. He was still stunned by the night, by Merry. He had never been with a virgin, had never wanted to be, but now it was as if he were seeing the world in a whole new way. He felt overwhelmed. Now he understood why some put a price on virginity; it was as if Merry had become his woman. His completely. He told himself he was being ridiculous, but his heart wasn't buying that. She was *his* woman, and she had given him the very special gift of herself.

When they were in the throes of passion, he knew he had called her "love"—something he had never done before. And he knew he wanted her to an extent he had never desired any other woman.

He remembered their conversation last night—an eon away—yet her words were too clear: *How'll you know when you meet the right person?*

I'll know.

Just like that? Like lightning striking or what?

I'll know the way anyone knows when she or he is in love. Surely you've been in love?

No, he hadn't ever been deeply in love, never experienced what he was beginning to feel now for Merry. Was he falling in love? How had she gotten past his defenses so swiftly and so thoroughly? This five feet of feisty female had stormed into his life and knocked him off his feet in every sense of the word.

He shifted onto his side to look at her. He couldn't get enough of touching or kissing her. *He wanted her again. Now.* Suddenly, when he had expected to be satisfied, to have gotten her out of his system, he wanted her more than ever. More than he had just hours ago.

"I could devour you," he said in a husky voice, kissing her throat. "Come here, Merry," he said, standing and picking her up to carry her to his shower again. This time they soaped each other slowly, until both were breathless, gasping with need. They rinsed off, their hands sliding over each other's slippery bodies. Jason braced himself against the wall of the shower, spread his feet and lifted Merry up to let her slide down slowly onto his hard shaft.

She held him, moving and crying out with pleasure, finally feeling a burst of release. Afterwards, she put her head on his shoulder. "You won't have to carry me to the shower this time. We're already here."

"My legs feel like pudding. We're getting to that bed before you have to carry me back to it."

She smiled at him as he set her on her feet, and they washed. As soon as they toweled each other dry, he carried her to bed to pull her close into his embrace again.

"Jason, will we know when the sun comes up? Your shutters are closed."

He groaned. "I don't want the sun to come up. I have an appointment with the insurance guy. Some firemen will be back to gather more evidence and check things over. I don't want to leave this room or let you go. I want to stay right here with you in my arms, in my bed for the next week."

"Sorry, cowboy, that's impossible."

He rolled her over and propped his head on his hand to study her. "Maybe I can try keeping you here, and we can just ignore everyone."

"No!" She sat up and reached for the shutters that were all tightly closed.

He caught her arm and kissed her wrist, looking at her solemnly. "Maybe I'm falling in love, Merry."

Merry's heart thudded at the words, but she reminded herself she was with Royal's number-one playboy. She had heard about his reputation. She smiled and patted him.

"That's nice, Jason," she said.

He drew his finger down her cheek. "I mean it. Don't patronize me."

"I wouldn't think of it," she said, kissing him lightly. His arm tightened around her and his lips touched hers, brushing so lightly. Then his mouth opened hers, kissing her deeply. Tongues touched and stroked while her heart pounded.

She pushed against him. "Wait a minute." She glanced at the clock on his desk. "Jason, that says it's almost eight in the morning. That's late for you to be getting up."

"Don't care. Come here, darlin'," he said in a husky voice.

By a quarter before nine, Jason groaned and stood. "I have an appointment in fifteen minutes." He caught her chin. "Merry, you're safe here, so you stay here today. I don't see how he would dare try anything again as long as you're out here and there will be someone around all the time. Promise me you'll stay.''

''I will,'' she said, knowing it was probably useless to argue, and Jason didn't seem the least concerned about risk to himself.

He picked up his cellular phone and switched it on, punching in a number. ''Rob, this is Jason. Yeah, we're okay. I need to see you and the others when we can. Definitely without Dorian.''

Eight

As Jason drove away from his ranch, he wanted to turn around and go back to be with Merry. The need he felt to be with her surprised him because the intensity of it was a unique experience. At the same time, his feelings tied him in knots.

He didn't want to fall in love. Not the forever till-death-do-us-part kind of love. Yet being with her was the best thing that had ever happened to him. He couldn't wait to get back to the ranch and see her, hold her and kiss her.

Even the danger and the boldness of Dorian—if Dorian was the one—couldn't take his thoughts off Merry.

Since childhood he had sworn he would never love deeply, never be caught in the trap his father had been in, loving a woman and becoming vulnerable. But now nothing seemed the same. If loving Merry made him vulnerable to hurt, he couldn't help it. He was as out of control as a shooting star. If this was love, he was in, head over heels, and it seemed damned good and right.

She was a beautiful, sexy woman. She was intelligent, fun to be with, kindhearted and exciting. He wanted to be with her all the time, and the thought of her walking out of his life made his breath catch.

He was the only man in her life. The first, the only. That thought tugged at him, and made the bond between them even stronger.

Stunned by his reactions, he marveled at how his feelings for her had changed his whole perspective on life.

In town, the day seemed interminable. Jason couldn't set up a meeting with the others from the Texas Cattleman's Club until tomorrow morning, but they knew about the bomb. Everyone in Royal knew his house had burned, but only his close Cattleman's Club friends knew the truth. The only information the media had still indicated a possible gas leak, and that suited him.

Through the busy day Jason struggled to concentrate on the problems facing him, yet Merry was constantly on his mind. It amazed him to feel this way—as if Merry were the most important person on earth. Earlier that day, he had almost walked in front of a moving car. His attorney had been with him and had reached out to stop him. Hal Worthington had chalked Jason's fog up to the night's calamity, talking nonstop to Jason about his loss and how sorry he was about the explosion and fire.

Jason had barely listened as Hal had rambled, and as soon as they parted, Jason called the florist and ordered a dozen red roses, saying he would pick them up on his way back to the ranch.

On his way to an appointment, he paused in the lobby of a building, finding a corner where he could call Merry undisturbed.

Her voice was lilting, making him remember the night too clearly.

"Merry. I wanted to talk to you."

"I'm glad you called."

"I've made reservations to take you to Claire's tonight."

"You don't think it's dangerous for us to be in Royal?"

"No, I don't. If the bomber was Dorian, I suspect he was after the disk or giving us a warning. I'll keep you safe, I promise."

"You can't promise me absolute protection."

"I'll do my best. Darlin', this morning seems a year away instead of hours."

"Yes, it does," she answered in a softer tone of voice.

"I hate being away from you, and I'll be home as soon as I can—probably half-past five before I can get there. I've gotta run now, but I had to talk to you."

"Thanks for calling," she said in that same low, breathless voice that made him want to cancel all the rest of his afternoon appointments and go home right now.

"'Bye, Merry," he said, wanting to say so much more, continually shocked by his intense reaction to her. As soon as she returned his farewell, he broke the connection, pocketed his cellular phone and left for a meeting with his accountant.

In a daze Merry replaced the receiver and walked to the bedroom they had shared the night before, staring at the bed while her thoughts spun vivid memories. She was in love with Jason, but she wasn't falling for any wild promises or lines from him because this was old stuff to him. He was a playboy and oh-so-clearly had let her know he didn't want to be involved in a serious commitment.

In spite of knowing about his past and his reputation, she loved him, and a broken heart seemed inevitable. She knew that she needed to move out of his house and get some distance between them because she was going to have to resist his sweet-talking, sexy charm if she didn't want to become as devastated as her sister.

In the meantime, she would be here tonight and she was going out with him this evening and for the next twenty-four hours, she was going to close her mind to the future.

At half past five she heard his pickup and saw him stop at the main house and get out to talk to one of the hands, then he climbed into the pickup and drove to the guest house. She wanted to run and throw herself into his arms. She looked down at her cutoffs and red T-shirt. Her hair was clipped behind her head and she smoothed wayward tendrils back into place.

The door of the pickup slammed shut, and as she watched his ground-eating stride, her pulse jumped. In his black Stetson, jeans and a white shirt, he looked sexy and appealing. In his hand was a crystal vase with a dozen deep-red roses.

He opened the door and tossed away his hat as his hot gaze met hers.

"Hi," he said in a husky voice. "I brought you flowers."

"They're beautiful," she said without taking her gaze from his. He set them on a table as he crossed the room to her.

Her racing pulse accelerated, and then she was flying to fling herself at him. The moment they were in each other's arms, Jason walked her backwards toward the bedroom.

While they kissed, her hands were all over him as much as his were all over her. She hadn't known it was possible to desire someone the way she did Jason. Still kissing him, she unbuttoned his shirt and tugged it out of his jeans frantically, barely aware when he pulled her T-shirt over her head and tossed it away. In their slow walk to the bedroom, clothing was strewn willy-nilly.

"I want you, Merry," he whispered hoarsely. "I haven't been able to think about anything else all day."

She wound her fingers in his hair, kissing him while her other hand trailed over his chest.

He cupped her bare breasts to fondle and kiss her while she closed her eyes and moaned with pleasure. Urgency tore at both of them. Her hungry need for him overwhelmed her. She caressed him as he lifted her onto the bed and moved between her legs, lowering himself and entering her swiftly.

She arched beneath him, clinging to him and moving with him, giving herself completely to him. She ran her hands over his smooth, muscled back, down to his thighs, memorizing each inch of him. Body against body, united, hearts beating together. How she wanted it to be forever!

When they crashed with release, ecstasy filled her and in that one moment, she held him, knowing they were one.

"I couldn't wait to see you," he said when their breathing slowed to normal. He held her close in his arms, his fingers smoothing her hair from her face. "I'm torn between wanting to take you to Claire's tonight and wanting to stay right here in bed and love you all night long."

She drew her fingers through his hair, feeling the thick strands, letting her hand slide down to his strong shoulder. "I suspect you'll get hungry later."

"Hungry for you," he said, nuzzling her neck. "Reservations are for half-past-eight. That gives us some time." He turned to kiss her throat. She ran her hand over his muscled back, still covered with a sheen of perspiration. She couldn't get enough of him either. She wanted him in her arms, loving her, more than she wanted anything else. And she really didn't care whether they went to Claire's or not.

"Merry, the club has an annual charity ball coming up—will you go with me?"

She looked into his thickly lashed eyes and kissed him lightly. "Yes, I'll be happy to go with you. What's the charity?"

"Sebastian headed up the ball this time. He decided to make a bet with all of us. This was back in his bachelor days. All of us were bachelors then."

"Sorry to interrupt your story, but who is *us?*"

"Sebastian, Rob Cole, Keith Owens, Will Bradford and I are the group. The bet was that the last bachelor left standing—since most of those guys are marriage-minded—"

"But one isn't," she interrupted him.

Smiling, Jason kissed her lightly. "Maybe. Maybe I'm changing."

"Like tigers lose their stripes. Go on. Tell me about this last bachelor."

"The last bachelor left standing will enjoy a 'consolation' party during the ball and get to choose the charity for the gala."

"So what's your favorite charity, Jason, since you'll win this bet, hands down."

"You're really sure about me," he said, studying her and toying with locks of her hair.

"You've made your feelings clear. What's your charity?" she insisted.

"There's a program for kids who need help with literacy. That's the charity I'd name."

"That's a good one."

"Actually, three of the guys are married now. Will, Sebastian and Rob. So it's down to a contest between Keith and me."

"Well, I know who'll win, and a lot of little kids will be helped."

"You're so sure about me," Jason repeated. He rolled over to prop his head on his hand and look down at her. "This would be nice to always come home to," he said solemnly, and Merry's heart lurched. Instantly she told herself to not be taken in by lines he may have said too many times.

He kissed her hungrily, a kiss that heated her from her head to her toes and made her forget the annual ball or the last bachelor or anything else they had talked about. She was lost in another dizzying spiral of lovemaking.

Two hours later Merry finished dressing and walked out to find Jason standing waiting in the living room. The moment she stepped into the room, her breath rushed out. In a dark suit and white shirt, Jason looked even more handsome and commanding than ever.

His gaze lighted with pleasure as he looked her over, making her tingle from head to toe.

"Darlin', we may go to Claire's more often," he drawled. "You're gorgeous, Merry."

"Thank you. I could say the same about you."

She wore a simple black dress with a V-neck and a low-cut back. It was a sheath, clinging to her figure and hitting her just above the knees.

He crossed the room to tilt her face up. "Now I've lost all appetite for anything at Claire's. What I'd rather have is you, but I'm going to take you out at least once."

"I think that's the best idea."

"No. My best idea is bed."

She linked her arm through his. "Let's go, Jason." She touched the bulge beneath his coat and patted his side, looking up at him questioningly while problems rushed back into her life.

"I might want my pistol," he said to her unasked question.

"That makes me want to stay home."

"You'll be safe," he said with a determination that gave her a chill.

"I'm glad I know you now and not when you were living a different life."

"Whether in the CIA or out of it, I'm still me. And I usually don't carry a weapon here in Royal, but the situation changed when someone blew the end of my house away."

They walked in silence to the car and he held the door. "Jason," Merry said after they were driving from the ranch, "if Dorian has a good alibi for the night of the murder, that leaves him out as a suspect. Other things, like the electronic journal and his shady past, indicate it was him, yet if he was sitting in the Royal Diner the whole time, he's not the killer."

"Laura Edwards testified that he was at the diner. The

police checked her background, and she seems honest enough.''

"That alibi really lets Dorian out."

"Probably, but it doesn't hurt to keep looking. You never know what you might uncover or where."

It was half past eight when they walked into the elegant entryway of Claire's. The lighting was dim and the carpet thick. A couple leaving the restaurant headed toward them and paused.

"Hi, Jason," the tall, handsome man greeted Jason. Merry looked at an attractive black-haired woman standing beside the man.

"Merry, this is Pamela and Aaron Black, some friends of mine. Meet Meredith Silver she's from Dallas.''

"I think we've met," Aaron said with a twinkle in his green eyes.

Meredith blushed as she nodded. "Aaron was outside the Texas Cattleman's Club when I first arrived and was searching for Dorian Brady," she explained to Jason.

"How's the baby?" Jason asked.

"As wonderful as ever," Pamela answered, smiling. "She's almost seven months old now."

"I just happen to have her latest picture," Aaron said, grinning and whisking a picture from his wallet. "This is our Amy," he said, and Merry looked at a picture of an adorable baby girl with huge blue eyes and wisps of black hair.

"She's beautiful," Merry remarked.

"Thanks. We think so, too," Aaron replied proudly.

"Put the picture away," Pamela said, laughing. "Aaron is immersed in fatherhood and he pins everyone down to show them pictures and tell them about Amy."

"That's great," Merry replied.

"Yeah, it is," Jason added. "Thanks again, Aaron, for coming to help fight the fire the other night."

"Glad to do it. You'd do the same for me. If you need any more help with anything, let me know," he added solemnly, and suddenly Merry didn't think he was talking about fires or ranching at all.

"I will."

"I hope you find the cause."

"We're working on it," Jason replied grimly, and Merry was certain Aaron knew more about the fire than the general public did. "When things settle and I get the house rebuilt, you two will have to come over and bring Amy for a cookout."

"Thanks," Aaron said. "We'd like that."

"It was nice to meet you," Pamela told Merry.

"We'll let y'all get to dinner," Aaron said, taking his wife's arm and heading toward the door.

"He's a fellow rancher and a fellow Texas Cattleman's Club member. He used to be in the diplomatic service. The worldly diplomat married the local school marm. I doubt if Pamela has ever been one hundred miles out of Royal. At least, not until she married Aaron."

"They seem very happy."

"Yeah, they are happy. This past year Aaron has been the happiest I've ever seen him."

"So marriage isn't always all bad," she teased.

"I never said it was bad. I just said it wasn't for me. And that was all before I met you."

"You come up with statements like that as easy as breathing," she accused, determined not to be taken in by a charming expert at seduction.

"I mean what I say, Merry," he said solemnly, and she tried to ignore the thud of her heart. "Here's the maître d'," Jason said, turning to the man.

In minutes Jason and Merry sat at a white-linen-covered table with a candle and a single rosebud in a crystal vase. Jason ordered steaks for both of them, but when hers came, Merry could barely eat. All she wanted was to be back in Jason's arms.

Halfway through dinner she sipped her red wine and lowered her glass, slanting her head. "What? You're looking at me and not saying anything, but something's on your mind."

"Yeah, it is," he said in a husky voice. "I was thinking about you, us, home together. That's where I want to be."

She drew a deep breath and last shred of her appetite fled. "Someday I'll have to tell you no, but it isn't going to be tonight."

"I don't ever want to hear no from you," he said solemnly.

"We won't argue that one now," she said. "This night is special."

He picked up her hand and brushed a kiss across her knuckles. "It's damn special. Ready to go home or do you want to finish your steak?"

"I'm ready, Jason," she said in a sultry voice, and his eyes darkened as they did in moments of passion.

He motioned to the waiter and in minutes they were in Jason's car, headed down Main and out of town. She saw Jason adjust the rearview mirror and watch it often.

"What are you looking at?"

"Traffic. We've picked up a tail. Why don't you get down."

Chilled to think they might be in danger, she slid low in the seat, loosening her seat belt.

"Don't take that seat belt off. We may be in for a bumpy ride. You hang on, because I'm going to do a turn in just a minute."

"Are you certain we're being followed?"

"Yep. I am."

Suddenly he jammed the brakes, spun the car in a U-turn on Main Street and sped back the way they had come. Merry half slid off the seat and scrambled to get back up.

"Dammit," Jason snapped.

"What's wrong?" she asked, sitting up to see what was happening.

"He's gone. Whoever it was moved quickly. When I turned, he shot across the street into an alley." Jason whipped down Main, spun around a corner and raced down the next street.

"You may hear sirens in a minute. You're more than over the speed limit," she said. "That wild turn you made in traffic on Main should have brought the law."

"He's gone," Jason said and hit the steering wheel with his palm. "Damn. I wanted to see who it was."

"We're safe and now we're not being followed," she said, resting her hand on Jason's thigh. The moment she touched him, she tingled with awareness that drove all thoughts of danger away. Jason looked around at her and drew a deep breath.

"We're going home," he said roughly.

They drove out of town on back roads, and, as town lights faded and darkness enveloped them, Jason drove swiftly. He held Merry's hand on his thigh. He wanted to stop, pull her into his arms and make love to her here, now, in the car. But he knew they would be safer to wait until they reached the ranch where alarms and guards would be a protection.

He listened while she talked, but his thoughts were only half on what she was telling him. He was thinking about being followed, and then his thoughts shifted to their discussion of the Cattleman's Club ball and the remarks on marriage. He'd told her that he wasn't the marrying kind. But was that really the truth?

Was he in love with Merry Silver? He knew he needed to sort through his own feelings, but he had never before been this way about a woman. Never wanted one with a need that was insatiable, a craving that was impossible to fully satisfy.

He thought about meeting and talking to the Blacks. Aaron looked happier than he had ever before in his life and Jason had known Aaron Black since childhood. Hell, all his married friends looked happier. And Pamela Black looked radiant. Jason had known Pamela merely as an acquaintance, but he had always thought her rather plain. She didn't look plain now. *Radiant* was the best description of her. And Merry tonight in her black dress had stolen his breath away. She was gorgeous, alluring, sexy. He thought about his past doubts and fears of commitment; they seemed to be melting like fog in summer sunshine.

Would Merry ever walk out on her family?

The question seemed absurd. No matter how tough the situation, he didn't think she would walk out on a commitment or responsibility. Look at her taking off work to take a little revenge on the man who'd hurt her sister so badly.

He had spent a lifetime swearing he would never marry. How could he throw over years of solid conviction after just a few days of knowing someone? Merry had turned his life upside down, stolen his heart, stormed his senses. He liked everything about her, which was crazy because he hadn't liked a lot of things about her when he met her. She was fiery, impetuous, impulsive, feisty. Not his type of woman.

Keep telling yourself that, he thought. But that wasn't what his heart and mind and soul were shouting inside him. He wanted her, needed her, *loved her*. There it was. He was in love with a woman—deeply, truly in love for the first time, in spite of his playboy reputation and the many previous women in his life. None of those affairs had been serious. Not one.

He looked at Merry, who sat serenely gazing out the window at the dark Texas countryside that was nothing but flat land and mesquite trees. How could she have become so damned necessary to him? So special. *He was in love.* He wanted to reach across the car seat, pull her beside him and kiss her.

Acknowledging what he felt was amazing. Never had he expected love to happen to him. He had guarded against commitment, fought it, shrugged it away as something that happened to other people, but would not be a part of his life. Now love had become vital.

He wanted to tell her exactly how he felt, but right now, speeding home through the empty night, was not the place for a very special announcement.

She would want children. He had never given children a thought because he had never expected to fall in love, much less marry. A baby with Meredith. Their baby. The notion was awe-inspiring.

But before that was love. Glorious, fire-and-dynamite loving. He remembered her in the throes of passion, her legs around him as she cried out his name. He increased the speed of the car slightly because he wanted to get her home.

He couldn't keep from glancing at her repeatedly. She seemed oblivious to his glances, and he wondered what was running through her mind.

"What are you thinking?" he asked finally, his voice a notch deeper because his thoughts were erotic.

"About Dorian having an alibi, yet so much points to him. And I'm thinking about being followed tonight. Whoever bombed your house, if the person was sending a warning—why follow us? If it was Dorian after the computer disk—why follow us? Unless whoever it is really intended to harm us and failed with the bomb," she added.

"We're safe. Don't worry about it, and no one is following us now."

"No, but if they know who you are and who I am, then they know exactly where we're going right now."

"I'm watching and I'm armed."

"Somehow that doesn't reassure me. I don't want to get into a shootout."

"We won't. Whoever this is, he or she doesn't work that way. So far, with the exception of Eric Chambers, there's been no direct confrontation."

"I'd call bombing your house about as direct a confrontation as you can get."

"Let me worry about the danger. I was hoping you had

other things on your mind.'' He stroked her nape lightly while he watched the road.

''What things?''

''Us. Making love,'' he answered in a husky voice.

She leaned close to him to flick her tongue out and kiss his ear. ''We did that, mister, not much over a couple of hours ago.''

''Merry,'' he groaned, ''this is the longest ride home I've ever had.''

She laughed softly and ran her fingers up his thigh. ''You keep your attention on the road.''

In the early hours of the morning Merry snuggled against Jason, who held her close. He lay on his side, his head propped on his hand as he studied her. She had a sheet pulled high under her arms, but her shoulders were bare, her hair a riot of silky auburn locks cascading over her pale skin. Jason ran his finger lightly along her hip, covered by the sheet.

He was in love, and he thought again about their conversation.

How'll you know he's the right person if you haven't gone with him some first?''

I'll know.

Just like that? Like lightning striking or what?

I'll know the way anyone knows when she or he is in love.

He had told her he had been in love, but it wasn't like this. This love was the real thing. He understood her now when she said she had never been truly, deeply in love. It shocked him to find himself head over heels in love. He had guarded against it, but had he really been preventing falling in love, or had it simply been that Merry had not yet come into his life?

Now the urge was growing stronger by the hour to get some kind of commitment from her. He didn't want her to go back to Dallas.

And even though she hadn't declared her love, she must feel it because she had given herself completely to him and only to him. He kissed her shoulder, then nuzzled her neck, wanting her fiercely again, as if they hadn't made love through most of the night. He pushed the sheet down to fondle her breast, lowering his head to take her nipple in his mouth and kiss her. When she stirred and moaned, he raised his head to look at her. Her eyes slowly opened and she smiled at him, wrapping one arm around his neck.

"I love you, Merry."

"You're nice, Jason."

He caught her chin in his hand. "I'm really in love with you."

She smiled at him, a mysterious, feminine smile that left him unable to discern what she truly felt. "I'm glad."

"I don't think you believe me."

"Of course I do, to a degree," she said, twisting to turn onto her back to wrap both arms around his neck and pull him down to her. "I'll show you, Jason."

It was noon the next day before he kissed her goodbye.

"I have appointments all afternoon, and at four, I'm meeting with Sebastian, Rob, Will and Keith to tell them what we found in Dorian's computer files and about my fire."

"Be careful in town."

"I will, and you stay on the ranch and don't disappear." He kissed her hard and long and then released her. "I have to break some bad news to my friends about our suspicions. See you tonight."

She watched him stride away and thought about his declarations of love and reminded herself not to be taken in by them. Once again, she told herself that she needed to pack and go home, back to her regular life instead of this life that had turned into a dream.

Nine

Late in the day, Jason sat in the meeting room at the Texas Cattleman's Club. The air-conditioned room was cool and quiet. Iced tea and cold beer had been served. Will and Sebastian had come from work and had shed their suit coats and ties and rolled up shirtsleeves. Leaning back in one of the comfortable leather chairs, Keith was in chinos and a green knit shirt while Rob was in jeans and a blue Western shirt like Jason.

Jason looked around the circle of solemn faces.

"Thanks for coming. I want to bring all of you up to date. I asked you to keep this meeting confidential," Jason said. "We've cut Dorian out of the meeting."

"Is there a good reason?" Sebastian asked with concern in his gray eyes, and Jason suspected Sebastian still wanted to believe the best about his half brother even though it was growing more difficult all the time.

"I think there is," Jason answered. "Merry and I got into Wescott Oil—"

"You're the burglars?" Will asked incredulously.

"Where and how is Merry?" Rob asked.

"She's fine and she's out at my ranch," Jason replied evenly.

"Well, she's not escaping now," Will observed with amusement. "Is there some reason for this?"

"Hey, maybe *I'm* going to be the last bachelor left standing," Keith said, staring at Jason. "I might win that bet after all," he said.

"You can't beat our resident playboy," Rob remarked, watching Jason closely even though he was grinning. Rob tilted his head. "That's right, isn't it?"

Thoughts flitted through Jason's mind as he hesitated before answering, a mistake, because instantly all of them were teasing and asking questions.

"Our playboy bites the dust," Rob said. "The wildcat gets her man."

"The wildcat lassos the cowboy, hog-ties and drags him to the altar," Keith said.

"She won't have to drag me," Jason replied, and whoops of laughter and disbelief burst from his friends. He grinned and waited for them to settle.

"You're going to be the last bachelor," Rob said to Keith.

"Well, not quite so fast," Jason cautioned. "The lady hasn't said yes. I haven't asked her yet."

"Oh! Sorry, Keith," Sebastian said, "The truth comes out. I can't see our playboy popping the question."

This brought more teasing which Jason put up with patiently.

"Okay, y'all," he said finally. "Enough's enough. We didn't meet to discuss my love life—"

"Which would fill two or three volumes," Rob interjected.

Jason waved his hand. "I'll keep you posted. In the meantime, Keith, you're not exactly the last bachelor, although I hope to change that soon."

"Will wonders never cease?" Will said.

"You better get to planning that ball and thinking about your charity, Keith. Looks like we've got our man," Sebastian said.

"For just a minute let's discuss why I called y'all here and why I asked you to keep this meeting quiet," Jason said.

"I think we were talking about the burglary at Wescott, which I now find out was done by you and your lady love," Will said.

"Yes," Jason admitted.

"I knew about their plan," Sebastian admitted. "I didn't tell you, Will, because I thought that the fewer people in on the plan, the better. And this way, when you got the news, your reactions were normal and sincere."

"Merry got into Dorian's computer files—"

"Dammit, I thought we had those so secure no one could get into them," Will snapped. "We had to open Eric Chambers's files for the police."

"Well, she got into them in about five minutes," Jason informed him dryly, and Keith laughed.

"That's embarrassing because we sold Wescott some of its software and set up the programs. The wildcat's not so crazy after all," Keith added.

"Anyway, we were interrupted because Dorian came to the office. Merry copied some files and got enough to indicate that Dorian kept an electronic journal. There's a reference that made it sound as though he was blackmailing Eric Chambers."

"Let me interrupt," Keith said. "Rob and I have copies. I can give you one, Sebastian, and then you can pass it to Will. All right?"

"Sure."

"The next thing…" Jason continued. "A statement went out on the news that the fire at my place may have been caused by a gas leak. There was no gas leak. I gave that to the press. The fire chief said that they were investigating what caused the fire, which was the truth on his part. He just didn't elaborate. But we knew that night that the explosion was caused by a bomb.''

''Why you?'' Sebastian asked. Before Jason could answer, Sebastian answered his own question, ''Was it because Meredith Silver is at your place?''

''We don't know, but one possibility is that it was done to wipe out my computer and any disks that were copied at Wescott Oil the other night.''

''That would have to be Dorian,'' Keith said.

''He's got that damned alibi for the murder,'' Rob reminded them. ''Laura Edwards swears he was sitting in the Royal Diner the whole time that Eric Chambers was murdered.''

''Yes, but Laura Edwards seems very much in love with Dorian,'' Will remarked dryly. ''There's always the possibility that he has pulled the wool over her eyes, and she's covering for him.''

''A lot points to Dorian,'' Jason reminded them grimly. ''And we have a mole in our group, so, more than likely it's one of us.''

''Damn,'' said Sebastian. ''If it's Dorian, I brought him into our group.''

''If it's Dorian,'' Jason said, ''then he's caused you a world of grief when you were trying to be a brother to him. We're all going to be sorry about that.''

A grim silence fell over the group. ''So where do we go from here?'' Will asked.

''I think we need to set a trap of some kind for Dorian,'' Rob suggested. ''If Dorian's the murderer, he's done too much and gone too far. Whoever is behind all this has killed Eric Chambers, tried to frame Sebastian, bombed Jason's house—''

''If it's Dorian, there's a possibility he has taken money from Meredith Silver's sister. She doesn't have proof though.''

''Dammit again,'' Sebastian said. ''I brought him into

our group, moved him into my business, my circle of friends. I did everything for him. Why would he do this? What's his motive? If something happens to me, he won't inherit what I have. He'll be worse off with me gone than if I'm alive. I can't see what motive he has, and he has a sound alibi.''

Another silence followed and Jason tried to keep his thoughts from drifting to Merry.

"Okay, back to where we go from here," Will said. "I agree with Rob that we need to set a trap. Let's think about what we can do, because we have to be careful. He's aware we suspect someone in our group, so that narrows suspicion to him instantly. He may get desperate, and if he's the guilty party, he's already murdered once, so he has nothing to lose if he does it again.''

"Sorry, but I have to go. I have an appointment," Will announced, standing.

"Everybody think about what we can do to set a trap," Jason suggested. "We'll meet again—a week from now, same time, all right?"

All heads nodded and Jason stood.

"And Keith," Will said, grinning, "you consider what charity you want. I think our playboy is losing his title."

"I might be," Jason admitted, thinking about Merry and how long it would take him to get to the ranch.

"I hope you're not so in love that you can't watch your back," Rob cautioned, moving beside him as they left the club.

"I'll be careful. I have guys guarding the ranch. Even though he may have just been after the computer and disks, I'm having an alarm system installed for the grounds around the house.''

"Maybe, but you don't know. She's annoyed him no end. And we need to find out for sure if it's Dorian. If we're chasing the wrong person, we're wasting time and putting everyone in more jeopardy.''

Rob paused to face Jason. "We talked about setting a

trap for Dorian. There is something that we might do that wouldn't involve a lot of risk. It might be just one more bit of proof. You could get Merry to confront him here in Royal.''

''Oh, no! I'm not jeopardizing her—''

''Look, this wouldn't be as dangerous as what the two of you did breaking into Wescott Oil. That could have got you shot.''

''Not in Royal. I don't want her in danger.'' Wind caught locks of Jason's hair as gazed at his friend.

''She's in danger just living at your ranch. Do you want to catch this guy or not? She isn't afraid to go after him.''

''All right,'' Jason relented reluctantly. He knew Merry wasn't afraid, and she would want to do whatever she could to help trap Dorian. ''What's your idea?''

''With Sebastian's help, because he works with Dorian and knows where he is from eight to five, we could arrange a seemingly casual meeting during the day between Merry and Dorian. They could encounter each other with people around and in daylight. I've got a mini-recorder that she can drop into her pocket and pick up every word he says. I don't need to tell you about those devices.''

''I hate to have her anywhere near the creep. It'll just be one more goad to a man who may be desperate now.''

''We need some proof. If he would own up to knowing her and her sister, that would be one more arrow pointing to guilt on his part. It wouldn't tie him to the murder, but it would show that he's been lying to us.''

Jason mulled the plan over. He wanted to refuse, yet he knew Merry would agree to doing it without hesitating one second.

Rob continued, ''If they met in broad daylight on the streets here in town, I don't think he would do anything. I could be in a car not far away. I wouldn't let her out of my sight and I wouldn't suggest it if I thought it would put her in any danger.''

''You don't need to bother watching her because I will.''

''If you want both of us to watch, even better.''

Jason nodded. ''I don't want to take any risks, and if she doesn't want to do it, that's it.''

''Good,'' Rob said while satisfaction lit his eyes. ''I know what her answer will be. You weren't there when she stormed into the club. The lady is determined, and she didn't act as if she would be scared of Old Ned himself.''

''She might not be,'' Jason agreed with a sigh, ''but that doesn't mean I want her at risk.''

''I swear I'll watch her and keep her safe.''

''Both of us will. I'll ask her about it tonight.''

''I'll call Sebastian. Tell Merry thanks.''

''You're so damned sure of yourself.''

''Nope. I'm sure of her. I think she's a good match for you, my friend. She'll keep you hopping.''

''She already does. I think Dorian's the one, but then, I never have liked the guy. If it's him, he knifed Sebastian in the back after all Sebastian did for him.''

''Yeah, but if he won't inherit, then why did he kill?''

Jason shrugged and headed for his pickup. ''That's what we have to figure out. See you.''

''Hey, Jason, wait up,'' Keith called and jogged across the lot to catch up with Jason.

''Does Meredith need work?'' he asked.

''She's a freelance programmer.''

''She must be damned good at what she does. I could use someone like her in my business. I'd like to talk to her about a job.''

''Get in line and give her a call. You know my number.''

''Get in line?''

''Rob wants her to do something for him. Go ahead, call her.''

''I will. Thanks.''

''I'll tell her that you'll call.''

''Great. See you later.'' Keith turned to go to his car and Jason slid into his pickup, forgetting about Keith instantly as his thoughts turned to Merry.

He didn't want her to confront Dorian ever, but he would leave the decision to her because Rob's plan didn't sound like it would put Merry in jeopardy.

As Jason drove along Main, he thought about her. He wanted to get her a ring. He wanted to buy her everything, wanted to give her the world. He was in love, and it was scary and marvelous and amazing. When could they marry?

This was May, and if he could have his way, they'd get married next week, but Merry had a big family and he did, too, so he suspected a wedding would be a major event. Could he get her to stay at his ranch until then? He wanted her with him constantly. He was more amazed at himself than his friends were. He had never, ever expected to be in love, never known he could feel like this about a woman. He was dazzled, unable to concentrate on anything else very long before she filled his thoughts. He loved her and he wanted to marry her—the sooner the better.

Jason drove to a jewelry store, and an hour an a half later he drove out of town with a ring in his pocket, roses beside him and a bubbling eagerness to see her again.

As he raced home, Jason glanced out the window and realized he had passed the road to his house. He groaned, swung in a U-turn and headed home.

"Woman, you better marry me before I lose it completely," he grumbled, knowing now it would be ten minutes longer before he would see her.

Merry lolled in a tub of sudsy water while she contemplated her future. She had to make decisions, because, since arriving in Royal, Texas, her life had changed completely. She needed to move out of Jason's house, get back to work and go on with her life.

Three more days. She would give Jason three more days and then she had to pack and go. She didn't think she would be in any danger if she moved back to Dallas. She lived in a gated apartment that was as secure as the one that she had rented here in Royal seemed to be. Right now, for tonight, she didn't want to think about leaving Jason, and she put it out of mind. The time would come soon enough.

She finished bathing, dried her hair and dressed carefully in a blue sundress with a halter top and full skirt. She slipped into sandals and looped and pinned her hair on top of her head.

Wayward tendrils escaped to curl around her face and she left them, making a face at them in her reflection in the mirror.

It seemed like forever before she heard Jason's pickup, and this time she did go out to meet him, flying into his arms. He caught her up, kissing her hard and long as he carried her into the house and kicked the door shut. He set down the vase of roses and turned to Merry.

"It's been an eternity," he said in a breathless voice and pulled her into his embrace.

An hour later Jason held Merry close against him. "I'll cook steaks unless you'd prefer I'd take you to town to Claire's again."

"Actually, the steaks right here sound like a deal."

"Steaks it is. Let's shower first."

She moaned softly and hugged him. "If we shower together, there won't be any steaks for hours."

"How hungry are you?"

She gave him a sultry, heated look that made him groan. He stood and scooped her into his arms and carried her to the bathroom and it was another hour before they were seated in the kitchen over thick, sizzling steaks and baked potatoes covered with melted butter and sprinkled with chives.

Glasses of red wine sat on the table along with warm slices of bread, crisp asparagus and slices of juicy red tomatoes.

"How was your meeting today?"

"I almost forgot. Keith Owens is going to call you. He wants to offer you a job with his company. He was impressed that you got into Dorian's computer files, because Keith's company sold software to Wescott and helped them set up some of their programs.''

''He's offering me a job here in Royal?''

''Yes. Think about it, all right?''

When she smiled at him, Jason thought about the ring upstairs in a drawer beside the bed. Their dinners were only half eaten, but he had lost his appetite.

''Come here,'' he said, taking her hand. ''Let's dance.''

He already had music playing, and he pulled her into his arms.

In his arms Merry moved with him as if they had danced together forever. They danced into the family room with its hardwood floor. In her sundress, her back and shoulders were bare and he caressed her while they danced.

When she raised her head, he leaned down to kiss her, wanting her as fiercely as he had when he had driven to the ranch earlier today.

''Merry, I love you,'' he whispered.

Something flickered in the depths of her smokey eyes, but she merely gazed at him solemnly and then stood on tiptoe, pulling his head to hers.

They kissed and Jason wanted to bury himself in her softness. He unfastened the buttons on the sundress and let it fall away while she tugged his shirt out of his pants.

She took his breath with her luminous gray eyes, hot kisses and fiery hair. He wanted her with a desperate urgency, but he wanted to make love to her for hours, to make it as good as possible for her, to drive her wild.

He peeled away the bits of lace underwear she wore and shed his own clothing, tossing it aside to pull her down on the sofa and kiss her from head to toe.

Merry was lost in sensations, aware of Jason murmuring endearments as he kissed her, trying to turn them off in her mind, to give herself to passion and feeling and not let her heart be talked into believing a dream he was weaving around her.

Hours later, they loved in the big bed until they lay exhausted, wrapped in each other's arms while their racing hearts slowed.

He kissed her tenderly, moving beside her and stroking her face. "I love you, Merry. Really love you. For the first time in my life, I'm truly in love."

She put her fingers over his lips. "Jason, it's good. Let's leave it that way."

"You don't believe me, but I'm telling you the truth."

She smiled at him, determined not to be completely taken in by the words. The man was the ultimate playboy, the consummate lover, and she wasn't falling for a line of love promises made in the throes of passion or right after loving.

He turned, opening the drawer beside the bed to fumble in the drawer. He rolled back over to place a small black box on her bare stomach.

She stared at it with curiosity, realized it was probably a jewelry box. Pulling the sheet beneath her arms, she sat up. Jason took the box from her hand and gazed at her solemnly while he opened it.

"Merry, I love you. Will you marry me?" he asked, leaning forward to kiss her lightly.

Stunned, Merry looked at the beautiful diamond catching glints of the soft light in its sparkling depths, and then she looked into Jason's blue-green eyes that made her heart thud. Everything inside her cried out acceptance. *If only...*

Ten

Unable to answer him, she looked down at the diamond. Why did it have to be this way? Inside, she hurt, a pain that spread and deepened, and she wondered whether it would completely consume her. She kept staring at the diamond until Jason tilted up her chin, and she gazed into his solemn eyes.

"I love you, Merry. You've changed my life and how I feel about things. How I feel about love."

She kissed him, long and slowly, barely aware of the salty taste of her tears, knowing that she was going to be heartbroken, but also knowing there was only one answer to give him.

"Tears?" he said, leaning back and framing her face to wipe away her tears with his thumbs. "Merry, I love you. I think you love me," he said, watching her intently.

"Jason, we haven't known each other long enough. This is too fast. Last month I didn't know you. Days ago you told me in no uncertain terms that you would never marry."

"Well, I hadn't fallen in love then. My life has changed because of knowing you."

"It's too soon to really know what you feel deep in your heart."

"I think you're the one who said something about you'd just know when you fell in love. Well, that's the way it's been with me. I know what I want and how I feel." He gazed into her eyes in a long, probing look. "Tell me you don't love me."

"You know I can't tell you that, but this is too fast. I don't want to rush into an engagement, rush into a marriage. Last month you were certain you'd never marry. You've spent a lifetime—your adult lifetime—going from woman to woman. For you to really know your feelings is going to take time."

"No, it isn't," he answered, and her pulse jumped because she wanted with all her heart to believe what he was saying.

"If we love each other, time will prove it."

"I don't want you to go back to Dallas. I want you here, just as you are now. I want you in my arms, in my bed every night. I want to come home to you, to call you when I need you, to have someone to share everything with."

"Jason, I want that so badly that I don't dare think about it."

"Let go and trust me. Acknowledge what you know you feel."

"You can't be so sure so fast. I don't know if you've done this with every other woman you've—"

"I haven't asked another woman to marry me," he interrupted her gruffly. "I swear to you, Merry, I've never told a woman I loved her. Not once, not ever. Not even as a teen. There was always a part of me that stood back and held back and kept quiet."

"Oh, Jason," she said, knowing that withdrawal was from old hurts, but that didn't mean he was so completely certain now. "I don't think you can change quickly and really know how you'll feel a year from now or two years from now. This is way too fast, way too superficial.''

''There's nothing superficial about it. I know to the depths of my soul, Merry. I've never been this way before. I know for certain.''

''Then date me and show me. There hasn't been anything normal or routine about the time we've been together—the bomb, I'm away from home, I'm living here—''

''The intimacy and the upheaval ought to allow us to know each other better and know our feelings better. In a crisis all civilized veneer is stripped away and what's real is left. And that's what we've seen of each other.''

''Maybe, but I think we need some time and space. I can't believe you really know your own heart. No one can have a complete turnaround the way you have. Not this fast. Jason, when I marry, I want it to be forever.''

''I do, too. And I know my heart. I know what I feel for you. I love you.''

She closed the ring box and placed it in his hand. ''Maybe in time, Jason. Not now. There's no way you can convince me that you deeply, truly love me. You were far too convincing only a short time ago when you said you would never fall in love, never marry.''

''I didn't really know you then.''

''You don't really, really know me now.''

''I think I do. And what I don't know, I want to find out.'' He held her face with his hands. ''Dammit, woman, I love you. I want you to marry me.''

She gazed into his eyes, blazing with determination and desire. He pulled her closer to lean forward and kiss her long and hard.

''Marry me,'' he urged after a lot of kisses.

She moved away, wrapping his fingers around the ring box. ''We can talk about it, and you can see how you feel after we get to know each other better.''

He caught her chin with his hand and his eyes burned

into hers. "I know exactly what I want. I love you, darlin'. And I'll convince you of it."

Her heart thudded, and she couldn't resist pulling him to her, taking them both down on the bed and kissing him wildly. Letting go with kisses and lovemaking, she couldn't get enough of him or give enough of herself to him. There were no barriers here, no holding back. Time did not exist. Love was all-encompassing, and she could pour out her love for him.

The next morning, Jason left the house shortly after dawn to round up steers to take to market.

A lot of the ranch work Jason did was from his pickup, but today he and the men were going on horseback. At the corral he saddled his gray horse and swung into the saddle, riding out to join the others.

All through the day, unless his attention was completely on his work, he thought about Merry and how to convince her he knew his own feelings. In late afternoon before he returned to the house, he flagged down his foreman.

Almost seven feet tall and thick through the shoulders and chest, Dusty Grant strode over to him.

"I want you to handle this sale tomorrow."

"Sure," the blond giant replied, taking off his hat and wiping sweat from his forehead and neck with a red bandana.

"I'd like to take a few days off. I'll be around the house if you need me, but I want some time off."

"Sure, boss. It's fine. Day after tomorrow you were going to that horse sale."

"I can do that, but you take over the rest."

"Will do," he said. "Men are standing watch around the clock."

"Until we find out who planted that bomb, keep a watch going. I don't want anything else to happen. Thanks, Dusty. I asked Henry to fly us to Houston tonight, and we'll be back sometime tomorrow."

"Sure thing."

Jason turned and headed for the house. He was flying Merry to Houston to dinner tonight and they'd return home tomorrow. His pulse speeded in anticipation. She knew they were going out to dinner, but he wanted the flight to be a surprise, so he hadn't told her.

He stretched out his stride, hurrying to the guest house, wanting to be with her, something he had yearned for since he'd told her goodbye this morning.

He crossed the porch and reached for the door as she stepped outside and into his arms. He caught her up and embraced her tightly, kissing her as he walked them both inside and kicked the door closed. Reaching behind him, he turned the lock. He wanted her desperately. "I'm dusty and hot—"

"I don't care," she whispered, and his pulse soared. She was cool, smelling sweet and enticing, so soft in his arms. He couldn't wait, peeling away her clothes and shedding his. His hands shook with haste and need. She was soft, wild, magical. In minutes he lifted her off the floor and she locked her legs around him while he entered her. Urgency drove them, and he felt as if it were the first time all over again.

"Merry! I love you. My love, my woman," he whispered, wondering how long it would take to convince her of the depth of his feelings.

Thoughts vanished as he relished loving her, swept into ecstasy with her and wanting it never to end.

Later, after they had showered, he carried her to bed to hold her close in his arms until they had to dress to leave for dinner.

He waited in the small living room, finally hearing her heels clicking, and then she walked through the door. Sexy and beautiful, she paused, her gaze warm enough to melt him as he drank in the sight of her in a clinging red dress with her hair looped and pinned on top of her head. Stray tendrils hung down, framing her face. As always, he was tempted to forget dinner and just go back to bed. But he wanted to court her and win her over, and taking her out was part of that.

"You're beautiful," he said, his voice husky. He couldn't keep his reactions to her from showing. Nor did he really want to.

"You look very handsome, too," she said breathlessly. "Sure you want to leave?"

"Hell no, I don't want to do anything except make love to you, but I want you to have some special moments besides when we're in bed. So let's go."

She took his arm and it wasn't until they turned and drove up to the small jet waiting at the Royal airport that she raised her eyebrows. "So what's this?"

"We're going to Houston for dinner and dancing."

She smiled and leaned close to kiss him. "Sounds great. Another very special evening with you."

"Let's see how special we can make it," he said quietly, wishing she would come home wearing his engagement ring.

Jason tried to be his charming best through a lobster dinner with glasses of chablis and a flaming dessert. The restaurant had an indoor waterfall and a pond with blooming lilies. There was a deserted dance floor because the combo would not commence playing for another hour. In the meantime, soft piano music added to the cozy atmosphere. Their table had candlelight, white linen and a vase of pink tulips and daisies.

His appetite had diminished since he'd met her, and it wasn't any stronger tonight.

"Jason, this is exciting and wonderful, but life goes on. Monday, I have an appointment with Keith. Whatever I do, I need to move out of your house."

"Merry—"

"Wait and let me finish," she said firmly. "I will either go back home to Dallas or I'll accept Keith's offer and move into the apartment I rented here in Royal."

"I don't want you to go."

"I have to. I can't keep staying at your house."

"I wish you'd marry me, and that would settle it. I love you. Can't you see that?"

"I'm flattered, but I don't think you know what you feel."

He groaned and wanted to pull her into his arms and stop all this nonsense by making love to her until she acknowledged what they both felt.

His past had caught up with him, something he had never given a thought to before. He sipped his wine and wondered how much time it would take to convince her that he meant what he was saying. This was a problem he had never expected to have. She was sexy and sweet and unfortunately, as strong-willed as he was. He took her hand, feeling her smooth, soft skin and looking into her smoke-colored eyes that held flames in their depths.

Until Merry, he had never found a female he couldn't charm or seduce or win over to his way if he wanted to. She was moving out Monday. The announcement was like the plunge of a knife into his heart. She might go back to Dallas. He hurt and he didn't want her to go. He didn't want time or distance between them, but he knew it was pointless to argue with her about it.

"You're a challenge, Merry. And you've been one since that first night at the club."

She smiled at him, a twinkle in her eyes. "You need a challenge every once in a while."

"What I need is you," he answered, his voice becoming a rasp. The band began to play and he glanced at the dance floor, standing. "Come dance with me," he said, taking her hand and wanting her in his arms.

As she danced with him, he tightened his arm around her waist, holding her close, frustrated because he couldn't convince her of his feelings.

He wasn't going to let her go, but he damned sure didn't want to court her for a year or longer and that's what she seemed to be hellbent on him doing. He kissed her soft cheek, blew lightly in her ear, and wished she could see that he knew his own heart.

"Merry, I've told you this before, but I'll say it again. I know what I want."

"If you're really in love, then time will prove it, Jason," she answered so sweetly he wanted to gnash his teeth and swear.

The music changed to a fast number and he watched her move around him, a flame in her red dress. He wanted to pull her hair down and peel her out of the dress and it took a major effort of will to keep dancing instead of taking her back to the hotel suite he had reserved for them. He didn't want to think about Monday and her leaving.

In the early hours of Monday morning, Merry lay awake in Jason's arms. Neither had slept well, loving most of the night, yet both aware of the deadline she had arbitrarily set. She knew the most difficult thing she had ever done would be to move out in a few hours. She had turned down his ring and proposal, now she was moving away from him, but she knew she had to.

This morning at half-past ten, she had an appointment with Keith Owens. It would have to be a very good offer to pull her away from her freelancing. She turned on her side to look at Jason as he slept. Locks of his unruly black hair fell over his forehead and his cheek. His muscled chest was bare, the sheet down below his waist. Her heart thudded, and she wanted so badly just to move into his arms and say yes, she would marry him, and forget all caution. But she didn't want major regrets later.

His arm was draped over her. He held her always in the night, moving her close against him, even in his sleep. She brushed locks off his forehead. "I love you," she whispered.

Sleep was impossible, and she was still awake when Jason stirred, tightened his arms around her and pulled her closer to kiss her.

They loved long and leisurely, yet with an underlying urgency. When she finally dressed to leave the ranch for her appointment with Keith, time was running out and she had to rush.

With her things packed and in her own car, she hurried through the house to find Jason waiting in the kitchen. He stood when she entered the room.

His gaze raked over her simple blue suit. "You look gorgeous."

"Thanks, Jason. I hope I look professional. I have to run or I'll be late to meet Keith."

"Keith will understand if you call and change the time."

"I'm keeping my appointment. Kiss me goodbye," she said, walking up to him with her heart thudding.

His arms wrapped around her tightly and he pulled her close, kissing her long and taking her breath. She knew she should stop him. He was drawing out his kiss, rekindling desire that smoldered all the time. She pushed against him. "I have to go now."

"No, you don't really," he said gruffly, his blue-green gaze intense and tearing into her. "And you could come home to me afterwards."

"We've been over that." She headed toward the door and he moved with her, holding the door of her car and closing it behind her.

Jason leaned down to take her chin in his hand. "I'll meet you for lunch at the Royal Diner after your interview."

When she nodded, he stepped away from the car.

She started the motor, shifted and drove away. Glancing in the rearview mirror, she saw Jason standing with his fists on his hips, his feet spread apart while he watched her drive away.

She hurt and wondered if she had just tossed aside a wonderful future. Was she making an incredible mistake by not saying yes and following her heart and rushing into marriage?

Tears streamed down her cheeks and she wiped at them hastily, not wanting to go to a job interview with clothes wet from tears. She didn't particularly care about the interview, but Keith Owens had sounded as if he could make her an interesting offer, and he was very complimentary about her skills, even though he was basing his opinion on her getting into Dorian's files.

When she walked into his office, he stood to offer her his hand. She looked into friendly brown eyes. "I'm glad to meet you again under better circumstances."

He laughed. "You stirred us all up, but we need that sometimes. Have a seat." Dressed in dark slacks and a button-down short-sleeved broadcloth shirt, he was casual in appearance and approach. He moved away from his desk, turning a chair to face her and looking relaxed. "Thanks for getting your résumé to me so quickly."

"My sister sent a copy to me, and it was easy to send one on to you."

"Your résumé is impressive. But getting into Dorian's files is even more impressive. We have an opening I think you would be perfect for."

She listened while he talked, and all through the interview, she kept thinking that if she took the job with Keith Owens's firm, she would live in Royal and not be separated from Jason.

The longer they talked, the more interested she became.

"Would you like a tour of the place?" he asked, and she nodded, standing when he did.

As they walked through offices, in between introductions and explanations of various departments, he gave her a brief history of his firm. When they finally returned to his office, he faced her.

"Any more questions?"

"I've asked you everything that's come to mind."

He grinned. "You don't know what salary I'm offering."

"Some of the other considerations are more important, and I knew we'd get to salary before I left."

He named an amount, and she whistled. "That's a very good salary."

"That's to start. In six months we'll review things and then you may get a raise. I hope you'll think about working here."

"I'm interested, and it's a very attractive offer," she replied. She stood, offering her hand. "Thanks so much. I'll be in touch with you soon with my answer."

"Good, Meredith."

"Call me Merry. I go by Merry more than Meredith."

Keith walked to the office door with her and told her goodbye again. As she crossed the shaded parking lot, she mulled over her choices. Stay here and date Jason and see what happened or go back to Dallas and date him on weekends or whenever they could get together. The job sounded worthwhile and the salary was fabulous.

Merry spent the afternoon picking up a few dishes, an air mattress, new sheets and a pillow so she could stay in her apartment until she had decided whether or not to accept Keith Owens's offer. She went ahead and had a telephone installed so she wouldn't have to rely completely on her cellular phone.

That night at Claire's she discussed the offer with Jason. His reaction was what she had expected. He wanted her to take the job.

He took her hand. "You've got my head spinning and I can't think about anything else except you and making love to you. There's something I was supposed to tell you days ago."

"Really? What's that?"

"Rob and I talked about setting a trap for Dorian. After our meeting, Rob talked to me alone and suggested that we could give you a small recorder. We'll find out when Dorian's leaving work or going to the Royal Diner and have you casually confront him. It'll be the two of you, but it will be daylight out in public with people around, and Rob and I will be watching so you won't be in danger."

"I'll do it tomorrow."

Jason ran his hand across his forehead. "Rob said you wouldn't be afraid."

"Why would I be afraid in public with you close at hand? Would you be afraid if you were the one to do it?"

"Hell, no, but that's different."

"I don't know why. You think I'm too weak to take care of myself?" she asked in a haughty voice, and Jason couldn't bite back a grin as he remembered how she had knocked him flat in the parking lot.

"Let's go home and let me check out your muscles."

She made a face at him. "Call Rob now and set something up. The sooner the better."

Jason sighed and shook his head. "I should have known what your reaction would be." He reached into his pocket and pulled out his cellular phone. In minutes he handed it to Merry.

"He wants to check things out with you. We're set."

He watched her while she listened and talked to Rob and all Jason could think about was taking her home. He wanted to talk her into coming back to the ranch with him. When had he ever had trouble talking a female into anything he wanted? Since he had met Merry. She could resist all his wiles. He reached across the table to run his fingers along her soft cheek. She returned the phone to him, and he talked to Rob, who said he would call back as soon as he talked to Sebastian, but they would plan on tomorrow afternoon when Dorian left work.

Jason put away the phone and stood to take her hand. "Let's dance."

He whispered endearments in her ear and then tried to talk her into going back to the ranch, but she was adamant about returning to her new apartment.

When he walked to the door of her apartment with her,

she turned to face him, and he realized she didn't even intend to invite him inside.

"Aren't you going to show me your apartment?"

"Not tonight. You won't like it because it doesn't have furniture in it."

"Come home with me," he said.

"We've been over that more than once. We need a little time and space. Or at least I do, and I think you should take a step back."

"That's crazy when I feel the way I do about you," he said, wrapping her in his arms. "You're not going to let me come in tonight?"

"No, I'm not."

"I love you, Merry."

Her heart thudded, and she wanted so badly to believe him, so badly to go home with him, but he had a history that worried her. "You were very convincing when I met you and you told me you never wanted to marry."

"I wish I had kept my mouth shut. Don't you know that I've fallen in love with you? It happens, Merry. Why can't you believe me?"

"I want to, and maybe I will, but I want us both to do a few things that are logical."

"Yeah? Well, where's logic in this?" He leaned down to kiss her, his mouth covering hers, opening it as his tongue touched hers. Her heart pounded and she stood on tiptoe and clung to him to kiss him back. She wanted him desperately, wanted him to really be in love with her and she poured herself into her kisses until they both were panting.

"Give me your key," he whispered.

She pushed against his chest. "As difficult as this is, I'm going to do what I said. I'll talk to you tomorrow, and tonight was fun." She unlocked her apartment, stepped inside and gazed into smoldering blue-green eyes that took her breath with blatant desire.

"'Night, Jason," she said, thinking it was the hardest

thing she had ever done and wondering how she was going to be able to leave him and go back to Dallas if that's the decision she eventually made.

She closed the door and locked it, standing in the empty darkened apartment and feeling forlorn. In minutes she heard his car drive away, and she wiped away tears. She wanted to be with him, wanted to accept his ring. Did he really mean his declarations of love? she asked herself for what seemed like the millionth time. Or would he gradually disappear out of her life and go on to another woman? That possibility hurt. "I love you," she whispered the words she had wanted to say to him so many times, yet she had to be sure about him.

She couldn't see how he could be so sure about himself when he had spent a lifetime fighting the idea of marriage.

She shifted restlessly and tried to think about their plan for her to meet Dorian face-to-face. She would welcome the opportunity. And then she could prove to Jason that Dorian was lying about knowing Holly and her.

Late in the afternoon the next day, Merry opened the gate for Jason and watched as he drove his black car to the front of her apartment. Wanting to avoid showing him the empty apartment, she stepped outside quickly. His gaze went over her in a swift assessment, and she saw a momentary relaxing of his somber expression. "You look great."

"Thank you."

He kissed her lightly on the mouth and looked down at her solemnly. "Sure you don't want to change your mind?"

"I'm dead certain. I want to talk to Dorian."

"Come on. Let's get this over with," he said, taking her arm. He opened the door of the car for her, closed it when she was seated and strode around the car to get behind the wheel. As they drove to Wescott Oil, she glanced at him. He was in a dark suit and crimson tie. She, too, had dressed for the occasion, wearing her navy suit and navy pumps. Her hair was twisted and pinned behind her head, and she hoped she had achieved a businesslike, no-nonsense appearance. All she could feel was anticipation; she would finally be able to confront Dorian. It was Jason who amazed her today. She was both surprised and amused by his concern for her safety.

"It's not too late to back out of this," Jason said.

"Will you stop worrying about me! You couldn't have been this edgy about yourself when you worked for the CIA."

"That was entirely different," he replied grimly. A muscle worked in his jaw, and she smiled, placing her hand on his thigh.

"I'll never be out of your sight. You're armed to the teeth. There's nothing he's going to do, and I'm looking forward to this because I want to tell him what I think of him. Now you stop worrying."

He glanced at her, swiftly returning his attention to his driving, but he put an arm around her shoulders and squeezed her. "All right, but if he tries anything, I'm moving in."

"Just don't do it if it isn't necessary."

"Don't get into a car with him."

"Jason—"

"All right. I'll stop, but I'm worried about you."

"I don't expect to talk to him very long."

"You better not."

She smiled and leaned over to kiss Jason's cheek. He shot another quick glance her way. "Come home with me after this. I deserve an evening with you after you've shredded my nerves."

"Your nerves are all right because you've been these kinds of situations before. You'll get through this."

Merry appreciated his concern and she wanted to go home with him, but she wasn't going to. Now every time she was with him, there was a tension between them that hadn't been there before. Nevertheless she stood fast in her determination to put some time and space between them to see if he really was in love. She settled back against the car seat and watched him drive.

He slowed to a stop in front of an office building across the street from Wescott Oil. "Wait in the lobby. Sebastian will call me when Dorian leaves his office. Then I'll call you. It'll give you time to go to the corner, cross the street and get to the front doors about the same time he does."

"Will do," she said cheerfully, but he gazed at her as solemnly as ever. She climbed out of the car and entered the building without looking back, knowing he would circle the block and park where he could watch the proceedings.

She stood waiting, glancing at her watch. It was thirty minutes after five, only five minutes since she'd last looked at the time. The sun was angled in the west and traffic had picked up on Main as people came out of offices to go home. The minute the high-pitched ring of her cellular phone came, she answered and heard Jason's voice.

"Sebastian said Dorian is leaving the building."

"I'm on my way."

"The recorder is on?"

"Yes," she replied, switching it on, still amused and touched by his concern. She was certain he had never been this way with any operatives he had worked with. "'Bye, Jason."

As she hurried out of the building and approached Wescott Oil, her pulse quickened. The glass doors reflected the sunlight, but most employees exited the back where the large employee parking lot was located. Only the executives could park near the front door. She kept walking toward the door, slowing because she would reach the front door before Dorian and she wanted it to look like a chance casual encounter out in front of the building.

And then Dorian strode through the door, sunlight catching glints in his brown hair. Dressed in a brown suit and tie, he was a handsome man who resembled his half brother, but there was something far kinder in Sebastian's usual expression than in Dorian's tight-lipped appearance.

She moved into Dorian's path, blocking the way, with the western sun behind her so he would be facing the sun. "Dorian," she said.

His gaze flew to hers and he stopped instantly.

Eleven

Briefly, she caught a flare of recognition in his eyes and then it was gone, but she knew she hadn't imagined it.

"I don't believe we know each other," he said curtly. "Should we?"

"Dorian, I'm Merry Silver, and we know each other very well."

"You must have mistaken me for someone else. Your reputation and actions precede you, Miss Silver, so of course, I do know you from your attacks on me. Am I safe or should I be screaming for help now?"

She moved a step closer, aware of a faint scent of his aftershave, remembering Jason's admonition to be careful. "You're safe enough from me. You know me and you know Holly. When you left, you broke her heart, and you were rotten to take her money."

"You do have the wrong person," he said with an in-furiating calm. "This is the first time we've met, albeit I doubt if it will be the last, since you persist in laboring under a delusion.''

"There's no delusion, Dorian, and you know it.''

"There are laws to protect people like me from people like you. You can't run around accosting me. I can go from here to the sheriff's office. The police are willing to protect people from stalkers.''

"I'm not stalking you, and we both know that, too, as well as we both knew each other in Dallas. I don't know why you're ignoring me or what purpose it serves you, Dorian, but the truth usually comes out.''

"I hope it does and you pack up and go home. Now, if you'll excuse me—'' he stated in an impassive voice. After that first flare of recognition, there had been nothing but coldness in his expression.

Frustration rocked Meredith. The man was blatantly lying, yet there was nothing she could do about it. Why would he continue to lie? Jilting Holly had nothing to do with what had happened in Royal.

"Dorian, tell the truth!'' she snapped.

"I'm going straight to the sheriff.''

"You can't do anything when all I've done is say hello.''

"I'm sorry for you and your poor deluded sister,'' he said. "Goodbye, miss.'' He started to walk away and all of Merry's frustration welled up. She shook with anger, clenching her fists more tightly.

"You're going to get caught,'' she said.

He looked over his shoulder at her and his eyes narrowed and for a few heart-stopping seconds, she felt a chill from the cold fury that glinted in his eyes. Then it was gone.

"I don't have any idea what you're babbling about, Miss Silver. I suggest you go home to Dallas before you end up in a psychiatric ward or in jail for stalking me.''

Turning, he strode past her to his car.

Merry watched helplessly, angry that she hadn't shaken him and he hadn't admitted one sentence of the truth.

She stood in the sunshine and watched Dorian climb into

his car in one of the Wescott executive parking slots. Through his car's tinted windows, he seemed to look into her eyes and it appeared that he smiled. She couldn't be certain.

Her fists were clenched and she was breathing hard. As they had agreed, she turned to walk to Claire's where she would meet Jason.

The moment she stepped into the restaurant's cool, quiet interior, she reached into the pocket of her suit to switch off the recorder. Claire's elegant interior and late-afternoon quiet was a relief to Merry. She realized that her nerves were stretched taut, and she took a deep breath, glancing beyond the entryway at the almost empty dining room with its linen-covered tables.

A minute later Jason came striding through the door. He was handsome, walking with an easy, self-assured stride, a faint smile on his face. At the sight of Jason, she forgot Dorian, her frustration and all the dashing of her hopes the past half hour had brought. She longed to walk into Jason's arms and hold him, to feel his strong arms around her.

"There you are," he said cheerfully, his easy-going, good nature having returned in full. "Have you been waiting long?"

"No, not at all," she answered, knowing that he knew exactly when she had walked into the restaurant, and she wondered why he was bothering to create a cover for what they had been doing. No one else except Dorian would know or care.

Jason brushed her cheek with a kiss, hugged her lightly. "Let me get us a table," he said quietly, and turned to talk to the maître d'.

In minutes they were seated in a corner, and Jason ordered chablis with appetizers of wild mushrooms with grated Asiago cheese. Looking at her over the plate of appetizers, he said, "I can tell—you struck out."

"Yes," she replied, scowling and not trying to hide what she felt. "I wanted to reach out and shake him."

"I'm glad you didn't. You know what I told you about goading him."

"I didn't touch him. He acted as if I was a total stranger to him. Not once did he say anything to indicate he had ever known me."

"The man's clever."

"But such a blatant liar!"

"If he's our man, he's done much worse than lie. When we leave here, I want to go to your apartment and hear the tape. Unless you'll come home with me and let me listen to it there?"

"You can come to my apartment," she said reluctantly, her thoughts still on Dorian. "I feel as though I've failed Holly again. And you."

"Don't be ridiculous. That was just one gambit and it didn't work." Tilting his head to one side, he studied her. "Do you know how long it's been since I kissed you?" he asked, and his voice lowered a notch.

She smiled. "About ten minutes ago when you came into the restaurant."

"I mean really kissed you, the way I want to," he replied in a husky voice that made her pulse beat faster.

"At my door after our date last night," she replied. "If that's the kind of kiss you're talking about."

"That's way too long," he said, taking her hand to brush warm kisses lightly over her knuckles. His kisses made her tingle as much as his words, and she forgot being with Dorian or the frustration she had been feeling. All her attention was on the breathtakingly handsome man gazing solemnly at her.

He raised his wineglass in a toast. "Here's to tonight."

She arched her brows and raised her glass to touch his. "Fine. What's tonight?"

"A special evening with you. Each one is a celebration of my love. I love you, Merry. Deeply, truly, always. Sooner or later you're going to realize that I'm telling the truth."

"Jason…" she said, turning to brush a kiss on the back of his hand.

Their roasted king salmon served with a lemon artichoke aioli arrived, and while they ate, Jason talked about his rodeo days when he was in college and immediately afterwards, keeping her laughing and her thoughts off Dorian and the afternoon.

"You and your brothers were a wild bunch!"

"I doubt if we were half as wild as your brother Hank."

"That's probably true. Hank has spent a few nights in jail for brawls. You probably charmed your way out of that."

"I don't recall charming too many cops, or having to charm them, either. And I seem to be striking out with you when it really counts."

She smiled at him. "You're not striking out at all. You're just not getting your way every single second."

"I'm not getting my way about anything where you're concerned."

"That's not true."

"I want you to marry me. I want you to come back home with me. I didn't want you to talk to Dorian today. Tell me when I get to something where I'm having my way."

She laughed. "Maybe you haven't been getting your way quite as much lately."

"I haven't gotten my way since I met you."

"I think you have, a few times. Like, what do you want to do right now?"

"Take you home and make love to you," he answered instantly.

"Then what are we waiting for?" she said, knowing she was breaking her own rule, but unable to resist him.

He was already on his feet and taking her arm. She smiled at him as she stood. He kissed her lightly and leaned close to whisper in her ear, "I could eat you up right here if you'd let me."

"Get going," she said, her heart racing in anticipation.

He slipped his arm around her waist as they left the restaurant.

At the door of her apartment, she put her hand against his chest. The May night was cool and beautiful with sparkling stars and a clear sky. Crickets chirped, but otherwise the apartment complex was quiet and far enough from Main that all sounds of traffic were muffled.

"We'll make love a little while, but I didn't mean you can stay the night."

"Merry, that's not—"

She placed her finger on his lips. "Take it or leave it."

"All right."

"And—" she added, and he groaned "—we'll listen to the recording first."

"How about last?"

"Nope. Cowboy, it's time you didn't get your way about a few things in life."

"Let's hear that damned tape, and then I want you in my arms."

"One more thing."

"Merry, stop it."

"You can't fuss about my apartment. I haven't decided whether I will take the job with Keith or not, so I don't want to furnish this until I make that decision. I'm quite comfortable living here, so don't tell me I should move back with you. Do you understand?"

"Lady, you've got more rules than the Texas Senate. But I know what I can do about yours. Come here." He hauled her into his arms and kissed her. The moment his tongue stroked hers, all of Merry's pent-up longing for him exploded. Her hands shook as she ran them over his shoulders and through his hair.

"Your key," he whispered, and kissed her before she could answer or think. When she held up her key, Jason took it from her without pausing in his kisses.

Merry didn't care, knowing only that he swung her into his arms, pushed open her door, and kicked the door shut behind him. He set her on her feet and began peeling away her clothing.

She removed his as swiftly, wanting him and knowing she was breaking all her promises to herself, yet how could she resist or stop him now?

"Where's your bed?"

"There isn't one. There's a mattress on my patio."

"The hell with that," he said between kisses and took her down on the bare floor with him to roll over and move her on top of him. Merry sat astride, letting him stroke and fondle and kiss her until he shifted her hips and eased her onto his hard shaft.

They rocked together, and she was in ecstasy, deeply in love with this wonderful man. They crashed over a brink. Release, rapture enveloped her and she sprawled over him, both of their bodies covered in a sheen of sweat.

Slowly, their breathing returned to normal. He stroked her back lightly, lifting her hair away from her face. She raised up slightly to look at him. "All right, you got your way again. What did I tell you?"

"Maybe I did this time, but it's only once out of a hundred times lately. He rolled her over beside him and looked beyond her. "Merry, this apartment doesn't have one—"

She put her fingers on his lips. "What did I tell you?"

"Okay. I'll try to keep quiet. I love you, lady. Really love you."

She hugged him, refusing to admit her feelings, knowing there hadn't been enough time to prove anything to her yet. She wriggled away and caught up her blouse. "I'm going to shower—alone. Then you shower, and then we'll listen to the recording. And no complaints from you, because for the last little while, you have certainly gotten your way."

He snagged her ankle. "Tell me you didn't like my way."

"I loved it," she admitted in a sultry voice. "Now let go."

"Merry, dammit, woman, I want you."

"I'll be back." She hurried to her small bathroom, shut and locked the door.

While Jason showered, Merry switched on kitchen lights, poured glasses of iced tea, took out the recorder and sat cross-legged on the floor. She had changed to cut-offs and a T-shirt, was barefoot and let her hair hang free.

Jason came into the kitchen. He wore only his jeans and her mouth went dry at the sight of him. She knew she was going to have to struggle to resist him during the next hour.

He crossed the room to her and the desire in his eyes made her hot and tingly and breathless. "Tape," she reminded him, yet her word came out as a breathless whisper.

"Yeah, sure," he answered in a husky voice and sat down facing her, sliding his hand behind her nape to pull her to him and kiss her. When she pushed lightly against his chest, he finally stopped.

She switched on the tape, and Jason listened without comment until the end, when she told Dorian he was going to get caught.

"Oh, hell, Merry," Jason said.

"What? I just told him he would get caught."

"Then he knows you think he's the murderer. There's nothing concerning Holly to get caught about."

"Of course there is—taking her money."

"That's old stuff now and it's her word against his unless you or Holly come up with some solid proof. Merry, don't goad him."

"I was so angry—"

"Just cool it. This man could be incredibly dangerous. He doesn't know what or how much you know. I'm staying here tonight."

"No, you're not."

"I swear, I'll sit in the living room. I'm worried about you."

She thought about the night the bomb exploded and nodded. "All right. Tonight you stay. Tomorrow night you go home. But you stay in the living room and I sleep on the patio.''

''Nope. Not tonight. You sleep in your bedroom where he can't scale a wall and get to you.''

She shivered and rubbed her arms. ''You're worrying me.''

''Good. I'm glad something is finally worrying you about Dorian.''

She leaned back against the wall and stretched her legs in front of her while they talked about the murder and their suspicions, and conversation gradually changed to other times and places. She glanced at her watch and then stared hard in amazement. ''Jason, it's after four in the morning! I'm going to bed.''

''I thought you'd never ask me.''

''I didn't ask you,'' she said pushing against his chest. ''I'll sleep in my bedroom, and I don't have a spare air mattress.''

''I'm not going to sleep anyway.''

She didn't think it was necessary because security was good at the apartment complex, but she didn't argue, going to the patio to retrieve her mattress and then carrying it to her tiny bedroom.

She fell asleep thinking about Jason making love to her, holding her, showering her with attention and kisses.

The next morning when she awakened, he was gone. He'd left a note, and she read his large scrawl.

I think you're safe now, so I'm heading home. See you tonight.

With a smile she held his note against her heart. In a few minutes she would get up, but right now, she just wanted to remember the night and Jason.

That morning, Merry called Keith Owens to accept his job offer, and then she began to make arrangements to have her things moved from her apartment in Dallas to her new apartment in Royal.

Merry was no closer to feeling certain about Jason's declarations of love, but she knew she was miserable seeing less of him. Even so, she kissed him good night at the door Friday after their date and went inside to spend another evening alone.

She closed shutters and switched on a small lamp she'd bought, moving through the empty apartment, her steps echoing faintly as her heels clicked on the bare hardwood floor. She changed to a frilly red teddy, switched off the lamp and lay down on the air mattress. She had washed the new sheets and had them draped on the mattress, but it wasn't the same as being in Jason's arms in his big bed, held close against him.

She woke to a terrible racket. Disoriented, she opened her eyes, trying to get her bearings, and remembering the empty apartment.

A band was playing, and someone was singing loudly and off-key. And she recognized the voice.

Twelve

Shocked, she jumped up. As she looked around for clothing, her phone rang. She yanked up the receiver while she grabbed her cutoffs.

"Miss Silver," came the distraught voice of Willard Smythe, her landlord. "Jason Windover is in front singing—I think to you. Get him to stop immediately."

"I'm going," she said, half hearing the landlord, half listening to Jason's raucous rendition of "I'll Always Love You."

"I will give you two minutes, Miss Silver, to put a stop to this infernal cacophony before I call the sheriff. Of course, your neighbors may already have called him."

"I'm going," she said, and hung up, yanking up a T-shirt to pull over her head and jamming her feet into sneakers. *How could he?* "Jason, stop!" she muttered, pushing buttons to open the gates.

Flinging open the door, she raced toward the front gate. Lights spilled over the grounds, banishing the night.

"Stop," she said under her breath. Jason was exciting, intelligent, capable, handsome, so many good things, but he was definitely not a singer.

"Shut up!" some deep male voice yelled loudly.

She groaned and ran faster, stunned to see a band outside. Jason, dressed in jeans and a plaid Western shirt, held a mike and flowers, and was on his knee while he sang to her.

"I love you," he called when he saw her. "Will you marry me?"

"Jason, stop!" Sirens screamed in the distance, and in spite of the hour of the morning, a crowd was beginning to appear. As a flashbulb popped, she heard the drone of a helicopter. She had lived all her life with a mother who had a nose for news, and in minutes, Merry knew, they would be on television. In minutes beyond that, Jason would probably be in a police car charged with disturbing the peace.

"Marry me," he called again.

"Yes!" she yelled. "Just stop singing! Come here."

The band cheered and gathering onlookers applauded as Jason tossed aside the mike, stood and sprinted through the gates. He wrapped his arm around her waist.

"Let's go before they haul you to jail, or my family sees me on the morning news."

They raced for her apartment, running inside and slamming the door. Laughing, he wrapped his arms around her and held her.

"Jason, you're crazy!"

"I heard you say yes."

She could tell him she did it to get him to stop singing, that it was the desperation of the moment. Or she could take a risk, let go of her fears and caution, believe this tall Texan who had stormed into her life, and love him in return.

While he waited, his blue-green eyes searched hers. Taking a deep breath, she stood on tiptoe to wrap her arms around his neck. "You get your way, cowboy, but you better mean what you say when you tell me you love me. When I marry, I want it to be forever."

"You'll marry me?"

"Yes, Jason, I'll marry you," she said firmly. "I love you."

"Ahh, Merry," he said, letting out his breath. "You've made me the happiest man on earth," he added before he leaned down to kiss her and end all conversation.

Midmorning he held her close against him, propping himself on his elbow to look down at her. "This is a hell of a thing to sleep on."

"I don't recall much sleeping since you arrived."

"Maybe not, but let's move back to my ranch."

"Not until we're married."

"Lordy, how long to I have to wait?" he asked, groaning.

"We both have families, and I'm the first child to marry in mine and my mother will want a big celebration."

"You'll set up vacation time?"

"I will, Keith said I can work at home, so my work hours will still be somewhat flexible. Of course, after last night, I may be evicted from this place."

"I'm sure you'll smooth it over and charm that stuffy landlord of yours. He pranced out and warned me he was calling the police."

"Which didn't scare you at all. Jason, that was really low."

"My singing is that bad? Don't answer. I know it is. I was desperate without you." He stretched out his arm and pulled his jeans close to search a pocket, withdrawing something. He took her hand and looked at her.

"Sure? It wasn't just to stop my singing?"

"I'm sure," she replied solemnly. He slid the dazzling ring on her finger while he kissed her, and in minutes she forgot her new ring as she wrapped her arms around Jason to love him in return.

Epilogue

The last weekend in May, Jason stood at the front of the church with Ethan, his oldest brother, beside him as best man. Luke, his other brother, Rob, Sebastian and another longtime friend, Matt Walker, were groomsmen. Jason had cajoled Merry into a hasty wedding, but both had the resources to hire enough people to help pull it together quickly. And, to his delight, Merry seemed as eager as he was.

Jason watched bridesmaids come down the aisle, friends and sisters of Merry's he had met at parties and seen again at the rehearsal last night. Holly was maid of honor. He had been surprised to find she was a beautiful young woman, several inches taller than Merry, with the same wide, smokey eyes and flawless skin. Several of the single guys from home had taken to her quickly, and Jason was glad to see that she had gone out with one of them the night before the rehearsal, then last night after the rehearsal she'd left with Porter Hammons, a cowboy from Royal who was one of the ushers for the wedding.

At the sound of a peal of music, Merry's mother stood and turned, and everyone else came to their feet, but from that moment on, Jason was aware only of Merry, who came down the aisle toward him on the arm of one of her uncles.

Her hair was piled on her head, hidden mostly by the gossamer white veil. She was radiant, glowing with love, taking his breath in her long, white dress, and then she was beside him, her hand in his as they repeated their vows.

As he promised to love, honor and cherish her the rest of his life, the vows seemed so right, something he had already promised her more than once in intimate moments. Now he felt as though he had waited all his life for her, the perfect woman for him.

"You may kiss your bride," the minister said, and Jason turned back her veil, looking into her eyes filled with warmth and love. He leaned down to brush her lips lightly, and then they walked back up the aisle together, Mr. and Mrs. Jason Windover, which sounded wonderful to him.

"I've got you, babe," he whispered in her ear as they entered the foyer.

"And I've got you, Jason. I love you."

"Let's cut this reception short."

"Be patient. This is a once-in-a-lifetime, and I want to enjoy dancing with you."

He grinned, wrapped his arm around her waist, and they went through a hallway to go back around to the front of the church to pose for pictures.

The reception was at a country club where Merry's mother was a member. To Merry's surprise, her brother, Hank, had come home for her wedding. She watched as he stood talking to Jason, suspecting Jason might be a good influence in Hank's life.

She studied her handsome husband, and her heart raced in anticipation of their honeymoon. In a black tux, Jason was incredibly handsome, and she had to struggle to pay attention to friends and relatives and mingle in the crowd.

She saw Holly surrounded by a cluster of guys from Royal. They had discovered her during parties there, and to Merry's enormous relief, Holly seemed to have forgotten Dorian.

"Your sister is having a good time."

Merry looked around to see Susan Wescott. "Yes, she is. It's funny how things turned out. She's getting over Dorian, I'm married to Jason now—"

"That day we met at the Cattleman's Club, I thought you were going to take the place by storm," Susan said, smiling, her silver-gray eyes holding a twinkle.

"I don't want to think about that," Merry said. "I was dreadful."

"They deserved to get their staid old club shaken up a little," Susan said. "I wish you and Jason the best. When you can, I want both of you to come visit."

"Thanks, Susan. I'd love that," Merry said, realizing she had a friend. Someone called to Susan, who moved away, sunlight catching red glints in her chestnut hair.

Merry thought about Dorian, who still raised so many unanswered questions. Her marriage to Jason had to have angered Dorian, particularly since she was determined to find out if he'd been involved in murdering Eric Chambers and trying to frame Sebastian.

Jason was talking to a circle of tall, handsome men, all members of the Texas Cattleman's Club. It was a diverse and close-knit group. Some of the men she had just met for the first time: ranchers Matt Walker and Forrest Cunningham; Blake Hunt; a doctor named Justin Webb; Sheikh Ben Rassad; Hank Langley; Dakota Lewis, a retired air force lieutenant; Greg Hunt, a lawyer; Sterling Churchill. Others she had met before: Aaron Black, Keith, Rob, Sebastian and Will Bradford.

While they talked, Jason looked around the circle of men,

well aware that Dorian had been excluded, yet feeling not one shred of remorse.

"Well, Keith, we ought to plan the ball and you better start thinking about the charity you want, because you are the last bachelor standing," Jason drawled with a smile.

"I can't believe I've won this. I never thought I'd see this happen," Keith grinned and replied to Jason, gesturing to include the reception festivities.

"Our playboy retires," Rob stated.

"It's about time," Aaron added. "Next thing you know, the playboy will be announcing a baby on the way."

Jason grinned, unable to stop smiling. "I leave the bachelor and playboy reputation to Keith, who outlasted all the rest of us."

All the men chimed in and Aaron raised his glass. "Here's a toast to the man who keeps bachelorhood alive in Royal—our own Keith Owens. Our confirmed old bachelor."

"All right, you guys. We'll see who has the most fun at that ball," Keith answered with a laugh.

"I know who will," Jason said, "all the married guys. Each of us will get to take home the woman he loves."

"To the women in our lives," Sebastian said, proposing another toast and immediately glasses were raised.

"What's your charity going to be?" Aaron asked Keith as they lowered their glasses.

"Y'all told me to think about it and I have," Keith said. "I've picked what I want."

"Tell us what it is," Jason said.

"The New Hope Charity for battered women," he said quietly.

And Jason nodded while Aaron said, "That's a good charity."

Others repeated Aaron's sentiments while Jason thought about Keith's old flame from college. If he remembered correctly, Andrea O'Rourke was a volunteer at New Hope.

"And how long is this honeymoon?" Rob asked, bringing Jason's thoughts back to the present. Jason realized there was a serious note in Rob's voice.

"Only a week and I will leave word with you—and only you—how you can get in touch with me if there is an emergency."

As all of them sobered, Jason suspected each one of them was thinking about Dorian.

"When you get back, we'll have another meeting and see where we go from here. There's still nothing that really pins anything on him," Rob stated.

"Even if it did, he has an alibi," Jason said, aware they didn't even have to say Dorian's name.

"If any of you need any kind of help from more of us," Aaron offered, "you know we'll be glad to do whatever we can."

"Thanks. Now, my friends, I think I'll go find my bride and I'll see y'all when we get back to Royal."

Jason and Merry left Royal, driving to Dallas to the bridal suite in an elegant hotel. Tomorrow they had a flight to Madrid, and then they were driving to a small town on the Mediterranean coast of Spain.

The moment the door closed behind the bellman, Jason reached for Merry to pull her into his arms. He still wore his tux, but she had changed to a simple navy dress and pumps. His arms tightened around her and he leaned down to kiss her.

"Mrs. Jason Windover. I've got you, love, and you'll see how much I mean it when I tell you I love you."

"Your playboy days are over, Jason."

"I was just waiting for you, darlin'. You're the one and only in my life forever."

He bent his head to kiss her and Merry stood on tiptoe, wrapping her arms around his neck as she clung to him and kissed him in return. Joy filled her, and she no longer had any doubts about the depth of Jason's love. And she didn't intend him to have any doubts about the depth of her love for him. She loved him with all her being, and she planned to spend a lifetime showing him so. She tightened her arms around his neck, whispering, ''I love you, my special cowboy.''

*   *   *   *   *

THE BACHELOR TAKES
A WIFE
by
Jackie Merritt

JACKIE MERRITT

is still writing, just not with the speed and constancy of years past. She and hubby are living in southern Nevada again, falling back on old habits of loving the long, warm or slightly cool winters and trying almost desperately to head north for the months of July and August, when the fiery sun bakes people and cacti alike.

Prologue

Keith Owens was well aware of Jason Windover's air of contentment as he and his friends prepared cups of coffee for themselves at a serving cart, then sat in comfortable chairs around a table in one of the Cattleman's Club's private meeting rooms. Jason good-naturedly laughed off the teasing remarks about his and Merry's honeymoon, from which they'd returned only the day before, because it was all in fun and he'd expected some tongue-in-cheek banter from his buddies. But he wasn't above giving back at least part of what he was getting, and Keith, being the only bachelor remaining in the group, just naturally seemed to be his best target.

"Just you wait, old pal," Jason drawled. "Some sweet-lookin' little gal is out there this very minute, just biding her time for the right moment to rope and hog-tie Royal's most elusive executive."

"Elusive executive?" Keith repeated with a laugh, and looked around the table for confirmation or denial from Sebastian Wescott, William Bradford, Robert Cole and, of course, Jason, all of whom wore big smiles. "Is that what I am?"

"Sounds like an apt description to me," Sebastian said. "Good work, Jason."

"Thanks," Jason said with a cocky grin at Keith.

"All right, I get it," Keith said. "I'm the last bachelor among you jokers, and you're not going to let me forget it. Well, put this in your pipes and smoke it, old friends. I happen to enjoy bachelorhood."

"So did we when we were young and foolish," Rob said with an overly dramatic sigh.

Everyone laughed, because they'd *all* been bachelors only five months ago and they'd been neither young nor foolish. Only one thing had happened to change their status from single to married—falling in love, which was a mighty powerful force, as they had discovered. And not a man around that table—other than Keith—believed that Royal's "elusive executive" would remain a bachelor for long. After all, hadn't he already tossed his hat in the ring by naming New Hope Charity for battered women as the beneficiary of the Cattleman's Club's annual charity benefit? That decision would bring Andrea O'Rourke, Keith's old college flame, back into his life, since she was the volunteer at New Hope who dealt firsthand with public donations. It seemed to the men around the table that if Keith hadn't wanted contact with Andrea, then he would have named an entirely different charity to receive this year's check.

No one said so, though, as some subjects weren't up for open and verbal conjecture. They could tease Jason, because he'd just come back from his honeymoon, but they couldn't make light of Keith's sudden interest in renewing ties with Andrea.

"Much as I'm enjoying this," Keith interjected, "I think it's time we got down to the reason we called this meeting. Dorian." The other four friends sobered at once. They all shared the strong suspicion that Dorian Brady had murdered

Eric Chambers, an accountant at Wescott Oil. But so far, they had no proof of his involvement.

Keith continued. "We've been doing our best to keep an eye on Dorian during your absence, Jason, and none of us have spotted anything suspicious. In fact, it appears that, if anything, Dorian has been deliberately maintaining a low profile."

"That's suspicious in itself," Jason said. "Don't you agree, Sebastian?"

"Dorian was never low-key before," Sebastian soberly agreed. He was understandably more deeply affected by recent events than the others, since Dorian was his half brother. "Except when it fitted his agenda. As you all know, his showing up out of the blue was one hell of a shock. We look so much alike, I never for a minute doubted his story about Dad being his father, and I still don't. Putting him to work at Wescott Oil was a bad error in judgment, however. My only excuse was that I really wanted to help him."

"None of what happened is your fault, Sebastian," Keith said quietly. "How do honest people deal with a snake like Dorian? He's deliberately gone out of his way to undermine your authority and good reputation with the company and the community in general. Don't blame yourself for anything Dorian's done."

"Considering his background with Merry's sister even before he came to Royal, he was a louse then and he's a louse now," Jason said stonily. No one could disagree with that summation, and the conversation changed directions.

"What we still can't figure out is his motive for murder. What was Eric Chambers to him, other than a co-worker? It simply doesn't add up."

"And let's not forget Dorian's alibi," Will said. "Maybe we should talk to Laura Edwards about that. Double-check her story about Dorian being at the diner at the time of Eric's murder."

"Why would she lie?" Sebastian asked and got up for a coffee refill. "I've wrestled with motive since the murder, and I have a hunch that it's somehow connected to me. Jason, I know you were uneasy about Dorian from the start.'' Sebastian resumed his seat. ''Why?''

''We've covered this ground before,'' Keith said.

''Yes, but obviously we're missing something,'' Sebastian said. He frowned slightly and added, ''What could it be?''

''His computer files imply that Dorian was blackmailing Eric,'' Jason reminded them all. ''Merry discovered that.''

''Yes, but those files do not explain the blackmail. What was Eric up to that Dorian was able to discover and use against him? Maybe if we knew more about Eric,'' he mused. ''What do we really know about him?''

''He worked for Wescott for quite a few years,'' Sebastian volunteered. ''He was a very private individual with a cat as his only companion. He was divorced long before coming to work for Wescott, so no one I know has ever met his ex. He lived alone—with his cat—in a small house. That struck me as odd, because he made a good annual salary.''

''Which he could have been paying to his ex-wife in alimony,'' Keith said.

''But he wasn't. His wife had remarried quite a while back, ending the alimony payments, and there were no children for Eric to support. He could've afforded a much better home, considering his earning power.''

''Follow the money,'' Jason said, half in jest.

But the simple concept simultaneously struck all five men as critically important. They looked at each other, and several of them nodded. Months ago, money had gone missing at Wescott Oil. Sebastian, accused of killing Eric and taking the money—a ridiculous charge when he owned the company and had more money than he could ever spend—had been completely exonerated and all charges against him had been dropped. Since then, everyone had been concentrating on Eric's murder. The missing money was still unexplained, a loose end left dangling.

It could be the clue they had been hoping to uncover and follow up on.

One

Andrea O'Rourke was given the good news on the first of June. "New Hope has been named by the Texas Cattleman's Club as the primary beneficiary of this year's charitable donation!" The other volunteers present at the time were overjoyed and began discussing what could be done with the money. New Hope's most crucial need was money for expansion, but how much would the donation be? Everyone knew the club's annual charity ball donations were legendary, but the sums distributed to needy causes were never publicized.

Andrea tried to appear as thankfully elated as the other volunteers in the meeting room of the big old house that served as a sanctuary for battered and abused women. The building was the heart and soul of New Hope Charity, and the meeting room was pleasant with comfortable mismatched chairs, several desks where paperwork was taken care of, and a table with the tools and supplies to brew coffee and tea.

While Andrea rejoiced at New Hope's good fortune in her

own quiet, subdued way, she also suffered an internal ache that she would never even attempt to explain to these good ladies. Residents of Royal, Texas, knew that she was the volunteer who acted as New Hope's representative for events that benefited the charity. The more Andrea thought about it, the more suspicious she became that Keith Owens, longtime member of the Cattleman's Club and the one citizen of Royal whom Andrea tried diligently to avoid, was behind the good deed that had the other ladies in the room giddy with delight.

I'll have to attend the club's annual charity ball! I'll have to accept the donation with thanks, probably even have to say a few words about New Hope. Well, I've done that before at other events, but not with Keith Owens looking on and undoubtedly smiling that overbearing, egotistical smile of his while I'm on stage!

Oh, my heavens! What if he's the member passing out the award?

No! I won't do it, I can't do it.

But of course she could do it, and she would, however painful to herself. Looking around at the generous women who gave time, energy, intelligence and individual talents to New Hope, Andrea was aware that none of them really knew her. They thought they did, and she encouraged that impression because her privacy was crucial to the quiet lifestyle she had fashioned for herself. She had lived alone since the death of her husband five years before, and her preference for dignity and serenity in everything from her home to her personal demeanor eliminated a good many people who had attempted a close friendship. Those friends who had made the cut were truly cherished by Andrea, and for the most part they enjoyed the same gentle entertainment that she did—primarily small dinner parties and elegant little luncheons at which intellectual discussions of literature, music, fashion and personal hobbies took place.

Keith Owens was not in that circle and never would be. Andrea had never stepped foot inside the Texas Cattleman's Club's sprawling two-and-a-half-story clubhouse—decorated, she'd heard, in dark paneling, heavy leather furniture and stuffed animal heads. Visualizing herself doing so the night of the charity ball actually made her shudder. She couldn't share that thought with the group, of course, and why would she? Were the intimate details of her life—past or present—anyone's business, but her own? Of course not.

Again scanning the women, Andrea uneasily wondered how many of them, if any, knew about her and Keith's commingled past. It seemed a silly concern when their history had ended almost twenty years ago—both she and Keith were thirty-eight years old now—but some people had such damnably long memories.

Andrea suddenly couldn't sit still a moment longer. Rising from her chair, she smiled at the group and said, "I'm terribly sorry, but I just remembered a very important appointment. I really must run."

The women accepted her story and bid her goodbye, and before Andrea had even gone through the door they were back to fantasizing about New Hope's windfall.

Andrea left with acidic resentment gnawing at her vitals. If it weren't for Keith Owens's participation in the club's gift to New Hope, she would have been as genuinely overjoyed as the other volunteers were.

Damn him! How dare he create disturbances on the smooth pathway of her daily existence after so many years?

Keith kept himself in good physical shape in his home gym. A personal trainer came to the house twice a week to put Keith through the paces, check his vitals and advise him on diet and general fitness. The rest of the week Keith worked out on his own. He liked exercising himself into a sweat, and his exertion, followed by a shower, always seemed to clear his head.

The morning after New Hope had been notified of the club's choice—most definitely an honor for any charity organization—Keith went to his gym with his usual good intentions. But he hadn't slept as well as he usually did, and instead of diving into his exercise program, he dawdled around for about ten minutes, then lost interest and went down to his kitchen for some coffee and the morning paper.

The coffee tasted good but he couldn't concentrate on the daily news. Frowning slightly he leaned back in his chair and stared off into space. He felt adrift, uncentered, and he didn't have to wonder why: It was all about anticipation and the knowledge that Andrea would be at the ball.

For years they had ignored each other, or *tried* to ignore each other. When something unforeseen and unpreventable brought them together—always briefly—they said hello, but Andrea's polite voice and unsmiling countenance emitted enough ice to chill to the bone anyone within hearing range. He had to ask himself why he was forcing them to meet again when Andrea had only tried to avoid him. He didn't doubt that she would be civil at the ball—he'd observed those cool, impeccable manners of hers more than once—but since when had an evening of distant, chilly civility from a woman held any appeal for him?

Deep down, Keith knew the answer to all of his questions about Andrea. He wanted things to be different between them. He wanted her to talk to him without that famous chill, to look at him and really see him, and to treat him as she once had. Would the ball change anything? Maybe not. *Probably* not, if he was completely honest about it. But it *was* an opportunity to spend some time with her.

Accepting that summation with a knot in his gut, Keith turned his thoughts to the problem of proving Dorian Brady's guilt. It was frustrating as hell to be certain of something and not be able to come up with enough evidence to take to the police. Mulling it over for at least the tenth time since his last meeting with Sebastian, Rob, Jason and Will, something that had been niggling at Keith abruptly rose to the surface. Getting up from the table, he went to the telephone, took it from its cradle and walked around the room while he dialed a number.

"Sebastian? I'm glad I caught you. Listen, I'd like to pick

up Eric's computer. I should've thought of it before. I know the police checked the computer and so did Rob. He found Eric's personal journal and that e-mail message and, believe me, I'm not minimizing Rob's...or the police expert's... computer abilities, but if there's one thing I know through and through, it's computers. There could be more information in disguised or hidden files that everyone thus far has missed. I think I should check it out.''

Keith's extremely successful career had been built around computer software, and no one got very far with software unless they understood computer *hard*ware—the nuts and bolts of the machine, so to speak. He could take a computer apart and put it back together in mere minutes. Hell, he could build one from scratch if he had the components on hand. In some cases he could actually *create* the components. Owens Techware was a well-known and highly respected contributor of technical software the world over.

''Yes, you're the logical person to do that,'' Sebastian agreed with a spark of excitement in his voice. ''You may be on to something, Keith. Pick it up anytime. I had it put in storage.''

''Great. I'll come by Wescott Oil sometime today.''

After hanging up the phone, Keith let Andrea enter his mind again, but only for a few moments. Heaving a sigh because he had never understood himself where Andrea was concerned, he went to take the shower he should have taken earlier.

The elegant old clubhouse and its immaculate grounds seemed magical on ball night. Hundreds of tiny white lights bedecked shrubbery and trees, and every window in the building glowed with warm, golden light.

The limousine in which Andrea was riding crept toward the club's entrance. It was following a long line of luxury cars and limousines that stopped only long enough to dispatch beautifully dressed guests, so it was stop and go, stop and go, for about ten minutes.

Seated in the limousine's back seat Andrea drew a long breath rife with disapproval and dissatisfaction. She had accepted being manipulated into attending this year's ball, but she was adamant about it not happening again under any circumstances. If club members chose to bestow some of their wealth on New Hope again, she was going to weasel out of this duty by hook or by crook. She absolutely hated the club's insistence on picking her up in a showy limousine. She was not a limousine person, and she felt completely out of place in it.

This, too, she blamed on Keith Owens. No one would ever convince her that he hadn't dreamed up this whole scenario just to embarrass her, and, however much she would like to cut him cold tonight, she was going to have to smile and chat and act as though she didn't resent the air he breathed.

She had not willingly given Keith the time of day since college, though they ran into each other every so often. Accidental meetings—inevitable in towns the size of Royal, Texas—never failed to unnerve her. Just the sight of Keith raised her blood pressure and made the fine hairs on the back of her neck stand up, a condition she attributed to a mix of extreme tension and dislike. He had, after all, nearly destroyed her that night so long ago. That night when she'd naively expected a marriage proposal, and instead Keith had proposed a business partnership. A business partnership! He'd been full of himself then, and from the little she'd seen of him over the years, he was *still* full of himself.

On that particular night she'd been totally crushed and had angrily let him have it, making it clear that she was going to major in education and wanted nothing to do with his business plans. To make matters worse, Keith had derided *her* choice of careers—teaching—and boasted about *his* ambitions. Although Keith had made a fortune in computer software, Andrea had felt in her heart that her career rewards as a teacher far exceeded Keith's. But he would never, ever understand putting joy in one's personal accomplishments ahead of an ever-increasing bank account.

Andrea shook her head just as the limousine braked precisely at the club's main entrance. She disliked these particular trips down memory lane. Usually she had no trouble avoiding these memories in favor of those that gave her pleasure instead of riling emotions that she would rather not poke and prod to life.

The limo door was opened by a uniformed greeter. Andrea took his outstretched hand and allowed him to assist her from the vehicle. People were everywhere, she saw—going into the club or standing outside to chat. Laughter and conversation mingled with the muted music inside the club and floated out on the evening air. The dress code for the ball was formal, which had once dictated that men wore black. Not these days. There were tuxedoes in many different colors, and the males in attendance were almost as flamboyantly clad as their female companions. The ladies, however, were also gleaming from the exquisite jewelry around their necks, in their hair, on their wrists and fingers, and anywhere else they could attach diamonds, emeralds, pearls and rubies to their person.

The limousine moved away and another vehicle immediately took its place. Andrea began walking toward the entrance and gasped in surprise when someone took her arm.

"Good evening," Keith said, his lips brazenly close to her ear. "I wasn't sure whether you would arrive alone or with an escort, so I've been out here watching for you. Since you're alone, I'm appointing myself your guide, counselor, escort and buddy for this evening's festivities."

Despite her annoyance, Andrea couldn't help but register his good looks, which shook her aplomb and irritated her no end. His tuxedo was a wonderful shade of tan that was almost exactly the color of his light-caramel-hued hair. The quirky smile that had captured her heart back in college was still his best feature, although his thickly lashed dark-brown eyes ran a very close second. Admiring and eventually drooling over Keith Owens's good looks had caused her pain and heartache in her college years. Maturity had provided her with some

advantages, thank goodness, one of which was an understanding of just how unimportant good looks really were.
She'd figured that out only a few years after college, because
the man she'd married had been wonderfully pleasant-
looking but not drop-dead handsome, as Keith was. Frankly,
everything about Keith galled her, especially his overbearing
assumption that he could appoint himself her escort for the
evening.

"I think not," she said coolly, trying to pull her arm out
of his.

"Think again. It's only good protocol for our guest of
honor to have an escort," Keith said smoothly while giving
her a head-to-foot inspection. She was utterly beautiful. In
college she'd been pretty, with long black hair and dark-blue
eyes. Hell, she'd been cute as a button when she'd been a
kid, a fact he remembered very well because they'd grown
up next door to each other. But *cute* and *pretty* simply
weren't the right words to describe how she looked now. Her
figure was incredible, especially provocative in that two-
piece ivory gown she was wearing. It fit like a dream, from
its high neckline all the way down its classic lines to a hem
incorporating one sexy slit that permitted brief glimpses of
the lower portion of her left leg. It was a marvelous dress,
Keith decided, its delightful color accenting Andrea's hair
and eyes. Her black hair was much shorter now, but its simple style was extremely becoming to her beautiful face.

"If I had wanted or believed I needed an escort, I would
have invited a friend to accompany me this evening. Your
protocol is about fifty years outdated. You may find this a
major shock to your good-old-country-boy beliefs, but now-
adays women actually walk and talk all on their own. Please
let go of my arm."

"I'll let go of yours if you'll take mine."

"How about if I kick you in the knee, put you out of
commission and get rid of you that way?"

"Resorting to violence already, are we?"

Andrea shook off his hand with one big jerk of her arm.

"That's enough childish horseplay!" She started walking toward the entrance, fully aware of Keith keeping up with her every step. He wasn't going away, however rude she might be. She heaved a sigh. The evening was going to be as unbearable as she'd anticipated.

Inside the club there was a receiving line, and while Keith bantered and laughed with his friends greeting the arriving guests, Andrea smiled congenially, and furtively checked out the décor. It was as dreadfully macho as she'd been told. Was that a boar's head over the mantel? She shook hands and made appropriate comments to people she recognized but just barely knew. *Her* friends were not members of this club, which admittedly did a lot of good for the community but was also known for some very rowdy escapades. Now that Andrea was inside she could tell that the band was playing some very lively songs, mostly with a country-and-western slant. *Well, what did you expect? Schubert? Beethoven? Chopin?*

"My dear, we're all so proud of this year's choice of charities," an older woman, Janice Morrison, wife to a lifetime member of the club, said while gripping Andrea's hand in a long handshake. Mrs. Morrison's diamond necklace alone would have financed the operation of New Hope for five years, Andrea thought, although she certainly did not begrudge the congenial woman her astounding necklace. Andrea was wearing very little jewelry herself—a pearl-and-diamond ring and matching earrings—but she had some very good pieces in her safe. They were gifts from Jerry, her deceased husband, which was the only reason she kept them, because she hadn't worn the items since his death.

"We at New Hope are both proud and delighted," Andrea murmured. "Be assured that all donations will be put to very good use."

"I'm sure they will. My, you two make a fine-looking couple," Mrs. Morrison gushed.

The woman was gazing from her to Keith, and Andrea's smile faded a little as she withdrew her hand. Keith saved the day by quipping, "We're just a couple of old friends, Janice."

Janice Morrison wasn't convinced. "Who do you think you're kidding, Keith Owens?"

Andrea wilted internally. Here was a lady with a long memory, and there were probably dozens of others attending the ball that also remembered when the Vances and the Owenses—her parents and Keith's—had lived next door to each other. This time, when Keith took Andrea's arm to steer her away from the receiving line, she felt too weak to protest. How in heaven's name was she going to make it through an entire evening of innuendo and reminders and still keep on smiling?

"Sorry about that," Keith said to her.

Andrea forgot about smiling and her eyes flashed angrily. "Why would you expect anything else when you're sticking to me like glue?"

"Would you really rather be left on your own in this crowd?"

"I'd *rather* not give anyone the wrong impression!" Andrea glanced around. "Do you have any idea of how many people are looking at us right now?"

Keith glanced around himself, then grinned wickedly. "Quite a few, by the looks of it. Wonder what they're whispering about. Maybe they're wondering if we're sleeping together."

Andrea gaped at him. "Are you mad? We didn't even sleep together when we dated!"

"That sure wasn't my fault."

"Of course it wasn't. Since you had—and probably still do have—the morals of an alley cat."

"Don't tell me the subject of sex still embarrasses you. Andrea, you're a big girl now. Actually, when I think about it, you were a big girl in college, but you had far too many hang-ups for a…" Keith wisely closed his mouth. He'd been about to say something about randy young college men, but decided to avoid that topic for the present. "How about a glass of champagne?" he asked instead.

"If I say no are you going to go off and find someone else to badger?"

"Nope."

"Then yes, I'd like a glass of champagne."

"Great." Placing his hand on the small of her back, and enjoying a delicious tingle in his lower regions from the physical contact, Keith steered her through the crowd to one of the bars and ordered two glasses of champagne. After handing one to Andrea he smiled and said, "Cheers, sweetheart, and let me add that you've got what it takes."

Andrea felt heat rising in her cheeks and knew that she'd turned pink. "What on earth are you talking about? Why didn't you stop at 'cheers' and make this a tolerable occasion?"

"You know, I should have. Sometimes I say things without thinking. I mean, that was obviously a compliment, but if I had thought about it before speaking, I would probably have postponed it until you'd had a couple of glasses of champagne."

Andrea glared at him. "Meaning I would appreciate crude remarks then? You didn't know me in college and you don't know me now. I *never* liked your crudity, which you would remember for yourself if your self-serving, smug, conceited head wasn't bigger than Rhode Island!"

Keith roared with laughter. "Andy, I absolutely adore you."

"Oh, give me a break," she drawled, although her heart was suddenly pounding unmercifully fast. He didn't mean what he'd said, for heaven's sake. He was just the kind of man who said outrageous things to women and then laughed at their reactions. He obviously believed he was God's gift to womankind, and maybe he was—for some women—but he was no gift in her estimation. He was a cad without a conscience, and he didn't even have the grace to pretend otherwise.

He peered, owl-like, at her over the rim of his glass as he took another swallow. "How about a game of tit for tat?"

"Which is?" she asked, frowning and suspicious.

"I'll give you a break if you get rid of that stick up your spine. You used to be a fun person to be with. You used to laugh a lot. You're arguably the most beautiful woman here and if people are staring and speculating, that's why. After all, I've been single and alone for four years. I'd have to be crazy to be talking with the loveliest lady here and not let you—and everyone else—know that I'm interested."

Andrea gasped. "Do you actually have the temerity to think I *care* if you're interested?" Fury set in then, and she felt herself start to tremble. She had to get away from him before she let the whole crowd know that she could happily murder Keith Owens where he stood. "Which way is the ladies' room?" she asked. It was at that moment that she realized she didn't have her handbag. "Oh, no, I left it in the limousine!"

"Left what in the limo?"

"My handbag." She glared into Keith's eyes. If she hadn't been so unnerved by the evening ahead at the time of arrival, she never would have left anything in that accursed limousine. This, too, was Keith's fault. "Where do they park the limousines? I need to get my bag."

"I'll show you."

Just then a man's voice intruded on them. "Well, this must be the guest of honor, Andrea O'Rourke."

Both Andrea and Keith turned a bit to see the man. Keith's expression was no longer flirtatious and friendly, Andrea saw with some surprise. In fact, he was actually glowering at a very attractive man in an elegantly tailored black tuxedo.

"Aren't you going to introduce me, Keith?" the man asked in a dangerously slick voice. Andrea could tell that Keith didn't want this stranger even saying hello to her.

The man gave a dry little laugh. "Apparently the cat has taken hold of Keith's tongue. Permit me to introduce myself, Andrea. I'm Dorian Brady." He reached out and took Andrea's hand. "This is an honor and a great pleasure," Dorian said.

Andrea was not pleased. Dorian might be physically attractive, but something about him made her uneasy. She pulled her hand from his and said, "Thank you." Keith was still scowling at Dorian, which was puzzling, since Keith seemed to be on friendly terms with all the other club members. "The directions to the parking lot, please?" Andrea asked him stiffly.

"Well, I can see that the two of you are quite involved. You will excuse me, won't you? Good evening, Andrea. Perhaps we will meet again." Dorian bowed slightly and departed.

"That creep," Keith mumbled. "Andrea, give that guy a very wide berth."

"I plan to, but not because of *your* orders," she replied sharply. "Now how do I find the limousine parking area?"

Keith pulled himself together. Dorian's unexpected intrusion had unnerved him. Actually, Keith had expected that Dorian would avoid the ball, especially since Merry and Jason were there. Maybe it was time the club members voted to revoke Dorian's membership. Keith couldn't remember a member ever being banned before, but there must be something in the bylaws about membership reversal.

Calmer again, he said to Andrea, "Why don't I go and get your handbag? I could do it in half the time it would take you."

"Just give me the directions," she repeated.

"Fine," Keith said with a disgusted shake of his head. He glanced around and was relieved to see nothing of Dorian. He didn't want Andrea wandering the grounds alone with Dorian hot on her trail. Maybe Dorian had shown his face just to prove he could and had already left. "Go through that far door, which leads to a patio restaurant, then leave the patio and follow the main path through the flower garden, go past the pool and you will reach the club's valet-parking area.

The limousines are usually parked on the right side of the lot.''

It sounded like a long walk to Andrea, and his offer to run and get her handbag made a lot more sense than her strolling that far on high heels. But she'd already refused his help, and pride wouldn't permit her to backtrack. Andrea handed him her glass. Then, with a stony expression and a clipped and unfriendly ''Thank you,'' she turned on her heel and headed for the far door.

Walking as fast as possible in her dressy high heels, Andrea easily followed Keith's directions. Her thoughts were still in a whirl from having to deal with Keith tonight. His mix of good looks, cocky personality and overwhelming self-confidence shouldn't be allowed. She'd fallen head over heels for him years before she should even have noticed that he was a boy and she a girl, and while it nearly killed her to admit such a thing tonight, he was still a dangerous distraction to her emotional well-being.

Did he affect every female that way, or was she particularly susceptible to him?

Impossible, she decided. He probably drew women the way honey drew bees. She was just feeling overheated because of a very old romance and she resented it so much that she had to blink back tears of frustration.

Keith had said she was fun in college, and that she had laughed a lot. Obviously he'd never seen beneath the laughter to the serious young woman underneath who had adored him since childhood. Much of it had been hero worship. He'd been her favorite playmate and the friend to whom she could tell anything. He'd been the first boy to kiss her. They'd been around eleven at the time and had decided that kissing wasn't nearly as much fun as swinging a bat in a softball game or doing cannonball leaps into a swimming pool.

High school had changed both of them. He'd become one of the swaggering superstar jocks, too cute to be believed and the target of every girl in school. Andrea had still adored him, but Keith's head had swelled intolerably from his sudden popularity and she hadn't been able to resist telling him to get real and to come back down to earth. He hadn't taken criticism well, and their friendship had cooled drastically so that they rarely had even said hello to one another. The summer after high-school graduation they'd gotten back together and were thrilled to learn they had both been accepted at the same college, their plan for many years before Keith had grown too big for his britches.

Oh, yes, she'd been fun and had laughed at everything. What girl wouldn't laugh a lot when she was in a wonderful college and had the best-looking, most popular boyfriend of any of her sorority sisters?

But then, of course, Keith began wanting more than kisses. And to be perfectly fair, she had wanted more than kisses, too. She'd explained her intention to wait for her wedding night to Keith, but he had never accepted her stand. Still, Andrea had been certain of their love, imagining Keith would get the message and propose to her.

The blinders had fallen from her eyes the fateful night she had eagerly anticipated a marriage proposal and had instead received a business proposition from the love of her life. That had been the end of everything. They had finished college without ever speaking another word to each other. She had married Jerrold O'Rourke—her sweet, sweet Jerry—six years later, and according to rumor, Keith had married about a year after that. His marriage had ended in divorce, hers by the terrible finality of death.

And now, after more years than she cared to add up, Keith was making overtures again? No, she would have no part of it. She didn't need or want his friendship, and she certainly could never want anything else from him. She would get through tonight and then retreat back into her own life. This foray into Keith's world would never be repeated. Never!

Andrea finally reached the parking area with its dozens upon dozens of cars. Veering right, she located the limousines and realized, to her dismay, they all looked alike. Her limo had been white, but most of them were white and she hadn't paid attention to exterior details.

Distraught and frowning, she stood there and wondered what to do next. Hearing footsteps behind her, she turned and saw Keith coming toward her. Instead of resenting his presence, she felt relief. Maybe *he* could identify the right limousine.

"Something wrong?" Keith called out before reaching her. He'd seen nothing at all of Dorian, thank goodness, and hoped again that the slime had left the ball and gone back under his rock.

"All of these limousines look alike," Andrea explained with a small frown.

Keith stopped next to her and studied the gleaming vehicles. "No, they don't. The one you arrived in is third from the left."

"It is?" Andrea peered at the one he'd named. To her it looked almost exactly like its neighbors, and she sighed. "I'll have to take your word for it." She started walking toward it. Keith kept stride—again—and she knew there was no shaking him tonight.

Keith opened the door of the limousine and peered inside. "I don't see a handbag," he said.

"Let me see." Andrea tried not to make contact as she moved around him, but felt the brush of their bodies as she peered inside. The distraction of the warmth he was emanating and her determination to ignore it made it difficult to focus on the task at hand. "I don't see it, either."

Turning a bit, she sat on the seat and began checking under it. Sliding along the soft leather seat she finally exclaimed, "Here it is! It must have fallen…" To her dismay, when she looked toward Keith, he wasn't patiently waiting at the door of the limousine, he was inside the car with her. "What on earth are you doing?" she demanded coldly.

"I *was* going to help you look for your bag."

"Well, I found it, so put your transmission in reverse!"

"I've got a better idea." He pulled the door shut and slid

her way in one fluid movement. "The formal segment of the ball is going to get started in about ten minutes, but that's long enough for former sweethearts to renew old acquaintances, don't you agree?"

Two

To Andrea's surprise, the closed door merely piqued her curiosity. Certainly there was no reason to fear Keith. Goodness knows, he'd never had a vicious or threatening bone in his body, and in spite of old resentments she couldn't imagine him changing in that regard.

"Whatever could you be thinking?" she murmured.

Keith wasn't a bit bashful. "There's a lot on my mind tonight. For quite some time now. For certain since our last meeting."

"Which was when?" There was false innocence in her voice because she recalled the last time they'd seen each other quite clearly. She had been dining with a very nice young woman, Rebecca Todman, who had come to her for advice over Rebecca's abusive past. Andrea's longtime, well-known connection with New Hope sometimes resulted in one-on-one discussions with distraught women seeking relief from emotional pain and scarring caused by abusive relationships.

At any rate, Andrea had listened to Rebecca's story throughout most of the meal and was in the process of assuring her that she seemed to be on the road to healing herself when Keith and Robert Cole, the detective hired by Wescott Oil to investigate the murder of Eric Chambers, came into the restaurant. Andrea had seen their entrance but could not have imagined them joining her and Rebecca. Robert's interest in Rebecca had been the big draw, not anything between her and Keith. She'd been only cool and distant with him, as usual, she recalled now, so whatever tidbit of association occurring that evening to cause "a lot on his mind" had completely escaped her notice.

"Surely you remember," Keith said. "You were with Rebecca and…"

"Yes," she said flatly, cutting him off.

In truth she had absolutely no desire to know what had happened that evening to reactivate his interest in her. The mere thought of Keith in her life again was stupefying. Why, they couldn't be more different! He was wealthy beyond belief and while she was far from poverty—she had inherited from both of her parents and then her husband—her style of living would bore Keith silly. *His* would destroy her. Loud and boisterous friends, too much money and living in an ostentatious mansion? Oh no, she couldn't even think of that sort of existence without shuddering.

The limousine's interior lights had gone out when Keith closed the door, but the parking lot lights illuminated his face. Andrea looked straight into his eyes and asked, "Isn't it time we returned to the clubhouse? If I remember correctly, dinner is to start promptly at eight. I don't have a watch. What time is it?"

Keith obligingly checked his watch. "Yes, we have to go back, but in a minute. Andy—do you remember when I called you Andy?—for some time now when I've seen you something inside of me does flip-flops. I've been trying to understand it, without a whole lot of success. But since I have that same sensation tonight, it has to mean something. Any ideas?''

''One springs to mind,'' she said dryly. ''Flopping organs could be serious. I would contact my cardiologist and request an EKG if I were you.''

Keith grinned. ''Ouch.''

''Then again, it could be gas. Come on, let's go.''

Keith stared at her, admiring her grit and knowing he couldn't let her get away with such brazen repartee at his expense. He moved quickly but smoothly, taking her by surprise, and ended up with his arms around her and his mouth on hers. He felt her shocked gasp on his lips but instantly forgot it within the hot whirlwind of emotions overwhelming him. Her mouth was incredible, soft and sensuous, and while she wasn't exactly kissing him back, she wasn't trying to scratch out his eyes, either.

He didn't overdo it and broke the kiss after only a few moments. ''Dear Andy,'' he murmured softly. ''Sweet as candy. We had the real thing once, or we almost did. Something tells me that *this* is our time.''

She was so outraged that she was trembling. ''This is *not* our time! I don't even know what you mean by that absurdity. Let go of me, Keith.''

''Let's go inside and have some fun,'' he said cheerfully, letting her go.

''I'm afraid your idea of fun and mine do not coincide.'' Instead of waiting for him to get out through the door they both had used to gain entrance to the limousine, she opened the one on her side of the vehicle and exited as gracefully as she could manage, considering the explosive nature of her mood.

Keith hastened to join her. ''When did you become a snob?'' he asked.

Andrea stiffened and almost gave him no answer at all. How dare he judge her? But after a few seconds she *had* to defend herself. ''I am not a snob,'' she said icily.

"Sure you are. You think you're superior to everyone here, especially me. You didn't feel that way in college."

"That was twenty years ago! I don't know who or what I was in college, other than stupid!" She was referring, of course, to her relationship with him and hoping he got the message.

He did, but not precisely as she'd meant it. "It wasn't twenty years ago, it was eighteen years ago, and we were both a little stupid in those days. But neither of us was a snob, Andy Pandy."

"Please stop calling me those ridiculous names!"

"I like those names. Be honest. Didn't you enjoy that kiss just a little?"

They had reached the patio, which was completely vacant. Everyone had gone into the ballroom for dinner. Andrea stopped at the door to send him a very poisonous look.

"You are my age, thirty-eight years old, and still you behave like an adolescent. No, Keith, I did not enjoy that kiss. Perhaps I liked being pawed in my youth, but *my* youth has long been spent. Apparently yours hasn't."

Swinging away, she opened the door for herself and went in. Shaking his head, Keith followed. "You act as though we're ready for the rocking chairs. You sure don't look like your nights should be spent a-rocking and a-reading. Hey, that's good. You used to rock and roll, and now you rock and read." He ducked his head to peer at her face. "Am I right or wrong?"

"What you are is incredibly vexing."

"Vexing? I'm vexing? You know, I've seen that word in novels but I've never heard anyone actually use it before. Vexing Keith." He chuckled. "Guess I'm a vexin' Texan."

"You're also not nearly as clever as you think you are."

"But I'm cute."

Andrea rolled her eyes. "Puppies, kittens and small children are cute. You're a middle-aged man, for pity's sake. Get over yourself."

"Middle-aged! Boy, you go right for the jugular, don't you? Now, that hurt, Dandy Andy."

"I hope so," she said sweetly and then said no more; they had reached the entrance to the ballroom. She could see that it had been festively decorated and set up for dinner with numerous tables, which were filled with chatting, excited, laughing people. Later, after dinner and the ceremony of presenting her with the club's donation, most of the tables would be removed to make room for dancing. Andrea planned to leave shortly thereafter, as soon as she could do so without appearing rude or ungrateful. She was, after all, representing New Hope, and she couldn't act solely on her own behalf. Of course, if she had only herself to consider, she wouldn't be here in the first place.

Keith offered his arm and said quietly, "Our table is across the room."

Gritting her teeth, Andrea forced herself to take his arm and to smile. Crossing that large room on Keith Owens's arm, with nearly every eye in the place on the two of them, was pure torture. She knew she shouldn't let it bother her. After all, she was there for the charity presentation, but how people did love to talk! To whisper and speculate and imagine. Andrea could see them doing it as she and her self-appointed escort moved among the tables. Escort indeed. What nerve!

"Here we are," Keith announced, stopping at a circular table with four couples and two vacant places. "I think you already know some of these people, but let's make this easy. Starting on the left we have Will and Diana Bradford, then Rob and Rebecca Cole, Sebastian and Susan Wescott and finally Jason and Merry Windover. Everyone, this lovely lady is Andrea O'Rourke."

Hellos were said, Andrea's chair was pulled out and then she and Keith sat down. Conversations began, and Andrea participated graciously. In mere minutes the first course of the meal was served, and Andrea found herself relaxing with these friendly people. From bits and pieces of the table talk she overheard while eating, she gathered that all of the men were members of the Cattleman's Club, which forced her to alter the hard-drinking, crude-talking, cigar-puffing image of the typical member of this club with which she'd arrived. These were intelligent, attractive people, every one of them, ranging in age from mid-twenties to early forties, and it occurred to Andrea that she could like them—some more than others, of course—if they weren't such bosom buddies with Keith.

She fell silent, while enjoying a delicious salad made with tender greens, warm mushrooms and crunchy pecans, and thought about the kiss he'd ambushed her with in the limousine. She was glad, of course, that she hadn't embarrassed herself by kissing him back. With his massive ego Keith would have taken even the slightest response from her as a green light and no telling what would have happened next.

Andrea suffered a sinking sensation over the scenario that idea conjured up. She knew *exactly* what would have happened if she had given Keith the encouragement he'd obviously hoped for. The problem with that relatively certain theory was the sensual ache it created in the pit of her stomach.

No! She would not ache for Keith Owens! For heaven's sake, had she lost her mind tonight? She *never* thought about sex. She wasn't looking for a man now, nor had she even considered another man since Jerry's death! *Lord love a duck, if you have to suddenly rediscover your libido, why pick Keith?*

Right in the middle of that horrifying question she felt Keith's leg press hers under the table. She moved her leg away from his and furtively reached under the tablecloth and pinched him on his nervy thigh, at the same time giving him a phony smile and saying in a low, for-his-ears-only voice, "Try that again and I'll sue you for sexual harassment. There are eight witnesses around this table, and friends of yours or not, if I suddenly stood up and told you to keep your hands to yourself, they would testify on my behalf in court."

"All I did was accidentally touch your leg with mine.

You're the one with the wandering hands. Who pinched whose thigh, you sneaky Pete?''

''Who kissed whom in the limousine, you Don Juan degenerate?''

''Oh, oh, the club photographer just snapped your picture. Could be one for the books, what with that accusing, vengeful expression on your pretty face.''

''You're lying through your teeth. I know how to maintain a normal expression however furious my thoughts.''

''Learn that trick during your marriage?''

Andrea gasped. ''How dare you? My marriage was...was wonderful!''

''Yeah,'' Keith drawled. ''So was mine. That's why I'm divorced.''

''You know perfectly well my husband passed away. We *never* would have gotten divorced!''

Keith regretted his comment at once. He never should have wisecracked about Andrea's marriage, not when he really knew nothing about it except that her husband had died. He just seemed to be more nervous around Andrea than he'd anticipated.

''I'm sorry,'' he said quietly. ''I shouldn't have implied anything.''

''No, you should not have!'' Andrea turned away. In a second she sent him another resentful look. ''And I am not a snob. You're incredibly rude, which, when I recall the past, you always were.''

''Rude, vexing Keith,'' he whispered with a dramatic sigh. He had to get over it, he knew, and forced himself to lighten up and ask, ''How did you ever put up with me for so many years?''

Andrea decided they were both going too far. If it hadn't been for the din of so many conversations plus background music, their dinner companions would already easily have overheard them. She didn't want to cause more gossip, since she was positive it was already occurring all around their table. It was better just to ignore Keith as much as she could.

Dishes were cleared away for the next course and Andrea looked up to see Laura Edwards, a waitress from the Royal Diner, working at another table. Laura wasn't a friend, but Andrea knew her from stopping into the diner occasionally to indulge in one of Manny, the cook's, fabulous hamburgers. The diner itself was an assault on one's senses with its red vinyl décor and smoke-stained walls and ceiling, but there was no question about Manny's burgers being the best in town.

Something about Laura tonight gave Andrea pause. The woman looked pale, pinched and—was *haunted* the right word for that wary, frightened expression on Laura's face? Or perhaps *hunted* was more appropriate. After a few moments of watching the waitress at work, and pondering her unusual demeanor, it occurred to Andrea that Laura looked exactly like the terrified women who came to New Hope's shelter to escape abuse!

Andrea pushed back her chair. "Please excuse me," she murmured to the table in general. Keith leaped up and the other men started to rise, also. Andrea smiled her thanks at them and walked toward the Ladies' Lounge sign. As planned, she intercepted Laura on her way to the kitchen with a tray of dirty dishes.

"Laura, hello," she said. "I'd like to speak to you. Can you take a minute?"

"Oh, Mrs. O'Rourke," Laura said in recognition. "It would have to be only a minute…we're all real busy…but let me get rid of this tray first."

"Of course. Can you meet me in the ladies' lounge?"

"Employees aren't supposed to use that facility, but I'll tell the boss that you asked to see me about something. That should clear it."

"Good. See you shortly." Andrea continued on to the lounge and Laura disappeared into the kitchen. Andrea was touching up her lipstick in front of a long beveled mirror over a pink marble counter—pink marble was the last thing she might have expected to see anywhere within the confines of this otherwise blatantly male retreat—when the door opened and Laura slipped silently into the room.

Andrea turned from the mirror. "Thanks. Laura, I can see from the look in your eyes and on your face that something is seriously wrong. I'm sure you're aware of my connection to New Hope and of the good the organization does for battered and abused women. You can talk to me, Laura. Nothing you say would ever be repeated, except perhaps to a counselor at the center, and only with your permission."

Laura was visibly squirming, obviously taken by surprise. "It…it's not that, Mrs. O'Rourke."

"Call me Andrea. I know how hard it is to talk about certain troubles, Laura, but if you're in an abusive relationship you really must get out of it. I can help. New Hope can help."

Laura wouldn't quite meet her eyes and something sighed within Andrea. It happened so often. Too many abused women simply couldn't speak of their torment and suffering until it got too horrible to bear. Andrea couldn't spot any bruises on Laura, but some men beat their women in places that were ordinarily covered by clothing. And then, too, emotional bruising wasn't visible.

Andrea reached into her small handbag for a business card, which she put in Laura's hand. "Please call me if you ever need to talk, Laura," she said gently. "Along with New Hope's number, my home number is on this card. Call anytime, day or night."

"Thank you," Laura said hoarsely, slipping the card into a pocket of her uniform. "I…I really have to get back to work."

"I understand." Andrea smiled. "I wish I knew what to say to put a smile on your face."

"You're a kind person." Laura smiled a little before hurrying out.

Andrea sighed again. That wan, mirthless smile that Laura had attempted spoke volumes, but the subject matter could only be guessed at. Obviously the woman was miserably unhappy over something, but was that something a man? An *abusive* man?

Leaving the ladies' lounge, Andrea returned to her table.

Three hours later Keith walked her to the waiting limousine. The check made out to New Hope Charity in Andrea's purse was such a generous sum that she had let its many zeroes influence her normal good judgment and had stayed at the ball much longer than she'd intended. Yes, she had even danced, with Keith and with several other men, and she regretted playing the social butterfly now because Keith was insistent about seeing her home.

"I'll just ride along, walk you to your door to make sure you get home safe and sound, and then leave."

Keith had been honestly concerned about Dorian forcing that introduction to Andrea, although Dorian must have left immediately after. Keith had watched all evening for him and had also alerted his friends to Dorian's presence and intrusion, so they'd been watching, as well. But just because he'd vanished from the ball didn't lessen Keith's concern about Andrea going home alone.

She, of course, only saw Keith's insistence as more attention than she wanted from him. "Please," she said. "I'm exhausted and I don't need anyone walking me to my door. I've lived alone for five years. I go home by myself after dark all the time."

"Well, maybe you shouldn't."

"Nonsense." Andrea extended her hand for a handshake. "Let's say good-night here, and thank you again for a most generous donation."

His dark eyes bored into her. "I'd rather kiss you than shake your hand."

She sucked in a sudden sharp breath. "Don't, Keith! You and I are *not* going to take up where we left off twenty years ago."

"Eighteen years, and why aren't we? Give me ten good reasons."

"I'll give you *one.* I don't want to. Good night." Andrea got into the limousine, the chauffeur closed the door and hurried around to the driver's door, and they drove off. Andrea looked out the back window and saw Keith standing there, watching, just watching. He looked disappointed and…worried? Why on earth would he be worrying about her?

Turning around to face front, she put her head back and told herself that she didn't care what was going on with him. They weren't friends or lovers, merely very old acquaintances, and she had absolutely no desire to change the status quo. He had his world, she had hers, and it was best that they each stay within the boundaries they had been living within for many years. Why he would suddenly want to cross over into her world, or coax her into his after so long was beyond her.

She only knew she couldn't let it happen.

Keith stood there until the limousine's taillights were out of sight, then avoided the clubhouse and the valet, and walked to the parking lot to get his car for himself. It was much cooler at midnight than it had been earlier and the fresh night air felt good to him. Even so, he walked with his head down.

The night had not gone as well as he'd hoped. Dorian's appearance had put everyone that knew the score on edge, of course, but even without that, Keith wasn't satisfied with the evening—all due to Andrea's adamant refusal to let down her guard with him. There was a wall around her that he hadn't been able to breach with teasing good humor, open and admitted admiration or a pass he probably shouldn't have made. It was odd how differently each of them saw the past. Possibly they'd been in love in college, but he couldn't be sure. His head had been so full of ambitious dreams and he'd honestly believed Andrea had felt the same way. Even now Keith was positive they hadn't been ready for the responsibilities of marriage back then; there were too many things to be done before taking that particular step.

Still, there had always been a serious connection between them, from their toddler sandbox days to that first experimental kiss and on through the rigors of high school. It was during the summer following high-school graduation, Keith recalled, that they had begun seeing each other as adults. And then in college they had gotten closer still. If it had been up to him they would have spent most of their free time in bed. Damn, he'd wanted her! Andrea was the one who'd kept things cool between them, but hadn't her attitude been rather childish? After all, they had ended up in a horrific fight that had completely destroyed what they'd had, and, thinking about it now, Keith couldn't help blaming Andrea's stubborn insistence on chastity as the cause of their breakup.

Oh, well, he thought with a heavy sigh as he reached his car and got into it. Tearing apart the past was useless. He needed to concentrate on the present, on his campaign to prove Dorian's guilt and on what he was going to do about Andrea now. They were completely separate issues, but each was seriously crucial to Keith's peace of mind.

He simply was not going to accept Andrea's avoidance any longer, that was all there was to it. Andy Vance O'Rourke was going to learn that he could be every bit as stubborn as she was, and what's more, he was going to have fun in the process.

And so was she. Seeing her tonight, watching her so closely, sensing her withdrawal from anything that didn't measure up to whatever high-handed rules she lived by had told him that she needed some fun in her life. Some *real* fun.

He was the guy to provide it, the guy to make her laugh and love and enjoy herself.

He knew it in his soul.

Andrea had an awful time sleeping that night, or what was left of it. She came wide awake at six the next morning, lay in her bed tired and resentful for an hour, then got up and stood under the shower until her head felt clearer.

Usually she ran in the morning. Rarely did a morning pass,

in fact, that she didn't run at least three miles. Her route took her from Pine Valley, Royal's upscale community in which she and nearly everyone who could afford it had their home, to Royal Park, which had a well-used hiking trail completely surrounding it. A couple of turns around that trail and then the return trip to Pine Valley added up to three miles, a good workout.

It bothered Andrea that Keith lived in Pine Valley, too, although his mansion was on Millionaire's Row, as that one particular area of Pine Valley was called by those in the know, and her house was quite some distance away. But she'd always known where he lived, even when she'd purchased her home, so she had eventually taken his presence—albeit mostly invisible—in stride.

Her house was lovely, small by Pine Valley standards, but very cozy and homey. It was a typical rancher but with lots of bells and whistles. After Jerry's death she had sold the house they'd lived in during their marriage and bought this one. It would never do for a family, but it was perfect for one or two people. She had decorated it exactly to her liking, the very first time she'd been able to do that, and the interior colors were soft and conducive to peaceful relaxation.

This Sunday morning Andrea felt neither peaceful nor relaxed. She didn't want to run, either. She was restless, barely able to sit still for more than a minute, but running held no appeal today, and these were very uncommon feelings for her to have. She knew who to blame for her unusual edginess.

How dared Keith kiss her last night? Memories of the entire evening seemed to bombard her from every direction.

It was noon before she felt halfway normal again, before she was calm enough to phone the officers of New Hope and relate the amount of the Texas Cattleman's Club's donation. They were, of course, overjoyed.

After that Andrea went back to bed, ignored several telephone calls that she let her voice mail pick up and spent a perfectly miserable afternoon switching channels on the large-screen television set in her bedroom.

It appeared that Keith Owens was succeeding in ruining her life, just as she'd feared would be the case if she were ever nice to him even one time.

Keith's Sunday was almost as unproductive as Andrea's, the main difference being the time he spent in searching the files in Eric Chambers's computer. Keith had brought the computer home rather than to his company office, as he wanted the club members' interest in this whole sad affair to remain as low-key as possible. That was the way the men of the club that were involved in saving lives and/or bringing criminals to justice worked—discreetly, strategically, invisibly.

The computer's hard disk was laden with accounting files, understandable since Eric had been vice president of accounting at Wescott Oil. But there were numerous sub-files with far more information about clients of Wescott Oil than Keith thought necessary, indicating to him that Eric had been obsessive about detail. Nowhere, however, were there any notations or entries regarding the missing money. Considering Eric's penchant for detail, Keith thought that strange.

After hours of searching, he opened Eric's personal journal file and looked for hidden attachments. He could find nothing more than Rob had, but that didn't satisfy Keith. He was positive that he had to be missing something, and he wasn't giving up on finding it after only one session. Still, he turned off the computer, got to his feet and stretched his back.

For the rest of the evening he thought about the ball and Andrea. Just as he couldn't give up on cracking Eric's computer secrets, neither could he give up on Andrea just because she hadn't encouraged his interest last night.

And he had an idea of what to do next to get her attention, too. He only hoped it would work.

Three

The following morning, a Monday, Andrea was back to normal except for one thing. She was thoroughly disgusted with herself for having wasted a beautiful day in June in maudlin self-denouncement and angry resentment of Keith. Ignoring church services and friends' telephone calls were things she just didn't do, and there were messages on her voice mail to remind her of yesterday's outlandishly childish behavior.

She did her running with a determined, almost grim expression on that sunny Monday morning, even while enjoying the diamond-like sparkle of dew on grass and flowers, and the fresh air. Running was one of her greatest pleasures and she was not going to allow Keith Owens to destroy the contentment of her daily routines. There was no reason ever to see him again, except by the whims of chance. Should another occasion such as the charity ball arise she would simply refuse to participate.

Andrea loved Royal Park with its little lake, botanical garden and striking gazebo that had been the center of many

Fourth of July celebrations. This was a park that was actually used, and even at this early hour she could see people walking, jogging or sitting on benches near the lake, some of them feeding the resident ducks.

After several turns around the park, Andrea headed for home. Sweaty, but feeling more at peace with herself, she entered her house and went straight to her shower. Twenty minutes later, she scanned the morning paper while eating fresh fruit and cold cereal for her breakfast. She tidied the kitchen, her bedroom and bathroom, then got dressed, choosing a simply styled blue-and-white cotton dress and flat shoes. Her hair was almost dry and she fluffed it slightly, applied makeup very sparingly, ignored perfume and cologne and decided she would do.

Taking up her workday purse, she located her car keys and used the connecting door between laundry and garage. Because she drove slowly with the windows down—very soon it would be much too hot to drive anywhere without the vehicle's air conditioner going full blast—and enjoyed the activity of the town, it took her a good fifteen minutes to reach Kiddie Kingdom, the nursery school at which she taught. Like New Hope Charity, the nursery school was situated in a very old house that had once been quite charming. Now its high-ceilinged rooms were used as classrooms for preschool children, and its once elegant backyard was a playground with swing sets, a sturdy slide and a merry-go-round. Huge ancient oaks shaded the play area, so even on the hottest days youngsters could spend some time outdoors.

Andrea's charges were three- and four-year-olds, wee boys and girls that she absolutely adored. Following college Andrea had taught fifth- and sixth-graders, and after her marriage she'd taken on some high-school classes, which had been quite an experience. Most teenage students, she had discovered, were bright, intelligent, witty and sweet, but some were so difficult and rude that Andrea had been forced to change her idealistic belief that no child was unteachable. She'd changed her tune after that and gone back to teaching youngsters. Now she couldn't be happier with her position. She wasn't working for the modest paycheck but because she loved children, and there was nothing more satisfying for her than watching them learn and knowing she was part of their expanding knowledge.

She and Jerry had both wanted children of their own, but none came along and they went in for testing. The tests revealed Jerry's sterility, along with a list of other medical conditions, including a weakened heart. Jerry had always avoided doctors so diligently that he honestly hadn't known that his aches and pains—everyone had 'em, so why stress over it? he'd always said with an infectious laugh—were signs of severe physical breakdown. But Jerry hadn't changed his stubborn ways just because of a serious diagnosis. He had worked as hard as ever, played tennis like a wild man and done anything else he'd pleased regardless of doctors' recommendations that he slow down and conduct both work and play at a less hectic pace.

Andrea had been more furious than grief-stricken when he had simply keeled over one day. He could have lived a much longer life—possibly into old age—had he listened to his doctors. But Jerry had been Jerry, and she'd loved him for his Irish wit, strength and temperament. No one had ever gotten away with telling him what to do, not his family, not the medical community, not her, even though Andrea knew he'd loved her with all his heart.

Finally she had tucked away her grief and built a life without him. She'd done a pretty good job of it, too, she felt. Until last Saturday night, that is.

No, she was not going to think of that again, she decided vehemently while entering her classroom and putting away her purse. The children were arriving, delivered to Kiddie Kingdom by parents or nannies.

"Good morning, Natalie," she said to a tiny blond girl, who responded with a shy little smile.

And so it went, as did every weekday morning. Andrea greeted each child by name as he or she came in, and when everyone had arrived she began the day's lessons. Teaching such young children was best accomplished in short segments, with songs and games interspersed among the lessons. Remarkably, some of these tots could already read. Others were just beginning to learn the alphabet. Andrea gave as much one-on-one attention to the children as she could squeeze into their three-hour school day, which to her seemed to fly by.

It was around ten-thirty when the door to her classroom opened and in walked Keith Owens, dressed in tan chinos and a casual, white, open-at-the-neck shirt. Andrea was so startled that she gaped at him with her mouth open. He smiled broadly, as though she shouldn't be at all surprised to see him, walked to the back of the room and sat on one of the tiny chairs provided for the pupils. He looked ridiculous to Andrea, but worse than that in her eyes, every one of the children had turned around to stare at him. He looked back at them unabashedly, with a friendly sort of half grin, and Andrea soon began seeing smiles on their little faces.

Clearing her throat, clinging to composure through sheer will power, she walked to where he was sitting, bent forward and whispered, "What's going on? What are you doing here?"

"I'm just visiting, so don't enroll me," he said with a devilish twinkle in his eyes.

"How cute," she said coldly. "You're a distraction. Please leave," she added, refusing to laugh at his feeble excuse for a joke.

"A distraction? For whom?"

"For the *children!* Get off that chair before you break it...and leave!"

"Nope."

It occurred to her that he might have a child. She didn't know *everything* about him, after all, and since she had never encouraged anyone to talk about him, it was possible that he and his ex-wife had children that she hadn't heard about.

"Do you have a child to enroll?" she asked bluntly.

"No, do you?"

Her heart seemed to flip in her chest. She'd wanted kids so much, and teaching these adorable tots satisfied some of her need to nurture, but not all of it. At that moment she hated Keith more than she had when they'd fought and broken up in college.

"You *know* I don't," she whispered harshly.

Keith could tell he'd struck a nerve, which wasn't his intention. He'd been hoping that she would laugh over his coming to Kiddie Kingdom and perching on a child-size chair. Didn't Andrea laugh at anything anymore? "Sorry," he murmured. "I'd like to watch the class for a while."

"Even if your presence is a distraction for the children?"

"It's bothering you a lot more than it is them, Teach," he said softly. If he let her chase him off every time he appeared, he'd *never* get anywhere with her. And he wanted to, very much, even if he really didn't comprehend why.

Andrea realized he wasn't going to budge. In no position to show her anger, she pivoted on her heel and returned to the front of the classroom. She did her best to ignore Keith while reciting the alphabet with the class, reading a story out loud and passing out cartons of juice, but she was almost lethally aware of him every second.

At recess time she led the children out to the playground, and when she brought them inside again about twenty minutes later, Keith was gone.

It didn't seem to matter. He had succeeded in turning her inside out once again, and when it was time to go home for the day, she felt totally drained. Andrea drove home with a very suspicious mist in her eyes, and she hated the possibility that she was crying over Keith Owens again. Hadn't she cried enough tears because of him eighteen years ago?

Pulling herself together, she stopped at the bank and deposited the check in New Hope's account, the usual routine with donations that she or other volunteers personally received. Tucking the receipt in her purse so she could later pass it to the charity's accountant, she returned to her car.

Underway again, her thoughts immediately returned to Keith's unmitigated gall that morning.

That *had* been a one-time intrusion, hadn't it?

Andrea's breath nearly stopped. Surely he wouldn't be back!

But what if he did come back? Maybe she should talk to the principal, but what on earth would she say? *Keith Owens is visiting my classroom and driving me up the wall. Would you please do something about it?*

Visitors were not unwelcome at Kiddie Kingdom. Besides, should principal Nancy Pringle take Andrea's complaint seriously and talk to Keith the next time he showed up—*if* he came by again—he would have Nancy tittering and tee-heeing all over the place with his good looks and glib way of conversing with women. Andrea saw through him, but would Nancy? Oh, he would undoubtedly charm his way out of any accusation Andrea made against him, make no mistake.

So if he *did* show up again, she was going to have to grin and bear it, Andrea thought with a groan of frustration. In the next instant, however, she switched from frustrated to furious. She might have to bear Keith's presence until he grew bored with the little game he was playing, but she didn't have to be nice to him and she was not going to be! He'd catch on. He might be a pain in the neck but he wasn't stupid. He'd get tired of being ignored very quickly.

Feeling much better, Andrea pulled into her garage, got out of the car and went into the house. Deciding that she needed something to take her mind off of Keith, she prepared some lunch then sat at the glass-topped kitchen table with a pad and pen. She had always enjoyed planning a dinner party, and by the time she finished eating she had five names on her pad, along with the start of a wonderful menu.

Since this was an impromptu affair for the coming Friday evening, she phoned her friends rather than send written invitations, which was a nicety to which she normally adhered. Delighted that everyone accepted on such short notice, An-

drea fluffed out the skeleton menu with some especially delicious side dishes, added two desserts, one made completely
of fresh fruit and the other a decadently rich strawberry
mousse served in a flaky pastry crust.

She occupied herself for another thirty minutes with a gro-
cery list, which she would fill on Friday afternoon, then sat
and stared blankly through one of the tall, undraped windows
that framed the splendor of her yard on three sides of the
kitchen's dining nook. A wide overhang shaded every window in the house, which allowed Andrea to leave curtains,
shutters, drapes and blinds open, if she wished.

But she wasn't enjoying the view of evenly trimmed grass
and symmetrically perfect beds of flowers as she ordinarily
did. She felt blue and lonely, she realized unhappily, and
even anticipation of Friday's dinner party—already a success
because everyone had eagerly accepted her invitation—
couldn't dispel the terrible aloneness gnawing at her.

The sensation frightened and then angered her, because
feeling like the last rose of summer was not her fault. Something she'd been fighting against believing was suddenly too
clear and real to thrust aside any longer: Keith had, for some
unknown reason, decided to become a part of her life again.
Just how far he wanted to take this new and extremely per-
turbing admiration of her she could only guess at, but she
could hardly assume he only intended them to be on friendly
speaking terms when he'd kissed her at the first opportunity.
So what did he want, an affair?

Andrea's stomach began churning in alarm. An affair was
so...so...well, it was something she'd never done and just
the thought of making love with Keith made her feel shaky
and weak. Actually she suddenly felt like going to bed and
hiding again, as she'd done yesterday, but she told herself to
stop it at once. *You cannot run to your bedroom every time
Keith and what he might want from you pops into your silly
head!*

Feeling like a total mess—a rare sensation for Andrea—

she dragged herself to her feet and forced herself to clear away the dishes she'd used for lunch.

The next morning Keith was back. Andrea felt her knees go weak when he strolled into the classroom as though he owned the school, the town and all of Texas. No one could ever say that Keith Owens lacked self-confidence, which, at the moment, didn't make her like him any better.

But, sad to say, even while disliking him intensely—or telling herself she did—she felt his magnetism even more than she had at the ball. And she'd let him kiss her that night! How far might she let him go?

Shaking her head to rid her brain of such nonsense, Andrea went on with the story she'd been reading before Keith's interruption. It was about frogs and turtles and a small boy on a farm, a sweet, well-written little story that the children had been enthralled with before Keith walked in. Now they were more interested in the big man sitting on the tiny chair at the back of the room.

Andrea said in the gentle way she spoke to her class, "Children, look at me, please." The little faces turned to her again. "Mr. Owens, unfortunately, was not allowed to attend nursery school when he was your age, and he came here yesterday and again today to learn all of the lovely things you are learning. But we shouldn't stare at him, should we? Staring is very impolite. Just think of him as another classmate...a much taller classmate, of course...but one who is about the same age as you are. Can you do that?"

Keith almost burst out laughing. Andrea's putting him in his place, cutting him down to size for intruding on her class, had surprised him. He gulped back waves of rolling laughter and decided again that he *had* to bring them together. Hell's bells, their past was so long ago it shouldn't matter to either of them now. They hadn't parted on friendly terms, true, but this was another lifetime. She was an intelligent woman, and while she was obviously wary of his intentions, she couldn't possibly still be holding a grudge after so many years.

"I'm five," a small boy boasted proudly.

"Not yet, Jason," Andrea said with a warm smile. "Next month, I believe? Yes, I'm sure of it. Your birthday is in July and *then* you will be five. Class, would you like to hear the rest of the story?"

"Yes," the tots all shouted.

"Very well." Andrea began reading again. At times during the story she was so aware of Keith's eyes on her that the fine hairs on the back of her neck prickled. She *had* to stop him from coming here, but how? What could she possibly do that would chase him off, yet appear sensible and necessary to anyone else?

After recess, Keith disappeared again, and Andrea breathed more easily for the remainder of the morning. After parents or nannies had picked up the children, she put away toys and books to tidy her classroom then gathered her purse and left the building. Another teacher walked out with her and remarked on the great weather they were having.

Andrea smiled and agreed. They stopped and chatted for a few minutes about their individual classes and the children they were teaching—there were always anecdotes to relate to other teachers at the school—then they went in different directions to reach their vehicles in the parking lot. Andrea could feel her face turning crimson when she spotted Keith leaning against the back of her car, but she wasn't sure if her high, hot color was caused by anger or by a large spurt of adrenaline associated with unexpected, instantaneous and extremely shocking sexual awareness.

You've lived a celibate life far too long a time if just the sight of Keith can do this to you. And you thought you had every phase of your life under control, you...you dolt. Pull yourself together this instant! Don't you dare humiliate yourself by letting him know how strongly he affects you. He's already unbearably full of himself. Don't give him more fuel to feed his massive ego, for goodness sake!

Andrea's cheeks might be pink, but the expression on her

face could not have been frostier when she walked past Keith without a word and unlocked the driver's door of her car.

"Good afternoon to you, too," Keith said teasingly while ambling toward her.

She whirled on him. "You know something? I'm glad you hung around today because there are a few things I'd like to say to you."

Keith nodded. "Good, glad to hear it. I've got a whole bunch of things I'd like to say to you, too, but how about us talking over dinner tonight? We could go to Claire's, or to any other place you'd like. We could even drive to Midland, if you prefer."

"If I prefer? If I *prefer?* You...you..." She stopped her furious outburst and took a calming breath. After a moment she said, "Please listen to me. I don't know why you suddenly decided to annoy me by intruding on my classroom, but..."

Keith broke in. "Andrea, the answer to that couldn't be easier. I wanted to see you. It's as simple as that."

"Do you actually believe that becoming an irritating pest is going to make me like you?"

"Are you saying you *don't* like me? Andrea, you like everyone. Or you used to. You've become a snob of course, so I guess that changes things, but you have no reason to dislike me."

"No reason? You obviously have a conveniently selective memory, nice for you but selfish as all get-out for everybody else."

"Andrea, I've never been selfish with anything," Keith said, because he could see that Andrea was just barely managing to keep her temper in check. In fact the blazing light in her eyes truly surprised him; he believed that time healed wounds, real or imagined, big or small, and God knows, eighteen years was a long time.

"Do you actually believe that?" she demanded with astonishment.

"Yes...I do. Look, I realize now that getting the two of

us back together isn't going to be as easy as I'd thought. Or hoped. You've obviously got resentments to put to rest, but don't *you* realize nothing will be put to rest for either of us if we don't try? Have dinner with me. Lay your cards on the table. Andy, take the first step with me.''

''Oh, Lordy,'' she whispered, turning her face away to avoid seeing the plea in his dark eyes. Gathering her courage, she looked at him again. ''I have no cards, nor do you. Any step I would take with you would detour my life into unknown territory that I do not wish to explore. It may be impossible for you to understand, but I have not been living an unhappy existence. My life is full and I'm a contented woman. Or I was. You seem to be doing your level best to upset my personal applecart, and if I resent anything about you, Keith, it's that. Now, please leave me alone.''

She got in her car, started the motor, checked to make sure he'd moved out of the way, then backed out of her parking place and drove away.

Try as she might, she could not rid her mind of the look on his face when she'd delivered her final statement. Had it been cruel? No, she decided, not cruel, merely honest.

After all, how much pussyfooting could a woman do around a man she didn't want? *Even if he does fan old, all-but-forgotten embers back to life? Especially* if he fans old embers back to life, she thought adamantly. A fiery affair at her age was unthinkable. She was a lady, for God's sake, not a…a…

She stopped that thought before it got out of hand because she could not condemn women for making love. That sort of thing just wasn't for her; that was really all there was to it.

That philosophy did raise one question, however. If the man pursuing her with such determination weren't Keith Owens, would she be less strict about her personal code of ethics and morality?

Keith called a meeting at the club late that afternoon. When everyone had arrived and gone to one of the private rooms, Jason said as they got settled, ''Something must have happened.''

''Nothing conclusive,'' Keith replied. ''Yet. But I've been going through Eric's computer with a fine-tooth comb and I found one totally unidentifiable file. There's nothing in it but numbers.''

''Rob missed that?'' Jason said, looking surprised.

''Rob did a darned good job, Jason. This particular file is not in any way connected to Eric's personal journal. It was and is attached to an accounting file and is obviously written in some sort of code. I printed it out so y'all could have a look at it.'' Keith went into the briefcase he'd brought and stashed next to his chair and came out with a sheaf of papers, which he passed around.

Sebastian spoke first, after studying the pages of numbers. ''Is this a crackable code, Jason? With your CIA background, you must know something about codes.''

''Any code is crackable,'' Jason said. ''But not always easily nor by just anybody. We might be able to figure it out ourselves, or we might not. Should we bring in an expert?''

''I think we should give it a try first,'' Will said. ''What do y'all think?'' he asked, including every man in the circle of chairs in his question. ''We're not cryptographers, but neither are we stupid. It's possible that we might make some sense out of this. And we've only used outside help in the past when absolutely necessary. If we're to maintain our practice of total privacy, we should only call on outsiders as a last resort.''

''Will's right,'' Keith said. ''I'd like each one of you to study those numbers and see if they make any sense. I've already thought of bank account numbers, but that idea was easily disproved. I believe it's a numerical code, with numbers representing letters or words or something else that can be transposed into words.''

''Eric was a damned good accountant,'' Sebastian said, ''but this is a pretty complex code...''

''Yes, I know what you mean,'' Keith said thoughtfully. ''But, Sebastian, what's accounting if not numbers?''

Four

Keith sat in his favorite chair in the den, sipping an excellent cognac and staring into the gas-log flames of the fireplace. The fire wasn't needed for heat nor was it throwing enough to notice, but Keith enjoyed dancing flames with his cognac and troubled thoughts.

Eric's numeric code gnawed at him, but at the moment, questions about Andrea took precedence. Had he really loved her in college and been too beset with ambition to assign importance to anything else? Well, of course he'd loved her. He'd loved her for as long as he'd known her, since they were children. But had he also loved her in that special way a man loves the woman with whom he wants to spend the rest of his life?

Frowning at the fire, Keith raised his snifter for another taste of cognac.

Then there was another question: Were his feelings for Andrea the underlying reason his marriage had failed? Candace had always told him his mind was somewhere else. He had attributed her complaints to his work ethic, which truly had driven him back then. It was one of the ironies of his life, he felt, because these days one would be hard-pressed to locate that same quality of ambition within Keith Owens in any way, shape or form, all because of money. He'd become so wealthy from his computer software company that striving to increase that wealth seemed almost obscene. He rarely showed up at his business anymore; he had the best talent available in every key position, and he honestly didn't know if it was good or bad but he couldn't doubt that his former burning ambition had waned almost to the point of indifference. He'd changed, obviously, changed a lot, and if he and Candace were married now they might have made it to old age together.

That was neither here nor there, though. Candace was long gone—she was the person who had rejoiced in this huge mansion and the one who'd spent a fortune and the first year of their marriage decorating it—and Keith never really missed her. She'd had some good points, of course; he couldn't hate her for demanding a divorce and an enormous property settlement from a husband who'd given her anything money could buy but precious little time and consideration. She'd grown weary of it all, as he had, and finally there'd been nothing between them but anger, reproach and bickering.

And all the while, without trying, without ever going out of his way for information, he'd kept track of Andrea. Running into her on the street or in a shop had disturbed him in ways he hadn't let himself explore, for she'd never been anything but cold and distant. Her marriage had set him back a pace, though and then later on, the death of Jerry O'Rourke had been a major shock. He'd sent a huge flower arrangement to the funeral home and a sympathy card to Andrea's house, on which he'd personally written, "I'm so very sorry. Please let me know if I can do anything to help you through this."

He'd received a formal thank-you card for the flowers and

nothing else; she had never acknowledged his sympathy and offer of help in any way.

Narrowing his eyes thoughtfully, still gazing at the fire, Keith again sipped his brandy. He could not regret his behavior during his college years. He'd been young, overflowing with exciting plans, absolutely unstoppable physically— running on very little sleep and barely noticing it—and living on a natural high so incredible that remembering it brought tears to his eyes.

He didn't live on that plane of youthful exuberance now and he was able to spot the flaws that had totally eluded him at the time. For one thing, it was entirely possible that he'd let his soul mate, his mirror image in many ways, the one woman in all the world born perfect for him, as he was for her, get away.

Recalling their college relationship, the laughs, the gang of friends they'd happily shared and finally their private times, their kisses and petting sessions, was depressing for Keith, because they'd been in complete harmony on every issue but one. Andrea would *not* permit sex between them. She had kissed him, told him she loved him, let him caress her and touched him intimately. But when things got to that fever pitch, she stopped everything. He'd begged, debated with her even, ridiculed her righteous attitude and nothing had worked. She had been determined to be a virgin on her wedding night and she probably had been.

Only, he hadn't been the lucky groom.

Muttering a curse under his breath, Keith turned his thoughts to his present courtship. Was it working at all? Was he making Andrea remember their good times, as he couldn't help doing?

She was incredible with those kids in her class, he mused, picturing her gentle way of speaking to them, the warm and wonderful smiles she bestowed upon them. In the past, hadn't she talked about kids quite a lot? Yes, he was sure of it. Andrea had wanted a big family; he could recall her saying those very words many times. She'd been an only child, same as him, and she had mourned her lack of siblings while growing up. Keith couldn't visualize her changing her mind on something that had been so consistently momentous to her, so *why* hadn't she had the family she'd so passionately dreamed of producing?

He, on the other hand, had never yearned for kids and neither had Candace. They'd been like-minded on that subject, if no other. He had spent precious little time in the company of kids of any age. Certainly he'd never classified noisy *small* people as either cute or smart. Those youngsters in Andrea's class were unquestionably adorable—he'd never even come close to an observation of that sort before, and yes, it was surprising. It was also obvious that Andrea loved each and every one of the tots in her class, so again, why hadn't she had kids of her own?

Keith finally had to admit that furtively keeping track of Andrea for eighteen years had never given him the kind of personal information he would like to have about her now. For instance, had she truly loved Jerry O'Rourke?

"Damn!" Keith exclaimed in sudden and startling frustration. Rising from his chair, he went to the fireplace and turned off the gas. Then he took his brandy glass to the kitchen and set it on the counter. Gabriella, his housekeeper who came in every weekday morning, would rinse the glass and put it in the dishwasher. It honestly never occurred to him to do that simple chore himself. She kept the house sparkling clean and also did some cooking. There were always casseroles, soups or stews in the refrigerator or freezer that he could warm up should he decide to eat at home, which was happening more and more of late. Keith had been raised with housekeepers, cooks, gardeners, et cetera, and he'd hired Gabriella to run his household as soon as he'd had a household to run. Candace had liked her, so Gabriella had been around a long time.

Keith climbed the spectacular circular stairway in the massive foyer of his home to the second floor and went to the large elegant master suite and ultimately to bed. Lying in the dark with his hands behind his head, he came to a decision. He couldn't let Andrea's objections stop him. Not yet, at any rate. She was still ticked over their breakup, which seemed utterly ridiculous after so long a time, but women were funny about things that men barely noticed.

So, he'd give her as much time and as many opportunities as she needed to come around to his way of thinking. It would happen, he was positive. She was too intelligent to carry a silly grudge to the grave.

Smiling in self-satisfaction over his decision, Keith turned on his side, got comfortable in his oversize bed and closed his eyes.

Andrea sighed when Keith walked into her classroom yet again. Had he completely lost his former pride, which she recalled as stiff-necked and a seemingly indestructible part of him? She pondered the past and present in genuine and most definitely unamused amazement. Could she have made her disapproval of his ridiculous behavior any clearer yesterday? If someone had made it so plain that she wasn't wanted, she certainly would not have returned the very next day.

Keith touched the tips of his fingers to his forehead in an informal salute and smiled at her. Andrea tensed defensively, and she did *not* smile back. Actually, she longed to throw the storybook in her hand at him as he made his way to the back of the room and that tiny chair. What in heaven's name was she going to do about this? It was all up to her, for she could not complain about it to anyone. Keith was a well-known, highly respected person in Royal, and the only thing complaining would do was to spread the news that he was hot on her trail.

The children, she noticed then, had grown tired of staring at Keith and were beginning to squirm. She had been getting ready to read to them, thus the book in her hand, and inspiration suddenly struck.

"Children," she said calmly. "How would you like Mr Owens to read to you today?"

"Yay!" they shouted, creating a din of high-pitched childish voices that could have jangled adult nerves within moments if Andrea had not quieted her tiny students.

Keith knew he'd been had. In fact, there was something about this sneaky tactic of Andrea's that smacked of polite warfare. It was if she'd thrown down a gauntlet, or fired the first shot. Oddly, what Keith perceived as a declaration of war didn't anger him in the least. Rather, it exhilarated him, awakened youthful energy that obviously—and happily—was still a part of him but that must have been in slumber mode.

With one eyebrow cocked and a devilish light gleaming in his dark eyes, he strolled to the front of the room. Andrea held out the book and he took it from her fingers. Before he even looked at it, he said, too quietly for the children to hear, "I accept your challenge."

"My what?" Confusion beset Andrea.

"You always did look good enough to eat...make that kiss...when you blushed. Now, let's take a look at this book."

Andrea wanted to wind up and sock him a good one. He aggravated her normal composure and stirred her anger much as a tornado shatters any earthly thing on which it descends.

"It was written for preschoolers, so I'm sure you'll be able to understand it," she said icily.

"Hmm," Keith murmured while perusing the cover art. "Yes," he added in a serious vein, "I probably will. Well, shall we get started?"

"Sit over there," Andrea told him, indicating the chair she always used when reading to the class. While Keith complied, she sat behind her desk. He began reading and the children stared wide-eyed at him.

Keith came to the phrase, "And the chicken said 'cluck, cluck, cluck,'" and each tiny child listening so spellbound shouted, "Cluck, cluck, cluck!" Startled, Keith looked over to Andrea for help, but she appeared to be writing something and was completely unaware of his quandary.

He figured it out for himself, though, when the pig in the story said, "Oink, oink, oink," and the children shouted the "oinks" as he read them. *These little ones know this story by heart!* From that moment on Keith began enjoying himself. He oinked and whinnied and clucked and mooed, and when the kids giggled because he sounded so funny, he laughed with them.

Andrea kept her pen in her hand, but she was watching Keith and the kids very closely. She'd never seen him with small children before, but the Keith she'd known in college would not have had one second of fun reading to them. He especially would not have done or said anything to make anyone—even small children—laugh at him!

She felt something shriveling within herself; it was her years-long resentment of Keith and it quickly diminished to a barely recognizable mass. *You're getting mushy and soft just because he's having fun with the kids, and they like him? Don't be a fool, Andrea. He's still the same man who broke your heart in college.*

From out of nowhere came a painful, unfamiliar urge to weep. Not to sob or bawl but to quietly weep for things that might have been. The feeling unnerved her. Her life had been good. Her life *was* good. She'd married a wonderful man, and Jerry would always hold a special place in her heart. She had good health, this job she loved, great friends and enough financial security to live comfortably for the rest of her days. And still she felt like weeping because a man who had no right at all to intrude on her safe, secure little world was making her tiny students laugh and clap their hands.

Andrea held back the tears, but her whole system felt jagged and torn as she wondered what *really* made Keith Owens tick these days. Was she being too hard on him? What if all he wanted was a renewal of the wonderful friendship they had enjoyed from childhood to college? Goodness, true friendship was something to cherish, and wasn't it also a rarity? Could she honestly say that her current friends were more valuable, more precious than Keith had been for such a very long time?

You ninny! If all he wants is friendship he would not have kissed you in the limousine! Don't kid yourself about what he wants. You know full well what's on his lecherous mind! You didn't sleep with him in college, and he's determined to move you from the "Got Away" to the "Nailed Her" columns of his journal of sexual conquests.

Andrea jumped when Keith touched her shoulder and said, "All done, Teach. Here's your book." He grinned at her. "Where were you, off in fantasy land?"

"Yes," she said dryly. "It was definitely a fantasy." Rising, she left her desk and walked closer to the children. "It's time for recess. Everyone stand, please, and walk with me. Remember that we always leave quietly."

Keith followed them out and for the first time really observed Andrea and her class on the playground. She was so great with those kids, he thought, and it was obvious to him that they adored her. She never raised her voice to get them to do something, or to stop them from doing something. They obeyed her without whining, dragging their feet or questioning her request. She would be—Keith's breath caught over the thought—an incredible mother.

He left when the class went back inside the building, but waited in his car in the parking lot. Andrea saw him the second she came through the front door and she stopped on the stoop to assess the situation. Actually she only had two choices: continue their ridiculous squabbling, for which she blamed herself, for Keith had not said one insulting or demeaning thing to her while she had lambasted him at every opportunity, or be nice to him. After all, pleasantness toward a man certainly did not have to include anything sexual, and she was many years away from awkwardness around the opposite sex. Actually, it was Keith's misfortune to have suddenly developed silly ideas about her, not hers. She could handle Keith, she thought with a squaring of her shoulders, and he would eventually get the message that she wished he would return to the past and stay there.

Andrea walked directly to her car, but she didn't pretend that Keith wasn't there. Instead, she looked his way and said clearly, "You did a marvelous job with that story. The children enjoyed your rendition very much."

Pleased as punch with her compliment, Keith got out of his car and walked over to her. "Do you want to hear something funny? I enjoyed it, too. Andrea, I'm beginning to see why you were so set on becoming a teacher."

It was a sore subject for Andrea, because she would never forget how cruelly he had accused her of wasting her talents, her education and certainly her future by teaching instead of going into the computer software business with him. He couldn't have forgotten that awful night, any more than she did. But she'd decided on the school's stoop to be nice, and so she smiled and nodded and acted as though he hadn't just slammed her with a painful reminder of the past.

"Well, I really must be going," she said cordially. "I have a thousand things to do today." She got into her car.

Before she could close herself in, though, Keith took hold of the door and bent from the waist to peer into the car at her.

"Andrea, would you have dinner with me sometime?" he asked softly.

"Uh...dinner?" Damn it, she'd given an inch and now he wanted a mile! "Keith, really...I...I rarely go out."

"You're not known for being a run-around," he replied with an amused grin, "but I've seen you eating out with friends with my own eyes."

"Well, of course...on occasion," she said rather sharply. "But...I can't...I just can't...go out...with you."

Keith narrowed his eyes. He'd been thrilled with what she'd given him today, but it wasn't enough. He didn't let his disappointment show, though. "All right, maybe some other time," he said congenially, and stepped away from her car.

Keith didn't have to follow closely behind her because he knew the way to her house, and he could tell from the route she was driving that home was where she was going.

Andrea couldn't get rid of the tremor in the pit of her stomach. No matter how she treated Keith—disdainfully or pleasantly—he stayed one step ahead of her. She raised her garage door with her remote and drove in, relieved to be home and…and safe from Keith's magnetism.

"Nooo," she moaned. Keith's magnetism? What was wrong with her?

In the next instant she realized Keith's car was precisely behind hers! He'd followed her home. She stared in the rearview mirror as though she'd lost the mobility to do anything but sit right where she was.

Keith got out, quietly shut the door of his car and walked into her garage. Using the button on the wall, he dropped the garage door, and Andrea's pulse went wild. They were so alone, so completely isolated from everyone else in Royal. She wasn't sure she could keep him at arm's length any longer. In spite of old hurts, his infectious grin, his good looks and now his sweetness with the little darlings in her class were working some sort of magic on her.

Keith opened the door of her car and she didn't move a muscle, just sat there rigidly and stared straight ahead through the windshield.

"Andy?" he said quietly.

She still wouldn't look at him. "This is too much, Keith. Why are you here, invading my home, my space?"

"Please don't put it that way." But, of course, she'd only said the truth. He *was* invading her space and he suddenly wasn't so sure of himself. "I never seem to do anything right with you," he said with a deep frown between his eyes.

The pathos in his voice caused Andrea to finally look at him. "Why do you want to? I…don't understand you," she said in a shaky, husky voice.

"I don't understand you, either, but I want to. Andrea, would you and I becoming friends again be so terrible?"

"Friendship isn't the only thing on your mind."

"That's true, but I'm willing to start there." He let a few moments of silence go by, then quietly asked, "Could I see the inside of your house? You couldn't begin to know how many times I've driven past this pretty house and wondered what you were doing."

"You haven't," she said, sounding totally deflated. "Tell me you haven't been doing that."

"Do you want me to lie?" He held out his hand to help her from the car. "Take me inside. Give me a glass of tea or a soda and talk to me. Treat me like an old friend, for that's what I am, Andy, what I'll always be no matter how determinedly you fight it."

Andrea looked at that hand, his hand, and knew that if she took it and invited him in for a soda and conversation that she would be making a grave mistake. He was stronger-willed than she was, and gradually he was wearing her down.

But then she raised her eyes to gaze into his, and she felt sixteen again, about the time in her teen years when he had changed from her best buddy to the center of her universe. She knew now, of course, that he'd done nothing to cause her such a drastic change of heart. To him she'd still been best "bud" and the girl next door.

Looking into his gloriously alive brown eyes, every memory she possessed about him went sailing through her brain, leaving behind a star-sprinkled trail of emotions she had thought were dead and buried.

Apparently not. She reached out and took his hand. "I'll fix some lunch for both of us," she said with a catch in her voice, knowing he'd won, that he'd negated her every objection and beaten her.

She could only hope now that he wouldn't make a pass because she'd never been so unsure of herself before. At least, not in a very long time.

Five

Keith liked Andrea's home the second he stepped inside. "It's nice, Andrea. Warm, very pleasant."

"Thank you. Look around, if you wish. I'll be in the kitchen."

"Thanks, I will."

When he strolled away she physically wilted against the refrigerator. It didn't seem possible that Keith was actually there, in her house. And not for a social gathering of friends and acquaintances, but alone, by himself!

Andrea quietly groaned. Her heart seemed to be fluttering nervously, as were her stomach and hands. Why had she let herself be drawn into this situation? She could have stood her ground in the garage and told him to leave her property at once. But no, she'd caved in and invited him to lunch!

Lunch. What on earth was she going to feed him? Quickly she turned and opened the door of the refrigerator. Scanning the shelves, she added up what she had on hand. Fine, she thought, and went to the sink to wash her hands. Returning to the refrigerator, she began taking out ingredients.

Keith came back while she was setting the table. They would eat in the kitchen's dining nook rather than in her formal dining room. Not that she wanted things cozy between them, but a spur-of-the-moment luncheon should be casually prepared and served.

"Can I help?" he asked.

"Everything's taken care of." Andrea walked from the nook to the counter, where she began putting the finishing touches to a bowl of chicken salad. "Have a seat," she said without looking at him.

Keith wandered over to the counter with its three stools and sat on one. "Do you remember when we were kids and you would go into your house, make a pile of peanut butter and jelly sandwiches and bring them outside to our fort?"

"Along with as many cartons of juice I could carry."

"You haven't forgotten our fort, then."

"Of course not. It was a big part of my childhood."

"Mine, too. One day it would be a spaceship and the next a rustler's hideout. We had great imaginations back then, Andy."

"Most children do." She wanted to ask him to please stick with her given name, and not to shorten it or alter it, but she refrained from doing so.

"Too bad we all have to grow up," Keith murmured. "It happens so fast."

"When childhood is thirty years ago, it seems that it flew by much too quickly. We never truly enjoy each and every phase of life until it's gone. I let my teens and then my twenties rush by without ever stopping my hectic pace long enough to relish any one particular age."

"I know what you mean. Now we're both eight years into our thirties. Are you still letting a hectic pace rule your heart?"

Andrea felt her cheeks turn pink. She'd said nothing at all

about her heart, and she was not going to be led down *that* path!

"Are you?" she asked, throwing him a challenging glance.

Keith smiled teasingly. "I asked you first."

"You used to pull that on me when we were kids, if I remember correctly," she said and gave her chicken salad a final stir. "Lunch is ready," she announced. "Please bring that pitcher of iced tea to the table."

When they were seated and eating, Keith began another conversation. "Do you ever feel old?"

Startled, Andrea lowered her fork. "I'm not sure that's a question I care to answer."

"You don't look much older than you did in college, you know, but you could dress younger."

"And what's wrong with this dress?" It was a pretty dress, pink cotton with white trim.

"Its style is too old for you."

"Good Lord, Keith, I'm a teacher! Should I wear short skirts and halter tops to teach youngsters?"

"I guess not, but do you even *own* a short skirt and a halter top?"

"That's none of your business," she grumbled. "Look, you worry about your wardrobe and I'll worry about mine."

"Sorry. Obviously I hit a nerve."

"You have no right even to comment on my clothing, let alone judge and censure it."

"Don't get all steamed up. You always look nice, whatever you're wearing."

"Then why say something as rude as that remark about my dressing younger?"

"I apologize again. You looked great at the ball."

"Young enough for your juvenile taste?" she drawled.

"You're all fired up and sarcastic. I take it back, okay? Anything I said that might have annoyed you, I take it back."

"You should."

"I do, but it wouldn't hurt you to answer my question."

"What question?"

"Do you ever feel old? I guess I'm asking because every so often I feel older than my dad was when he passed away. He was sixty. Mother was sixty-two when she died."

"About the same ages as my parents were when they died," Andrea said quietly. "They all died too young. I have friends well into their seventies and eighties who are active and great fun to be with. Of course, they're in reasonably good health, which makes a major difference, but I also think a sense of humor helps to keep people young."

"Could be. You used to have a great sense of humor."

"Meaning I don't now?"

"Now don't go getting all puffed up again. All I said was…"

"I know what you said."

"Well, how would I know if you still love to laugh when we rarely see each other? Andrea, when you really think about it, isn't it silly for you and I to be anything but the closest of friends?"

Instantly wary, Andrea covered her fluster by picking up the pitcher of tea and refilling their glasses. She had to say something, give him some kind of reply, but what?

She finally said, rather stiffly, "It's not so silly, Keith. We didn't part on the best of terms, you know."

"But that was a hundred years ago! Andy, I have so many feelings for you. What should I do with them?"

"They're all *old* feelings, Keith, part of the past! Leave them there."

"Sometimes old things are the best. Can new friends really replace old ones? I don't think so. Andy, I'm lonely."

Her jaw dropped. "Now, *that's* a lie!"

"No, sweetheart, it isn't. Yes, I have friends, lots of them, and I've got money and community respect. But there's a hole right about here…" He laid his hand on his abdomen. "…that I can't seem to fill."

"Have some more chicken salad," she said dryly, giving him a glib answer. What a con artist!

Keith couldn't help laughing. "Well, I can see that your

sense of humor is still alive and thriving. That's good.'' After a few silent moments he said, ''But I wasn't lying about being lonely.''

''Maybe not, but why tell me about it? Every adult in the world who lives alone probably has moments of loneliness. It's hardly a fatal affliction.''

''You're thinking that I'm looking for sympathy.''

''You are,'' she said flatly. ''But you're looking in the wrong place, and from the wrong person.''

''I never dreamed you could be so cold.''

''If a realistic take on life translates to a cold attitude to you, there's not much I can do about it.''

''You're not cold with the kids in your class.'' Keith put his elbows on the table and leaned forward to look directly into her eyes. ''You're magnificent with those children, and it's obvious as anything I've ever seen that they adore you. You love them, don't you? You pour all your emotion like a stream of liquid gold into that one glorious outlet, and you can do it day after day, month after month because it's safe. There's not a sliver of danger from loving children, is there? Nothing at all like what can happen if you let yourself love a grown-up.''

Andrea refused to look away from the smug expression on his face. In a way it amused her that he actually believed that he'd figured her out so easily, but there *was* a grain of truth in his analysis. The ''safety'' factor he'd mentioned wasn't entirely incorrect, but neither was it accurate. Should she set him straight on that or let him wallow in his misconceptions?

''If you're expecting me to debate with you over my affection for young children, you're going to be sadly disappointed.''

''Then everything I said must be true.''

Andrea shrugged. ''Think so if you wish. I don't owe you anything, Keith, least of all an explanation of why I behave as I do. The truth is, I don't owe anything to anyone and I like it that way.''

Keith narrowed his eyes on her. "In other words, you're *never* lonely."

"We're back to that? Sorry, but that bait still isn't going to work."

"Bait?"

"You're fishing, Keith. What you're hoping to unearth from deep within my psyche is beyond me, but you've got something in mind."

He leaned back in his chair and regarded her solemnly. "I already explained it. I want us to be friends."

She was suddenly furious. "*Kissing* friends?" she spat. "We might have stood a chance if you hadn't made that insulting pass the night of the ball. What did you think I was going to do, fall into your arms like some...some sex-starved tart?"

"It was only a kiss, Andy. You really didn't hate it that much, did you?"

"It was a shock that I hope will never be repeated." Pushing back her chair, Andrea got up and began clearing the table.

Keith rose to help. Carrying dishes, cutlery and leftover food they passed each other twice before everything was on the counter and Andrea could wipe down the table. Andrea's mind wished Keith would say "Thanks, goodbye," and leave, but there was a different tune playing elsewhere in her body. She didn't want the feelings there, she *hated* the tingles and flutterings of her own female system caused by a man that intellectually she wanted no part of.

Such feelings were confusing her to the point that she wasn't sure of what to do next. Considering her "marvelous hostess" reputation, she was behaving out of character. Her friends would not have recognized the woman she was today, for none of them had ever seen this uncertain side of her. Keith had. She hadn't always been resolute and confident. She'd been soft in her youth, starry-eyed over anything that smacked of romance. She'd seen love where there'd been none. The partnership *Keith* had been thinking about had been all business. She might as well have been his cousin.

Why didn't he leave? He'd had his lunch and his say, and it was all he was going to get from her. Should she come right out and ask him to leave?

She tried to ignore his watchful gaze as she rinsed the lunch dishes and put them in the dishwasher. "Did you see the backyard?" she asked, striving for a casualness she was far from feeling.

"Only through the windows. Your yard is beautiful."

"I designed it."

"The pool, too?"

"All of it. When I bought this house it was extremely plain. It had this great floor plan and it was exactly the size home I was looking for, but the former owners had done very little to it in the way of interior décor and exterior landscaping. The entire yard was grass and a few trees, and since I intended to live my life here, I wanted everything perfect. Perfect for me, that is."

"You did a good job."

"I think so. I'm sure the whole house would fit in the foyer of yours, but..."

"Totally irrelevant," Keith said before she'd finished speaking. "Why didn't you stay in the house that you lived in during your marriage?"

Andrea stiffened. "I didn't want to," she said sharply.

"That's no answer. Your leaving that house for this one makes me wonder: you didn't love Jerry O'Rourke, did you?"

She gasped out loud and swung around to face him. "I most certainly did love Jerry! What gives you the right to even mention my marriage? I had a good marriage and I was happy. I will never get over losing Jerry."

"If that's all true, then I owe you an apology. Thing is, Andy darlin', it sounds more like a fairy tale than the truth."

"Why?" she demanded angrily. "Because *your* marriage was such a bust?"

"Maybe," he said, sounding speculative. "One question springs to mind, doesn't it? Am I petty enough to doubt your happy marriage because mine wasn't?"

"And how could the great Keith Owens *ever* acknowledge something so human as pettiness, right?"

"Well, the idea does sort of pinch," he replied with a grin.

"You're impossible."

"I've heard that before, so you could be right."

Andrea closed the door of the dishwasher, rinsed her hands at the sink and dried them with a paper towel.

"You're the only man I know who's proud of his faults," she said with a scorching look at him.

"You're beautiful when your fire's up and burning," he told her.

"*Nothing's* burning. Nothing's even warm, so don't waste your breath, Keith." She realized that he'd taken two steps toward her, and she backed up. "If you try anything I swear I'll brain you with a skillet!"

"No, you won't." He advanced farther, and she found her backside against the counter. "Tell me you don't feel anything," he said in a low, husky voice that alarmed her more than his proximity.

"This is the reason you followed me home, isn't it?" she said accusingly. "Not to reestablish friendship but to make another pass. Well, maybe we should just go to bed and get it over with. Once should be enough, don't you think?"

He was so stunned he couldn't say a word for a very long moment. Finally he cleared his throat and managed a hoarse, "You never used to talk like that."

"I could talk plainer," she snapped. "You're not irresistible, Keith. I live alone because I want to. I do not want another man, another husband. I'm without a man by choice! Do you get my drift? If I've been too subtle, say so and I'll draw you a picture!"

Keith held up his hands in total surrender. "You win. I won't try to kiss you again, though I'd like you to remember that kissing you and making love to you are the uppermost thoughts in my mind every time I'm near you.''

Andrea stared. ''You're planning to be near me again?''

''Every chance I get, darlin', every chance I get. Thank you for lunch and I enjoyed our conversation, before I went and ruined everything by behaving like a man who admires a woman more than he can express in mere words. That's when the need for kissing and all that other stuff overwhelms one's good sense. I won't be at the preschool tomorrow because I have a meeting, but I will be seeing you again very soon.''

He walked out of Andrea's kitchen, whistling a merry tune. She stared after him like a sleepwalker, dazed both in eye and spirit. No matter how she treated him, no matter what she said or did, he always seemed to get the last word. How could he always stay one step ahead of her?

But the worst, most painful, question to ponder was why she had relented so drastically and actually invited him into her home. Something told her there was no eradicating what she'd done today. He had a foothold now, and *she'd given it to him!*

''My God, why?'' she whispered.

The rest of the day was a bust for Andrea. There were a dozen things she could—and probably should—have done, but she couldn't seem to get herself together enough to accomplish anything constructive. After Keith left she had donned yard clothes and forced herself outside to search the beds of flowers for weeds. The man she employed for yard work did an excellent job, and he didn't need her to keep the flowers and grass free of weeds.

And so she sat in the shade on the patio, gazed upon her beautiful backyard and brooded over Keith. It was awful to feel so helpless about something, for she *wasn't* helpless. Not ordinarily, anyway. But this…this invasion of her privacy, of her personal life, had her frustrated and stymied.

Hoping to relieve her mind of anything remotely connected

to Keith, she deliberately thought of the people she paid to keep her home in A1 condition. There was Lucyanne, the lady who came to the house once a week and made the whole place shine and smell good from aromatic cleaning products and elbow grease. Hector came twice a week to clean the pool and check the chemical balance of the water, and finally there was Jake, whom she rarely saw because he kindly coincided his lawn-mowing with her morning classes at Kiddie Kingdom.

She had it good and knew it. Or she *had* known it, believed it with all her heart, but now, watching the sun creating silver streaks in the aquamarine water of her pool, there was a restlessness within her that she couldn't seem to dent. Well, yes, her loyal household helpers were blessings, and so were her friends and her job and the investments inherited from her parents and from Jerry. Everything she had was a blessing, for there were so many people with so very little in the way of material comfort. She understood that very well, thanked her lucky stars and was more than generous with donations to worthy charities. Plus, of course, she gave more than money to New Hope, she gave some of herself—her time, perhaps the most intrinsically valuable donation of all.

Andrea heaved a long-drawn-out sigh and blamed Keith for causing her such an awful case of the blues. She'd been hard on him and in a way she was sorry, mostly because she wasn't normally unkind to anyone. But Keith scared her. He was a disruption in every way possible. She'd been completely contented before the Cattleman's Club ball and now she wasn't, and who or what else *should* she blame for that? No, Keith was definitely the cause of her discontentment, and by his own words, he was not going to leave her alone.

How to deal with this? How to deal with an unwanted Romeo? The questions went around and around in her mind. If someone had noticed Keith's dark-blue SUV in her driveway today—and it seemed pretty farfetched to assume that no one had noticed it—then it was probably all over town by now that he'd been to her house.

"Who cares?" she mumbled. There were those in the area who never forgot anything, so a lot of Royal residents remembered that she and Keith had once been an item. A fresh new rumor might titillate imaginations for a while, but so what?

Sighing again, Andrea realized the afternoon was practically gone. She'd wasted hours brooding over Keith's brazenness. Whenever Keith had wanted something, even as a child, he'd gone after it like a hound on the scent of a rabbit.

Well, in this case, she, apparently, was the rabbit!

"Damn you, Keith," she muttered and got up from her patio chair and went inside.

On Friday, Keith did not come to her classroom. He'd told her he wouldn't be there, but Andrea really didn't believe anything he said. Oddly, that empty little chair at the back of the room bothered her in some unfathomable way, because she found herself looking at it far too often.

It also bothered some of the children, whom Andrea saw glancing toward the back of the room several times. For the first time since she'd begun teaching at Kiddie Kingdom, she was glad when school was out for the day and she could go home. Telling herself it was only because she had so many things to do to prepare for her dinner party that evening, she drove from the school to her favorite supermarket.

That afternoon she accomplished a great deal. With five good friends coming for dinner, she couldn't just sit around and worry today. She shopped, she drove home with a back seat full of groceries, she cooked and she tried almost desperately to lock Keith out of her thoughts.

By six-thirty the dinner menu was ready except for a few final touches that could only be done just before serving, Andrea was dressed in a lovely hostess gown the same color as her eyes, and, of course, thanks to Lucyanne, the house was perfect. To the spotlessly clean rooms, Andrea had added numerous vases of freshly cut flowers. She loved candles, but omitted them this evening because one of her guests was allergic to the smoke.

Ten minutes before seven her guests began arriving. Everyone there knew Andrea's routine. Cocktails at seven, dinner at seven-thirty. She poured herself a glass of wine and joined her friends already involved in a rather humorous dissection of a recent bestselling book. Andrea wasn't quite through reading it, but when she stated rather flatly that she didn't like the book and probably *wouldn't* finish it, five sets of eyes looked at her in surprise.

Then the arguments began. Her friends were going to convince her that the book might have flaws, but wasn't it possible the author deliberately included them to make readers think?

For the first time ever Andrea didn't give a whit about the friendly, rapid-fire debate. Realizing that startled her, for she had always loved intellectual debates with these wonderful friends. She excused herself on a kitchen-duty pretext and fled the room.

Breathing hard, as though she'd just run her usual three miles, she strode through the kitchen and went outside through the garage. Standing in the shadows of garage and house, she breathed in the cool night air and tried to pull herself together. Nothing was the same as it had been before the Cattleman's Club ball, and she had the most awful urge just to let go and cry her eyes out.

Which she couldn't do. She had to return to her guests. She had to smile and talk and act as though her life was the same smooth and serene routine it had been for years. She had to serve her marvelous dinner and talk again while everyone ate it. And then she had to offer after-dinner drinks, which everyone would accept, and talk again. For hours. At least until eleven, although some of her dinner parties had run past midnight.

She was just turning to go back inside when she heard a car on her street. It was moving slowly and when she looked she saw that it was a dark SUV. That was Keith's SUV, she'd bet her life on it! Now he was driving past her house at night? What next?

Keith saw the cars in Andrea's driveway. She had guests. He turned at the end of her street and drove home.

When he got there he turned on Eric's computer once again and opened the numeric file he'd found. Studying the rows of unbroken double-spaced numbers, which made absolutely no sense, as every type of written record contained vacant spaces, he began playing around, trying various tests, such as eliminating certain numbers or combinations of numbers.

He worked for several hours, accomplished nothing concrete or conclusive, and finally went to bed. The second his head hit the pillow there wasn't a number anywhere in his brain. In fact the only thing occupying that particular part of his anatomy was an image of Andrea's face. And she wasn't looking at him with a kindly expression, either.

Grunting in frustration, he punched his pillow.

Six

Andrea bid her guests good-night with her usual warm, winning smile. They complimented her delicious dinner and exemplary hospitality and departed in high spirits shortly before eleven. Relieved that no one seemed to have picked up on her jittery mood, Andrea busied herself picking up glasses from various tables in the living room and carrying them to the kitchen.

She went to her bedroom then to change into her night-gown and summer-weight robe, for comfort mostly, but also to avoid the risk of spilling or splashing something onto the exquisite fabric of her blue dress, and returned to the kitchen.

All the while her mind jumped from one thing to another, mostly from her established routine to Keith, who had disrupted longtime habits and rituals. She resented him terribly. If he stayed on his side of Pine Valley, she wouldn't have to resent him at all. She would hardly be aware of his existence, which was precisely how their non-relationship had flowed along—with only an occasional discomfiting lurch—for years and years.

But he did what he wanted. He always had, if she looked back and recalled the bossy, mouthy little boy he'd been, even though he'd also been her best friend. And then, at thirty-eight years old, from out of the blue, some weird event had made him see her in a brand-new way. And he had the bloody gall to think she should be thrilled about it! What exactly could she do about such arrogance?

She was still deep in thought on the subject when her front doorbell chimed, startling her so much that she nearly dropped the plate in her hand. Quickly gathering her wits— a guest must have accidentally left something behind—she dried her hands and hurried to the foyer.

Switching on the outside light, which she'd turned off once her dinner guests had driven away, she peered through the peephole in the door. Her jaw dropped, her stomach knotted and her pulse began racing: It was Keith!

The bell chimed again. Drawing a huge breath, Andrea unlocked and opened the door a crack. "It's late. Why are you here?"

"I saw your lights. May I come in?"

"What for?"

"Because I need a friend."

"Oh, you're in one of your lonely moods." She knew she sounded cruel, and she really didn't want to hurt Keith. But who else did she know who would ring her doorbell at this time of night? *Her* friends were considerate. *Her* friends called before dropping in.

Keith slapped at a moth that had been drawn by the light. "To be perfectly honest, I thought about what you said yesterday, and I think you just might be right."

"What did I say?"

Another moth buzzed Keith's head and he made a swipe at it. "Could I please come inside and escape these critters?"

Grudgingly she opened the door and stepped back so he

could enter. "What did I say yesterday?" she repeated stonily.

"Hey, do I smell coffee? Would it be too much trouble to give me a cup?"

She shook her head disgustedly. "You have more bullish brass than Texas longhorns. If you want some coffee it's in the kitchen." Spinning on her heel, she walked away.

Grinning all over his face, positive that she wasn't really angry with him for dropping in uninvited but she had to act that way, he stayed right behind her. "How'd your party go? Ended kind of early, didn't it? What happened? Wasn't it any fun? Did you make the mistake of inviting a bunch of boring people over?"

She swung around to face him. "My friends are not boring! We had a perfectly lovely evening."

"A lovely evening that stopped dead before the clock struck eleven, let alone twelve?"

"I suppose *your* parties are just beginning at eleven, probably with every guest falling down drunk by twelve! Well, my friends don't happen to enjoy that sort of sport, old *sport!*"

He reached out and gently brushed a strand of hair from her cheek, shocking her to immobility, and said softly, "How come I rile you so much, sweetheart?"

Andrea swallowed hard and forced her feet to step away from him. Going to the coffeemaker, she filled a cup and then brought it to the counter. "Sugar, cream?" she asked in a voice she barely recognized as her own. He changed who she normally was, she thought unhappily. That was his secret, his power; he had the ability to eradicate all the gentility she'd acquired through the years and leave her with nothing but a raw inner core.

"Black, just the way it is." Keith sat on a counter stool and lifted the cup to his lips for a sip, keeping his eyes on her all the while. Her robe had not been designed for seduction, but it seduced him, probably because it *was* a robe, which hinted at a flimsy gown and nothing else under it.

"Was your party a shower of some sort?" he asked.

"A shower! Why on earth would you think that?"

"Because of your robe."

It took a second for her to make the connection between *shower* and *robe,* and when she did she couldn't help smiling.

"You're incorrigible," she said.

Keith smiled at her. "Have some coffee with me."

"Might as well," she muttered, totally giving up on ever besting him. "I already knew I wasn't going to get much sleep tonight."

"Why not, hon?"

His endearment caused a shiver to travel her spine. Holding her cup of coffee in front of her, she hit him with a hard look. "You know damned well why not."

"Not because of anything I've done. Maybe because your party was a bust?"

"It was *not* a bust! Damn, you're irritating."

"Did you just now come to that conclusion?"

"Hardly."

"Well, if I'm so irritating and you thought so before now, how come you let me in?"

"Yes, let's get back to that. What did I say yesterday that you decided was so agreeable that you had to come by in the middle of the night to remind me of it? And I would appreciate a straightforward answer, if you don't mind."

Keith slowly took another swallow of coffee and tested her patience further by narrowing his eyes as though deep in thought.

"Will you please get to it?" she demanded hotly.

"Well, on second thought maybe I shouldn't."

"Oh, for crying out loud!"

"You might get upset."

"I'm *already* upset!"

"Yeah, I guess you are. I upset you pretty easily, don't I?"

"I don't have words to describe *how* easily."

He ignored her sarcasm and mused aloud, "I wonder why that is."

The red-hot anger rising within her wasn't a pleasant sensation, and she was honestly afraid of where it might lead. She gritted her teeth and forced herself to speak normally.

"I don't have to wonder, I know. Now, take this any way you wish, but either tell me what I said yesterday that intrigued you so...the *only* reason I opened my door to you at this hour...or leave. Those are your choices."

"Okay, but remember you insisted on candor. You said that we should probably go to bed together and get it out of our systems. I'd like to take you up on that offer."

Andrea slumped against the refrigerator and just stared at him. "You're insane."

"Did you or did you not say those very words?"

"Not in the context you're construing them!"

"Oh. Well, what other meaning could an invitation to join you in bed have?"

"I didn't invite you to join me in bed!" she shrieked. "That is not what I said!"

"I'm afraid it is, Andy," he said with a smile she would just love to smear across his face with a hard slap.

"Leave!" she shouted. "Get your butt off that stool and leave my house!"

"Well, if you're going to get all bent out of shape over some simple conversation, then fine, I'll be happy to go." Keith set down his cup and got off the stool.

Andrea was breathing hard, so full of righteous fury that her color was high and her bosom heaving. There was also discomfort in her chest, not a piercing physical pain that would frighten a person, but a thudding ache without a name. It was there, and she knew nothing about its cause or meaning, other than it was somehow connected to Keith. Or maybe it was a reminder of Keith, perhaps a ball of memories that had wound around itself so tightly for so many years in her effort to forget all that had been good between them that it was now wizened and almost unrecognizable.

Then, with a swiftness and strength that took her breath, some part of herself that was alien to the woman she'd been for a very long time urged her to find her voice and call him back, to ask him to stay and finish his coffee. Surely they could talk without anger, couldn't they? She opened her mouth, but nothing came out of it.

Keith walked around the counter and started to leave the kitchen, but then he took her completely by surprise and reversed direction in a fast-moving blur. Her back still to the refrigerator, he pinned her with his body pressed against hers and looked deeply into her shell-shocked eyes.

"You're a beauty, Andy," he said huskily. "You clearly said that we should go to bed together, and I did *not* misinterpret your meaning. You were thinking that we stir each other's emotions far too much to pretend we're unaware of it, and that maybe it was because we never really made love when we should have. You were hoping, I think, that one time together would kill the bad case of nerves we have around each other. You could be right, although I'm not positive of that. One time together might only open a dam of desire that neither of us could even imagine. But I'm willing to take that chance, if you are."

"I…didn't mean it the way you…took it."

"Oh?"

"I think I was…uh, trying to get across to you a completely different kind of…message." Truthfully she couldn't remember why she'd said something so unbelievably stupid. She should have known how he would take it. And she was still reacting stupidly to him, thinking that the ache in her chest could be a bunch of old memories that refused to stay buried.

But she had another, more urgent concern at the moment, an unfamiliar physical weakness. Her muscles felt rubbery and all but useless, her legs threatening to buckle, and if he wasn't pressed so tightly against her, she was quite certain that she would slide down the face of the refrigerator like a wave of hot liquid.

Nervously she licked her lips. Whatever else she did or didn't know, one thing was clear: she had to break this up and get him out of her house.

"You...I..." Stumbling over simple words was foreign and embarrassing, and she felt impossibly adolescent.

"What, sweetheart? Say it." Keith lowered his head so his lips were but a breath from hers. "Tell me what you want," he whispered.

What you want...what you want. The words repeated in her bewildered brain, for what she wanted was something she *hadn't* wanted in years. Even more painful to contemplate was why she would feel all silky and sensual now because of a man she didn't even like. She wished she weren't thinking such things.

Only now she couldn't push the tantalizing topic from her mind. Keith's body was hard and yet yielded to her female curves. She was dazed and yearning, aching in places that had felt nothing for so long.

So, what did she want? Her heart could have said the words if it could speak, but the part of her that *could* speak, her mouth, simply would not cooperate.

"I...I want you to leave," she said and stunned herself by sounding like a rusty spring.

Keith's dark eyes were traveling her face with a smoldering light. "And I want you," he said in a low-pitched, gravelly voice. "How are we going to align our differing desires?"

"We...we aren't," she whispered. "We...can't. We..." It was the last word she said before his lips settled on hers. A moan rose in her throat as her body caught fire. His nervy connecting of their bodies, his nearness, that low, bedroom voice in which he'd been speaking had all been foreplay, and it had worked. She slid her hands up his chest, locked them together behind his head and opened her mouth to suck on his tongue. Oh, what joy, she thought dizzily. *Why* had she relegated these incredible feelings to the trash bin after

Jerry's death? Other widows grieved and then lived again. Why hadn't she?

She wriggled herself closer to Keith and kissed him with a rare, ravenous hunger. Her feverish passion startled Keith so much that he broke the kiss and tilted his head back to scrutinize the features of her face. Was this real? He'd been hoping to arouse her, but had he really believed in his ability to do so? Something didn't feel quite right, though for the life of him he couldn't figure out what it might be. Andrea had never kissed him like this when they were both young and randy in college. Something was *very* odd here.

It struck him then that he could have her tonight, right now, in her own kitchen or wherever he chose. If ever a woman was ripe and lushly ready for lovemaking, it was Andrea, and it just didn't add up. Running hot and cold was one thing, but this was…well, it was astounding. Keith's heart sank. Something told him to get the hell out of there, and it seemed so ludicrous when this was what he'd been wanting from Andrea. But he couldn't take this to the next level. Not tonight, he couldn't.

He slid her arms from around his neck, kissed her lips lightly and said, "You were right, it's late. May I call you tomorrow?"

She was almost too thunderstruck to speak. Why had he stopped? She didn't want him to stop!

"Yes…I suppose," she mumbled.

"Good night. Sleep well." Keith walked out of the kitchen and in a few seconds she heard the front door open and close. What had just happened? she asked herself. Dazed and confused, she stumbled to a chair and fell into it. She sat there numbly and tried to find some sense in Keith's visit.

She couldn't do it. There was no sense to it, certainly none in the way he'd talked about making love and then kissed her the way he had, only to back off when she kissed back.

Strangely, though, when she finally went to bed and stared at the darkened ceiling, her thoughts were more on herself than on Keith's peculiar behavior. In fact, her own behavior was far more peculiar than his, and it made her cry to think about it.

She finally fell asleep with wet, teary eyes and a heavy heart.

Keith didn't go straight home from Andrea's house. Instead, he drove to the Cattleman's Club, parked and turned off the engine of his SUV. There were times when the club was more welcoming than his own home, and he started to get out to go inside when he spotted vehicles belonging to friends parked in the lot. They would call him over, ask him to join them, and those that knew him best would see that something was wrong and, with all good intentions, even ask him about his downcast demeanor.

And what would he say? You're looking at a fool. I had her in the palm of my hand and I walked away.

Heaving a sigh, he decided against going in but he didn't immediately restart the motor and leave. He sat behind the wheel staring through the windshield at nothing in particular, remembering that kiss and wondering…wondering with every cell in his body. Surely Andrea's response hadn't scared him off. No, he hadn't been scared. He'd been stunned, but why, for God's sake? Why wouldn't she be more passionate now? She'd been married, she was a mature woman and everyone learned and changed with time.

But as logical as that explanation was, it didn't sit right. The problem hadn't been Andrea's response, it had been his! How could he be so damned ambiguous about something he'd been so positive of wanting? He *still* wanted her! Didn't he?

Sighing, Keith tried and couldn't put it all together, the old memories—so many of them pure gold—with Andrea's consistently distant treatment of him since college, and now this. Why in heaven's name hadn't he stayed? Not just to make love, but to talk. To *really* talk. Damn, instead of confronting her ardent mood he'd run away like a schoolboy, red-faced after his first kiss.

He finally drove home, disgusted with himself and wondering who the real Andrea was these days.

Andrea began her early-morning run on Saturday with none of her normal exuberance. She felt listless, in fact, and hoped that some extra oxygen in her blood from physical exertion would bring her back to life. She always spent time at New Hope on Saturdays, and she didn't want to go in looking like the last rose of summer.

It was how she felt, though, and she only got as far as Royal Park when her willpower totally deserted her. Stumbling to one of the benches near the lake, she collapsed on it. In seconds, tears began filling her eyes, a humiliation in public. But it was very early and while there were some other early birds in the park, no one was close enough to see Andrea O'Rourke crying without a sound, just sitting there while tears dribbled down her cheeks.

She angrily dashed them away. There was something wrong with her, and she fully intended to find out what it was. Kissing Keith the way she had last night and then being turned down was more humiliating than crying in the park, for heaven's sake.

"Oh, stop it," she muttered and got up from the bench and ran for home.

Andrea put in her time at New Hope that day, but though she tried not to be impatient to be out of there, she couldn't enjoy her hours at the charity facility as she usually did. Perhaps *enjoyment* wasn't the right word to describe her work with New Hope, for every woman seeking shelter and protection there had a sad and sometimes brutal story to tell. But helping people who truly needed it had been giving Andrea a satisfying sense of purpose. Today, while not proud of it, she was more concerned with herself than anyone in the shelter.

Finally she was able to leave, and she drove home wishing she could shake her dark and gloomy mood. When she got home, she sat at her small, elegant desk in her den, checked her voice mail and listened to messages from last night's guests thanking her. Courtesy was a high priority with her friends, and the additional thanks were no surprise.

Neither was Keith's voice in her ear. "Andy, you said it was all right to phone today, so that's what I'm doing. Sorry I missed you, but maybe you'll call me back. My number is 555-2777. I'd like us to get together. We could have dinner out or simply meet at your house or mine for some conversation. Anywhere is fine with me, so name it if you have a preference. I'd just like to see you. Uh, guess that's it. Call me, please."

Andrea put down the phone and then sat numbly. For her, the day had been emotionally painful. She'd teetered all day on the very edge of a really powerful crying spell, and would seeing Keith again so soon change that? She found it hard to believe that it might.

Why was this happening to her? She hadn't found celibacy trying before this, probably because no other man had moved her in the way Keith had last night. Also, she really hadn't given any other man an opportunity to move her. Keith Owens had brought that obviously ignored and hidden side of herself into the sun, and why? How? Why him?

Why *not* him? she thought woefully. He *had* been her first love, after all.

Only she'd really known nothing at all about love at the time...certainly nothing of the physical side of love in college. All her fault, of course. She'd been so determined to be a virgin on her wedding night that she'd probably driven Keith away.

You most certainly did not drive him away! He did that himself by offering you a business proposition instead of offering you an engagement ring!

Yes, she'd been embarrassingly naive, but that had been a long time ago. She *hadn't* been even slightly naive last night and he'd walked away from her! Dammit, after all the chasing after her he'd done lately, she had a right to know why.

Reaching for the phone, she punched out Keith's number. He answered on the third ring.

"Hello," she replied to his greeting. "This is Andrea. I'm returning your call, and this may surprise you but I would like to get together this evening."

"This evening?" Keith echoed in surprise.

"Oh, didn't you mean tonight?"

"Yes...uh, yes! Tonight is great. Would you like to have dinner out?"

"No, I don't think so. Let's meet somewhere after dinner." She realized that she wasn't especially keen about his SUV showing up in her driveway again tonight, even though she really didn't care what the neighbors might think. But Keith was so well known in Royal, and deliberately inviting gossip didn't seem sensible, either. "How about..." She searched her mind for a place of privacy.

"Come to my house," Keith said brusquely. "I'll leave one of the garage doors open and you can park inside. No one will ever know you fell off the wagon and actually went to see a man."

She gasped. "Must you be so crude?"

"I was just beginning to believe that we both finally grew up," he retorted.

"Keith, I don't understand what's going on with us. Does that make me immature? I thought maybe if we did some talking...well, that's the reason I called. I...I'm not sure I know myself anymore and I sure as the devil don't know the man you are now."

"So all tonight is to you is a means to pick my brain. Okay, fine, I can live with that. I've been thinking we should do some talking anyhow. Maybe I don't know you anymore, either, and I want to, Andy, I want to know you in every way possible. What time should I expect you?"

After his statement of wanting to know her in every way possible she wondered if she shouldn't just cancel the whole thing. But she couldn't let sleeping dogs lie, not about this. He had finally succeeded in opening her eyes to the past, to the boy he'd been, the young man, to the many wonderful old memories she'd tried to bury, and he was *not* walking out of her life again as easily as he'd done in college.

"Around nine," she said flatly. "No, make it ten."

"After dark, huh?"

"Did you think I would deny it?"

"Andy, my sweet, I don't know *what* to think about anything you might say or do these days. But I'd like to. See you at ten."

Seven

Andrea paced and worried. Going to Keith's home bothered her. She wasn't ready for that step and should have thought the whole bizarre thing through better and had a specific meeting place in mind before calling him.

Irritated at her own reckless haste, she made a decision and dialed Keith's number again. When he answered she came right to the point.

"Andrea here. Are you free now?"

Keith was taken aback. "I'm hot and sweaty from working out in my home gym, but sure, I'm free. Well, maybe not free. You know the old joke. I might not be free, but I'm cheap."

"Yes," she said dryly. "I know the old joke. It doesn't apply, Keith. Not to me and not to you. We each come with loads of baggage."

"Meaning?"

"Thirty-eight years of baggage needs explanation?"

"Oh, I see what you mean. Okay, what's the pitch?"

"I've changed my mind about coming to your house and concealing my car in your garage. Lurking around in the shadows seems a bit too melodramatic. Anyhow, if you have the time now, I'd like us to meet in the park."

"Any particular place in the park?" he asked in his most pronounced Texas drawl, his way of letting someone know that he thought they just might be an egg or two short of a full dozen. Truth was, Andrea kept surprising him, and while some of her surprises were great, some were pretty far out and tough to swallow.

"Are you making fun of me?"

"Wouldn't dream of it. Where do you want to meet? It'll take me about twenty minutes to shower and make the drive."

"I intend to walk, so twenty minutes should be just about right. You remember where the old cannon is, don't you?"

"I know where it is, yes."

"Well, that's where I'll be."

"Fine. See you in a few."

Andrea hung up, then hurried to her bedroom to change into slacks and walking shoes. In minutes she was leaving the house and heading for the park. It was a glorious evening. Night was just beginning to fall, and the darkening of the sky combined with a spectacular sunset created a golden twilight. Hurrying along, she said hello to the people she encountered in her neighborhood without stopping to chat. An evening like this got folks outside, and she began worrying about how populated the park might be.

When she reached Royal Park, she relaxed considerably. There were people, quite a few of them, but no one was close to the old cannon, which resided on a square of cement and bore a bronze plaque honoring the bravery and patriotism of Texas men and women. Someone kept both the cannon and plaque polished, which always pleased Andrea although her thoughts were not on that small pleasure this evening.

She was on pins and needles, actually, anxious to talk to Keith and yet apprehensive. The truth was, now that she was here, what exactly was she so adamant about discussing with Keith? His college attitude? Hers? Good Lord, no.

Several benches faced the cannon, and Andrea chose one. She couldn't see the parking area from where she sat, which made watching for Keith rather difficult. She waited, grew impatient, checked her watch and waited some more. He was late.

Becoming more annoyed with his inconsiderate tardiness by the minute, she realized that people, especially those with small children, were leaving as darkness encroached on the lovely twilight. The park was emptying for the night and she was sitting in a particularly isolated spot. The old cannon was not near the children's play areas, nor was it near the lake or gazebo. It was, in fact, quite by itself on the south end of the large park, the main reason she'd chosen it for this meeting. But Keith wasn't there, and dusk was settling in quickly. There were lights in the park, of course, and heaven knew she wasn't normally a fraidy cat. Royal had a very low crime rate, but ever since the murder of that man who worked for Wescott Oil, Eric Chambers, everyone in town had been just a little bit on edge, a little more watchful. After all, the police appeared to be baffled and Eric's murderer could be anyone—even someone she knew!

That thought took her breath. Surely no one she knew could commit murder! Oh, what a horrible thing to think about at this particular time and place.

"Andrea?"

She nearly jumped out of her skin. Keith bounded around the bench and sat next to her. "Sorry I'm late. Just as I was about to leave, I received an important phone call. I couldn't cut it short. A business thing."

A "business" thing solely about Dorian Brady, which Keith couldn't possibly explain to Andrea. It was Sebastian who had called with the unnerving news that Dorian appeared to be preparing to leave town. "It's not certain, Keith, but it's a possibility. We have to step up our surveillance." They had set a meeting for first thing in the morning.

"And, of course, business *always* comes first," she intoned.

Frowning because she sounded much more knowledgeable than was possible, Keith peered at her. The only "business" of his she knew about was Owens Techware, and he replied in that vein. "At one time yes, but not anymore." He turned on the bench and settled his arm along the top of its back.

His arm touched Andrea's shoulders lightly. She was beautiful in the dusky light, her complexion glowing with good health and her dark hair a perfect frame for her perfect face. Oddly, they were dressed alike, in khaki slacks and white shirts. It would have been fun to kid about the two of them in matching outfits, but Andrea didn't laugh easily these days. Something deeply personal kept Andrea walking a very straight line, in fact, and Keith had only bits and pieces of clues about what it might be. All he could think of was that her marriage hadn't been as magical as she'd tried to make him believe.

But he had as many questions about himself as he did about Andrea. Last night's kiss between them had sizzled, and he'd run. That still puzzled him and even made him wonder if he would run again.

At any rate, he wasn't making a pass at the moment, he was merely getting more comfortably positioned to view Andrea as they talked. "Actually, my ex called my dedication to business ruthless. She said I had tunnel vision," he added.

"You're sorry about all that now, of course."

"Sorry? No, I'm not sorry. I accomplished what I set out to do, and Candace knew who and what I was when we married. I didn't change, she did. While we were dating she couldn't praise and encourage my ambition enough. In her eyes I was perfect, and I was besotted enough to believe she meant it. Well, she meant it until after the ceremony and I swear to God that we weren't married five minutes before she started trying to change me into someone else."

"I'm sure you're exaggerating. Five minutes?"

"I'm not exaggerating by much, Andy. Answer me this, did you change your husband?"

"Marriage changes everyone to a certain extent."

"But did you deliberately *try* to turn him into someone other than the man you married?"

Andrea paused to think, to remember, and if she were to be totally honest, she would have to say yes, because she had tried desperately to make Jerry listen to his doctors. One could say she'd nagged him all the way to the grave.

Oh, God, what a morbid subject! "Let's talk about something else," she said sharply.

"My question made you uncomfortable."

"Yes, it did!"

"Which leads me to believe you tried as hard to change Jerry as Candace did me."

"Look, that's all over with, for each of us. I don't care to discuss your marriage or mine. It's certainly not the reason I asked you to meet with me."

"Okay, what *is* the reason?"

With tension tightening her every cell, Andrea stared off across the darkening park. Only a few people were still there, and they were sitting or strolling near the lake.

Finally, reluctantly she spoke. It might not be the best beginning to a conversation with such a blurred topic, but it was the best she could come up with. "I don't know who I am anymore."

Keith cocked his eyebrow. "And you're blaming me?"

"Maybe. The only thing I know for sure is that this…the discontentment and confusion I've been feeling lately were *not* part of my personality before the Cattleman's Club's charity ball." She turned her head to look at him. "If you're not to blame, what is?"

He returned her gaze and they sat without moving and looked at each other for a long time. Finally he said softly, "I never forgot you, Andy."

She jerked her head around to break their locked gazes. "You have no right to tell me that. It…it's only upsetting and I don't believe it anyway. You forgot me the minute you walked out after our big fight in college. I made a fool of myself screaming and crying and you had no more sympathy for me than you would've had for a dog with a splinter in its paw.''

''That's not true.''

''It bloody *is* true! Forget it. I don't want to talk about that, either.''

''Well, at least we're gaining ground through the process of elimination,'' he drawled. ''I expect that eventually you'll get to the topic that really brought about this meeting. I say bless it, whatever it is, because it's getting harder and harder for me to come up with an excuse or a ploy to see you. Of course, I can always hang around Kiddie Kingdom.''

She stiffened. ''I wish you would stop doing that.''

''I know you do, and if you'd start seeing me…as in man takes woman to dinner…or something of that nature…then I wouldn't have to attend your classes. Those kids sure are cute, though.''

''When did you start liking children? Or even seeing them and admitting they are part and parcel of this world, for that matter?'' There was nothing complimentary in her questions or tone of voice.

''I didn't,'' he said flatly. ''Until now. What I'd like to know…and have asked myself more than once…is why I never wanted kids and now…'' He stopped, because he'd only recently been having these peculiar thoughts about sons and daughters, wondering why nearly everyone else he knew wanted babies and he never had. ''I really don't know my own mind on that subject,'' he said quietly.

''Except for the fact that you never liked kids and now you do. Maybe you're in the process of becoming a nice guy. Have you considered that possibility?''

He let out a surprised laugh. ''Andy, I've *always* been a nice guy.'' He crooked his arm behind her and gently touched her hair.

''No, you weren't, and please don't start getting all touchy-feely." She slanted her head away from his hand. "I'm here to talk, nothing more." Was that true? she wondered. Just sitting next to him was warming her blood, so maybe all that need-to-talk stuff was pure nonsense.

"So talk," Keith said. "Tell me what's on your mind."

Andrea swallowed nervously. How did a woman discuss really personal problems with the guy causing them? There really was only one way, wasn't there? By beating around the bush?

"I...I've been wondering if you, uh, remember my parents," she said, stumbling over her own tongue because she never had been a proficient liar.

"Your parents?" Keith frowned, for she'd really surprised him with that remark. "Well, I guess I do. Not very clearly, though. And more from a child's point of view than from later years. Do you remember mine?"

"Yours?" she said densely, before grasping his side of this strange conversation. "Oh, your parents. Well, yes, I have some memories of them."

"Is that why we're here, meeting in a public place to discuss our parents? Andy, that's pretty weird," he said teasingly.

"I know it is," she replied grimly, not at all amused by his attempt to make her laugh. She immediately realized her mistake, for she could feel his eyes boring into her, looking for answers. She'd aroused his curiosity, and there wasn't a reason in the world for them to be talking about their parents. Especially since she'd requested this meeting and given him the impression that she needed to talk about something important.

She forced a laugh, because now she was boxed in and *had* to play along. "It's *very* weird," she agreed with false cheerfulness. "But my childhood memories of Mother and Dad are so sketchy that lately I've been bothered by it something awful. Unlike you, I remember their later years better. It's the kid stuff that eludes me. Would you mind telling me what you recall of them? Tell me anything...events...things they said…things you might have overheard or seen by accident.''

Keith was truly taken aback. After last night he'd expected some sort of discussion, possibly accusatory and disapproving about one of two things, his kissing her or his *not* kissing her more.

But he decided to play along and see where this led. ''Andy, my childhood memories are mostly about us, you and me. Both your parents and mine are shadowy background figures. Hell, my folks were so busy with social obligations that I rarely got to eat dinner with them. Dad was a dynamo, I recall that quite vividly, and Mother shopped.'' He laughed and sounded genuinely amused. ''She shopped in Houston and Dallas and New York and Paris. Can you even imagine making shopping the highlight of your life?''

''And my folks?'' she prompted.

''They were around more, but I think you answered mostly to the housekeeper, or whatever she was. Yes, I'm sure of it. She was a heavyset lady that came outside and called your name every hour or so. Do you remember her?''

''Mrs. Dorsett! We called her Ducky Dorsett behind her back because she waddled when she walked. I haven't thought of Ducky in years.'' Andrea was beginning to get a real sense of the distant past. ''My mother was a very beautiful woman,'' she murmured.

''Was she?''

''Extremely beautiful. I have boxes of photos and snapshots in the attic to prove it. There's one of her and Dad in my bedroom, and I swear they both look like movie stars. He was handsome and she was glamorous, with never a hair out of place and always, *always* dressed to the nines. Now I remember that very well.'' Andrea laughed quietly and added nostalgically, ''Sometimes when I went into a room where she was, she would say, 'There's that dirty little girl of mine,' for I was forever making mud pies or doing something outdoors that soiled my clothes.''

Keith chuckled softly. "We started out clean every morning, but we sure never worried about getting dirty."

"Very true."

Was this innocuous conversation actually the reason for this after-dark meeting? Keith wondered. He couldn't make himself believe it. This had to be about last night, about why he'd kissed her so passionately and then abruptly left. But how could he explain it to Andrea when he didn't understand it himself?

Gently he took her hand. "You're really thinking about last night, aren't you?" he said in a low voice.

She turned her head to look at him. "I've thought about it, yes. Haven't you?"

"Constantly."

She was glad he'd forced the issue. It was time to *stop* beating around the bush. "Keith, what happened?"

"I wish to hell I knew."

"But…" They had only scratched the tip of the iceberg, and she wanted to keep talking.

It had gotten so dark that Keith could just barely make out her face. All the same he could tell how troubled she was. He hadn't been kind last night, and she deserved better.

"I'm sorry," he whispered.

"That…that's it, all you can say about it?"

He searched for an addendum to his apology. "You said that you haven't been happy since the charity ball. I hope you know that it wasn't my intent *ever* to make you unhappy."

"Did I say unhappy? I believe I said confused and discontented."

"Well, a woman could hardly be in a rollicking happy mood if she's all confused and dissatisfied."

"Did I say dissatisfied? Stop putting words in my mouth, for heaven's sake. The ones I used are disturbing enough. I certainly don't need your suggestions to add to the list. Besides, why would you even think the word *dissatisfied* in connection with me?"

"Because of last night," he said in a low, barely audible voice. "I wish I hadn't left when I did. I've wished it all day. We wanted each other...we *needed* each other...and for some crazy, incomprehensible reason I walked out instead of doing what my heart and body ached for. I'm still aching, in case you're wondering."

"I...I'm not," she whispered, too deeply shaken to do anything but lie. Certainly she couldn't admit to the aches and yearnings she'd endured and tried so hard to ignore all day. All of last night, as well. Desires she'd never felt so intensely before were the reason she was on this park bench tonight, after all, the *only* reason she'd returned his phone call, in all honesty.

"After the explosive passion between us last night, I find it pretty hard to believe that you don't give a damn about my feelings tonight. Andy, I *care* about you, won't you at least consider that?"

"How can I worry about your feelings when my own are overwhelming me?"

"They are?" Keith moved closer to her and curled his arm around the back of her neck. "Sweetheart, if you only know what hearing that does to me."

No! She couldn't pretend everything was all right when it wasn't. She jerked loose of his embrace and got to her feet. "I'm in an emotional quandary and all you can think of is..."

Keith had gotten up when she did, and he put his arms around her and pulled her up against himself. "I can cure your emotional quandary," he said gruffly before uniting their lips in a breath-stealing kiss.

At first Andrea tried to push him away, but then she began kissing him back, exactly as she'd done last night in her kitchen. Moaning deep in her throat, she leaned into him. He slid his big hands down her back, cupped her buttocks and urged her forward. What she felt against her belly was perfectly normal and not surprising; what *she* felt because of

such undeniable proof of his desire made her dizzy as a spinning top.

"Andy...sweet, sweet Andy," he whispered raggedly between hungry kisses.

Was *he* sweet? No, she couldn't call him sweet. He was
big and sexy and overpowering her senses. She wanted what
he did, and to worry over *why* seemed utterly silly. What did
it matter when her body was reacting all on its own?

But when he unbuttoned her shirt and buried his face in
the cleavage of her breasts, she gasped, "Not here, Keith.
Not in the park."

He didn't argue. Instead he buttoned her shirt, took her
hand and began leading her to the parking lot and his car.
His SUV, actually, with its marvelous fold-down seats. It
took him about one minute to create a lovers' nook in the
back of his vehicle, and since his windows were tinted
against the glare of the hot Texas sun, no passerby would be
able to see in.

She didn't say no when he beckoned her inside, but she
did steal a long, shaky breath. It was time she knew it all,
felt everything she should have felt in college with him.

She wasn't thinking with her brain at all. Her body was
directing the play, every act of it, and it did not want to say
no. She lay down with him, and when he removed his shirt,
rolled it into a ball and put it under her head for a pillow,
she laid her hand on his cheek and whispered, "Maybe you
are sweet."

"What I am is on fire," he said thickly, and spread himself
across her legs and warm, sexy body to take her mouth in a
kiss that conveyed the truth of his words. His bare skin was
hot, and his heat even came through his pants. She reveled
in that heat, for it intensified her own.

Gasping for air between kisses they wriggled out of their
clothes. Andrea had never made love in the back of a car,
and she suffered a momentary regret over doing something
at her age that she probably should have done twenty years
ago. Unquestionably she should have experienced this ur-

gency of wildfire desire before, whether in a car, a bed or leaning against a wall. Oh, yes, she'd read about this kind of feeling, this wild lovemaking, she just hadn't experienced it herself.

She dug her fingertips into Keith's back and writhed beneath him, absorbing every tiny nuance of hot bare skin deliciously chafing hot bare skin.

Keith groaned silently. He didn't have protection with him. Why would he? It was pretty lax of him to be without it tonight, though, because he'd known in advance that he was meeting Andrea and had still been frustrated as hell over his stupidity last night. He should have been prepared for what was happening, given all that had been going on between them since the ball.

But he wasn't prepared, and he would cut off his tongue before telling Andrea they couldn't make love. Besides, would a baby upset the applecart for him? It sure would have in times past, but now?

Hadn't he recently read somewhere that many, many women were choosing to have their babies after forty? Why, Andrea wasn't *even* forty yet, so she would undoubtedly create an incredible child.

"I adore you...love you," he whispered against her lips.

She knew he'd said something, but she was in another world, one in which everything was sensation and pleasure and joyful surrender, and she didn't ask him to repeat it. She gave him everything she was, her heart, her soul, her body, without even knowing how deeply she was involving herself in the dangerous game of truly great sex.

When he entered her she cried out. He froze in alarm. "Andy...darlin'...am I hurting you?"

"No...no." Her head moved back and forth on her shirt-pillow, and she clutched at him. "Don't stop...don't stop," she moaned.

He tried to be especially gentle, but he couldn't be, not when it was Andy beneath him, the woman he'd wanted all of his life. Nearly blinded by passion and the fierce pounding of his own blood, he rode her hard. Her legs rose to encircle his hips, and as dazed as he was he was still aware of every sound she made, from her gasping little breaths to her hoarse cries of unabashed pleasure.

And then she cried out, ''Oh, Keith…Keith…'' and he knew she was almost there. He held himself in check through sheer willpower, and when she went over the top, so did he. They rocked together for an eternity, it seemed, squeezing every drop of pleasure from their simultaneous release.

But that particular eternity ended, as that sort of bliss always does, and Andrea found herself sweaty and wide-eyed, pinned beneath Keith in the back of his SUV in Royal Park.

Eight

After dropping Andrea off, the drive home didn't take long, nor was there much traffic. That was a relief, as Keith couldn't keep his mind on the road no matter what he did. This night's events were burned into his brain, all but blurring his vision, certainly making concentration on anything else particularly difficult. The physical effects he felt were surprising and confusing. After such incredible lovemaking he should be relaxed and serenely happy, and instead he felt tight as a drum.

After driving Andrea to her home from the park, he'd asked to go in with her. She had stammered out a few words, "No...please...not tonight," and he'd experienced the strangest rush of relief. That was something to wonder about: Why in heaven's name would he be relieved over Andrea's haste to end an absolute dream of an evening?

Keith's eyebrows nearly met in a troubled frown. There was something terribly wrong in his attitude at the moment, but what was it? Certainly he wasn't afraid of serious involvement, was he? For days he'd done everything but stand on his head to capture Andrea's notice, to regain her attention, to make her see him as she once had, and he'd succeeded, too, or they never would have made love. And now, when everything seemed to be going his way, he was fearful?

"Preposterous," he muttered. Hitting the remote control that opened the iron gate securing his driveway, he drove in, pushed another button and opened one of the four doors on his garage. He walked into his house with a scowl on his face, for he didn't like the direction of either his feelings or his thoughts.

His relationship with Andrea was different from any other. Vastly different from that he'd had with his ex and those he'd had with women he'd dated before and after his marriage. Actually, he hardly remembered them; they simply hadn't been important. He respected women but...but *he loved Andrea!*

That was the crux of his startling misery, he realized in one fell, rather shocking swoop: he was totally, madly and almost painfully in love with Andrea. He'd suspected it before, but there were miles of variances, discrepancies and disparities between suspecting something and knowing it for fact. Doubts and what-ifs had flown the coop, completely deserting him. He was on his own now, a man who had fervently pursued one very special woman, had reached the finish line and was now in a sweat over what to do next.

He didn't understand himself and it was a foreign, discomfiting sensation. What he needed was some time to sort through this whole thing, to figure out what was really going on in the pit of his stomach and to come up with some answers.

Instead of going to bed, Keith wrote a note for Gabriella, phoned Sebastian to tell him that he wouldn't be at tomorrow morning's meeting and where he'd be if he was truly needed, packed a bag with some changes of clothing, then carried it and his briefcase out to the garage. He drove from town heading south, refusing to look at his departure as running away. There was nothing wrong with a man taking a few days by himself to do a little soul-searching.

At least, that was what he kept telling himself.

Andrea awoke at two in the morning, uneasy and apprehensive. She lay still and listened, wondering if some outside noise had brought her out of a sound sleep so abruptly, but she heard nothing unusual. Still not satisfied, she got out of bed and walked through the dark house. Everything was normal; obviously her middle-of-the-night-jitters were internally caused.

Well, she thought with a sigh, why wouldn't she have jumpy nerves? Actually, it was surprising that she'd gotten any sleep at all tonight.

Then, suddenly, she knew what had awakened her: a dream. It was vague and fuzzy now, mostly unconnected images of the past, not frightening, certainly not eerie enough to pull her from sleep, and yet it had. She didn't normally pay much attention to dreams, but considering her free and easy behavior with Keith in his SUV—and the emotional turmoil with which she'd fallen asleep, wasn't she bound to have suffered a few disturbing dreams?

Doubting that she would sleep again right away if she went back to bed, and with a decided sense of nostalgia, she went to the attic and returned to the living room with an armful of family photo albums. Before starting on them, though, she went to the kitchen, prepared a pot of herbal tea—she certainly didn't need caffeine tonight—and finally settled down on the sofa with tea at the ready and the stack of albums.

Some rated only a quick glance and she turned the pages swiftly. But then she came to the one filled with snapshots of her. Who had taken all of these she wondered—her mother, her father, Mrs. Dorsett?

Almost immediately she realized that Keith was in nearly every picture with her. A little brown boy, usually without a shirt, often without shoes, making faces at the camera or caught unaware while in the midst of a game. There he was in his pirate hat, Andrea thought with a soft smile of remembrance. For a while one summer they'd been on a pirate kick and their fort had been a ship at sea. For weeks they had fought off imaginary bad pirates—they'd been *good* pirates, of course—and saved innocent people from their evil clutches.

As she turned pages, the boy got bigger. She must have been growing, too, but her growth wasn't as obvious as Keith's. His shoulders became broader, bony for a while, then gradually filled out with muscle. He'd been a handsome little boy, a beautiful, adorable child, to be perfectly honest, and he'd grown into an extremely handsome adult. He had remarkable good looks, above-average intelligence and an athletic, muscular body. Andrea had to admit he was pretty much the perfect specimen.

She picked up her cup for a swallow of tea. Keith should have had children. He would have fathered incredible children...attractive, smart, active little replicas of himself. Of course, his ex-wife's genes would have shown in their children, as well. What was her name? Andrea couldn't remember the woman's name, but she did recall how pretty she'd been. And only from a few brief sightings, too. Funny what one stored in one's memory banks, Andrea thought.

For instance, the fact that she and Keith had made love without protection last night. Not that she would ever forget one second of last night. How could she, when she was so torn between resentment for having missed the blood-boiling excitement of wild, raw sex for so long and an uneasy joy over discovering her sensual side again?

Andrea sighed, for she hadn't encouraged one single man's interest since Jerry's demise. There'd been several very nice men who had asked her out, or at least given her the impression that they would like to ask her out, if she would only give them some indication of interest. She hadn't, of course, not ever. Her hands-off attitude had always served her just fine, but now she wondered about it.

She pondered that for a while, then for some reason again mulled over Keith's carelessness about protection. Not that he'd been the only careless person in that passion pit of a vehicle he owned. After all, she was as responsible for what they'd done as he was.

But surely she needn't worry about pregnancy, need she? Frowning suddenly, she got up and raced for a calendar.

"Oh my God," she whispered after calculating dates. She was smack dab in the middle of her fertile period. Feeling weak as a newborn kitten she stumbled back to the sofa and collapsed. She could be pregnant this very minute! What if she was? What if she and Keith had made a baby at Royal Park?

Andrea's body was suddenly taut with nervous tension. Just how would Keith take *that* bit of news, should it be true? Why in God's name hadn't he been concerned about the possible outcome of unprotected sex? Had he simply gotten too carried away to remember protection? That explanation made the most sense, although it really made no sense at all. Mature men and women did not take chances like that.

You did!

Yes, she had, and if she *had* conceived…? Her heart began pounding. A baby? A child?

Stacking the photo albums on the far end of the sofa, Andrea curled her legs under her to think about this very startling possibility.

At the same time something began coalescing in her brain…all the fragments of her thoughts since scanning the snapshots…Keith's beauty and intelligence…the odds of his fathering beautiful, healthy children…her excellent health. She could be pregnant with Keith's baby, and could any woman hope for a more physically and intellectually perfect father for her child?

But he didn't love her, and she didn't…well, she couldn't possibly love him, could she? Not that she hadn't loved him in the past. She'd all but worshipped the ground Keith Owens had walked on, but she'd buried all of those lovely feelings after the night of their big fight.

Why, it was utterly ridiculous to even wonder if she loved

Keith. What she felt was simply desire, just her response to his ability to transport her to the stars with kisses and surely the most incredible male body in all of Texas.

They had proved their feelings—or lack of—in the back of Keith's SUV, hadn't they? Sexual desire had run rampant, but love? Romance? No, indeed, there had been neither of those emotions spurring them on.

If she really were pregnant, should she even tell him about it? He might figure it out, but would he care? One thing was certain, she would not marry a man she didn't love and who didn't love her merely because of a child. She knew how to raise a child without a father. Dozens of women right here in Royal were single moms doing a very good job of it. And who understood toddlers better than a nursery-school teacher?

But what would she tell her friends? Pouring more tea into her cup, telling herself to calm down and not succeeding, she pondered people's reactions to her having a child without a husband.

But it was such a simple solution, really. Women all over the globe were having babies with the use of sperm banks. That was what she could tell her friends, prepare them ahead of time for the big event, in fact. "I want a child and I'm going to that fertility clinic in Dallas." Everyone would understand; everyone would *accept*, because her friends knew how much she adored children. A few might be surprised that she would go to such lengths to have a baby at her age, but perhaps her age would work in her favor. After all, how many years did she still have to conceive, carry and give birth to her own child?

And Keith probably wouldn't care even if he *did* figure it out. He'd wanted her sexually, perhaps he always had. It was entirely possible that one time in her arms was enough for him. She might never hear from him again!

Andrea's heart sank. Considering his sweet good-night kiss after driving her home and then his plea to come in with her, once probably wasn't enough. It was undoubtedly going to be up to her to end their relationship and put plenty of time between tonight—if she was actually pregnant, of course—and the future.

Could she do it? She had mastered her facade of dignity and decorum to protect and guard her privacy, but she could not claim to be overloaded with courage. This would take a shocking amount of deceit. Not just once or twice, either, but for the rest of her life. She couldn't factor leaving Royal in her plan, for it was home and the thought of living anywhere else, where she knew no one, was horrifying. No, she would stay put and should her and Keith's paths cross in the future—it was bound to happen—she would deal with it.

It all seemed so feasible, so possible if she kept her cool. Envisioning telling Keith that she was pregnant and watching him wriggle out of any sort of permanent arrangement because he was going to be a father would be more painful for Andrea than not telling him at all.

And so, she decided again and with a tear in her eye, if it were true she would have her baby by herself and raise it by herself. Tears suddenly dribbled down her cheeks. She'd given up long ago on ever having a child, but here was her dearest wish in the palm of her hand, or it seemed to be. Something very powerful—instinct, female intuition—told her that she *had* conceived tonight. She'd heard women say, "I knew I was pregnant the moment we made love," and now she knew exactly how they had felt. She wept with both joy and sadness.

She finally returned to bed and eventually slept again, but what had seemed sane, sensible and attainable in the middle of the night seemed nothing short of appallingly dishonest in the morning. Rubbing her eyes wearily, totally discarding her ridiculous notion of being pregnant after making love only one time and then deliberately keeping it from Keith because he didn't love her, she hauled herself out of bed, changed to running clothes and left the house. But she ran with more care, as she knew she would do everything until she found out if she was pregnant or not.

A long hot shower felt wonderful when she got back, and after some fruit and cereal for breakfast she got dressed for church.

That Sunday morning she drove past the church she usually attended and took the road to Midland. It was only fifty miles away, and she would make the eleven o'clock service. She did that occasionally, but never had she made that drive with such a heavy conscience. The serenity of the lovely old church and the beauty of the holy songs from the choir soothed Andrea's troubled spirit.

Back in Royal she decided to stop at the diner for lunch before going home. After locating a parking place only a short distance from the eatery, Andrea went in. If one wanted to touch base with stability or some sense of longevity, this was the place to come, she thought as she looked around for an empty booth. The Royal Diner never changed. Various employees had come and gone through the years, but the cracked red Formica that topped counter, tables and booths was almost comforting in its constancy. Also, any patron who had eaten there before knew that Manny, the cook, served up some mighty fine fare, especially his burgers and coconut cream pies.

Andrea walked to the only empty booth, sat down and then took note of the other people in the place. Recognizing several, she smiled, nodded and tried to look as cool and collected as she usually did. The courtesy was returned, but no one got up and came over to her booth. Glad that the other patrons were only acquaintances and she wouldn't have to get involved in any sort of conversation, she waited for the waitress.

A glass of water and a plastic-coated menu were set in front of her. Andrea looked up to say thanks and saw Laura Edwards, who seemed to be even more haggard than she'd been at the Cattleman's Ball.

"Hello, Laura," Andrea said quietly, forgetting her own problems for the moment.

"Hello."

"You remember me, don't you?"

"Yes, ma'am. Would you like a few minutes to look over the menu, or are you ready to order now?"

Andrea frowned slightly, for Laura's entire demeanor was distant and unfriendly. "I'll order now…a hamburger, well done, and a chocolate malt."

"Thanks." Laura hurried away.

Andrea felt truly rebuffed, but Laura's unnecessary coldness only made Andrea more certain than ever that something was terribly amiss in the waitress's life. Laura had lost weight, and the circles under her eyes evidenced a rocky road of some sort; those signs pointed to an abusive relationship in Andrea's opinion, for she'd seen that same haunted, scared-rabbit expression on the faces of battered women who'd sought safety at the New Hope shelter.

Sighing over her helplessness with Laura—neither she nor anyone else could ease another person's burdens if they refused all offers of assistance—Andrea turned her thoughts back to her own worries. If Keith decided to stay hot on her trail, there was no way she could keep him away. Hadn't she tried to do exactly that since the ball? She could decide to ignore him *and* tell him to leave her alone till she was blue in the face and he would still keep turning up like a bad penny, if he chose to. What did he want from her, other than the obvious?

Thinking of herself as any man's sex toy made her feel squeamish in the stomach and she hailed Laura. When the waitress came over, Andrea asked, "Is it too late to cancel my order? I'm not feeling very well."

"Came on you just like that?" Laura intoned.

"I'm sorry, but there's no way I could eat…anything. If you can't cancel, I'll just pay for it now and leave."

"Let me check with Manny." She hurried off.

Andrea took a sip of water and tried to will away the nausea. Everyone has problems, she told herself. You certainly can't get so upset that you become physically ill over yours.

Laura came back. "It's fine. You don't have to pay."

"Thank you, Laura." Andrea laid down two one-dollar bills. "For your trouble," she murmured.

"You weren't any trouble."

"Laura, do you still have the card I gave you the night of the ball?" Andrea had to ask. Whether Laura wanted help or not, she had to offer it.

"I...think so."

Andrea quickly dug in her purse. "I'm going to give you another one. I know something's wrong, and while I suspect what it is, I can't be sure unless you talk about it. At the same time I understand your reluctance to confide in anyone. But if things get too bad to deal with on your own, please, please call me."

Laura took the card and slipped it in a pocket of her uniform. "Thanks, Andrea."

"You're welcome." Andrea slid from the booth.

"I hope you feel better."

"I'm sure I will." Actually, Andrea started feeling better the second she was outside. It must have been the smell of all that greasy food, she thought as she began walking toward her car. She'd have a bowl of soup at home. Besides, she really wasn't all that hungry.

She had so much to think about that the afternoon flew by without her realizing it. It was about seven that evening that Keith's silence began to seem unusual. He really didn't give a damn about her, she thought morosely, not even a little, nor did he respect her enough to call the morning after. The entire *day* after, to be more accurate.

After an hour or so of beating herself up with that sort of self-inflicted misery, something finally gelled in her brain. Keith hadn't called because he wasn't going to call. Not ever again. He'd gotten what he'd wanted all along, and that had been the end of it for him.

Andrea had considered that scenario before, but now that she believed it with all her heart, her legs got shaky and she had to sit down. After a few minutes her pulse rate had quickened fearfully and her throat had gotten too dry to even swallow. Hurrying to the kitchen for a glass of water, she stood at the sink to drink it while tears coursed down her cheeks. *Keith had gotten the only thing he'd wanted from her!*

"You fool," she whispered raggedly, nearly choking on a sob. Why did this hurt so much? Wasn't it what she'd wanted all along?

Or had she really been hoping for the opposite and kidding herself?

Nine

Two weeks later, Andrea tended her class of toddlers with only half her mind on them; the other half was focused on that small empty chair at the back of the room and the painful fact of Keith's ongoing silence. She was past cursing herself for a fool and now she merely felt empty.

Using flash cards bearing numbers and letters of the alphabet in bright colors, she numbly went through the motions of testing her little ones' level of recognition. Later, when she read to them she recalled how enchantingly Keith had read the "cluck-cluck" story. Wondering if she should really believe that he'd suddenly started to like children, as he'd told her, Andrea pursed her lips angrily.

Oddly, anger revived her pride and sense of dignity, and when it came time to leave for the day she exited the building with her head held high and not so much as a glimmer of hope that Keith would be waiting for her in the parking lot. He wasn't, of course, and she got in her car and drove home actually relishing the fury she felt. She might never get the chance to tell him face-to-face how much she despised him, but then again she might, and *that* would give her boundless pleasure!

By the middle of the week, Andrea was weary of living on rage.

That morning, she had driven to an unfamiliar shopping center with a massive drug store and purchased two home pregnancy tests. The drive back to Royal had been conducted with a great deal of anxiety, all because of those upcoming tests. She wanted to know and she *didn't* want to know, and it bothered Andrea terribly to be so ambiguous. But this was not a trivial matter. This was quite possibly the most *un*trivial undertaking of her life.

The first thing she had done when she'd gotten home was to check her voice mail. There had been brief messages from two women friends who had merely called to chat. That was all. Andrea had been disappointed that Keith had not called, even though she wasn't sure she wanted to hear from him.

She sat on her bed and gingerly took out the two packaged pregnancy tests, almost as though they had teeth and the ability to bite her. This was nerve-wracking, she acknowledged, probably because she wanted so passionately to have a child. She'd *always* wanted a child, and if the tests came out negative she was going to be terribly disappointed.

An hour later she was weeping quietly, but not from disappointment. Both tests had come out positive: she was pregnant! She had some decisions to make, primarily whether she was going to follow her usual routine of not teaching during the summer months. Kiddie Kingdom was open year-around, with two- to four-week break intervals scattered among four approximately two-month terms. Most of the school's employees took one of those terms off and Andrea had always chosen the summer term for her annual break. This year, of course, was different from any other. Her decision now wasn't about taking one break but whether she should completely retire from teaching. First, though, before she did anything so rash as that, she planned to see an obstetrician. She was convinced of her condition, but she *was* thirty-eight and this was her first child. Making sure that everything was all right seemed crucial to her.

Her friend Rebecca surprised her with a phone call and some questions that afternoon. "Andrea, is something wrong? I haven't heard from you recently and I was worried. What's the matter, Andrea? Surely you know you can tell me anything."

The only thing Andrea knew for sure was that she couldn't tell anyone anything. Her friends were good people, wonderful people, but Andrea did not feel close enough to any one of them to let go of her natural reticence and tell all. After all, there'd been nothing to confide for years and years. Her life had been an open book until Keith had manipulated his way back into it, and what could she say about that? "Oh, by the way, I made love with Keith Owens in the back of his SUV, and now I'm pregnant." The mere thought of such a confession gave her cold chills.

Andrea's fury finally diminished enough to permit her to wonder about Keith. While she pondered her teaching career and a summer break versus retirement, something in the back of her mind urged her to locate him. Just knowing where he was and what he was doing would relieve a lot of her tension. And if by some small miracle she actually got to speak to him, she could coldly and calmly tell him what a louse he was and then hang up. Why it would be so satisfying to lambaste him with dignity and then be the one to hang up, she didn't know, especially when she considered the situation. But she was just so darned hurt by his ongoing silence. How dared he treat her so shabbily?

She finally did it. Nervous and rattled, she dialed Keith's home number. His phone rang twice before a female voice said, "Owens residence."

Andrea asked for Mr. Owens and heard, "Mr. Owens is not at home. Would you like to leave a message?"

"Uh, no. No, thank you. I'll call again, uh, later." Andrea

hung up and weakly fell into a chair to recoup her courage, for now that she'd made one call, she *had* to make a second.

It took about five minutes to gather enough courage to dial Keith's computer software business. A woman answered again. "Owens Techware. How may I direct your call?"

"I need to speak to Mr. Owens, please."

"I'm sorry, but Mr. Owens is not in."

"Oh. Well, do you know when he will be in?"

"I'm sorry, I do not. Would you care to leave your name and number?"

"No, thank you." Again Andrea hung up. He wasn't home and he wasn't at his place of business. Could he possibly be hanging out at the Cattleman's Club today?

She looked up the number and dialed it. "Cattleman's Club," a male voice said in her ear.

"Hello. I'm trying to locate Keith Owens. It's not an emergency but it is important that I speak to him. Is he there, by any chance?"

"Nope. Sorry. Do you wanna leave a message in case he comes in? We got a bulletin board, you know. I could post your call."

"No…no, thank you." Shuddering at the thought of her name and phone number being posted for all to see on a bulletin board in the Cattleman's Club, Andrea hung up for the third and final time. Either Keith was out of town or in hiding.

She opted for "in hiding," the big jerk.

Even with the consistent use of sunscreen, Keith's skin had darkened to its usual summer mahogany. He'd driven nonstop from Royal to the house he owned just south of the border in Mexico, a long drive but worth it. His flat-roof, southwestern-style house was situated within a stone's throw from the lapping waves of the Gulf of Mexico and had been his private getaway since his divorce. A small fishing village was within walking distance, and he took the walk every day to purchase fresh fish, shrimp, locally grown vegetables and homemade bread baked by some of the ladies of the town. He also bought Mexican beer and ice, and he spent most of his time on the verandah of his house sipping ice-cold beer and watching seagulls and the water.

After two weeks he still had no answers. Or at least not the definitive answer he wanted, the one that satisfied the restlessness of his mind and body. Thus, the question remained to haunt him: Why had he so fervently chased Andrea and then gotten confused when he caught her? Good Lord, he'd even had thoughts of babies and Andrea as his wife before everything went weird on him.

Yes, everything, he told himself. Andrea hadn't been at all thrilled over his successful breach of her personal ethics, which she'd conveyed very effectively by refusing his request to go in with her after he'd driven her home. That night with Andrea, she'd been hotter than live coals in the back of his SUV and then, for no reason he could give logic to, she'd reverted back to pure ice. Strange woman, no doubt about it.

At any rate, the only conclusion Keith had reached in two weeks of soul-searching was that he and Andrea probably weren't destined to be together. Wasted time, he thought, wasted effort. He might as well go home.

But the next morning was so incredibly beautiful, with a cool breeze off the Gulf and that perfect view from his verandah of the water and small fishing craft that he never tired of looking at, he decided to stay for one more day.

It was that afternoon that he thought of asking Andrea to join him. Maybe they still had a chance of making things work for them. She might very well refuse for legitimate reasons, or she could simply cut him cold, but he really did want to figure the two of them out and why shouldn't she be here going through the stress of the inquisition with him? Besides, she might enjoy the view as much as he did.

After debating the issue until long after the sun had set, he finally placed the call.

Andrea was reading—or trying to read—in bed that night while gentle, soft music wafted from the concealed speakers of her CD system. She'd seen an obstetrician that day, been given the ultimate medical test for suspected pregnancy and a thorough physical exam, been told she was definitely pregnant and in excellent health and part of her was quietly thrilled.

But that other part, the one that mightily resented Keith Owens, wouldn't relent and let her retain one word she read. Soothing music generally relaxed her, but it wasn't working tonight and neither was the book. The text kept getting lost among the uncountable questions about Keith that felt like rodents gnawing great gaping holes in her brain. Questions about herself, as well. She could hardly classify herself as unaccountable for letting Keith seduce her, after all.

Who was she now? Certainly not the same well-adjusted, clean-living Texas widow she'd been before the Cattleman's Club charity ball. *That* woman would never have succumbed to a man's desire in the back of his vehicle!

Sighing, Andrea closed her book; there was little point in staring at it. She was reaching to turn off the lamp on the nightstand when the phone rang. It was a bit startling, for her friends rarely called after eight at night and it was now after ten. Still, it did happen occasionally, and so she unsuspectingly picked up the receiver and said a calm, quiet, "Hello?"

"Hi, Andy. How are you?"

It was Keith. Her pulse went crazy and she suddenly couldn't breathe. "Hold on a second," she gasped. "I...I have something on the stove." She held the receiver against her chest, cursed her stupid lie and wondered frantically how to deal with this. He hadn't called for...well, it was over two weeks...and now he expected...what?

Wait a minute, she thought. Did it matter what he expected from this call? She had herself to think of, her trampled-in-the-mud pride to resurrect, her child to protect from the unmitigated selfishness of its own father. Yes, this was an opportunity to call Keith foul names at full volume and let him know how much she loathed him, but would that *really* make her feel better? Probably not. One thing might, though.

Raising the phone to her ear, she spoke with studied calm. "Sorry, my pot of gravy runneth over."

"You're cooking gravy at this time of night?"

"A lovely brown sauce, really. It's for a late supper with a…friend. Oh, excuse me for another second, Keith." This time she laid the receiver on the bed, got up and walked around the room, murmuring as she went. "Do have more wine. Supper's almost ready and feel free to turn up the music, if you wish." She had a volume control in her bedroom and she gave it a twist so Keith would be sure to hear the music.

Then she returned to the bed and retrieved the phone. "I'm sorry. What were you saying?"

"I wasn't saying anything." Keith was trying to keep his wits intact, but what he was hearing over the telephone was damned confounding. Andrea was obviously entertaining a man with wine, a late supper and some extremely sensual music. She had never invited *him* to a late supper, damn it, and dining alone together late at night conveyed a special intimacy. "I was *trying,* but I wasn't getting very far," he added, sounding very much like a sullen child.

His tone of voice truly gladdened Andrea's heart. Gladdened her entire system, for that matter, her wounded female pride, especially. "I can only apologize again," she said without the slightest inflection in her voice. He would get nothing from her tone, not so much as a hint of her true state of mind. This was much better, much more gratifying. "You must have had a reason for calling," she said.

"What about your lovely brown sauce?" he asked sarcastically.

"It's fine. Everything's fine. Now, why did you call?"

"Because I had the misguided notion that you might enjoy a few days in Mexico."

Andrea's eyes widened in surprise, but she had to play out the hand she'd dealt herself. "When are you going?"

"When am I going? I'm here!" he shouted. Andrea had to put her hand over her mouth to stifle the laughter bubbling up in her throat. "I've *been* here for two weeks! Didn't you notice I wasn't around?"

"Well…no, actually. You've really been out of town for two weeks? Time goes so quickly, doesn't it?"

"Are you putting me on?"

"Now Keith, why would I do that?"

"I have no idea. Anyhow, would you like to come down here for the weekend? I have a nice house on the Gulf, and it's peaceful and quiet and a great place to unwind."

"It sounds marvelous, but I've made all sorts of plans for the weekend and I couldn't possibly disappoint my friends, especially on such short notice."

"But you don't care if you disappoint me."

"Why on earth would that disappoint you? You've obviously been enjoying yourself for all this time without my company. I'm sure the weekend will be equally enjoyable. Keith, I really must sign off. It was very nice of you to call."

"Wait! Don't hang up yet! Andrea, *please* come down. You could fly to Corpus Christi and I would pick you up there. Andy…we could…" He stopped to clear his throat. "…talk. I think we need to talk. I do, anyway. I've been doing a lot of thinking, but the problem with looking for answers by yourself is that everything's one-sided."

Recalling her own long hours and days of probing for answers, she could only agree. "That's true," she said, still speaking without inflection, although there was a noticeable ache in the vicinity of her heart and she honestly felt like crying. "But when one lives alone…for myself I wouldn't have it any other way…but I know that living alone makes for some very solitary conversations. I'm sorry, Keith, I simply cannot get away this weekend. I have to say good-night now. Pleasant dreams." She hung up.

But instead of feeling great over finally besting Keith at his own double-dealing game, she buried her face in her pillow and bawled like a baby.

In Mexico, watching the reflections of moonlight on the Gulf waters, Keith scowled and pondered the phone call. He hadn't known Andrea was seeing other men, although he was aware that her circle of friends included men. She had never seemed unhappy, he mused with a sinking sensation. They hadn't run into each other that often through the years, but when it had happened he'd never seen signs of unhappiness on her beautiful face. She didn't sound unhappy tonight, either, not when she was cooking and entertaining a male guest at this hour.

Then the full impact of what he'd discovered with that phone call hit Keith. Andrea was serving one special guy a candlelit supper, and that was so painful it was physically jarring. Jealousy ripped through his guts like a hot knife through butter. Unable just to sit there and take it, Keith jumped up from his chair on the verandah and headed for the beach.

His mind ran faster than his legs, torturing him with another spate of questions without logical answers. Whatever was going on in Royal, did he have the power to do anything about it? For that matter, regardless of that painful burst of jealousy that still hadn't completely disappeared, did he really *want* to do anything about it?

Maybe he should have stayed in Royal and figured everything out there. Fat lot of good running away had done. He'd been in Mexico for weeks, and did he know his own feelings any better tonight than he had during that long drive from Royal?

Realizing that he was now looking at his departure from Royal as *running away*—the night he left he wouldn't even consider that possibility—caused him to grimace.

"You are one sorry piece of humanity," he muttered.

Andrea could not remember a time when her emotions had been so jumbled. She'd had her bouts with love before, and with sorrow and grief, of course; losing loved ones—her parents and Jerry—had put her through an emotional wringer three different times. But she was discovering a new type of misery that seemed to spring from within her very own self. Thinking of the baby helped, but even that joy didn't cure her malady.

Finally she unearthed and faced what was really at the core of her melancholy. She'd been applauding herself for putting Keith in his place when he called, and she deserved no applause. She'd been unkind and deceitful with that stupid charade and she regretted her playacting.

Why was there so much pushing and pulling between them? Right now they should *both* be thrilled and happy about their baby. Instead she couldn't even tell him about it. Nothing would ever convince her that he hadn't gotten all unnerved over their passionate interlude and run away to nurse his wounds…or his *imagined* wounds. He'd begun his campaign the night of the ball and hadn't let up for a minute. And he'd won the trophy, too, hadn't he?

No, she thought then. Keith hadn't won the trophy, she had!

When she looked at the wide-screen perspective of this whole affair, she was astonished that Keith ran off to Mexico instead of swaggering all over Royal crowing about how his irresistible machismo had finally overcome Andrea O'Rourke's defenses against men in general and him in particular.

And now he believed there was another man in her life. How could he believe anything else after her dramatic rendering of "The Widow and the Late-Night-Supper Lothario?" It disgusted Andrea that she'd resorted to such cruel tactics. If she'd been so bent on giving Keith some attitude and even on letting him know what a low-down dirty dog she considered him to be, she hadn't had to make a run for the best-actress-in-Texas award like some melodramatic teenager. She was a mature adult, after all. *And* a mother-to-be!

If Keith *hadn't* relentlessly pursued her she would not be a mother-to-be. She supposed he deserved thanks, not censure. Besides, maybe a woman needed a man like Keith to lean on during bad times and to rejoice with during the good times.

But that of course would involve telling Keith everything, and she really didn't know how he would take the news of impending fatherhood resulting from one belated sexual conquest. Somehow, given what she remembered about him, she really couldn't see him jumping up and down for joy.

By Friday afternoon Andrea had gotten herself into such a state that when a woman friend, Linda Vartan, called with a casual invitation to drop by her house on Saturday for grilled steaks and ribs, to be cooked by her husband at poolside, Andrea couldn't say yes fast enough. Sitting around and wallowing in all sorts of emotionally dark dungeons for two days was an unbearable prospect. Thus, on Saturday she tried on her two new bathing suits—purchased during a shopping trip to Dallas in April—and took her time in deciding which one to wear to the Vartans' today.

It was gratifying to be firm and fit enough for a two-piece suit—all that running really paid off—but she'd also bought a stunning one-piece in jewel-tone colors and she decided on it. After taking it off and slipping into a comfortable cotton wrapper to do her makeup, she sat at her dressing table. She had just applied a glossy light-coral lipstick when the front doorbell rang.

"Oh, for pity's sake," she mumbled. She wasn't dressed for company, nor was she expecting any. She had to leave for Linda's in less than an hour and she didn't want to get hung up with some inconsiderate caller and arrive late.

Rising from the dressing-table stool, she tied the sash of the wrapper and took a look at her reflection in the mirror. She was not appropriately clad for this time of day, but she was decently covered. Sliding her bare feet into terry slippers, she hurried to the front door. Whoever was out there was an impatient soul, because he or she was practically leaning on the bell. Terribly annoyed over that alone, Andrea jerked open the door. Then she stood with her mouth open and stared at Keith, who sported the most incredible tan and looked positively devastating in white duck pants, sneakers and a white-and-blue polo shirt.

Keith stared, too. Andrea was wearing a rose, teal and royal blue something or other. It looked to him like some kind of robe, or maybe a bathing suit cover-up. Hell, he didn't know what it was, other than damned sexy, which sort of ticked him off. She hadn't known *he* was coming by, so she was obviously dressed for that late-supper jerk.

"Aren't you going to invite me in?" he asked gruffly.

"I...I'm getting ready to...go out." Andrea felt hot all over and wished she could free her overheated body from the wrapper and get some air on her feverish skin. He was much too handsome with that tan. Damn it, he was much too handsome *without* a tan! And all she could think of was how he'd made her feel in the back of his SUV.

"I'm sure you can spare a few minutes."

"Uh, no, I really can't. Not if I'm going to be on time."

Her flushed face said more to Keith than the words formed by her full luscious lips. She was *afraid* of inviting him in! She knew what could happen...and just might...if they were alone in her house. And that robe or casual dress or whatever it was she was wearing looked pretty darned flimsy. In fact, it looked to him as though she had nothing on under it.

He cleared his throat in an attempt to ignore—and reverse, if possible—what was happening in his pants. "You should either let me come in or shut the door in my face. It's hotter than hell out here and your air conditioners are running full throttle."

"Oh, yes, you're right," she mumbled. One didn't stand with the door open in hot weather in Texas or, she supposed, any other place where temperatures soared above the century mark. She stepped back and opened the door wider. "Come in...but as impolite as it sounds I have to say that you can't stay for long."

He stepped inside and she closed the door behind him. "I hope you understand. I believe I mentioned having plans for the weekend when you called the other night."

"I understand more than you think."

She stiffened from sudden fear. He didn't know about the baby, did he? How could he know? Deciding that he couldn't and it was ridiculous even to think he might, she asked coolly, "What's that supposed to mean?"

"Nothing and it wasn't true, anyhow. Andy, I don't understand a damn thing that's been happening between us. Okay, you have plans and I won't ask you to break a date. But how about later on today? Or this evening? I just want to talk. In fact, I'm being eaten alive by a need to sort things out. I can tell you right now that's never happened to me before, and I have got to get to the bottom of it."

She didn't completely believe him, but it didn't matter. If she agreed to another talk, it would probably evolve into the same thing that had occurred between them at the park. She really had to keep her distance from him. "I'm sorry, but I'm sure I won't be home until quite late this evening."

"That's okay. I could come back then." He had things to do anyhow, such as talking to the guys and catching up on their recent observations of Dorian. Also, he needed to work on breaking that code of Eric's.

"No!"

"Why not?" He moved in and put his hands on her waist before she could get out of his way. "You don't have a stitch on under this thing, do you?"

"That's none of your business," she whispered and realized that she was trembling, just from his touch, his scent, his nearness.

The color of his already dark eyes seemed to get darker. "I want you, but you know that, don't you?"

She swallowed nervously. He *did* want her again. She *hadn't* been a one-night stand. Oh, how could a once clear-thinking woman be so confused that she couldn't tell up from down, or right from wrong?

He pulled her forward and kissed her hard on the mouth. Then he let go of her. "I promise I won't do that tonight. I meant it when I said we needed to talk. That's all we'll do, I swear it. See you tonight.''

He walked out of her house and left her standing in her own foyer with a benumbed expression on her face, as though she had no clear concept of what had just taken place.

Ten

Andrea was relieved to see so many cars when she arrived at the Vartans', as she had worried about being the only guest when she wasn't in a party mood. The presence of others—quite a few, by the look of it—took a major burden off of her.

She tried to appear relaxed and delighted with pool volleyball and tasty grilled food. Her heart just wasn't in it, though, and she mostly sat in the shade of the patio roof and thought about the sameness of every function this crowd created and attended. There simply was no excitement in that lovely backyard and it made Andrea sad to realize it, for she had enjoyed these genteel people and their conventional attitudes and well-bred activities for quite some time. Finding fault with them now was terribly unnerving.

In truth, the word *excitement* had taken on a whole new meaning for Andrea. It occurred to her with a touch of sadness that she was no longer satisfied with her solitary lifestyle. Most of her friends were married or had seriously committed partners. The few single men in the group were well-read and great conversationalists, but they were…well, dull.

Andrea flushed. How could she sit there and deem her unwed male friends dull? From behind her dark sunglasses she studied one fellow—Jim Bailey—whom she'd known for years. He had on perfectly hideous bathing trunks that were so long and baggy they reached his bony knees, and he had a caved-in skinny chest with about three hairs more than the few on his balding head. Jim was a super-nice guy, always ready for a long discussion on any subject anyone mentioned, and Andrea liked him, but was he even slightly exciting?

No one was, she thought dismally. No one but Keith.

Was he back in town for another romp in his SUV? Maybe he'd class it up a bit by luring her into an actual bed, but the result would be just as degrading if all she was to him was the pushover of the week. Would he treat her differently if he knew she was carrying his child? She honestly didn't know the answer to that question, which depressed her further.

Wishing the day away one minute and hoping it would drag on forever the next, Andrea put in hours of phony good cheer and forced smiles with her friends. Around five, the Vartans took cocktail orders from their guests, and Andrea's request for plain ice water drew some good-natured teasing, which she laughed off.

Drinking was not normal routine for this crowd's social affairs, but a pool party was always a bit looser than those events held in more formal settings and it wasn't long until some of them were dancing to Latin music and having a high old time.

Andrea was coaxed into dancing a few numbers, but then she returned to her chair in the shade and her ice water. But it had felt good to let go and forget—if briefly—Keith and his brand of excitement and all of the worries and heartaches that had unbalanced her equilibrium since the ball. While the others got sillier and funnier, Andrea mostly watched from her chair on the patio. Even without her complete participation she knew that this party had turned out well for the Vartans.

It was around seven when she began feeling queasy. She should have gone home hours ago, and would have if Keith hadn't been lurking in the shadows again. With so much on her mind, Keith asking questions—or making another pass—was more than she'd wanted to deal with. Thus, she had stayed outdoors longer than she should have. The heat was stifling, even in the shade, and her occasional dips into the pool to cool off hadn't done much good.

Making the rounds she said goodbye to everyone and then shocked herself and her friends by getting so dizzy she reeled and nearly fell flat on her face. No one laughed. They rushed to help her to a chair, to ask how she felt, to talk about heat sickness, to comment that she must not have felt all that great all day because, after all, she'd refused even a glass of chilled wine. Andrea hemmed and hawed and finally said something about the heat being a little much for her today, then announced that she was fine now and really should go home.

But everyone agreed that she shouldn't be driving. Not when she was already dizzy, for heaven's sake. She really couldn't argue that point, not when she felt like hell and longed almost desperately for the cool comfort of her bedroom.

And so she left her car at the Vartans' and let Harry Vartan drive her home. Andrea tried to focus on him as he chatted, but her head was spinning too much to concentrate on anything. Harry walked her to the door of her house, unlocked it for her and then asked, "Are you going to be okay if I leave now?"

"Yes. I just need to lie down." Her head had started throbbing painfully, also caused by the heat, she was sure, and she blessed the obstetrician she'd seen for giving her some samples of safe medication in case of a headache.

"Are you sure?" Harry asked. "I could come in and check the house for intruders, if you'd like."

"Thanks, Harry, but my security system is very good." Even lightheaded and unfocused she managed to press the right sequence of numbers to disarm the security system.

"Well, if you're sure. Linda and I will drive your car over tomorrow."

"Thank you. Good night." She shut the door and then stumbled her way through the house to her bedroom. Doffing her swimsuit, she fell on the bed without a stitch. Her ceiling fan was running and the moving air felt cool and wonderful on her hot skin. Even without medication she began feeling better. And sleepy, she realized drowsily. Very, very sleepy.

She was almost asleep when the front doorbell chimed. "Go away," she mumbled, for she was in that lovely zone of half sleep, utterly relaxed and almost floating.

A few minutes later she heard someone rapping on the French doors that led from her bedroom to the patio. She opened her eyes to see Keith looking in at her. It was getting dark and she couldn't clearly make out his expression, but he seemed to be totally mesmerized by the sight of her.

Keith *was* mesmerized. Never in a million years could he have imagined Andrea lying on her bed stark naked. He'd come around her house because she hadn't answered the doorbell. Suspecting that she'd decided not to see him tonight and swearing not to let her get away with it, he'd knocked on every door he'd come to.

This was the big-prize door, he realized. He'd hit the jackpot with this one, because there she was, naked, incredibly beautiful and…and… He frowned, because she was just lying there, not in a panic because he *was* outside filling his eyes, or even acting as though she was aware that he was outside. What was wrong with her? Something was. The Andrea he knew wouldn't just lie there and let a man—*any* man—watch her when she was naked as the day she was born.

"Hey," he called, alarmed now, and he rapped on the French door again.

"Go away!" Andrea yelled. She honestly didn't care if he

saw her naked; she cared that he was out there trying to get in!

Keith's jaw dropped. "What's wrong with you?" he called. "Are you sick or something?" Pounding on the door he called her name. "Open up, Andy, or I'll call the police."

He'd call the police? What on earth for? She tried to make sense of his threat, but she couldn't do it. Suddenly furious, she slid off the bed, walked to the door and unlocked it.

"What the hell are you doing?" she demanded to know when the door was open.

Keith stepped inside. "What the hell are *you* doing?" he retorted. Was she drunk, he wondered. But no, she didn't look, act or sound tipsy. "Apparently you had a good time today."

"So what if I did? What're you doing here?"

"We had a date."

"We most certainly did not!" Her nudity suddenly became an embarrassment, and she turned to go and put something on.

But Keith had other ideas. "Not yet," he said softly and stopped her retreat by pulling her into his arms and lowering his lips to hers. The warmth of her struck him hard, and the kiss that had begun soft and gentle became hungry. Holding her naked was an incredible high, and he wanted nothing more than to *continue* holding her.

But why in heaven's name was she naked in the first place? Too curious to ignore the questions stacking up in his mind, he broke the kiss, raised his head and peered at her in the dimming light.

"Something happened today," he said. "You're different."

Andrea wished at that moment that she could tell him about the baby. She was dizzy again, she realized, but not from the sun this time, although Keith's heat was almost as potent.

"No, I'm not," she said, denying her difference only because she couldn't be honest. But she was different, all right, in more ways than one. Standing naked in his arms was so foreign to the woman she'd once been that even she found it hard to believe.

Keith slowly slid his hands up and down the smooth warm skin of her back. "Why were you lying in the dark like this?" he asked softly.

Andrea sighed. If she told him one truth she might tell him everything. Besides, they had *not* had a date tonight. She had not agreed to his coming over and talking tonight. He was being his usual pushy self, and she was letting it happen again!

"Keith, don't!" She escaped his embrace and went for a robe.

Keith walked over to the bathing suit she'd dropped on the floor and picked it up. "It was a bathing-suit party?" he drawled, conveying sarcasm with tone of voice and his most pronounced Texas accent.

It annoyed Andrea. "Don't grill me," she snapped. "Whatever I did today is none of your affair." She realized that her head was beginning to ache again. What she needed more than anything else right now was a shower. But first she had to get rid of Keith. "Would you please leave? I want a shower, a bite to eat and then a good night's sleep."

"Take your shower. Who's stopping you?"

"Damn it, Keith, don't you know when you're not wanted?"

He laughed. "Go take your shower. I'll wait in the living room...or maybe the kitchen."

She gave up. It was either that or stand there and argue with him, and the only time she'd gotten the better of him—and that really hadn't been an argument—was the night he'd called from Mexico. Maybe her deceit that night was part of the reason she shut up and marched into her bathroom. Without a doubt she was truly sorry about it.

Twenty minutes later when she exited the bathroom she was so much more alive it seemed a small miracle. Her headache was gone, she had no sign at all of nausea, and, in fact she even felt a little hungry. The aroma of coffee reminded her that Keith was somewhere in the house, but she felt stronger and more able to deal with him. Figuring there was little point to maidenly modesty after that major-motion-picture nude scene before her shower, she donned a light-weight, knee-length robe, ran her fingers through her still-damp hair and left her bedroom. The odor of coffee became stronger as she walked to the kitchen. It was probably where he was lying in wait of her, she thought dryly.

She was right on the money. Andrea hesitated at the doorway for a moment and saw a very cozy little scene—Keith seated at the kitchen table with a cup of coffee and the newspaper, which still resided where she'd left it that morning. He either heard or sensed her presence because he looked up and smiled.

"Hi."

She walked in and headed for the coffeepot. Her "Hi" wasn't nearly as friendly as his had been, but at least she hadn't immediately shrieked at him. She pulled a cup from a cabinet and picked up the coffeepot.

Keith got up and hurried over to her. "Let me do that. Go over to the table and sit down."

"I am perfectly capable of filling a cup with coffee!" She proved it.

"Fine. Just trying to help. Are you feeling better now?"

"I'm feeling just fine, and I'm going to have a piece of toast."

"Sit down with your coffee and I'll make your toast."

"I don't have a broken leg, for God's sake! I'll make my own toast. *You* sit down."

"Okay, okay, you don't have to get mad. I was just trying to help." Keith returned to the table and sat down.

"Would you like some toast?" she asked stiffly.

"Sure, I'll have a piece. Thanks."

His thanks annoyed her, as well. Obviously she was easily annoyed tonight, but why wouldn't she be? Why didn't Keith just leave? Surely he had to realize how distressing all of this was for her.

When the toast popped up, she put each slice on its own plate and brought them to the table dry. After getting her coffee she returned to the table and sat down.

"I'm eating mine dry. If you want butter or jelly, they're in the refrigerator. Just help yourself."

He grinned, got up, went to the refrigerator and then into a drawer, and ultimately returned to the table carrying a jar of strawberry jam and a spoon. Seated again he spooned jam onto his toast.

Andrea couldn't help glaring at him. "You seem quite amused over something. Care to share it?"

"Well, when I first saw you on the bed without a stitch on, I thought you might be tanked."

Her voice dripped icicles. "I do not get 'tanked,' and for your information, although it's none of your business, all I drank today was lemonade and ice water."

"Maybe you should've tried something stronger. That ice water can be lethal."

"Funny, very funny. You probably thought I was looped because you're so familiar with the malady."

"Well, not really. I haven't overdone it in that department for quite a spell, actually."

"How marvelous," she drawled. "Mr. Perfect."

"Now, that hurts. Even if you had been tanked I wouldn't have judged you for it, Ms. Andy Pandy. And why wouldn't I think you might have drunk a little too much when you'd been at a bathing-suit party all day?"

His blatant enjoyment of this discussion was more than Andrea could take and remain calm. "You didn't *know* it was a pool party, so don't pull that high-and-mighty face and act as though I drink at every excuse! I *rarely* drink, and then it's only a glass or two of wine."

"Hey, don't you think I know that? The whole town knows it."

"Yes, and now the whole town also probably knows you're here, in my house right now!"

Keith laughed again. "Not the biggest crime of the century by anyone's measure," he remarked. He liked her cosmetic-free face. With her hair finger-combed and no makeup she looked like a young girl. "Andrea, I'm not going to apologize for sticking around in case you needed someone. Before you showered, you looked pretty shaky."

She sipped coffee from her cup and dared to meet his eyes. "I'm not shaky now."

"I can see you're not."

"Well, doesn't my excellent physical condition give you any ideas?" She was hoping he would take another extremely unsubtle hint and go home.

"One or two," Keith said softly, then just sat and looked at her. Finally, when he could see that she was getting uncomfortable over such a long silence and his unbroken gaze, he changed gears and said, "I was remembering something when you were showering. Do you remember when I filched a bottle of crème de menthe from my father's liquor cabinet and we drank it in the fort? I think we were about thirteen. You didn't like it very much and only drank a little but I chugged most of the bottle…playing big man, I suppose. Anyhow, I got sick as a dog and you took care of me. We both knew if I went in the house that sick my folks would cart me off to the emergency room, and then everyone would know that not only had we drunk alcohol but that one of us had stolen it.

"So you took care of me. You brought in pans of water and clean towels…you must have sneaked into your house for them…and you kept bathing my face, and I kept heaving. It went on all afternoon and we were scared spitless of what would happen when we had to go in for dinner. But by then I was weak but able to walk into the house without giving anything away. I remember telling my folks some story about getting too much sun and losing my appetite over it. I recall receiving their sympathy instead of their wrath, which made me feel guilty, but not guilty enough to confess the truth.

"The point of all this is that you helped me through a killer hangover one time and tonight I wanted to help you, even though you're so dead certain you didn't need it. It was no big deal, Andy, so don't turn it into one."

"What we did as children cannot be compared to our behavior as adults."

"Why not? We're taller and maybe a little smarter, but we're basically the same people. When one gets down to hard facts, the only real difference between a man and his childhood is the type of games he plays. I doubt that women are all that different."

"You certainly have your own way of interpreting things. Speaking for myself, which *you* cannot do, there are few similarities in the person I am now to the child I was so many years ago."

"There are more similarities than I can count. You really can't see them? Or feel them?"

"I'm not overly pleased with every memory, as you seem to be. For one thing I was your shadow as a kid. I'm certainly not that now, nor would I ever be again."

"Andy, you weren't my shadow, you were my pal, my best friend, my buddy."

"Until high school," she said with an infusion of ice in her voice, for his transformation from best buddy to swaggering, conceited star jock in high school still smarted. "You turned into a complete jerk in high school."

"Well, hormones do strange things to boys. Girls, too, I suspect. Anyhow, everything evened out in college, didn't it?"

"To a point," she grudgingly agreed.

"That point was the bedroom door, wasn't it? Damn, I wanted you. I ached for you, every damned minute of every damned day. And you kept talking about your wedding night. I sure as hell hope Jerry O'Rourke appreciated your virginity, because you guarded it like something sacred. And maybe it was. Maybe you were right and I was wrong about that. It's hard to know now. So much has happened since then. You got married, I got married..." Keith's voice trailed off.

Then he spoke again. "But we're not married to other people now, Andy," he said softly. "And neither are we kids. Our connection is still strong, just as it was when we *were* kids, only it's even better now because we both have more sense. I do, anyway."

Her hands were under the table, in her lap, and she couldn't stop herself from wringing them. It was the perfect opportunity to tell him that he was going to be a father, if she was ever going to do it. That was the problem. Was she going to stand firm on her decision to keep him in the dark?

"Andy," he said quietly, "don't you love me even a little bit?"

She'd been wondering just how personal he was going to get with this conversation but never could she have dreamed up a question like that.

"I...Keith...don't ask me things...like that," she stammered.

His gaze never lost its directness. "Why not?"

Andrea was sure her face was crimson, because it felt hot as a furnace. It angered her—she couldn't let something like this, probably just another ploy to get her into bed, influence her decision about the baby—and she spoke harshly. "All right! I suppose some childish part of me will always...I can't bring myself to use the word *love*, so I'll say that because of our intertwined pasts, some part of me will probably always care for some part of you."

"And that's the best you can give me?" Keith sat back, shoved his hands into his pants pockets and stared across the table at her with a challenging, unblinking gaze. "I've been thinking of a lot more than that, you know."

"No, I'm afraid I don't know. What's more, I don't *want* to know." Shaken, she got up for the coffeepot, which she brought back to the table, and refilled his cup. She'd intended to fill hers, as well, but more coffee suddenly didn't sound so good.

Returning the pot to the coffeemaker, she was taken completely by surprise when she felt him standing right behind her. In the very next instant his arms moved around her and his face was in her hair.

"No, Keith," she whispered shakily, but his hands were moving over her breasts, her waist and abdomen. He pressed his body against hers and continued to caress her through her robe. She told herself that she didn't want this, but her heartbeat had gone wild and an intense craving in the pit of her stomach was torturing her. She felt the way she had that night in the park, all soft and boneless, and she could not stop herself from leaning against him.

"Andy...sweetheart," he whispered raggedly. "If just touching each other makes us want so much, it has to mean something."

"You...you're not just touching me," she gasped as his hand worked up the front of her robe. "Keith...we can't keep doing things like this." How could she maintain a charade about the child in her womb and keep on making love with its completely-in-the-dark father? She groaned.

"We can, damn it, we can!" Keith exclaimed.

"You're just as...as leery of commitment as...I am." She was on fire from the gentle but extremely knowledgeable stroking of his fingers between her legs.

"Maybe...I'm not sure anymore. Why do you think I left town? After we made love that night I needed to do some heavy-duty thinking."

"And?" she whispered thickly while moving her feet farther apart to give him all the space he needed to keep on working his magic. She'd never been so overcome—not even in his SUV—from one rather simple caress from a man. "Did you figure out anything?" Had he? Oh, if he only said the right things right now she would crumple and tell him everything.

"No. A man can't figure out those kinds of answers all by

himself. I should have stayed in town and talked to you. Opened up with you and begged you to do the same with me.''

She moaned with intense pleasure and totally forgot the theme of their conversation.

"Feels good, huh? Andy, we're almost like one person, don't you realize that? We were the same way as kids, always together, playing together, getting into trouble together. You must remember at least as much of it as I do.''

"Don't...don't talk now,'' she mumbled. She couldn't stand there a moment longer, not even with him doing all the supporting. "Let's take this...out of the kitchen.''

"Are you inviting me into your bed?'' he whispered huskily.

"Don't put it into words,'' she groaned, afraid even to think, let alone talk. "I'm telling you that talking right now will stop...everything.''

He didn't say another word. Instead, he released his hold on her, took her hand and hurried them both from the kitchen to her bedroom.

Kissing almost frantically, they began undressing each other. Tearing each other's clothes off was a more accurate description of their haste and hunger. Finally down to bare skin they fell on the bed together, wrapped in each other's arms. Andrea was so ready that she pleaded, "Do it now. Please, do it now.''

Keith became so excited by her passionate request that he plunged into her at once. "Andy...Andy,'' he repeated gruffly as he almost roughly moved in and out of her.

She was in another world, the same one she'd touched on in his SUV, but tonight it was even more mind-boggling. She writhed freely beneath him, giving him everything, following his lead and rhythm, and she wanted it never to stop. This had to be...love.

No! she thought wildly and immediately buried the word beneath layers of sexual pleasure. Love was something else.

This was physical sensation and love was…well, it wasn't this.

Keith too wanted it to go on forever, for once it was over they would have to talk again. Talking was the best medicine in most cases, but Andrea was so guarded with her inner thoughts that he was afraid of another dead end, or even of inadvertently angering her. She didn't take demands well, so he knew he had to be tactful in any discussion without appearing to be a wimp. He *wasn't* a wimp and never had been, but Andrea scared him. Not in a physical way, that would be too ridiculous to consider, but she was strong-minded and set in her ways, and he knew she could turn on him in the blink of an eye.

Except right where she was, under him and moaning and whimpering from the pleasure he was giving her. In bed, making love, he was the stronger. At least for the time being. Who knew the next time they made love? Andrea might take the initiative. He didn't doubt that she'd do anything she wanted to do.

There's the key! He became even more excited because unearthing what Andrea really wanted was the key to any future they might have together. Riding her harder, faster, he brought them both to the brink. She cried out his name…"Keith…oh, Keith"…and he knew the moment had come. In seconds they went over the edge, in perfect harmony again, which completely amazed him.

Supporting himself on his forearms so he could look at her face he said softly, "Do you realize what a rare couple we really are?"

Eleven

"A...couple?" Andrea echoed hoarsely. Out of all the words he'd just said, *couple* registered with the most impact. She didn't know to react to it. Could he actually be thinking of them as a couple? A *committed* couple?

She peered into his velvety dark eyes and realized that she hadn't seen them looking this soft and shiny since...well, she couldn't remember when. "Your eyes look like chocolate kisses," she had teased as a child. And he'd teased back by calling her "blue-color-crayon eyes." He'd even taken out the cobalt-blue crayon and shown her which one matched her eyes. She had giggled.

She didn't feel like giggling now. She felt like a puddle of something soft and oozy. He'd done that to her. He was the only man who'd done that so well, and maybe she should tell him that.

"You're looking awfully serious," he said with a bit of a grin. "Does the idea of our being a couple scare you?"

Andrea recognized it as his *teasing* grin. She'd seen it

often enough, after all, and it contained exactly the same amount of daring and fun that it had years ago. He wasn't committed to anything but his own pleasure, same as he'd always been.

She wasn't angry, just very, very hurt. She showed him nothing of her true feelings and smiled. "We're a couple, all right," she quipped. "A couple of nuts. Let me get up, please." For humorous emphasis she slapped him on his arm.

With a broader grin he rolled onto the bed. "Don't take your time," he told her as she picked up her robe and hurried into the bathroom.

"Funny," she dryly said over her shoulder. "You're a funny guy."

"And you're my sweetheart," he called out just as she was disappearing behind the closed bathroom door. Locking his hands behind his head, he lay uncovered and let the ceiling fan cool his feverish body. He was positive that he had never felt more contented or satisfied than he did at that moment.

Andrea took a quick shower and thought about his parting shot. She was the mother of his child, but she wasn't his sweetheart. At least she didn't feel that particular role.

But if she was so certain about that, why had she let him make love to her again? The first time had taken her by surprise, but today? No, today she'd been fully cognizant of the meaning behind his first touch. And now he was in her bed, waiting for her, probably with all sorts of erotic ideas whirling around in his head.

Trembling from so many emotions warring within her system, Andrea felt tears fill her eyes. This relationship had moved into emotionally dangerous territory. She had tried everything she knew to avoid this very thing, but Keith had kept coming, hot and strong. Then he ran away, then he came back, and then...? Well, who knew what Keith's next move would be? How could she risk her baby's future with such an on-again, off-again man for a father?

By the time she was ready to leave the bathroom she ha

decided her most sensible course was to treat Keith and everything going on between them as ordinary adult entertainment—and *not* tell him anything. If at all possible, she would keep it light and shoot for laughs. *Yeah, you're just a laugh a minute these days.* The wry observation of the little voice in her head was somewhat discouraging, but it wasn't as if she had a week to figure this out. Keith was here now, she had to put on a happy face and act as though going to bed with him was no big deal.

Bracing herself, she walked into the bedroom with a smile. It was phony as a three-dollar bill, but only she knew that.

"Hey, you're dressed," Keith exclaimed.

"Hey, you're not! And I don't think wearing a robe constitutes being dressed," she retorted. "What're you going to do, lie there naked all night in hope of more action? Forget that, sport. I'm totally done in. See you in the kitchen…or wherever." She walked out with her own erratic but powerful heartbeat nearly choking her.

He was too much for a woman like her to deal with, she thought breathlessly. Lying naked on her bed like that, with every part of him in plain sight. No shame at all, no *modesty* at all.

In the kitchen she stuffed the half of her toast she hadn't eaten before into her mouth. Her stomach was as shaky as her legs, and she hoped the small piece of toast would ease that particular ailment. The table was really a mess, she realized, with dirty dishes and newspaper strewn all over it.

But she couldn't deal with that, either, and she left the kitchen and went to the den. Going to a window she looked outside at Keith's SUV in her driveway, but her bad nerves wouldn't permit her to dwell on that big masculine vehicle or the destruction of her reputation it had caused.

Finally she sat down and waited for Keith to show his face. She wasn't at all comfortable because she couldn't get past the seriousness of her situation and when Keith did appear she was going to have to act as though going to bed with him was no more than a bit of Saturday-night fun.

Fun.

Groaning quietly, Andrea put her head back. Her mind was swimming with thoughts, all of them disturbing. She was sitting in the same chair and wearing an agonized expression when Keith walked in.

"Oh, here you are," he said.

Startled, she drew a quick breath and composed herself. "I see you got dressed."

"An easily reversed process, leave us not forget." There was a devilish twinkle in his eyes, a true reflection of the joyful excitement he was feeling over the evening's events.

His gist was so apparent that there was no way Andrea could misinterpret it. *Remember to keep it light!* her little voice reminded.

"I suppose we could always make a contest out of who could get undressed the quickest," she drawled.

"I would win."

"You still believe you're the best, the fastest, the smartest, the absolute cat's meow, don't you?"

Keith chuckled. "The cat's meow? I haven't heard that in a long time."

He sat on the end of the sofa closest to her chair and Andrea's gaze moved from him to the opposite end of the sofa with its stack of photo albums. Her housekeeping, her almost obsessive penchant for having everything in the house clean, tidy and in its place, had obviously gone to hell the same as her moral standards had or else she would have put those albums away once she'd looked through them.

For some reason those albums being on the sofa instead of in the attic made her completely forget her vow to keep things light between her and this overbearing man. This distracting, conceited *male* who had grown up thinking he was the center of the universe. Why wouldn't he intrude on her life? On anyone's life, for that matter. When the entire universe revolved around you, you intruded on anything you wished without once thinking you could possibly *be* an intrusion. Oh, the gall of him, the bloody, damned gall!

She simply could not hold her tongue, and there was a caustic edge to her voice when she spoke. "I'm going to tell you something, Keith, which, given your massive ego, you won't want to believe, but when we were kids I *let* you win our swimming and running races. I let you beat me at checkers, chess and games. I deliberately fumbled the ball when throwing it so that you would throw it a greater distance than me. And I constantly fed your ego with praise for how much better at everything you were."

He looked first surprised then amused. "Now why would you manufacture a story like that? Anytime I beat you, it was fair and square."

"I knew you wouldn't believe me."

"Andy, I didn't *always* beat you."

"Only because I figured you'd catch on or even lose interest in our games if you won every time. I didn't want you losing interest, because you were my best friend and my hero. There was no one to take your place, should you go off and leave me behind." She paused briefly, then added, "Which is exactly what you did in high school."

"Well, teenagers can be cruel."

"Not *all* teenagers. You were a jerk, and if you had one honest cell in your body you'd admit it."

Keith grinned. "Since you put it that way, what can I do but admit it? I was a jerk in high school. There, does that make you happy?"

"Don't be absurd."

"Andy, I'm trying to be agreeable. What would you like me to say?"

"Well, for one thing you could say that you *knew* I was letting you win most of the time."

Keith couldn't help laughing. "But I didn't know, and I still don't. You played your heart out, whether it was a game of checkers or tag. Besides we were really young when we played together. In middle school I was on the softball team and you weren't. As I remember it, you joined the girl's volleyball team."

"And the soccer team, and the tennis team, and... Oh, what difference does it make now? Yes, in middle school we weren't constant companions. We couldn't be...except during summer breaks."

"So in truth," Keith said, "we began growing apart in middle school, not high school. Andy, you're right about one thing. What in hell difference does it make now?"

"Then you believe me? About my letting you win most of the time?"

"No, I don't believe you. I was always twice your size. I could always outrun and outswim you. I still could."

"You most certainly could not! Do you run almost every day, as I do? I could beat you with one hand tied behind my back."

"Or one foot?"

"Don't make fun of me!"

"Then change the subject. I couldn't care less which of us is the fastest runner."

"Well, you cared when we were kids!"

"We were *both* competitive, Andy." Keith wasn't grinning now. In fact he was getting more upset by the moment. In his opinion this was a stupid, adolescent conversation, and he wished he could get Andrea on another track. Still, he couldn't lie and tell her he believed that she'd let him win when they were kids. His good nature could be stretched only so far, even if it was the woman he loved doing the needling.

He sucked in a startled breath, not because his being in love with Andrea was a brand-new thought but because it seemed so permanently embedded now, so much a part of who and what he was, of who and what he wanted to be in the future.

A clap of thunder so loud that it seemed to rock the house took them both by surprise. In mere seconds the sky opened up and began spilling rain, sheets of rain.

Keith jumped up. "I think I left a window open."

He ran from the den and Andrea heard an outside door open and close. It occurred to her to get up and arm th security system so he couldn't get back in, but she merely contemplated the idea for a few enjoyable moments. Then, sighing, she got up and walked through the house to look out various windows at the severity of the sudden storm. It was while frowning at the sight of flowers bent to the ground from the heavy rainfall that she realized the headway she and Keith were making, regardless of the childish bent of their conversation. The childishness was her fault, she'd searched for a safe subject to discuss to keep his mind out of the bedroom, and she'd come up with that ludicrous tale of letting him win all the time. Small wonder he'd gotten miffed.

But if they kept talking...they'd covered childhood, middle school and some of high school...wouldn't they eventually get to the topic of their college relationship, at which time she could let him know how cruel he'd been? Wasn't that what she'd been wanting to say to him all along, certainly since the ball but also during all of those years after their breakup? This was her chance; she should take it.

Returning to the chair in the den she'd used before, Andrea wearily laid the back of her hand on her forehead. She wasn't physically tired, but the thought of fighting, arguing or debating the past with Keith again was emotionally exhausting. Should she really put herself through that to finally say to his face, "You were a wretched, cruel person that night." Would he care if she did say it?

Ask yourself this, Andrea O'Rourke, do you really want to run Keith off? Do you truly want to succeed in causing a division so permanent and irreversible that the two of you would go out of your way to avoid each other for the rest of your lives, just as you did the last eighteen years?

Andrea sighed. She didn't know what she wanted, except for one utterly impossible thing: to turn back the clock to the day she'd been told about the Cattleman's Club donation. If she could go back to that day she would tell the other New Hope volunteers that she could not attend the ball as the charity's representative and someone else would have to do it.

Everything that had happened concerning Keith since the night of the ball would be erased with that one small change of history. He wouldn't be here tonight; he would never have been here. Nor would they have met in the park, or ever made love. Her life would be serene again, the placid stillness of her daily existence would never have been disrupted.

But you wouldn't be pregnant. She wanted this baby. She wanted it more than she'd ever wanted anything.

"Andrea!"

"What?"

"I'm dripping water all over your laundry room. Bring me something to wrap up in and I'll toss my clothes in the dryer."

She got to her feet and called, "I'll get some towels."

"Thanks," Keith called back. He'd started undressing the minute he came in, so by the time Andrea appeared with an armful of clean towels, he was stark naked.

"Well, honestly," she drawled with deliberate sarcasm "You drop your drawers faster than anyone *I* ever knew." She set the stack of towels on the folding counter.

Keith grinned. "You just don't know the right people, sweetheart." Helping himself to what looked like the largest towel in the stack, he wrapped it around his hips and tucked it together at his waist. "There, all covered up again. How do you get this dryer going?"

"Probably the same way you get *your* dryer going."

"That's not something I do, Handy Andy."

"So we'll let Handy Andy do it, right?"

Keith shrugged. "I know it's a tough job, but someone's gotta do it."

"Who wipes your nose and washes your back when Handy Andy's not around?" Andrea turned the dryer dials and pushed the Start button.

"Believe it or not, I can manage to wipe my own nose. But back-washing's a whole other ball game." He moved closer to her—she was still facing the dryer—and put his arms around her. "I'll bet you're a hell of a back-washer," he said, burrowing his face into her hair. "Damn, you smell good. You *always* smell good. What kind of perfume do you use?"

"I rarely use perfume. All you're smelling is body lotion and…and shampoo. Keith, please, don't do this."

"Can't help it, sweetheart," he said huskily. "You're all I think about anymore."

"Which, of course, is the reason you fled to Mexico after our…uh, first time together."

Keith cooled down in the space of two seconds. He could lure her into bed again, of that he was positive, but there was still something huge and forbidding between them. It felt like a locked door, and even when they made love that door remained securely bolted. If their relationship was going to make it to the finish line—which seemed to be what he wanted, at least, it was what he wanted tonight—then he had to unearth the key to that lock.

Even as kids it hadn't been easy to get Andrea to talk about something she would rather not discuss. She'd been mule-headed stubborn as a child and it appeared to Keith that she hadn't changed much. Which made him wonder why she was willing to have sex with him when she'd made it so plain on numerous occasions that she'd wished he would disappear from the face of the earth.

He dipped his head and kissed the side of her neck and said softly, "Let's light the fireplace in the den and listen to the rain together." He let go of her.

"Uh, fine. Good idea." Andrea hurried from the laundry room.

Keith stayed right behind her, watched the delightfully feminine way she walked and wished that she were wrapped in a towel, too. Not that her robe was much of an obstacle, should they both get in the mood again. Maybe they would. What better way could a man pass a stormy night than to spend it with a woman who made him feel young and glad to be alive? Andrea did that for him. Yes, on second thought he was *certain* about their relationship reaching the finish line. All he had to do now was convince her.

"Since you're so helpless around a house, I'll light the fireplace," Andrea said as they walked into the den.

Keith smiled. "Yes, dear."

"How do you survive on your own?" Shooting him a rather disgusted look she turned on the gas and pushed the striker button. The flames leapt to life at once.

"Oh, I have plenty of help."

"You must."

"Paid help, Andy."

"Yes, well, one can buy anything with enough money."

"That's not true."

"Name one thing." She sat in the same chair again and Keith returned to the sofa.

"Love. Sex can be bought, even companionship can be bought, but not love, Andy."

"I'm sure you could buy a pretty good facsimile, considering how many single women would give their eyeteeth to nail a man like you."

"I'm special because of my bank account?"

"Uh, well, you're not unattractive, you have to know." *Especially with that dark tan and those incredible eyes. Damn it, do you* have *to be so good-looking?*

"So you think I'm attractive?" Keith asked innocently.

"Not nearly as devoutly as *you* think it, but yes, I see you as an attractive man."

"Devoutly?" Keith laughed. "You do have a way with words...or should I say subtle insults?"

"If you consider what I said an insult, how do you deal with the real thing?"

"Honey, one thing you are is the real thing."

Andrea bristled. "And what's *that* supposed to mean?"

"Only that you're the genuine article. Andy, it was a compliment."

"Well, since you don't know me well enough to judge me as genuine *or* phony, I really had no clue as to what it was."

"You really think I don't know you?"

"That's right. You don't know me any more than I know you. Everything between us is strictly superficial."

"Superficial? You're calling each of us depthless and our feelings trivial." He leaned forward. "Is what you feel in bed with me trivial?"

She cast her eyes downward, for his seemed too full of feverish emotions to comfortably look at. "What...would you call those kinds of feelings?"

"Not trivial!"

"Okay, fine. Answer me this. Why did you run off to Mexico after we made love in the park?"

"You actually said it without hemming and hawing."

"You're trying to turn the tables on me, and I'm not going to let you do that. Give me an answer."

Keith finally sat back, and he turned his face from her to the fireplace. "I wish I hadn't gone."

"Now you're going to play on my sympathy? No way, Keith. Why did you go?"

"I needed to think."

"About?"

He looked at her again. "About us. About you, about me, about what was happening between us. For all the answers I came up with I might as well have stayed here."

Andrea felt suddenly weak. "You...you must have found some sort of answer. You came back and...and..."

"And we made love again," he said softly. "Maybe we should get married."

She gaped, she gasped and she nearly stopped breathing. Rising, she went to the window and looked out, mostly at the rain running down the glass.

"I know you don't mean that, so why did you say it?" she said.

"Maybe I do mean it."

"But you're not sure."

"Oh, Andy, are you? Are you sure you want me out of

your life, or would you rather I hung around and we got it on every so often?''

She whirled around. ''Don't you dare talk to me like that.''

''Why in hell not? That's what we've been doing, isn't it?''

''Twice does not an affair make!'' Turning around again she found herself looking at her empty driveway. ''What did you do with your car?''

''I put it in your garage.''

''Next to mine?''

''Your car's not in the garage. Someone obviously drove you home today. It was probably your new boyfriend, the guy you cook fancy little suppers for at midnight.''

''You're jealous!''

''Am not.''

''You sound exactly like a sullen child, so don't try to con me, Keith. I don't care anyway. I do not have a boyfriend, and what you heard over the phone the night you called was precisely what I wanted you to hear. I lied, Keith. I wanted to get back at you. When you called I was in bed...alone...with the CD player on. I fabricated everything else.''

Keith slowly got to his feet. ''I never would have guessed it.'' He tried to smile but it came off as feeble. ''You didn't let me win that night, did you?''

''We're not in a contest, Keith.''

''What would you call it?''

''I've been trying to figure that out, and so, apparently, have you.'' She glanced back at the window again. ''Harry Vartan drove me home because I wasn't feeling well. He and his wife are good friends of mine and the party was at their house.''

''You weren't feeling well?'' Keith frowned. ''How come?''

Probably because I'm pregnant! ''Too much sun, I think.''

''Are you sure that's all it was? How are you feeling now?''

"Obviously I recovered or I never would have let you in!" she replied waspishly. This whole thing was really getting her down. Tell him…don't tell him. Ask him to leave…let him stay as long as he wants.

They looked at each other for a very long moment, and then Andrea's eyes filled. Wiping away leaking tears, she returned to her chair and sat down.

Keith sighed, shook his head then headed for the laundry room. His clothes were probably dry by now.

Twelve

Fully dressed again, Keith stood at a window in the den and watched the storm, visible through the many yard lights on Andrea's property. What he couldn't get past was Andrea's surprising deceit the night he'd called from Mexico. She'd been mad as hell or she wouldn't have gone to such lengths to make him think she was entertaining a man. Had his leaving town caused so much anger? Or was it—and this supposition was much more serious than his first—the aftermath of their making love in the back of his SUV?

Keith's frown intensified. He seemed to be suddenly bombarded by guilt and it was coming at him from all directions. He had pushed Andrea too hard. He'd kept after her and kept after her, completely ignoring her protests, and he could claim success, if luring a woman into bed was the yardstick with which he measured victory in a personal relationship.

But he hadn't only wanted sex from Andrea. In fact, he was annoyed by the mess he'd made of something that had started with the very best of intentions. Uneasy and troubled

Keith wondered if there was any chance of setting them on the right track. He loved her. But for some reason he hadn't been honest with her.

"Damn," he muttered, shoving his hands into the pockets of his pants.

Glancing back at Andrea, Keith saw the distress on her face. His heart sank. Neither of them was happy with the way things stood between them, and if they didn't come to some sort of understanding, nothing was apt to change. Maybe tonight was do-or-die, he thought grimly. Maybe this was it—the real beginning or the bitter end.

He noticed the stack of photo albums on the sofa—they had piqued his interest when he'd first come into the den. Seating himself next to them, he transferred the top album to his lap and asked, "Is it okay if I look at this?" It was really just something to do until he thought of an opening line to get them communicating with no-holds-barred. Nothing else would alter the status quo, he now believed, nothing but complete and sincere honesty from each of them.

"Sure, go ahead," she said listlessly. She honestly had no fight left in her. Massive amounts of emotion, but not enough strength to put on a defense against anything Keith might do or say.

"Thanks." He began turning pages and his speed slowed to a snail's pace when he realized the snapshots he was looking at were all of Andrea, from when she was about five to—he took a quick peek at the album's last page—her early teens. And he was in almost every one of them!

Looking at those old photos brought back so many memories—most of which he'd long forgotten.

His interest surprised Andrea, and she watched him. Seeing Keith while he was so immersed, she could see both the boy he'd been and the man he was now, and for the very first time she began to grasp that they were one and the same. It seemed like a revelation of sorts, although of course he was the same person. Why wouldn't he be? It was just that she hadn't been thinking of him in that way. If she'd loved him so much before, she should love him still.

Did she?

Her heart began pounding, and she tried desperately to think of something else, something trivial, something that wouldn't rip her from stem to stern. He'd always been the best-looking male in her life, always! Andrea's breath caught. She'd loved and adored Keith the boy and, she had discovered, she loved and adored Keith the man, now.

Keith chuckled, startling Andrea out of her reverie. "What so funny?" she asked, relieved to have a distraction. Rising from her chair, she went to the sofa to see for herself which picture had made him laugh.

"Look at this," Keith said.

Andrea sat next to him to peer at the photo he was indicating. It was a snapshot of her draped in pink chiffon—she recalled that playtime outfit as some old curtains, although where on earth she'd gotten them was a mystery—and Keith in his pirate hat and brandishing a cardboard sword. They were about six or seven years old, she figured.

"Do you remember the day this was taken?" he asked.

"Well…no. Should I? Do you?"

"Yes, I remember it. We both got hell for playing doctor."

"We were playing doctor with you in your pirate hat and me in pink curtains? I don't remember that."

"We weren't in them for long." Again Keith chuckled. "After Ducky took this picture…"

Andrea broke in. "I was wondering who had taken all these snaps. Was it Mrs. Dorsett?"

"Mostly, yes. Anyhow, after she snapped us in our favorite getups that day, she went in the house and we returned to our fort. I'm not sure exactly how we evolved from pirate and harem girl to doctor and nurse…or maybe it was doctor and patient…but we got totally naked and were busily examining each other when Ducky appeared to announce that lunch was ready. The poor woman nearly had a stroke when she saw us."

"That's not true. You made that up. I never played doctor with you."

"Andy, why would I make up something like that? Hell, we were little more than babies. I honestly don't recall how we even figured out that our bodies were different, but it apparently happened and innocent little beings that we were, we were curious about the differences."

Andrea was unwilling to admit to something *she* couldn't recall at all. "I don't believe it," she said stiffly.

Keith laughed. "Fine, *don't* believe it. It's not important anyhow."

But it was. It was one more shared event—even funny when she really thought about it—and further proof that their life on the same cosmic plane had begun over thirty years ago.

He turned his head to peer at her; she was close enough for him to see the flecks of black in her blue, blue eyes. He also saw a mist of tears and an alarming intensity.

"Let's not blow this out of proportion," he said quietly, hoping to soothe her. Why a simple little memory from their childhood would bother her to this degree escaped him, but her agitation was obvious. After moving the album back to the stack, he put his arm around her and gently urged her head down to his shoulder. "It can't be that bad," he said softly.

"It...it's not bad," she whispered, "just disturbing."

She began crying, and her flood of tears soaked Keith's shirt in seconds. He was dismayed by so much emotion over a perfectly normal childhood incident, but he sat there, held her and let her have her cry while he gently stroked her hair. He hoped that this might be that beginning he'd deemed necessary for their relationship to progress, but he wasn't impatient about it.

Then, without warning, Andrea got up, mumbled "I'll be back," and left the room. Keith got to his feet and frowned at the vacant doorway. What had that trip down memory lane done to Andy? The only thing it had done to him was to give him a few laughs, but she hadn't laughed over it, she had cried.

Andrea walked in with a box of tissues. Her eyes were red from weeping and the tip of her nose was pink, but she was much calmer, and she sat in a chair and asked him to please sit down again. "I have something to tell you," she said.

Wary and more than a little concerned, Keith slowly sank to the sofa again. Something told him he'd been right. This was either a new beginning or an irreversible ending for them. He hesitated to speak at all, but she seemed to want to hear from him.

"Is something wrong?" he asked slowly, cautiously.

She thought a moment, then said, "Maybe something's right, but right now I don't know."

He frowned at her. "You're worrying me, Andy."

"I know." She dove in, head-first. "Keith...I...I'm pregnant."

Keith froze solid. His mouth would hardly form words. "You're what?" he finally got out.

"I'm pregnant," she repeated. She could see his throat bob up and down as he swallowed. While she'd expected some show of surprise, she had not anticipated an almost fatal case of panic. Was he wondering if he should get out of there and run like hell? That was what he looked like. She had finally faced the truth of her own feelings for him and decided that she couldn't possibly withhold the existence of his child from him, and he was reacting as she had expected. She was never going to learn, was she?

"You can...uh, know that this soon?" he mumbled.

The damage was done. As much as she wished it, she couldn't take it back. She squared her shoulders, looked him right in the eyes and said coldly, "I've taken several tests, seen an obstetrician and there's no doubt."

Life was beginning to return to Keith's benumbed system. She was pregnant. They were going to have a baby! My God, this was a miracle. Shocking, yes, but definitely a miracle.

He got up and walked over to her. "When did you know?"

She sank deeper into her chair because she didn't want him getting too close. "I knew it was a possibility after our night in the park. I knew for certain once I took the tests."

He was so tall, and he was looming over her. She knew he was beginning to guess it all, and rather than let him flounder for a while longer, she decided to give it to him straight.

"I wasn't going to tell you at all." The fire in her eyes dared him to say something insolent or insulting.

His dark tan became noticeably lighter by several shades, right before those blazing eyes of hers. "You're not serious?"

She was *not* going to back down on this, or cower and act all weepy and wrong. From the look of him, as though she'd just taken away his very last toy and now he would *have* to grow up, she never should have even hinted at her condition.

"I'm *very* serious," she snapped. "Why should I want to tell you? You ran away like a scared little boy after seducing me!"

He recoiled as though physically struck. "Andy, that's not what happened."

Andrea watched him move around the room, feeling as though her heart weighed a ton. He wasn't happy about the baby, and why had she gotten maudlin over some old memories and decided he should know about his impending fatherhood? No, that hadn't been it. It had been that realization that she had never really stopped loving him. Oh, the flames had dimmed for a while, no question about it, but they'd always been lurking somewhere in her system.

He finally stopped pacing and looked at her. "I've never ever done anything right with you, have I?"

She could lie and agree with him, but she was through with lies and pretense. "Of course you have."

"In college?"

"Well...no...but..." She hesitated, but only for a second. This was something else that had to be said. "I always blamed you for our breakup in college. You were cruel."

Oddly the one thing she'd really wanted to say to him for weeks—for years, actually—didn't do a thing for her. It was all so long ago, and what did it signify now? She'd been much too unforgiving—a foolish, naive, unforgiving young girl. Even maturity hadn't softened her judgment, she had clung to the hurt for years, steadfastly believing that she had been wronged.

"I didn't mean to be," Keith said. "I thought you understood. That you wanted a business partnership just like I did. I guess I figured you'd know that eventually, when we became financially secure, which I was positive would happen, we'd get married."

"You never said that."

"I should have. I was so boiling over with ideas, plans and ambition. Regardless of all that, I did love you, Andy." He walked another circle around the room, then stopped directly in front of her, leaned over, put his hands on the arms of the chair and said, "I still do."

She swallowed. His face was close to hers and there was no avoiding his eyes. "I loved you, too," she said huskily. "Back then."

"But not now?"

She was afraid of giving too much too soon. "How can I know for sure what I feel? You weren't always so certain, either, or you wouldn't have hightailed it to Mexico to figure it out."

"Everything's different now. Andy, I want my baby."

"Which could be the reason you're talking about still loving me. Keith, it's not *your* baby until I say it is."

He frowned. "Wait a minute. Are you saying…?"

She broke in. "No! It's your baby, but that doesn't mean you can have it."

"What *does* it mean, then? If you intended to withhold our child from me, why did you tell me about it?"

"I got sentimental."

"And now you're sorry you did?"

"I don't know what I am!"

"Well, maybe you should figure it out!"

"Don't you dare yell at me!"

To preserve his own sanity and self-control, Keith walked away from her. Again he paced the room, thinking, remembering. They had more intertwined memories at thirty-eight than a lot of couples had at sixty. And he *did* love her, but she was so damn stubborn, and if she had it in her head that he'd only told her he loved her because of the baby, it would be almost impossible to change her mind.

He had to try, though. "Andy, how were you going to explain a baby without a husband?"

"There are lots of ways. Sperm banks, for one. Women don't need a man to have a baby these days, Keith."

"That's just great," he muttered darkly.

She felt awful. They should be rejoicing together, laughing, crying, making plans. Instead they were still fighting, still on different roads. Not even that, actually. Same road, different lanes was more like it, she thought sadly.

She thought of the baby then and laid her hand on her lower abdomen. It was so new, just beginning to form, but in her mind it was a fully developed infant. That was how she would always think of it till the day of its birth. Until that momentous day, she and nature would be its protectors, but then, didn't her precious son or daughter deserve to have both parents?

She could tell how hurt Keith was, and she could certainly feel her own pain. But she still loved him and it *was* possible that he hadn't said he loved her just to be part of his child's life.

She took a shaky breath. "Maybe…maybe we should try something."

Keith stopped and looked at her. "Try what?"

"To…to stop bickering and maybe…make it work…between us."

"Even though you don't love me?"

"Keith, that's not fair."

"But is it accurate?" He rushed over to her chair and knelt

at her knees. "Andy, you've denied my existence for eighteen years. Was I really that terrible in college?"

She was having trouble meeting his eyes. "No, but I thought you were."

"You still thought it the night of the ball, didn't you?"

"I was afraid of you."

"Because I made you feel things you didn't want to feel?"

"Possibly." After a second she added, "Probably."

"Look at me." He put his hands on her face, one on each side, and repeated softly, "Look at me, Andy." When she finally did, he said, "I think you do love me. What do you propose we do to try and make it work between us?"

She was losing her nerve again. "How about designing a board indicating all possible choices and then throwing darts at it?"

"I thought you were serious." He got up. "Maybe we should sleep on it and talk again tomorrow."

It was Andrea's turn to panic. She got to her feet. "No, don't go. I'm thinking that we might have been married to each other for years and already have had children. Instead, because of our fight and our own blindness, we went our separate ways. We're going to have a baby. I already love this child and you said you want it. Do you love it, too, or do you merely want to preserve the Owens dynasty?" She held up a hand to stop him from speaking. "Let me finish. I think I do love you, and if you can honestly say that you love me *and* the baby, then…"

Thunderstruck, Keith couldn't remain silent a moment longer. "Then we should get married!" He pulled her into his arms and began kissing her forehead, her cheeks and her lips. None lingered in any one spot, and she closed her eyes and savored the delicious sensation of his lips wandering and exploring her face. For the first time since the ball she *felt* loved.

"I truly adore you," he said huskily. "I mean it. I love you, I love you, I love you. I always have. I love the baby, and I swear to be the best father ever. I admit I ran off to think. I admit loving you so much scared me, but that was mostly because I wasn't sure of your feelings. Even making love with me wasn't proof of love, sweetheart. So there it is. I love everything about you, every single thing, and now I want you to say it.''

''Are we playing another game?'' she whispered, for truly, his speech had stunned her.

''Not this time.''

She dampened her lips with her tongue and sucked in a breath. ''All right, I'll say it. I adore you,'' she whispered as tears gathered in her eyes. ''Keith, I'm so weary of all the pulling and pushing we did. I just want to be happy.''

''With me and our child.''

''Yes, with you and our child.''

He hugged her so tightly she laughed. ''Keith, I can't breathe!''

Laughing, he loosened his hold on her and leaned his head back enough to look into her eyes. ''You are so beautiful.''

''Keith, I'm not.''

''Fishing for more compliments, are we?'' he teased. ''Let me start with…''

''No! Stop that now. We need to talk.''

''Fine. We could get married as soon as Texas law permits, if that's what you want, or we could fly to Las Vegas and do it tomorrow.''

''Let's be sensible about this and not rush the…the wedding. I'd really like to spend some quality time together, now that we're both out in the open with our feelings.''

''I guess that makes sense. All right, how about if we see each other every day and call each other at least three times a day. We should also go to every public place in town so everyone knows we are now a couple. I should meet your friends and you should meet mine. And we should make love at least once every day, no, make that twice a day. At *least* twice a day.''

Andrea was too breathlessly ecstatic to speak, for the dream she'd lived on in college was finally happening and it wasn't easy to believe. Had she hoped or even suspected Keith might go this far when she finally admitted—out loud and to his face—her love?

"And when we're ready...we'll know when the time is right...we'll get married," Keith continued. "Did I hit the right choice on the dart board?" he asked with an adorably enchanting grin.

"You did...yes."

Keith looked off across the room and after a few moments murmured, "It's still raining, coming down in buckets, it sounds like." Then he brought his gaze back to Andrea, who was by this time dangerously weak in the knees.

"Let's go to bed, sweetheart," he said, low and seductively.

"Yes," she whispered. She could say nothing else.

Thirteen

Three days remained of Kiddie Kingdom's spring term. On Monday, Andrea talked to Nancy Pringle, the principal, and asked if she could have a few more weeks to decide which term she wanted to take off this year. Her request surprised Nancy, and Andrea didn't explain that she couldn't go forward with either retirement or her normal summer-term break without a little more thought. Teaching had always meant so much to her, and she was finding it hard to imagine life without it. After all, she taught at a liberal preschool that permitted teacher-moms to bring their babies—and, of course, their toddlers—to class. If she wanted to continue teaching she would really only need to take off a month or so after the baby's birth. She hadn't yet discussed it with Keith, but she would.

Nancy said yes to her request, which pleased Andrea, but for a fact, nearly everything, even a simple "Good morning" from a stranger, pleased her now. Her mood was remarkably upbeat, there seemed to be a permanent smile on her face, and just thinking of Keith warmed her.

In truth she had never known the power and magic of the kind of love she felt from and for Keith. Her self-confidence soared because of it; her energy level rose because of it; the sky was bluer because of it. She was so glad and thrilled to be alive and in love, so thankful, and in gratitude for this miracle of fate or gift from above she would not let herself lament past mistakes and misjudgments, not her own, not Keith's.

They spent every possible moment together. When she got home from school on Monday he was waiting for her. That afternoon he invited her to *his* house, and indeed it was a mansion, enormous, overly decorated and not at all the kind of home she admired. But she walked through the rooms with him and in one of the bedrooms—not the master suite, she noted—they made such sweet and tender love that she wept.

Then they talked. "When we're married, where would you like to live?" Keith asked.

"Well…" She didn't want to say that she didn't like his mansion, because he must like it or he wouldn't be living in it.

"I opt for your house or a new one that we would plan and build together," he said.

His sweet unselfishness moved her, and she kissed him with all the love in her heart. Later they discussed her teaching career, and he told her to do whatever she wanted. "You know you'll never have to work a day of your life, but I know you love teaching, and now I even know why you do. It's up to you, sweetheart."

She thought that was sweet, as well.

They ate out that night, choosing Claire's, Royal's fine French restaurant. They saw people they knew and people they knew saw them. They smiled at each other because people would know they were a couple. It was what they wanted.

On Tuesday they went to Claire's with some of the Cattleman's Club members for dinner. Despite Andrea's in creased self-confidence, she felt a bit nervous about that. But Keith's friends seemed genuinely pleased to meet her—she'd met some of them at the charity ball, though she hadn't even tried to remember names and faces at the time—and the evening turned out to be great fun.

Wednesday was the last day of the spring term, and Andrea brought cookies to school as a special treat for her tiny students. She also invited Keith to the party, and when he arrived she asked him to read the "cluck-cluck" story to the class.

This time while he read she could not keep tears at bay. She was looking at such a beautiful, touching scene, her beloved reading aloud to ten adorable children, and it made her think of the tiny life she was carrying. Keith talked often of the baby—asking dozens of questions about how she felt and could she feel it inside her yet—and she now believed with all her heart that he was as elated with their impending parenthood as she was.

That night Andrea entertained her friends and introduced Keith to them. She saw a few surprised faces in the group, but all in all the evening went well and Keith was accepted. After everyone had gone home, he hugged Andrea and laughingly said, "I think I passed muster."

"Indeed you did, darling," she agreed and snuggled closer to him.

Thursday was their first completely free day, and they decided to take a long, lazy drive and just enjoy themselves *by* themselves. It was a fabulous day, full of kisses, teasing and laughter with some reminiscing thrown in—How could they not talk about their conjoined childhood on occasion?—and they got back to Royal a little before eight that evening, ecstatically happy, a little tired and very hungry.

"Let's stop at the diner for one of Manny's burgers," Keith suggested.

"And a slice of his coconut-cream pie," Andrea agreed. "Oh, that sounds perfect. I'm famished."

And so they went to the diner. Because of the hour only

a few other people were there, and, to their surprise, the customers were all strangers, no one either of them knew.

Keith led the way to one of the back booths, then excused himself and went to the men's room. Two glasses of water in plastic glasses were placed on the table, along with two menus. Andrea glanced up and saw Laura Edwards. Laura looked, Andrea realized with a sad and sinking sensation, even more haggard than the last time she'd seen her.

"Hello, Laura," she said quietly.

"Andrea," Laura acknowledged while looking around, as though expecting someone to pounce on her from behind. Andrea experienced a chill, for she was positive now that Laura was desperately afraid of someone. "Is it still all right if I call you at home?" the waitress whispered. "I'm off tomorrow and I think I could find a way to call without…without…" Her voice broke, convincing Andrea even more of her terror. But then she managed to add, "Maybe we could meet somewhere."

"Of course we could. I'll meet you anywhere you wish."

Keith returned and Laura scurried away. He smiled at Andrea and asked, "Did you order for us?"

Andrea leaned forward. "Laura and I were talking. Keith, she's scared to death of someone and she's going to call me tomorrow to set up a meeting. I think she's reached the point of having to talk about it and I…"

Keith was so stunned he couldn't immediately speak. Laura Edwards was the key person providing Dorian's alibi for the night of Eric Chamber's murder. They hadn't been able to disprove Dorian's claim, not when Laura claimed he was at the Royal Diner most of the night. Laura had stuck to her story. Did he want Andrea involved with this woman?

"Andrea, I don't want you getting hurt over someone else's troubles," he said, forcing calmness in his voice and sounding as though his stomach wasn't doing flips.

Andrea was startled. His objection was a complete surprise and puzzling. "Keith, I've helped quite a few women get through some very bad times and I've never once been in danger. Laura is in trouble and if I can help, I have to. That's what New Hope is all about. You wouldn't believe how many women are in abusive relationships, and I strongly suspect that's Laura's problem. Every time I see her she looks worse. Please understand.''

It wasn't a matter of understanding. He nearly broke his vow of silence about the club's covert activities and told her what he and the other members were working on right now. He was so concerned about her and the baby that he even opened his mouth to fill her in on the real facts of Laura Edward's desperation, even if they weren't completely clear in Keith's mind. But it made sense to him that Dorian might be a threatening force in her life now simply because she knew too much. Actually, if Andrea weren't involved—or *trying* to get involved—Keith would be elated about stumbling across Laura's present state of mind. But it was impossible for him to be elated over anything with Andrea crossing a line she didn't even know existed.

''Andy, tell her to go to New Hope. Isn't that what they do, take in women who are in trouble?''

Andrea frowned slightly. ''That's exactly what New Hope does, thanks to the generosity of people like you and your club friends, but it takes some abused women a very long time to reach the point of public acknowledgment of something that's been going on privately, possibly for years. Keith, darling, I have to do it her way. I *have* to. I'm going to wait for her call tomorrow. I'm sorry you disapprove but I know what I must do.''

Her determined expression wilted Keith's protests. He couldn't demand she stay away from Laura without a lengthy explanation he couldn't provide. He would watch over her and their baby in another way.

Internally shaken, he reached across the table and took her hand. ''I don't disapprove. Just be careful, okay?''

He only wanted to protect her from any possible harm, the darling man. She loved him so much at that moment that she had to blink back tears. ''I promise.''

* * *

The following morning, Keith told Andrea that he really should spend some time at his office—a lie—but he would call her around noon. He also asked—nicely—if she would call him when Laura Edwards phoned her, just so he would know where they were meeting. Holding her in his arms he said emotionally, "Maybe I shouldn't worry about you and the baby, but I do. Take care, sweetheart." He kissed her goodbye and left.

Andrea closed and locked the door behind him, then watched him drive away in his SUV through a side window. He'd stayed all night. Everyone in Royal had to know by now that Andrea O'Rourke and Keith Owens were lovers. Some of them were undoubtedly speculating about the duration of the romantic affair and if it would lead to marriage. Given her loner status for so long, Andrea couldn't fault normal curiosity.

Since she couldn't just sit around and wait for the phone to ring she sorted clothes and organized closets, and all the while, events since the ball passed through her mind. Her and Keith together again—and, perhaps, at long last— seemed like a fantasy. But it wasn't a fantasy, she reminded herself with a serene smile, it was real. Very real and very wonderful.

She was organizing her shoes when the phone rang. A glance at her watch as she went to answer told her it was noon. Time had really gotten away from her.

She picked up the phone. "Hello?"

It was Keith. "Hello, sweetheart. Any word from Laura?"

"Not yet. I hope something didn't happen to change her mind."

He hoped exactly the opposite, but he didn't say so. "You sound worried. Please don't let this get you down."

"I'll try. Are you still at your office?"

"No, I'm at the club." He'd been at the club all morning along with Will, Rob, Sebastian and Jason. They'd broken Eric's numeric code; it was merely a record of his gambling wins and losses, with dates and sums. His losses had far exceeded his wins, and the dates coincided with money taken from Wescott Oil bank accounts. They had deduced the rest of the story. Dorian had discovered Eric's embezzlement and then blackmailed him into churning the accounting records to make Sebastian responsible, using more money to open an account in his name. Apparently Eric had done something to enrage Dorian and Dorian had killed him.

Problem was, they still had no proof of Dorian's guilt, mostly because of the airtight alibi provided by Laura Edwards. When Keith told them about Laura's plan to call Andrea for a meeting, their hopes had gone sky-high; maybe Laura was ready to turn the tables on that lie. They had literally sat on the edges of their seats, same as Keith had, all morning, waiting to hear from Andrea.

"It's business, too, sweetheart," Keith told Andrea, "a lunch meeting." He didn't like deceiving her like this, but he had to do what they all thought was right. Dorian was a dangerous individual, and now they were very close to acquiring the proof needed to send him to prison. At least it appeared that way. Keith swallowed but concealed the nervous tension in his gut. He was, after all, permitting the woman he loved to put herself at risk by even talking to Laura, even though he and the others in the group were prepared to protect Andrea at any cost. "The fastest way to reach me is by cell phone, Andy," he said quietly. "You know the number."

"Yes, I do. I also have the club's number."

"Andy, the second Laura calls, you call me. Promise?"

"Yes, dear, I promise," she replied teasingly. His concern was touching, if a bit silly. Well, maybe not silly, she amended. Some spouses and boyfriends were truly dangerous men, and if Laura was trying to escape a really horrible relationship, there was always the chance her brutal companion might blame anyone attempting to assist her.

But it had never happened to her with any other woman

seeking help, and Andrea couldn't get too worried that it might with Laura. She put it out of her mind.

It was three-thirty when the phone finally rang again. A bundle of nerves by then, Andrea raced for the instrument as though it were a direct line to life itself. "Hello?" she said anxiously.

"Andrea...this is Laura...you know, from the diner?"

"Yes...yes...I've been expecting your call. Laura, are you all right?"

"Yes, I'm fine. I...just couldn't get away until now. Andrea, I really can't talk on the phone."

Andrea drew a calming breath, but she still felt rattled. "We'll talk face to face. Where would you like to meet? Do you have a particular place in mind?"

"No...I...just don't know," Laura stammered. "Do you know someplace, uh, safe?"

Andrea was beginning to think more clearly. Laura might still be in danger but she hadn't yet been harmed. She, Andrea, had to keep them both on the right track.

"Yes, I do," she said firmly. "Where are you now?"

"At the pay phone on the corner of Jennings and Fifth. Do you know where that is?"

"Yes. Laura, let me pick you up and bring you to my house."

"Your house? I was afraid you were going to say New Hope. I can't go there, Andrea. Too many people would see me."

"No one will see you at my home. Laura, are you afraid that someone's watching you now?"

"It's...possible," Laura whispered. "Maybe it's my imagination. I...really don't know."

Laura's fear gave Andrea a shiver. She'd never experienced that kind of fear herself, but she'd seen it in women's eyes. Hearing it in Laura's voice increased Andrea's determination to help.

"All right, here's what we'll do," she said into the phone. "Hang up and go into that little bookstore near the corner. I think it's the second shop from the corner. Act as though you're browsing the shelves but keep an eye on the street. My car is a dark-blue sedan. I'll double-park directly in front of the bookstore and wait for you. It shouldn't take more than ten minutes to get there, but wait twenty minutes just in case some unforeseen traffic problem slows me down.''

"All right. Bye…and thanks.''

"I'll see you shortly.'' Andrea hung up, then dialed Keith's cell phone. She didn't know if he was still at the club—it seemed a long time for him to have been there, even for a business meeting—but with his cell phone he was reachable anywhere in Royal.

"Andrea?'' he said by way of greeting after one ring. "Did she call?''

"Yes.'' Andrea explained that she was picking Laura up at Jennings and Fifth and bringing her back to the house.

"Good. But if anything at all happens that you don't expect, call me at once.''

"Keith, is something wrong? Nothing unexpected is going to happen. Well, I suppose the person she's afraid of could…''

"Andrea, listen to me. Don't let anyone but Laura get in your car. Keep the back doors locked and once you have Laura, drive directly home.''

"You big worrywart,'' she said adoringly. "I'll be fine.''

"And call me the minute you get home.''

"Yes, dear. I have to run. Laura will be standing around worrying. Love you. Bye.'' She hung up, gathered her purse and car keys from where she'd placed them in anticipation of Laura's call and then hurried to the garage. Jennings and Fifth was in downtown Royal, which seemed busier than normal to Andrea, and it took almost fifteen minutes for her to get there. She double-parked in front of the bookstore, Laura bounded outside and jumped into the car and Andrea immediately drove away.

Oddly, Andrea felt a strong sense of relief. Her tension had probably been caused by Keith's long list of cautions, she decided, but could she fault him for loving her so much? And he was thinking of the baby, too, of course.

"This is so good of you," Laura said while dabbing at her eyes with a wad of tissues. "I...I guess I've been wondering why a woman like you would put herself at risk to help someone like me."

At risk? A chill traveled Andrea's spine. "Am I in danger, Laura?"

"Well...I guess you could be...if he saw me get in your car...I guess." She sounded miserable, very apologetic and she said again, "I can't believe a woman like you would go out of her way to help someone like me."

Andrea began checking the rearview mirror, although she suspected she wouldn't know if they were being followed unless someone hooked his front bumper onto her back bumper. She wasn't a detective, after all. Unquestionably she was vastly more concerned now than she'd been, but she was also committed and had to see this through.

"We're not as different from each other as you might think, Laura," she said, striving for her normal composure in dealing with an abused woman.

"You're wrong," Laura said listlessly. "I know in my soul that you could never do what I did."

Andrea sent her passenger a sharp look. "What *you* did?"

"I...I have to tell someone about it," Laura whispered hoarsely. "I can't live with it any longer."

Andrea's alert alarm went off the scale. She'd been so certain that Laura's problem was an abusive partner, and now Laura was talking about something *she* had done.

Andrea's grip on the steering wheel tightened and her stomach tensed. She could be in over her head with Laura, but she couldn't just put her off now, could she? The woman was in trouble, trapped in a torment of emotional agony, and she was seeking relief. No, Andrea thought, she couldn't turn her back on Laura, whatever her story.

She couldn't help being on edge, though, and she kept driving with one eye on the rearview mirror, just in case she *was* able to spot someone following them. She saw nothing out of the ordinary, just what appeared to her eyes as Royal's usual traffic, but a clever driver could outwit an amateur like her any day of the week. It was incredibly relieving to finally drive through the gates of Pine Valley and ultimately turn onto her street. A look in the rearview mirror was reassuring; not one other car was in sight.

At her house Andrea parked in the garage and immediately lowered the door. The two women went inside and in the kitchen Andrea asked, "Do you like herbal tea, Laura?" As jumpy as Laura was, Andrea didn't think feeding her caffeine was a good idea.

"Uh, sure…yes…thanks," Laura mumbled.

"Don't be nervous. You're perfectly safe here. Sit at the table. It won't take a minute to prepare the tea." Andrea put the teakettle on the stove and said, "I have to make a phone call, Laura. I'll only be a minute." She hurried to the den and dialed Keith's cell phone.

"She's here," she said at once. "Keith, she hinted at something *she* did. I think I was wrong about her being trapped in an abusive relationship."

Keith clenched his free fist. He was positive now about what Laura was going to tell Andrea, and while he gave a nod to his friends, no one smiled. This was serious business for all of them.

But he couldn't stop himself from cautioning her again. "Andy, I'm going to have this phone in my hand until I hear from you again. If even one tiny thing occurs that seems out of sync, you are to call me immediately."

This time Andrea wasn't flippant. Something was wrong. She had no idea what it might be, but she sensed that it was crucial that she do exactly as Keith asked. "I will, darling." She hung up and hurried back to the kitchen.

"Your house is nice," Laura said shyly when Andrea walked in.

"Thank you. I like it."

"I live in an apartment. It's…pretty nice."

"Which apartment complex, Laura?"

"The Caplan Arms."

"Oh, yes, I know the place. There's the teakettle." Andrea quickly prepared the tea and brought it to the table. She sat across from Laura and smiled, though she realized that she honestly did not feel like smiling. In fact there seemed to be a sizable knot of nerves in her stomach. "Now we can talk. A cup of tea always relaxes me."

Laura managed a wan smile. "Tea is nice."

And then Andrea sipped tea and forced herself to wait quietly for Laura to begin the conversation. Finally Laura asked, "Do you know about the investigation of the murder of Eric Chambers?"

Andrea was so stunned—she never could have imagined *that* subject coming out of Laura's mouth—that she lowered her cup and actually gaped wide-eyed at the woman. Laura hadn't committed murder, had she?

"Not entirely," she managed to say, albeit rather weakly. "Why?"

"I...I think...no, I'm certain...of who the murderer is."

Andrea could feel the color drain from her face. "How...how would you know that?"

"I provided the killer's alibi," Laura whispered. "Actually, I *am* the killer's alibi. Oh, Andrea, it's all so awful." She started crying and Andrea rushed—albeit on shaky legs—to get her some fresh tissues. Her heart was pounding so furiously that her hands were trembling when she placed a box of tissues on the table next to Laura's cup. "Thank you," Laura managed to gasp between great heaving sobs.

Returning to her chair, Andrea wondered frantically what she should do. Did she want to hear Laura's story now? Laura was talking about murder, the murder of that poor man who had worked at Wescott Oil. She should be talking to the police, not to a New Hope volunteer!

But dare she say something of that nature to Laura? The woman felt safe in talking to her. She couldn't destroy that trust and tell Laura to take her story to the police. She would listen and then decide how to deal with this shocking turn. She would call Keith, of course, but first she would listen.

Laura eventually calmed down, got control of her emotions and began speaking. "I had a crush on Sebastian Wescott for years and years. He never knew I was alive, but I still fantasized about him. I know it was silly, but I couldn't help myself." Laura sighed. "Then about six months ago his half brother, Dorian Brady, came to Royal. Do you know Sebastian and Dorian?"

"I've met them, yes." Dorian Brady? That man who had insisted on an introduction at the ball? "Please go on."

"Dorian's very handsome with his chestnut brown hair and silver-gray eyes. He began paying attention to me, and I was flattered. I mean, he looked so much like Sebastian and I...I guess I was a fool for falling for his line...but he was so charming and I was so lonely and frustrated over Sebastian never noticing me. I began seeing Dorian. For a while it was nice between us, but then one night he told me that he was going to come into the diner quite late. He asked me to seat him in a back booth, bring him some food and then go about my business. He...he slipped out the back door, unnoticed by anyone else in the place, and...and I think he must have killed Mr. Chambers. He made me swear to tell anyone who asked that he'd never left the diner, and I've done that, Andrea. I've lied to the police and to Sebastian's friends who keep asking me."

Andrea whispered, "Are you sure he did it?"

"I'm pretty sure. He's got a terrible temper. He's a dangerous man, and...and I'm scared to death of him."

Andrea was so unnerved she could barely think. But one question suddenly formed clear as glass in her stunned brain. "Sebastian's friends?" she repeated slowly, and then added, "Who are?"

"Members of the Cattleman's Club. It's a very close-knit society. They made Dorian a member, so I can't say anything to them, because then he'd know!"

Keith was involved in that investigation, she knew it now.

It was the reason he'd been so concerned about her having anything to do with Laura.

It hurt to learn there were facets to Keith she knew nothing about; she'd been so positive of knowing Keith through and through now. But this secret involvement, this secret society wearing the face of an ordinary club for men…he could have told her about it, couldn't he? Didn't he trust her?

"Why…why would Dorian kill Eric?" Andrea asked in a choked voice. "Did he tell you that?"

"He's rambled on about it several times, but I kind of pieced it together for myself. Mr. Chambers was an accountant at Wescott Oil. Dorian said he had Mr. Chambers in his back pocket. I think Dorian talked him into accessing some computer accounts and moving money around to make it look like Sebastian was stealing from the company. I know Dorian was trying to get Sebastian in trouble. He's told me often enough how he resents Sebastian because *he* was never acknowledged by their father and Sebastian was the apple of Jack Wescott's eye. I think Eric Chambers threatened to go to Sebastian because Dorian was furious with him."

"I see," Andrea murmured, and then made a decision. "Laura, I hate saying this but you might be in terrible danger. If Dorian killed Eric then he could be planning the same fate for you."

"I know. I've been half-crazy ever since it happened." Laura's eyes filled again. "Andrea, I didn't know Dorian was planning murder that night. I thought he was merely going to do something to get back at Sebastian."

"And you couldn't help resenting Sebastian because he never noticed you as a woman."

"It was so stupid."

"Well, we're not always sensible and smart, are we? Laura, do you want my advice?"

"Yes. I…I'm afraid to go to the police on my own."

"You need a good lawyer. I'm going to call one and set up a meeting for you."

Laura looked downcast, but she nodded. "All right."

Andrea left the kitchen and hurried to the den, where she looked up a telephone number and dialed it. In minutes she had permission to bring Laura to the lawyer's office immediately. She put down the phone without calling Keith.

Returning to the kitchen, she picked up her purse from the counter and said, "Let's go, Laura. You need to get this awful mess straightened out, once and for all."

Laura got to her feet. "Do you think I'll have to go to jail?"

"I don't know. I hope not, but I simply do not know. Do you still want to see that lawyer?"

Laura nodded. "I have to do something. I can't live like this anymore. Let's go."

Andrea was back home in thirty minutes. She'd left Laura in capable, sympathetic hands, and now she knew she should talk to Keith and let him know that she didn't like being deliberately left out of what appeared to be an important part of his life. Yes, he was a businessman, but he was also a…a what? A private investigator, a soldier of fortune, damn it, what?

She paced and stewed and shed a few tears and asked herself how she could ever trust him again. And she'd just *learned* to trust him! Did he love her or didn't he? After this it was very easy to think that his "in love" behavior was an act to gain possession of his child.

She *had* to call him. There was too much bottled up inside her to go on like this. She punched out his cell number and he answered on the first ring again.

"Are you okay?" he asked right out of the starting gate.

She got right to the heart of it. "Keith, are you involved in the investigation of Eric Chamber's murder?"

Keith's heart sank. "Andy, where are you?"

"Home. Alone." She quickly and in a razor-sharp voice related what had taken place with Laura. "I'm not very happy right now, Keith. You've been lying to me."

"No, honey, no! I never lied, I just omitted some things because of a vow of silence."

"A vow of silence! What in hell is that club, a branch of the CIA?"

"I swear I was going to tell you everything after we were married."

"Meaning I'm not trustworthy now?"

"Andy, please don't take it like that. I was just trying to do what was best for all concerned."

"Well, I don't mind admitting that I'm a little disappointed in you, Keith. Oh, my God, what's that noise?"

"Andrea, I hear it. What is it?"

"I think…it sounded like shattering glass! Keith, I think someone's in the house! I didn't set the alarm when I got home!"

"Get out of the house, now! I'm on my way!" The phone went dead. Andrea had hung up, or someone had hung up for her. "Someone's in Andrea's house! It's probably Dorian!" he yelled as he slammed down the phone.

Everyone jumped up and followed him outside, where they piled into cars and left the club's parking lot with their tires squealing. Keith drove with a murderous rage pumping adrenaline through his system. Somehow he'd gotten ahead of the pack in his SUV, though they weren't far behind him. But he increased the distance by skidding around corners and driving like a maniac, swearing he would kill Dorian if he had harmed Andrea.

Andrea found herself looking down the barrel of a gun. It was in the right hand of Dorian Brady. He'd been on Laura's trail all day, and he'd figured out that she'd told Andrea everything. Well, if he thought she was going to weep and whimper, he had another thought coming.

"You can't kill the whole town, Dorian," she said in the steadiest voice she could manage. "Laura is talking to a lawyer right now, and then he will talk to the police and it will go on and on, ad infinitum. Your goose is cooked, face it."

"You meddling busybody," he hissed. "Forever passing out cards with your phone number so women who deserve exactly what they're getting from men can call you and lap up your sickeningly sweet sympathy."

"Oh, you're going straight to the penitentiary, mister, and that's what *you* deserve!"

"Not before I make sure you never ruin another man's life, you bitch!" Dorian straightened his right arm and took aim, and Andrea shut her eyes, for she could already feel the red-hot bullet ripping through her flesh.

Only, instead of a gunshot, she heard a loud thud and a yelp. Her eyes flew open; Keith had Dorian down on the floor and was using him for a punching bag. The gun had slid under a chair.

Andrea was afraid that Keith was going to kill Dorian, the way he was punching him. "No, Keith, don't! Stop, you're going too far!"

"He was going to shoot you!" Keith said through furiously clenched teeth.

"But he didn't, and I don't want you killing him! Please, just stop."

Keith's head dropped forward for a moment, then he climbed off Dorian and staggered to his feet. He put his arms around Andrea. "Thank God I got here in time."

Dorian was bloodied and beaten, and he knew what was in store for him. Moving cautiously and slowly he scooted over until he could reach his gun under the chair.

Then he stumbled to his feet, with the gun. "Stay where you are or I'll kill you both."

Andrea could feel Keith stiffen. "I knew I should have knocked you cold," he said angrily.

"I'm not going to jail for this. Don't do anything stupid and force me to shoot you." Dorian darted from the room just seconds before the arrival of the rest of the Cattleman's Club posse.

"It's Dorian, just as we suspected. He went out the back way," Keith announced, and all of them ran through the house. Just as they reached the door with the shattered glass window, they heard a gunshot.

Stunned, they peered outside and saw Dorian on the ground near the pool. "He shot himself," Keith announced. "I'm sorry, Sebastian."

"It's probably best, Keith," Sebastian said soberly. "Sad and unnecessary, but best, considering his criminal behavior."

They trooped over to the body, made sure Dorian didn't still have a pulse and then returned to the house. Keith phoned for the police.

The rest of the day was a nightmare. A number of police cars, an ambulance, the coroner's vehicle and even a fire truck had answered Keith's 911 call.

"There goes the neighborhood," Keith said dryly when everyone had finally departed.

Andrea tried to smile, but it simply wasn't in her. However evil Dorian Brady had been, he'd still been a human being and he'd killed himself in *her* backyard. She would not easily get over today's devastating events, she knew.

Keith made sure the doors were locked and the security system armed for Andrea's benefit. She truly looked as though she couldn't take one more scare, not even a small one. Then he returned to the living room, sat next to her on the sofa and pulled her into his arms.

"Try to relax and forget," he murmured, his lips in her hair. "It's over and done with."

She snuggled closer to him. "I feel safe with you."

"Good. Andy..." He held her all during his explanation of the Cattleman's Club involvement in secret missions to save innocent people's lives. "But you have to understand that what we do is not for publication, sweetheart."

"I'm sorry I got all upset when Laura told me about the club. Dorian must have told her. Anyhow, I won't breathe a word of it, but is that, uh, practice going to continue? I mean anytime you're not at home should I worry that you might be off on some dangerous mission?"

Keith laughed. "Of course not." What other answer could he give her? *Yes, my love, it's entirely possible that when I'm off on some supposed business trip, I'm really up to my eyeballs in a covert mission.* No, he couldn't lay that on her now, not after all she'd gone through today. And he would never, ever do or say anything that might endanger the safety of the baby in her body.

"Then I can count on you to let me know if another...if another Dorian enters the picture, and you're involved and you might be in danger?"

"You were the one in danger today, Andy," he said gently. "Not me. Are you going to continue your work for New Hope?"

"I'd...like to."

"I feel exactly the same about what I've been doing."

They hugged each other tightly for a long time. They were both committed to helping less fortunate people than themselves, and neither could ask the other to stop.

"How much time do you need to plan a wedding?" Keith asked softly.

Andrea's pulse quickened. "A formal wedding or a simple affair?"

"Which do you prefer?"

"Simple." Her face was against his chest and she could hear the beating of his heart.

"Then let's do it as soon as the big day can be arranged."

"Oh, Keith!" She adjusted her position on the sofa so she could throw her arms around his neck. "I love you so much!"

"Honey, uh, I just have one request. I'd like to hold a reception...after the ceremony, of course...at the club. Can you deal with that?"

"If you can deal with my friends, I can deal with yours."

"Then we have no problem." Keith's eyes were suddenly misty. "Oh, Andy, we should have always been together. Why did I let you get away in college?"

"Far more important than that question is what made you

start chasing me again after so many years. I think it was because we hadn't slept together before. I was the one that got away and you couldn't stand it.''

"But you didn't *really* get away, did you? It just took me a lot longer to nail you than it should have.''

Andrea slugged him a good one on his arm. "You toad!''

Keith grinned. "Come here, sweetheart, and show me how much you love me.''

Sighing happily, she did exactly that.

Two weeks later the local newspaper reported the wedding. Along with photographs of the bride and groom, there was an article. It read:

Keith Owens, sole owner and operator of Owens Tech-ware Company, and Andrea O'Rourke, nursery-school teacher and volunteer for numerous charities, were married in a private ceremony yesterday. A reception was held at the Texas Cattleman's Club immediately after, and it was indeed a splendid event.

The new Mrs. Owens was radiant in a white on white, ankle-length gown and Mr. Owens wore a pale gray Western-cut suit. An extremely handsome couple, they greeted hundreds of guests as they arrived at the club with a gift of a wrist corsage of white orchids for the ladies and an orchid boutonniere for the gentlemen.

Dinner was served buffet-style and consisted of baron of beef, barbecued ribs, turkey, ham, delightful and de-licious salads and side dishes, and last but far from least a number of Mexican favorites, such as enchiladas and tamales. An excellent champagne was served throughout the reception.

Some of the guests, to name a few, were Sterling and Susan Churchill, Blake and Joselyn Hunt, Aaron and Pamela Black, Dakota and Kathy Lewis, William and Diana Bradford and Sebastian and Susan Wescott. All in all it was a grand affair and it appeared that everyone had a marvelous time.

Before saying good-night to everyone, the groom announced that he was whisking his bride to the Bahamas for a romantic honeymoon, after which he said they would return to Royal to plan the construction of their new home.

Congratulations and best wishes to Royal's newest married couple, Keith and Andrea Owens!

*   *   *   *   *

SILHOUETTE®
DESIRE™ 2-IN-1
AVAILABLE FROM 18TH JULY 2003

0703/51a

HIS MAJESTY, MD Leanne Banks

The Royal Dumonts

A fake engagement to 'ugly duckling' Tara York would get Prince Nicholas some peace from matchmakers. But she was turning into a *swan*—a confident, sensual woman he ached to claim as his princess...

A COWBOY'S PURSUIT Anne McAllister

Code of the West

Celie O'Meara had blamed Jace Tucker when his friend jilted her. But ten years later, Jace was back, and intent on marrying her himself! Could the sexy bachelor convince her that they were meant for each other?

THE ROYAL & THE RUNAWAY BRIDE
Kathryn Jensen

Dynasties: The Connellys

Runaway bride Alexandra Connelly was posing as a horse trainer— she only wanted an afternoon of fun with Phillip, dashing Prince of Silverdorn. But his intoxicating kisses made her long to tell him who she really was...

HIS E-MAIL ORDER WIFE Kristi Gold

Dynasties: The Connellys

Tycoon Drew Connelly had no intention of marrying curvaceous Kristina Simmons, the bride his daughter had found him on the Internet. But he was unprepared for the sizzling attraction between them...

TALL, DARK AND CRANKY Kate Little

After his accident, corporate mogul Grant Berringer needed help getting out of bed in the morning. But with physiotherapist Rebecca Calloway by his side, bed was looking more and more appealing...

MILLIONAIRE COP & MUM-TO-BE Charlotte Hughes

When pregnant Katie Jonas was left at the altar, her old friend, millionaire Neil Logan, asked her to marry him—for the baby's sake. But could she settle for anything less than a *real* marriage?

AVAILABLE FROM 18TH JULY 2003

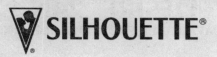

Sensation™

Passionate, dramatic, thrilling romances

LOVERS AND OTHER STRANGERS Dallas Schulze
SECRETS OF A PREGNANT PRINCESS Carla Cassidy
A CRY IN THE NIGHT Linda Castillo
GRAYSON'S SURRENDER Catherine Mann
IN HARM'S WAY Lyn Stone
STILL THE ONE Debra Cowan

Special Edition™

Vivid, satisfying romances full of family, life and love

THE ROYAL MacALLISTER Joan Elliott Pickart
HIS EXECUTIVE SWEETHEART Christine Rimmer
TALL, DARK AND DIFFICULT Patricia Coughlin
WHITE DOVE'S PROMISE Stella Bagwell
DRIVE ME WILD Elizabeth Harbison
UNDERCOVER HONEYMOON Leigh Greenwood

Superromance™

*Enjoy the drama, explore the emotions,
experience the relationship*

THE SHERIFF OF SHELTER VALLEY Tara Taylor Quinn
MARRIAGE TO A STRANGER Kay David
TWO MUCH ALIKE Pamela Bauer
OPERATION: KATIE Roxanne Rustand

Intrigue™

Danger, deception and suspense

RAFE SINCLAIR'S REVENGE Gayle Wilson
WHEN LIGHTNING STRIKES Aimée Thurlo
THE NIGHT IN QUESTION Harper Allen
COWBOY PROTECTOR Patricia Rosemoor

Three sexy, passionate romances

The Heart's Command

Rachel Lee
Merline Lovelace
Lindsay McKenna

*There's nothing like a sexy man—or woman—
in uniform to set the heart racing!*

Available from 18th July 2003

*Available at most branches of WH Smith,
Tesco, Martins, Borders, Eason, Sainsbury's
and all good paperback bookshops.*

0803/009/SH56

Maitland Maternity

Maitland Maternity

Where the luckiest babies are born!

Cassidy's Kids
by Tara Taylor Quinn

Troublesome twins… A single father…
An old flame…

Sloan Cassidy is a single dad with eighteen-month-old twins and he needs help! He knows one person who could help him, somebody he would love to see again. The trouble is, he hasn't been in touch with her for ten years…

Ellie Maitland has always had a soft spot for children and Sloan's little girls. But everyone knows this gorgeous rancher broke her heart. Everyone that is, except Sloan!

Maitland Maternity

Where the luckiest babies are born!

Married to the Boss
by Lori Foster

A practical proposal... A convenient
wedding... A passionate wedding night...

RJ Maitland, is forced into desperate measures.
The allegation that he is the father of the
abandoned baby boy have left his reputation in
tatters and the clinic in jeopardy. The solution
seems obvious—he has to get married!

Dana Dillinger, RJ's
secretary, has long been
hopelessly in love with her
boss. So when he makes his
entirely practical proposal she
is more than willing to
agree—with one exception...

SILHOUETTE® SPECIAL EDITION™

*is proud to present the all-new trilogy continuing
the Bravo family saga from*

CHRISTINE RIMMER

THE SONS OF CAITLIN BRAVO

Aaron, Cade and Will—
can any woman tame them?

HIS EXECUTIVE SWEETHEART
August 2003

MERCURY RISING
October 2003

SCROOGE AND THE SINGLE GIRL
December 2003

0803/SH/LC67

SILHOUETTE®
SPECIAL EDITION™

and

Joan Elliott Pickart

proudly present more wealth and
excitement from this powerful family in

THE BABY BET: MacALLISTER'S GIFTS

A new MacAllister generation ready for
love, laughter and babies...

August 2003
THE ROYAL MACALLISTER
(Silhouette Special Edition)

October 2003
PLAIN JANE MACALLISTER
(Silhouette Desire)

November 2003
TALL, DARK AND IRRESISTIBLE
(Silhouette Special Edition)

0803/SH/LC68

SILHOUETTE® SENSATION™

proudly presents
a brand-new trilogy from popular author

CATHERINE MANN

WINGMEN WARRIORS

Hot, passionate and strong—these
brave heroes will leave you breathless!

August 2003
GRAYSON'S SURRENDER

October 2003
TAKING COVER

December 2003
UNDER SIEGE

February 2004
PRIVATE MANOEUVRES

0803/SH/LC69

2 FREE

books and a surprise gift!

We would like to take this opportunity to thank you for reading this Silhouette® book by offering you the chance to take TWO specially selected titles from the Desire™ series absolutely FREE! We're also making this offer to introduce you to the benefits of the Reader Service™—

- ★ FREE home delivery
- ★ FREE gifts and competitions
- ★ FREE monthly Newsletter
- ★ Exclusive Reader Service discount
- ★ Books available before they're in the shops

Accepting these FREE books and gift places you under no obligation to buy, you may cancel at any time, even after receiving your free shipment. Simply complete your details below and return the entire page to the address below. *You don't even need a stamp!*

YES! Please send me 2 free Desire books and a surprise gift. I understand that unless you hear from me, I will receive 3 superb new titles every month for just £4.99 each, postage and packing free. I am under no obligation to purchase any books and may cancel my subscription at any time. The free book and gift will be mine to keep in any case.

D3ZEE

Ms/Mrs/Miss/Mr ....Initials....................................
BLOCK CAPITALS PLEASE

Surname ....

Address ....

....

....Postcode................................

Send this whole page to:
UK: FREEPOST CN81, Croydon, CR9 3WZ
EIRE: PO Box 4546, Kilcock, County Kildare (stamp required)